P9-CRN-777

Johanna Lindsey

Keeper OF THE Heart

AVON BOOKS ◆ NEW YORK

KEEPER OF THE HEART is an original publication of Avon Books. This work has never before appeared in book form. This work is a novel. Any similarity to actual persons or events is purely coincidental.

AVON BOOKS
A division of
The Hearst Corporation
1350 Avenue of the Americas
New York, New York 10019

Copyright © 1993 by Johanna Lindsey
Front cover art by Walter Wick
Inside front cover art by Elaine Duillo
Inside cover author photograph by Jerry Chong
Published by arrangement with the author
Library of Congress Catalog Card Number: 93-90387
ISBN: 0-380-77493-3

First Avon Books Printing: November 1993

AVON TRADEMARK REG. U.S. PAT. OFF. AND IN OTHER COUNTRIES, MARCA REGISTRADA, HECHO EN U.S.A.

Printed in the U.S.A.

RA 10 9 8 7 6 5 4 3 2 1

Shanelle Ly-San-Ter hit the cushioned exercise mat flat on her back, temporarily losing her breath. Score one for Corth. She'd told him not to go easy on her, and the android had taken her at her word.

"Why do you let it do that to you?" she heard from behind her.

Shanelle got her breath back and it came out in a near growl. She really resented that remark from Jadd Ce Moerr, one of her fellow graduates from World Discovery, where she had just spent the past nine months. When she had impulsively invited some of her new friends to come home with her for the three-month vacation they had earned before starting their life-careers, she hadn't counted on any of the *male* cadets taking her up on the offer.

Like most of the graduates from her class, with the exception of herself, Jadd was only eighteen years old. He was also short by her standards, no taller than a Darash male of the servant class on her home planet of Sha-Ka'an. But his relatively diminutive stature, coupled with his age, made him look like the boy he was. When her brother, Dalden, had turned eighteen, no one had doubted that *he* was a man fully grown. But she supposed Jadd's sandy-brown hair, gray eyes, and usually eager expression, along with his occasional tactless remarks like the one he'd just made, kept her from seeing him as anything but a boy.

She sat up now, tossing her long golden braid over her shoulder as she swung around and pinned the Kystrani male with narrowed amber eyes. "Corth isn't an *it*, Mr. Ce Moerr—he's just like family to me."

It wasn't hard to tell he'd gotten her angry. Those large, almond-shaped eyes could be disconcerting when they narrowed like that. And Shanelle Ly-San-Ter was not a small woman. She was, in fact, almost as tall as he was, and Jadd was above-average Kystrani height at five feet ten. Of course, she was only half Kystrani herself on her mother's side. The other half was pure Sha-Ka'ani, and everyone knew that the Sha-Ka'ani were of the warrior caste.

But the last thing Jadd had wanted to do was to get her annoyed with him, for the simple reason that he'd been trying to get her to file double occupancy with him ever since they had graduated. He would have tried it before they had graduated, but students were disallowed sex-sharing before then. And it had driven him crazy, being in the same class with Shanelle but not able to touch her. It was still driving him crazy, because she had flatly refused to share sex with him, let alone file for something more permanent. But he couldn't give up. She was, without a doubt, the most beautiful woman he'd ever seen.

He tried placating her now, not really sure what she was angry about, since the concept of "family" was alien to him. Just having a mother and father as she did was alien to him, though he had learned about such things in the portion of his studies that dealt with what might be found on other planets. On Kystran, children were born in artificial wombs and raised in Centers. On Sha-Ka'an, they were barbarically born by females.

"Come on, Shanelle, your android is just a machine. Even I learned families are made up of live persons," Jadd said.

"That's true, which is why I said 'just like.' But just like is pretty damn close as far as I'm concerned. And Corth not only looks lifelike, but my mother's Mock II computer has had years to tamper with his programming, so he's now almost as free-thinking as she is. Besides that, he has been my companion-protector since the day I was born, so he might not take offense at being called an 'it,' but you better believe I do."

Protector was a rather archaic word, but *companion* wasn't, and you only had to look at the handsome exterior of the android to know what he had been created for—a woman's entertainment. Real men had a hard time competing with something that perfect in looks and ability, and most men resented the entertainment models. This one was black-haired and green-eyed, and an unheard-of six feet four inches in height. The tallest any Kystrani male ever got was six feet max, and those men were all slotted for careers in Security. Jadd could have just made the height requirement for Security himself, but he didn't have what it took to bash people to bits, as those in Security were sometimes required to do. He had the feeling, though, that Shanelle had what it took. Her mother certainly did. Her mother, Tedra De Arr, had been a Sec 1, one of the top Sec 1s on the whole planet of Kystran. She had also become a national heroine some twenty years ago when she had brought an army of barbarian warriors to liberate Kystran from the mad dictator who had taken control of the planet. One of those barbarians was Shanelle's father.

Jadd felt he understood now why Shanelle had been turning him down repeatedly. She had a machine whose main function was to give pleasure to its owner. How was he supposed to compete with perfection?

He looked at the android with impotent fury, though his words were addressed to Shanelle. "You should have said he was your *companion*. Caris said your mother owned him, so I assumed you wouldn't be sharing sex with him, but—"

Shanelle's soft laughter cut him off. It was melodious and infectious, the kind of laugh that forced a smile even from strangers who merely heard it in passing. It had the ability to take the edge off his own jealous anger, particularly since it was genuine humor he was hearing, not anything ridiculing or sarcastic.

"I'm sorry, Jadd," she said after a moment, "but if you knew my father, you wouldn't have jumped to such a conclusion. Tell him, Corth."

Without expression, the android replied, "The Challen Ly-San-Ter would not allow me near his daughter until the Martha agreed to reprogram my abilities. I am no longer capable of sex-sharing."

"Oh, that's real tough, Corth." Jadd grinned with immense relief.

"I wouldn't gloat if I were you, Jadd," Shanelle came back with a grin of her own. "There was another thing my father insisted on when he allowed Corth to be my protector. Corth can't share sex with me, but neither can anyone else until I'm given to my lifemate. If you don't believe me, just try touching me when Corth is around, and you'll find out what it's like to be stomped into the ground."

"But that's—that's—it can't be!" Jadd exclaimed. "It's against the laws of the Centura League for an android to be programmed to hurt people. They're too strong, ten times stronger than any man could be. If they attacked someone, they'd end up killing him!"

"That's true, and Corth draws the line at killing, merely doing a lot of hurting instead. And that *is* what my father had in mind when he insisted on that particular programming."

"But the law—"

"Doesn't apply to Sha-Ka'an, Jadd. We aren't part of the Centura League, and my father is *shodan* of Sha-Ka-Ra, a law unto himself. Besides, what Corth would do to any man who touched me is mild compared to what my father or brother would do if they heard about it." Then she made a face. "Unless, of course, they approved of the man. Then I might be given to him for a lifemate."

Jadd didn't sympathize, no matter how barbaric he found the concept. It was one of the things Caris, their mutual friend, had told him that Shanelle had mentioned to her. Shanelle's father must approve of the man she would be given to, or he would choose the man himself, whether *she* agreed or not.

The final decision would be her father's. She could bring forth candidates, but only for his approval. It was for that reason that Jadd had gone on this jaunt to the Niva Star System and the barbaric planet of Sha-Ka'an. He'd already struck out trying to get Shanelle to accept him. He now intended to ask her father for her. With her father's permission, she would be his, and she wouldn't have anything to say about it. She would be his . . .

"You're as easy to read as computer basics, Mr. Ce Moerr." A female voice dripping with disgust came through the intercom on the wall behind them. "You don't really think her father will give her to you just because you ask him, do you? His own warriors have been asking for her for years with no luck. What makes you think he will favor a puny Kystrani still wet behind the ears?"

Mortified, Jadd flushed with color. Before he had come aboard Shanelle's Transport Rover, he hadn't known it was possible to hate a computer. In the past two weeks, he'd found out it was indeed possible.

"I will see you for dinner, Shanelle," Jadd said stiffly and stalked out of the exercise room.

Shanelle watched him go, then glanced at the intercom on the wall. "That wasn't very nice, Martha."

"I'm not programmed to be nice, kiddo. How many times do you have to tell that boy no before he takes the hint? Your mother wouldn't have put up with that kind of irritating persistence, so why should you?"

Shanelle sighed. "I'm not my mother."

"No, you're not. You're too damn softhearted. Not that Tedra couldn't be softhearted on occasion— she just never let anyone know it like you do."

"Martha, I'm in no mood for another lecture on my deficiencies. *When* are you going to stop trying to turn me into another Tedra De Arr?"

"When are *you* going to realize that that's something I wouldn't do even if I could? Besides, it isn't necessary. You're already more like her than you know. You just take a little longer to assert your wishes, but you *do* get around to asserting them."

Shanelle chuckled as she came up off the mat with easy grace. "Sure I do. That's why that obnoxious little boy is on his way to Sha-Ka'an with the rest of us."

"You just aren't fed up enough with him, because you know he won't try to take what he wants like a warrior would. Second, you knew as well as I did that the boy intends to ask your father for you, and you've decided to let Challen give him the facts of Sha-Ka'ani life. He would never give you to a man who couldn't protect you as well as he could. Third and more to the point, you're tickled pink that one of your worries has been permanently put to rest, a ridiculous worry, but no less real for that, that men other than warriors wouldn't find you attractive. The kid's determination reinforces the fact that you were worried for no good reason, which is why you don't really object to having him around."

Those facts had Shanelle glaring at the intercom, because they *were* facts. "Martha, when in the farden hell are you going to stop reading minds?"

"I don't have to read minds, kiddo," Martha replied smugly. "Motives, on the other hand, I tend to read even before you're aware of them."

With less anger but with a good deal of dread, Shanelle asked, "Then you know what I intend to do?"

"Am I the absolute best example of modern technology in this day and age, or what?" Martha asked in one of her more superior-than-thou voices.

Shanelle moved over and plopped down in an adjustichair, barely noticing the movement under her as it accommodated her slumped position. Corth came up behind her and gently began to massage the tenseness from her neck muscles. It didn't ease the disappointment she felt.

"I don't suppose for once you might consider not interfering and keep this our little secret?" Shanelle asked with little hope of getting an affirmative answer.

A perfect simulation of chuckling came out of the intercom. "I won't have to say a word. Your mother isn't dumb. But don't look so miserable. She wants what you want. Haven't you figured that out yet?"

"Not this time she won't."

"Wanna bet? You're her baby, Shani, her creation. She never knew what that would mean until she had you, and the feelings that released in her knocked her on her ass. She may love your father to the depth of her soul, but she wouldn't think twice about opposing him for you or your brother. It's called motherhood, and it took my Tedra by storm."

"This is different."

"How do you figure? Who was it who browbeat your father for six long months to get his permission for you to go to Kystran for some hands-on flight instruction? Who was it who fought with him, argued him down, and even challenged him and ended up having to obey his every little request for a whole month? She'd stopped challenging him years ago because she knew she couldn't beat him, but she still gave it another shot for you. And if you think she didn't *know* that that excuse you gave her for wanting to fly was a bunch of crap, then think again."

Shanelle squirmed in her chair, feeling a dose of guilt for not having been completely honest with her mother. "That *was* a legitimate excuse," she said defensively.

"Maybe five years ago it would have been," Martha replied with a snort. "But you know, and I know, and *she* knows that you no longer just want to fly the airobuses to the outer districts to bring the warriors in for trading. That *used* to be the reason you wanted to learn how to pilot, but it's not your reason now. Do you think your mother isn't aware that *I* could have taught you how to pilot

the airobuses, just as I taught you all the basics?
You wanted to go to Kystran to learn how to pilot
deep-space ships."

"But does she know the real reason?"

"She's got eyes, doesn't she? She's seen how you
shy away from Challen's warriors, giving none of
them the least bit of encouragement. She sees how
their attraction to you upsets you. And she's seen
how you close yourself up in your room whenever
it's common knowledge that one of the women has
been punished by her warrior, in that particular way
a warrior will punish his own woman. She's also
seen how you won't talk to your father for weeks on
the rare occasions that he punishes her in that way."

Shanelle shot out of her chair in total agitation.
"That way" for a warrior was to drive his woman
absolutely wild with sexual desire. The punishment was in leaving her like that, without any
hope of attaining relief. And it could go on for
hours, depending on the seriousness of the woman's
offense.

Only a lifemate or lover doled out that kind of
barbaric "discipline," so Shanelle had never experienced it firsthand herself. But she had heard enough
stories when women gathered to talk, about how
humiliating it was, how they begged and cried, all
to no effect. One of her greatest fears was that
she would have to suffer the same someday but
wouldn't be able to endure it. She was acquainted
with too many other cultures, knew for a fact how
barbaric that Sha-Ka'ani custom was, and knew that
no matter how much she might love her lifemate,
she would come to resent him because of it. She

wasn't like her mother, who got even with her father for punishing her that way. Her mother . . .

"How *can* he do that to her—to *her*!" she cried vehemently. "Sometimes I hate him!"

"No, you don't." Martha chuckled. "You love him to pieces, just like he loves you. You just can't accept that part of Sha-Ka'ani life any more than your mother ever did."

"Then why does she accept it?" Shanelle wanted to know, and in a small, bewildered voice added, "He makes her scream, Martha."

"Not in pain, kiddo, merely in frustration. But haven't you ever noticed that that big father of yours is easily bruised? He doesn't come out of one of those punishment sessions unscathed anymore, at least not when Tedra isn't restricted from retaliating by a challenge loss."

A challenge loss was a period of time that the loser of a fight owed the winner in service. This was usually manual labor, or a specific task. But for her mother, it was and always had been complete obedience in the bedchamber.

"They treat a challenge loss like a joke these days," Shanelle scoffed.

"Don't you believe it. They may kid around about it, but your mother takes all challenges seriously, because of that silly thing she terms honor. But she's smart enough not to be governed by challenge loss when she gets the urge to break some of the rules. And you don't see *her* staying mad at Challen for long afterwards, do you?"

"But she's a Sec 1. She knows *how* to give as good as she gets. I don't."

"But that hasn't stopped you from trying," Martha said with some more of her rendition of chuckling. "Corth tells me you spent nearly as much time in Security exercise classes as you did in your pilot classes."

It was true. As soon as she learned that there were ways to throw and take down large, usually immovable objects, she had insisted on finding out how it was done. It was all in the motion, in the propulsion, and in taking the object by surprise. It was a sport the Kystrani called downing, and it was very strenuous, but very effective. Only there hadn't been time to master the techniques. She would have stayed longer in Kystran to do so if her family wasn't expecting her home, and knew to the day when she should arrive.

"Fat lot of good it will do me against warriors," she grumbled now, only to hear more chuckling, which was really starting to get on her nerves.

"How many times has she tossed you on your butt this morning, Corth?" Martha asked him in a purring tone.

"Three, but I am not counting."

Even Shanelle couldn't help grinning at his answer. Martha had given the android a sense of humor a number of years ago, and it came out at the most inappropriate times.

"That doesn't count, Martha, and you know it. He isn't allowed to use his strength on me, so he's nothing like a warrior would be."

"You've got me there," Martha admitted. "That happens to be why your mother refused to teach you her own style of fighting. Because she felt it wouldn't do you any good. But that didn't stop you from learning on your own, now, did it?"

"No."

"And that didn't stop her from seeing that you were taught another style of fighting."

Shanelle made a face and dropped back in her chair. "Which won't be worth a damn against a lifemate, now, will it, who I wouldn't dare to hurt seriously? I can just see him now, laughing his head off, before he punishes me for years."

"Well, Tedra didn't know how you were going to end up feeling about warriors when she got it into her head that you should learn a warrior's skills. She wanted you to have the means to protect yourself, particularly after you got carted off in that raid when you were only ten. Your father took that in stride, since raiding is a fact of Sha-Ka'ani life and he knew he could buy you back. But your mother nearly went crazy before it was over."

Shanelle didn't like being reminded of the most terrifying experience in her life. It should have been no more than a simple raid, with nothing for her to really fear. The leader, Keedan, merely wanted a shipment of gaali stones in exchange for her return, which he was sure to get. But one of Keedan's warriors by the name of Hogar hadn't been quite right in the head. Hogar liked to hurt people.

Shanelle had had to ride with him for a day, and with the gag over her mouth, no one had heard her screams as he viciously twisted and pinched her everywhere he could reach. He'd only inflicted bruises on her, but the terror of what he was doing combined with the pain had made her faint four times. And she had had a deep, unreasonable fear of pain ever since.

But she had never told anyone what Hogar had done, not even her mother when she was safe at home again. She had been too ashamed of her own cowardice to mention bruises that had faded by then.

Martha didn't know she had stirred up unpleasant memories, however, and she was still making her point. "Tedra also couldn't stand the thought of your being helpless someday against a brute who decided he wanted to claim you despite Corth's being there to protect you. Corth is ample protection, but not against a warrior wielding a sword. He can get chopped up just like the real thing."

Shanelle put a hand over her eyes, but that wasn't going to put Martha off. She knew all this. There was no refuting it. She *was* like her mother in so many ways, but in one way they were glaringly different. Her mother had been born a fighter, a physical fighter, and she absolutely loved to take on men, her lifemate in particular, though she never had a chance of beating him and knew it. But Shanelle didn't like to fight with anyone, physically or even verbally. The former type of fighting led to pain, and the latter was frustrating beyond belief, because you couldn't argue with warriors. They didn't get mad and they rarely ever conceded on any point.

Tedra had insisted she learn how to fight, though. Instead of teaching her her own style of hand-to-hand combat, which worked fine on other worlds but was next to useless against barbarians, Tedra had decided that Shanelle needed to learn how to use a sword. This was an unheard-of notion on Sha-Ka'an for a female to have because there was a Kan-is-Tran law, still in effect, that didn't allow women to use weapons. That hadn't stopped Tedra, however. It had taken two whole years, but she had finally got Challen to agree with her by simply demanding, "Do you want *your* daughter at the mercy of some warrior who will walk all over her just because he can, someone like Falder La-Mar-Tel?" Falder happened to be someone whom Challen had never liked or gotten along with, so that did it. And once Challen had agreed, there was nothing Shanelle could say.

But Shanelle had hated all those lessons. She hadn't *wanted* any part of them. She might have finally got over her fear of a few bruises—her determination and her downing class had seen to that—but she hadn't back then. And she'd still rather run away than use a sword, rather use her wits if nothing else would do. She hated confrontations, period, and this one she was having with Martha was a prime example. You couldn't argue with or get the better of a Mock II computer any more than you could with a Sha-Ka'ani warrior. Both were extremely stubborn and both were utterly undefeatable.

"Maybe what you've learned of downing will come in handy someday—"

"Go ahead and say it!" Shanelle snapped. "On another world it might come in handy. *Not* on my world."

"Well, you knew that," Martha said reasonably. "That's why you wanted to learn it, because you

don't intend to stay on your world much longer."
Shanelle just covered her eyes again, but this time
it got a sigh out of Martha. "Tedra said it more than
once, that she did you a disservice by raising you to
her way of looking at things. You don't hear other
Sha-Ka'ani women objecting to the way things are,
do you?"

"But she did raise me differently. And I know
that the women on other planets aren't treated the
way our women are. Even on Kystran, if a couple
living in double occupancy has a disagreement, they
talk about it, with the one in the wrong ending up
feeling tons of guilt, which is more than enough
punishment as far as I'm concerned."

"But did you find a male there that you would
want to share sex with? You're twenty years old,
and your mother has given you her wholehearted
approval to make up your own mind about sex, to
go for it as soon as you find you want it, whether your father would approve or not. So did you
find it?"

"You farden well have all the answers," Shanelle
grumbled. "You tell me."

"All right, kiddo, but you aren't going to like it.
Sha-Ka'ani males may frighten you, but not because
of their size. Their size is something you happen to
appreciate, and in that respect you're just like your
mother. In your case, it can't be helped. You were
raised among them. They're the only kind of men
you are accustomed to. In fact, if a man *isn't* a
good deal over six feet tall and twice as wide
as you are, you won't be the least bit interested
in him."

"There are hundreds of planets that I am now capable of visiting, Martha. Are you going to tell me that in all those other worlds I won't find any other men with a little extra height and a little extra brawn?"

"Sure you will. So let's look again at what you're objecting to on your own world, the way warriors deal with their women when they break the rules."

"It's demeaning, humiliating—"

"But absolutely painless," Martha cut in. "There are worlds where lawbreakers are still executed. Worlds where they are still imprisoned for life. There are some worlds where the skin is whipped off their backs. And some worlds where advanced means are used to inflict excruciating pain without leaving a single mark. And that's just a few of the little niceties you'll find out there when you go hunting for your ideal mate. In comparison, what the Sha-Ka'ani do can only be considered merciful and harmless."

"There are also worlds out there that aren't so violent, worlds that don't have so many ridiculous rules either."

"You've been raised not to break the rules. Challen saw to that. So I don't know what you're really worried about."

"Yes, you do, and I don't want to talk about it anymore."

As usual, Martha listened only to what she wanted to hear. "Did you ever wonder why your mother puts up with those punishments you're so terrified of, that and everything else that she still objects to on that world?"

"Because she loves my father."

"There's that, yes, but there's also the fact that he knocked her socks off the first time she saw him, and he continues to knock them off every time he takes her to bed. To have something like that to look forward to for the rest of your life is worth putting up with a few things you don't like. And maybe what *you* don't like isn't even as bad as you think it is."

"It's not only that," Shanelle mumbled.

"What was that? Did I hear that we've wasted all this time on only half of the problem?"

"Cut it out, Martha. If you know so much, then you know what the main problem is, and there isn't any of your high-tech logic or reasoning to refute the fact that warriors don't feel love. They feel lust, and a measure of caring for their lifemates, but they don't experience love like women do. And before you throw it in my face that my father does, I happen to know how hard mother had to fight with him to get him to realize it and admit to it. And besides, father is an exception. There is no other warrior like him. Even my brother admits he doesn't understand what father feels for mother. He's never experienced it and *he's* only half Sha-Ka'ani."

Silence. Depressing silence. Why had she thought that Martha might be able to dispute that glaring fact of Sha-Ka'ani life? Martha had been studying and analyzing warriors for the past twenty years. If she couldn't reassure Shanelle at this point, then there *was* no reassurance to be found. And Shanelle was *not* going to hook up with a man for life who could only offer her great sex-sharing and a little fondness. She wanted more. She wanted what her mother had found, but she wouldn't find it on Sha-Ka'an.

2

"I don't know about you, Shani, but I'm so excited about getting to see your world, I can barely contain it."

Caris looked it, too, Shanelle noted, but she didn't understand why her friend felt this way. Sha-Ka'an was *not* a world she would want to visit if she didn't have a reason to. But she supposed a visit there became so enticing because it was forbidden to the average citizens of other worlds.

Caris confirmed that by adding for Yari's and Cira's benefit, "It was open for a while to tourism after Shani's mother first discovered it. But a few idiots didn't obey the local laws and ruined it for the rest of us. Now the planet is closed up tight with one of those Global Shields that prevent even the most sophisticated spacecraft from entering the atmosphere outside the designated Spaceport. If you want to land, you have to have permission from the Visitor's Center, and you better be a Trade Ambassador or in a dire emergency, or you can forget it. Only the ambassadors are allowed there now, and even they can't go any farther than the Visitor's Center. Without your invitation, Shani, we would never have had this opportunity. I hope you know how much we appreciate it."

Shanelle felt uncomfortable with that kind of gratitude. All she'd done was invite a few of her new friends home for a free vacation, since graduates didn't have enough earned Exchange Tokens to afford to go off-planet, while she had a Transport Rover at her disposal, a spaceship big enough to accommodate a thousand people comfortably. It didn't even need a crew, since Martha was capable of running the entire ship.

But Shanelle had invited only the three girls, Caris, Yari, and Cira. The two young men, Jadd and Dren Ce Rostt, Yari's first and only sex-sharer, had invited themselves along, Jadd for deluded reasons and Dren for almost the same reason, because he couldn't bear to be parted from Yari, sex-sharing being new and apparently wonderful for both of them.

Actually, they were inseparable, and they had been having a great deal of fun in the two weeks since they had left Kystran, and that could be taken both ways, since one of the Sha-Ka'ani expressions for lovemaking was "having fun." It certainly made Caris and Cira jealous, and both had remarked that they intended to pounce on the first males they came across as soon as they landed. They had also both tried to interest Jadd in a little sex-sharing, but he had decided that if he couldn't have Shanelle, he wouldn't have anyone.

Shanelle had also been feeling a little jealous of Yari's happiness, but not as much as the other two girls, since she didn't know what she was missing out on, whereas they did. It was expected that every cadet would spend the first night after graduation getting acquainted with sex-sharing, and that was exactly what this group had done, all except Shanelle. She had spent graduation night with Garr Ce Bernn, who was presently in his third ten-year term as Director of Kystran. It was Garr who had got Shanelle into the World Discovery class as a favor to Tedra, and Garr who had got her into the Sec exercise class, too. He had, in fact, made the past nine months very easy and enjoyable for her. Anytime she got lonely, she was able to visit him, and he would cheer her up with stories about her mother, since Garr used to be Tedra's boss.

She had had to make many adjustments, mostly in her way of looking at things, despite the fact that Martha had been her teacher for most of her life and had prepared her for such an advanced culture as Kystran's. Because she had been an otherworld student, which was a rarity on Kystran, she hadn't been required to live in the Learning Center complex like the rest of the students, so she had had daily dealings with Kystrani adults, and had learned that everything her mother and Martha had told her about Kystran was true.

The citizens really did look at lovemaking differently than the inhabitants of any other world. Sex-sharing, they called it, and because they'd discovered some healthful benefits from it, it was now mandatory for all citizens except students, to whom it was forbidden until graduation. They even had laws to govern it, it was such an integral part of their culture.

But their culture wasn't Shanelle's. Unfortunately, neither was her own culture, which was why she was having such a hard time dealing with the fact that she would have so little say in the choice of her lifemate, a man who would have complete control of her for the rest of her life, a man whom she was expected to obey, respect, and supposedly love. Fat chance, she thought, not once he started punishing her.

The only reason she hadn't yet been mated for life was because Tedra had put it off by finding fault with every warrior Challen had considered. And then the pilot training had come up, and Tedra had got her way in that, too. But Tedra wasn't going to be able to delay the momentous event much longer. Shanelle was two years past the average age for starting her own family. In fact, she might be returning home to find the decision already made.

She would have to ask Martha to contact Tedra to find out. She just might not be returning after all . . .

Stars, *what* was she going to do? Perhaps her mother *had* done her a disservice by encouraging her to think for herself. If she had had any other mother besides Tedra, she wouldn't be agonizing over this issue now. Instead she would be happy to let her father decide her future, without the least doubt that he would make the perfect choice for her, because, above all, he wanted her happiness. But the plain truth was, she preferred her mother's philosophy when it came to sex-sharing.

Though Tedra came from the Kystrani culture, she didn't subscribe to all of it, especially having something as personal as sex governed by someone else. What she did subscribe to was individual choice, and Shanelle wanted that individual choice. *She* wanted to choose, and she was more than ready to choose, more than ready to find out what was making Yari so happy, what had made her mother so happy all these years.

She was ready. She just hadn't found the man who could "knock her socks off," didn't even know what that was supposed to feel like. Her mother had assured her she would know when it happened, and when it happened, she was to take full advantage of it if she wanted to. It would be *her* choice. And her father either could approve of the man after the fact or not. She would still have made her choice. But Tedra seemed to think she could get around Challen's displeasure. Shanelle was counting on that being so.

Shanelle was drawn back to the conversation in progress when she was asked a question. They were gathered in the Rec Lounge, having finished the last meal for the day. Shanelle would have liked to retire already, but her friends were too excited to sleep.

"What was that?"

Caris answered, "Cira wants to know if she'll be allowed to sample the local wares when we arrive."

"Wares?"

"The barbarians."

Shanelle groaned inwardly. She really should have gone to bed. But she offered her friends a half smile.

"The Sha-Ka'ani don't like to be called barbarians, now that they know what meaning advanced worlds give that name. And they aren't really true barbarians anyway, though they might seem like it at first. But yes, you can share sex with a warrior if he's interested. You just have to make sure you tell him beforehand that you are protected by the *shodan*, to avoid any misunderstandings."

"What kind of misunderstandings are you talking about?" Cira asked. "Was this mentioned in those rules and laws Martha supplied us with?"

"Martha gave you the standard stats supplied to all visitors, but as you've already realized, your case is unique. Usually, the only visitors allowed to leave the Center are those who have requested an audience with the *shodan*. If he agrees to see them, they are escorted to the palace by the Center's Security. They take care of their business quickly and then they are escorted right back to the Center. If there is a female in the party, she isn't going to stop along the way to share sex with a warrior, so there's no reason to mention something like this in the stats."

Caris's green eyes widened considerably. "My Stars, you're talking about that claiming business you once mentioned to me, aren't you?"

"I'm afraid so," Shanelle replied, and explained further for Cira's and Yari's benefit. "If a warrior thinks you aren't protected, and you don't have a male escorting you, then he is within his rights to claim you if he wants to, and there won't be anything anyone on my planet or yours can do about it once he does. But as long as you tell him up front that you're under a warrior's protection, he'll make sure you're telling the truth before he does any claiming."

"Are *you* sure about that?" Cira queried.

Shanelle could understand that they might not be so eager now to sample the local males, but she hadn't meant to dissuade them from having a little Sha-Ka'ani fun, just to be cautious. "Only two female visitors have been claimed in all these years, and those two wanted to be claimed, so no one got upset about it, least of all the females. And claiming protection does work, because a warrior who tries to claim a protected woman knows he'll have to end up fighting her protector, and warriors don't fight over women."

"Why not?" Yari asked with interest.

Shanelle anticipated their reaction with a mixture of dread and disgust because of her own feelings on the subject. "Any warrior will tell you he doesn't know what jealousy is—or love."

"Oh, come on, Shani," Caris said doubtfully. "You've said that your father loves your mother, and we all know he's a warrior."

"My father happens to be an exception." But Shanelle's tone turned dry as she added, "You could say my mother has been a bad influence on him."

Caris and Cira laughed, but Yari put in, "Well,

I think it's great. Imagine not having to deal with possessiveness and jealousy."

"Is that right?" Dren asked with a twinge of annoyance in his voice. He was even shorter than Shanelle was, and too slim of frame by half, but he'd been the most handsome boy in their class. "You weren't thinking of trying any of these warriors yourself, were you?"

Yari grinned and wrapped herself around him on the adjusticouch they shared. He was short, but she was still shorter. In fact, not one of the girls was taller than five and a half feet, which made Shanelle occasionally feel uncomfortable with her own height and lushly rounded figure.

"Don't get your nose bent out of joint, babe," the petite brunette told him. "From what I've heard, those warriors are just *too* big for me. I like my skin white and creamy, not black-and-blue."

"Farden hell, I never thought of that," Cira groaned in complaint.

Shanelle chuckled and sat back with her goblet of Antury wine. "*That* doesn't happen to be something you need to worry about. There is no man more gentle with a woman than a warrior because he *is* always conscious of his size and strength. The female Darasha of the servant class are much shorter than you are, Cira, and they have no complaints."

"Are these females someone Jadd and I might like to sample?" Dren asked, to get back some of his own, but what he got was a poke in the belly from Yari.

Shanelle answered anyway. "The Darash females

are available for anyone's use, and they don't mind.
I sometimes wonder if they even know how to
say no."

"*You* certainly know how to say no," Jadd said
as he brought his wine over and sat down next to
Shanelle on her own couch. "I wonder if—"

He didn't get to finish. He'd no sooner taken
the new seat than Corth was there and about to sit
right on top of him if Jadd didn't move himself
real fast. He did scramble out of the way, spilling
his wine in the process. Two robocleaners came
out from two different sides of the huge room to
clean up the mess, but no one noticed them. Jadd
was glowering at Corth, Shanelle was laughing—
she simply couldn't help herself—and the others
were all staring at Corth as if he'd malfunctioned.

"Why did he *do* that, Shani?" Caris finally asked
for the lot of them.

Shanelle was too busy laughing to come up with
an answer, but Jadd wasn't. "He's her *protector*,"
he said, making it sound like a dirty word. "No
one can share sex with her while he's around. They
can't even *touch* her!"

"That's not precisely true, Mr. Ce Moerr,"
Martha's voice intruded, proving she'd been following the entire conversation. It was a wonder
she'd kept quiet until now. "If Shani wants
to do a little sex-sharing with a man, Corth
wouldn't interfere. He might even help her take
her clothes off."

Shanelle stiffened, thinking about throwing her
wine at the intercom panel. "That was rather crude-
ly put, Martha."

"You know me, doll. I like to get my point across in a big way."

"Thanks a lot."

Martha started to laugh, but Jadd demanded indignantly, "What kind of protector is that, I'd like to know? I thought he was supposed to keep *all* men away from you, Shani!"

Shanelle was annoyed enough to snap, "No, just those I've already refused."

Jadd's color heightened in embarrassment, making him sneer, "I doubt that's what your father had in mind."

"You're absolutely right, Jadd," Shanelle replied. "It's something my mother added to Corth's programming without my father knowing. She is a Kystrani, after all, just like you. She believes in saying no when she feels like it, and yes when she feels like it."

"But do you *ever* feel like saying yes?"

It was a question too personal even for a man in the grip of frustration to ask. Jadd regretted it immediately and looked away, not expecting an answer. Shanelle wouldn't have answered him anyway. But Martha, that miscreant of metal parts, had no such qualms.

"It wouldn't do her any good to say yes on Sha-Ka'an. She's a daughter with a hale and hearty father who no one will challenge for the position of *shodan*, much less for a woman. There isn't a warrior who knows her who will even approach her. All they can do is think about it, and try to prove to her father that they are worthy of being her lifemate. She won't be sharing sex until then.

She doesn't dare go against the natural order of things."

Shanelle was no longer thinking about throwing wine at the intercom. She was definitely going to smash it to bits. And she knew what Martha was doing. She was trying to goad Shanelle into standing up for her rights, by showing her how others would see her situation. And those others were looking at her in differing degrees of horror right now. Just what she needed, their pity on top of her own self-pity.

"Is that really how it works, Shani?" Caris asked. "Do you have to go straight to a permanent commitment without even getting to try the guy out first?"

"Most Sha-Ka'ani females don't mind that at all—" Shanelle began, only to have Martha butt in again.

"They don't know how to buck the system."

"Tradition, Martha, not system, and stay the hell out of this!"

"But, Shani, you're half Kystrani," Cira pointed out.

"That's right," Shanelle replied. "Something Martha conveniently forgets about just to make her points. I do happen to have other options, one I've already decided on."

"The coward's way out," Martha said with a snort. "You can find what you're looking for right at home. You don't have to go to another Star System and end up breaking your mother's heart in the process."

There it was, what Shanelle should have realized

from the start. Martha was only on loan to her. She was first and foremost Tedra's, and everything she said and did was ultimately for Tedra's benefit.

Shanelle sighed. "All right, Martha, I'll look, I really will, right up until my father makes his choice. But if I don't agree with his choice, then I'm gone, and my mother will back me on that."

"I know she will. All I'm asking for is a little effort on your part so it won't come to that, and now that you've agreed to make it, you'll have my complete support."

"Well, I hope you realize one of the undesirable possibilities of your underhanded goading."

"Of course I do. Dense isn't in my programming." And suddenly Jadd disappeared from his perch on the end of the couch only to reappear a few moments later looking mighty shook up. Martha's voice was now purring as she addressed the young man. "That was just a preview of what will happen to you, Mr. Ce Moerr, if you mention any of what you've heard here tonight to a certain somebody's father. Only next time you won't be Transferred to your cabin and back, you'll be dropped in deep space."

Even Shanelle was impressed by that threat. Molecular Transfer was the means to get from ship to planet surface without landing or using Transfer craft. It literally Transferred your body from one point to the other in less time than it took to blink. And Martha was in control of the Rover's Transfer system.

"That's—that's against the laws of Life Appreciation," Jadd said in a horrified whisper.

"That's rich," the computer was heard to chuckle. "I'm a Mock II, kid. I don't obey any laws other than my own. Everyone knows—" There was a long pause, and then Martha actually screeched, "Get the hell out of my terminal, Brock!"

Shanelle blinked in pleased surprise. She hadn't realized they were close enough to contact Sha-Ka'an yet, but the deep, masculine voice that now came through the intercom proved that they were.

"Be quiet, woman," the voice sternly ordered Martha. "I have come at the request of Shanelle's parents, *both* of her parents."

That "both" was all that was necessary to calm Martha's outrage, but of course Brock knew that, which was why he'd included it. He could be just as high-handed or underhanded as Martha was, but then he was also a free-thinking Mock II computer. And he happened to belong to Shanelle's father, which meant Brock had been programmed to be compatible with no one but Challen. To this day, Martha still complained that *she* was the one who had helped to create him by supplying Challen's statistics. But she had done it for Tedra, because Tedra had wanted to surprise Challen with his own Mock II.

Some surprise. For a year Challen wouldn't even go near Brock. He didn't *want* anything that ultramodern belonging to him. And after he did finally give in and start talking to the computer, it had taken nearly another year of arguing between the two of them to establish dominance, which each felt they had won. But now they got along perfectly. And lately, much to everyone's amusement other than Martha's, Brock had been trying to exert a warriorlike dominance over Martha as well, an impossibility if there ever was one.

Martha's outrage might have been put on temporary hold, but her grumbling certainly wasn't. "Just say what you have to say, then get your tin ass out of my terminal. And the next time you think to drop in, you damn well better ask permission first.

"A *tin* warrior can get his circuits fried," Martha actually growled.

"Now, now," Shanelle said with a grin. "If you two have forgotten, you have an avid audience here who has never heard computers fighting before, and quite frankly, you're shocking the hell out of them."

"We weren't fighting," Martha insisted.

"Your amusement is uncalled-for, Shanelle," Brock gently scolded.

"That's right." Shanelle sighed. "When you come, you come fully equipped, including sight. Just how long have you been with us, Brock?"

"Not to worry, kiddo," Martha assured her. "He's sneaky, but he's not sneaky enough to arrive without *my* knowing it immediately. Now state your business, Brock, and go home."

There was a long pause, as if Brock were debating whether to do as instructed or upbraid Martha on the inadvisability of giving *him* orders. He finally addressed Shanelle.

"I bring you greetings from your parents, child. They have sorely missed you, and eagerly await your arrival on the next rising."

"Is my mother there, Brock?" Shanelle asked eagerly. "Can I talk to her?"

"I am sorry," Brock replied. "But Challen and Tedra are presently at the competitions, where they will remain until this moonrise."

"What competitions?" Martha demanded before Shanelle even thought to. If there was anything Martha hated, it was not knowing about something *before* anyone else did, and before Brock in particular.

"Warriors throughout the land have been invited to Sha-Ka-Ra to test their skills against each other. It began this rising and will continue until a champion of all is declared. Challen, of course, is the ultimate judge, and so his presence is required for each event, as is your Tedra's. Otherwise they would meet Shanelle at the Visitor's Center. Since they cannot leave the competitions, an escort will await Shanelle at the bus station to take her to her parents' pavilion in the park."

"Just like that?" Martha's voice remained testy. "Well, you won't mind if I check with the Center to verify these facts, will you?"

"Woman, you are being deliberately disagreeable." Brock didn't even try to hide his annoyance now.

"Aren't I just," Martha shot back, and then added sweetly, "Good-bye, Brock."

There was silence from the intercom, long enough for Caris to lean over and whisper to Shanelle, "Does he really think she's a woman?"

Shanelle could have said that whispering didn't do a damn bit of good when a Mock II was around, but Martha made that perfectly clear by replying, "Damned right he does, but then he's an idiot, beyond salvation."

Only Martha didn't sound quite so annoyed any longer. She sounded—proud, which had Shanelle grinning. "I thought you liked Brock."

"Only when he displays a modicum of his vast intelligence, which is rarely these days. He has become, for some male-oriented reason, no doubt, the quintessential barbarian. And when he spouts that condescending warriorlike nonsense, he drives me up a wall."

"But you can handle that?" Shanelle asked.

" 'Course I can," Martha replied with a very loud snort.

3

Shanelle woke the next morning feeling a good deal of the excitement her friends had been feeling last night, but for different reasons. As much as she wasn't looking forward to what might happen soon after her homecoming, she was definitely looking forward to seeing her family again. She had missed them terribly, and her friends, too, even the servants, even her spacious home.

For the past nine months she had lived in a box of a room; at least it was boxlike in comparison to what she was used to. Of course, the Kystrani knew how to make good use of a little space, using movable walls to section off whatever room was desired at the push of a button, so that you could have four or five rooms in the space of one single room, everything coming out of the walls, even the toilet and bath.

She had seen some pretty incredible things on

Kystran, but no less incredible than some of the things she had grown up with. The Sha-Ka'ani might disdain the modern conveniences of other worlds, but Tedra certainly didn't, and whatever Tedra bought for herself, she also bought for her daughter.

Tedra would have done the same for her son and lifemate, but like the rest of the male populace, they stubbornly wouldn't touch anything not made on their world, or was closely similar to what *could* be made on their world—except for meditech units. Warriors weren't stupid, after all, and this was one modern wonder that beat the hell out of slapdash healers. Anything that could actually save lives given up for lost, repair tissue, and leave no scars was worth having, and just about every town on the planet now had at least one meditech unit; some, like Sha-Ka-Ra, had more than one.

"Rise and shine, kiddo." Martha's voice floated into the room at the exact moment Shanelle sat up, deactivating her air blanket by the movement. "I've been having a long chat with the Visitor's Center, and it looks like my good buddy Brock didn't tell us even half of what's going on."

"You really get a kick out of that Ancient's lingo, don't you, old girl?"

"Me and my Tedra both." Martha chuckled. "But if you haven't noticed, the same 'lingo' pops out of your own sweet mouth."

"How could it not, listening to you two all my life? So what didn't Brock tell us? I assume you mean about the competitions?"

"You got it. It seems your father was planning

this competition a good month or two before he got around to telling your mother about it, and he didn't mention it to her until *after* I'd left to pick you up. But the ambassadors somehow got wind of it months ago, and they've had time to inform their home planets in case anyone wanted to participate. Apparently competitions like these appeal to one hell of a lot of people, because the Visitor's Center is just about overflowing."

"But that would mean—"

"You got it again, kiddo. Sha-Ka-Ra has been opened to visitors—at least the park is. Anyone can come into our fair city for the duration, even if it's only to watch."

"And father *agreed* to that?"

"Shocking, huh?"

Shanelle just stared wide-eyed at the audiovisual console the Commander's cabin contained, trying to grasp the implications. She finally concluded, "Mother must have talked him into it."

"When he's been adamant all these years about keeping visitors *out* of Sha-Ka-Ra? When it was his idea to set the Visitor's Center out in the middle of nowhere, and do that *before* the trouble? When the airobuses have to go out of their way to fly above the atmosphere just so they won't be noticed? When all bus stations are inconveniently located well outside city limits?"

"What's your *point*, Martha?"

"Your mother may wield a lot of influence where your father is concerned, but not when it comes to the well-being of his Sha-Ka'ani. This sounds more like a warrior idea, a little proof positive of who's the superior fighter. I just wonder what brought it on."

"You should have asked Brock."

"That cretin wouldn't tell. He just *loves* keeping Challen's motives secret. For whatever miscircuited reason that had him class me with every other female, he now has it in his mind that I have no business involving myself in *warrior* business. He also won't admit that I'm his superior, when any fool knows that a Mock II's intelligence and capabilities increase with age, and I'm *older* than he is."

"You don't have to convince me, Martha." Shanelle grinned.

She headed for the Sanitary corner, activating the walls for a little privacy. Of course, the walls didn't affect the Rover's communications system, which meant Martha's voice could follow her anywhere. It did.

"You do realize," Martha was saying now, "what this competition means, don't you? There will be warriors down there who don't *know* you. And with the city open to visitors, you won't even have to show up in a *chauri*, which would declare you a Kan-is-Tran woman. As far as the out-of-town warriors will know, you could be a visitor yourself. That means you won't be off limits, and neither will they. Are you catching my drift, kiddo?"

"Loud and clear, Martha."

But Shanelle had already realized the implications for herself, and was now feeling a new kind of excitement that had nothing to do with home-coming. This really was a golden opportunity, one she had no intention of passing up—but not for the same reason Martha had in mind. If there were going to be a great many warriors down there, there were bound to be a great many male visitors, too, possibly the best-of-the-best from other planets. Not even possibly. They *had* to be the best if they were here to compete with warriors. Talk about saving time and energy. Instead of her having to go to their planets to find them, they had come to hers.

"Well?" Martha prompted.

"So maybe I'll sample a warrior before I leave, just so I'll know what I'm escaping from."

"That's the spirit."

"Or maybe I'll find a visitor I like even better."

"Pull Martha's leg, why don't you?" the computer scoffed.

"You don't think that's a possibility?"

"It's a well-known fact that of all humanoids, Sha-Ka'ani males are superior. They don't put them together any better, or are any better-looking, than right at home."

"That's a whopper and you know it." Shanelle laughed. "Every world has its fine examples of manhood, even if they end up being the exception to the norm."

"You didn't find any to tempt you on Kystran, and how could you, being spoiled by what you've got at home?"

"I wasn't there long enough, Martha, nor did I leave Gallion City to tour the rest of the planet."

"All right, all right," Martha said in exasperation.

"There's no point in arguing about it when the truth will tell. I'll be monitoring your vital stats while you're down there, so I'll know *exactly* when your libido gets snagged."

"Well, keep it to yourself. If it's going to happen, and I do mean *if*, I'd like to figure it out for myself."

The head of the Visitor's Center was on hand to welcome Shanelle back to the planet. She was surprised, because Mr. Rampon usually didn't leave his plush office unless Tedra or Challen made an appearance at the Center, or unless they were expecting some really important visitor.

"Welcome, Miss Ly-San-Ter, welcome," he began effusively. "Your mother has purchased an airobus for you, and a good thing, too. Our airobuses can't keep up with the demand, because of the competitions. We've had *waiting* lines, if you can believe it."

All Shanelle heard was that she had her own airobus, and her smile turned brilliant. "Did mother tell you I wouldn't need a pilot?"

"She mentioned it, and a good thing, too, since we don't *have* any extra pilots just now. She also mentioned that you might be flying for us in the near future."

"I just might." Shanelle grinned.

"Well, if you'll step this way, I'll sign your guests through personally, to save time."

Shanelle was again surprised. "Why, thank you Mr. Rampon."

"Just ask him what he wants, Shani." Martha's

voice drifted up from Shanelle's waist where the computer link was attached to her belt.

Shanelle's cheeks pinkened, but not nearly as much as Mr. Rampon's. He cleared his voice and said uncomfortably, "As it happens, I do have a small favor to ask. One of the High Kings of Century III arrived a while ago. We were able to fly him and his party to the bus station below Sha-Ka-Ra, but the pilot returned to inform me that Ground Transport has run out of *hataari* to rent, and even after all the extra mounts that were brought in."

"You're saying he's stuck at the station?"

"Exactly. And as you know, it's not a short walk from the station to the city, and it's all uphill. Not that such an esteemed personage would even consider walking, nor can we suggest it. Those High Kings take insult so easily."

Shanelle pictured a pompous, overweight king trying to climb the steep, winding road to Sha-Ka-Ra and almost laughed. "No, we can't have him walking."

"Then you wouldn't mind taking his party up with yours?"

"Not at all. One *hataar* does seat two, even three people quite comfortably."

"And a good thing, too, or we would have even more visitors stranded at the bus station. And I do appreciate this. I will consider it a personal favor."

Shanelle said a few more words about its being no problem, then left her friends with the administrator while she and Corth went to look over her new airobus at the front of the Center. It took at least five minutes just to get there, for the Center's main building was huge.

The entire complex sat on about two square miles of land, with the port taking up half that area, and now it was overly crowded with spacecraft from dozens of different worlds. The warehouses took up another big section where the trade goods were stored. Then there was housing for the Trade Ambassadors, more quarters for Security and personnel, still more for visitors who weren't staying long. Then there were the buildings for maintenance, repair, storage, and everything else necessary to run what was in effect a small city.

"And yet they can't get a few people up to Sha-Ka-Ra," Shanelle mumbled to herself.

Martha didn't ask what she was talking about; she just put her two cents in. "Your father may have relaxed the rules enough to let visitors into the city, or to be more exact, into the park, but I didn't think he'd relax them far enough to let the buses land in the city. That's a law for the whole planet, not just here. Sha-Ka-Ra is the only city visitors *can* still get into, even if just to see your father. They are forbidden to travel anywhere else."

"I know the laws, Martha."

"Then stop complaining."

"I wasn't. It just seems to me that if father was going to let them in for these competitions, he should have made it a bit easier for them to get there."

"When has he *ever* tried to make things easy for visitors?"

Shanelle laughed. It was true. Even before the planet had been closed to tourism, Challen hadn't got along well with the men from other worlds, but no worse than any warrior. Tedra had once summed it up nicely. "Visitors are either too frightened of warriors, and subsequently too subservient, or too condescending, thinking of them as nothing but barbarians in need of civilizing. They don't leave a warrior a middle ground to deal with them."

But they had to be dealt with. The natural resources of the planet were too much in demand, in particular gaali stones, which had turned out to be such an incredible power source that they even took the place of crysillium, once again cutting long-distance space travel time down by nearly half.

The Sha-Ka'ani had used gaali stones raw, merely for lighting. Advanced worlds had the technology to put a single stone to work to power a whole city, or a whole spaceship the size of a Transport Rover. And one stone was inexhaustible. The energy in the stones never depleted. Small wonder energy-poor worlds might have gone to war with Sha-Ka'an if gaali stones couldn't be traded for. And the Ly-San-Ter family owned the largest source on the planet, half a mountain full, which had made them one of the wealthiest families in two Star Systems.

But when war was threatened, it wasn't from the outside worlds, but from right at home. Too many visitors had flaunted the laws too many times, traveling where they weren't welcome, helping themselves to women they weren't allowed to have, stealing the planet's resources instead of trading for them. Shanelle wasn't sure which particular incident had set off the fireworks, since she had been too young at the time. But she knew a huge army of warriors from the eastern country of Ba-Har-an had ridden to Kan-is-Tra, a journey taking months because Ba-Har-an was so far away. And there would have been widespread bloodshed of the visitor kind if the perpetrators of the incident hadn't been turned over to them and the planet closed down.

Of course, the planet couldn't be closed down completely. Compromises had to be made. So bus stations had been installed outside every town and city, inconspicuous, mere telecomms where a Transport airobus could be sent for if someone had something he wished to trade. The airobuses brought the Sha-Ka'ani merchants to the Visitor's Center, then returned them to their towns. The Trade Ambassadors no longer got to go seeking for what they wanted, but had to wait and hope it would come to them. Not surprising, the Ba-Har-ani never traded again with anyone outside their own country.

"Did you know about this, Martha?" Shanelle asked as she looked over the brand-new, shiny sky-blue Transport airobus.

" 'Course I did. Tedra ordered it right after you left for Kystran. Of course, that was before she figured out that piloting for the Center wasn't all you were planning to do."

"Let's not rehash that again. I will make a sincere effort to fall in love very quickly, at least before my father makes his decision and it's out of my hands."

"Mutual lust will do for starters. After all, Tedra didn't love Challen right off. It took at least a week."

4

Shanelle touched down on the solidite landing pad at the bottom of Mount Raik without a hitch. The airobus handled like a dream. It was much larger than the one-seater Fleetwing II that she had been using on Kystran to get around in, but then she had learned in her World Discovery class how to fly all of the more modern single-pilot ships known in the Centura Star System. The airobus seated twenty comfortably, with a large cargo bay in the back for trade goods.

Shanelle opened the hatch just before turning to her friends. "This is the end of the easy part. From here on we rough it."

"You don't mean on *those*, do you?" Jadd asked, staring in horror at the waiting *hataari* on one end of the solidite paving.

Shanelle grinned, following his gaze. The four-legged Sha-Ka'ani beasts did take getting used to.

Huge, shaggy-haired, with long, wide backs that were as high off the ground as Shanelle was tall. But they were placid creatures, well adjusted to working with man.

But before she could reassure Jadd, Caris said with a good deal of awe, "My Stars, Shani, so that's what they look like!" She wasn't even look-ing at the *hataari*, but at the four warriors waiting with them. "I expected them to be big, but not *that* big."

"Shani said they're gentle with women," Cira reminded her, her own voice sounding eager. "I'm willing to find out."

"You may have to wait on that," Yari put in. "Looks like we got trouble coming."

Shanelle glanced toward the other end of the landing pad as she stepped off the airobus, and sure enough, a party of five men was heading in her direction, none of them looking very friendly. In fact, the short, rotund fellow in the lead looked as if he was just short of hopping-around mad.

Corth moved in front of Shanelle to block her view of the group just as it arrived. Six feet four and dressed in the leather *bracs* of a warrior, com-plete with sword—Shanelle's sword, to be exact—Corth brought the round, little man up short, but not too short. The fellow was still seething with belligerence.

"Get out of my way, man," he ordered Corth. "I demand to speak with the pilot of this bus."

Corth, of course, didn't budge, so Shanelle stepped to the side of him to say, "That would be me."

"Then I will inform you, young woman, that I will have the job of every incompetent at your Center. How dare you people treat His Eminence, the High King, in such a shoddy manner. Do you even know who you're dealing with? This is intolerable—"

Shanelle had the feeling he was only working up to a really good tirade, so she cut in. "It's not the Center's fault that so many visitors showed up for the competitions and that there weren't enough *hataari* to carry them all. But I'm here to offer you a ride if you want it."

"Well, that's more like it," the man huffed. "You will fly us immediately—"

"Sorry, but if you want a ride, it will have to be on those *hataari* over there. I'm not going back to the Center, and even I can't land an airobus within the city, or didn't you people read the laws of this planet to know that isn't allowed?"

The man visibly bristled at that. "Then you are as stranded here as we are, because we have already been informed by those ignorant savages that those particular animals are not for rent."

Shanelle did some bristling of her own at that point. "Those men happen to be my father's warriors, under his orders to escort me to him, so they wouldn't give up *hataari* brought for my use no matter who the hell you say you are. And I'll have an apology on their behalf, or you can—"

"How dare you speak to me so! How *dare* you—"

"Oh, for Star's sake," Shanelle said in disgust and turned away, finished with trying to get through to someone *that* pompous.

Only she came face-to-face with the four warriors who had quietly come to join the group, and who were each looking down at her in what was so obviously amusement. Likely they had heard what had been said, and that was what they were so amused about, that she had come to *their* defense. They wouldn't have taken insult themselves, not from someone so beneath their notice as the rotund visitor was.

"The little man with the big voice requires your assistance, Shanelle," she was told by Lowen, a brown-haired warrior with eyes almost as light an amber as her own. "Best you see to it."

She thought she was being reminded of the ride she had offered, until she heard the groan. She swung around to find that the visitor must have tried to stop her from turning away from him, because Corth now had the man's fingers closed in his own fist and was bending those fingers back in such a way that the visitor dropped to his knees under the pressure.

"Let him go, Corth."

The man was released instantly, but another voice was heard from, quietly commanding, "You should have known by the way she was dressed that she was Ly-San-Ter's daughter. Apologize, Alrid."

"But, Jorran—"

"Apologize!"

The little man, still on his knees, began a long spiel about how sorry he was to have offended the daughter of the *shodan*, and damned if he didn't sound sincere. But Shanelle was barely listening.

She was looking down at herself and trying to figure out how they had guessed her identity by what she was wearing. She wasn't wearing the *chauri* that all Kan-is-Tran women wore. Her calf-length skirt might be of the same length as the *chauri*, her blouse also sleeveless, but there the similarities ended. Her outfit didn't consist of the semi-sheer scarves that made up the skirt and top of the *chauri*, but was solid white with muted silver glitter, thin, surely, but in no way transparent. The skirt was narrow; the short blouse hung loose, but conformed to her ribs and waist in the way it was draped, outlining her figure. She wore white boots instead of sandals, and even her hair was tightly rolled at her nape instead of left unbound.

Of course, she was forgetting the one item that she took for granted, that would make her father send her straight home to the palace if she wasn't wearing it: the white cloak thrown back over her shoulders that said clearly she was under the protection of the *shodan*. A blue cloak would have done just as well, blue being the color of the Ly-San-Ter family. But no Kan-is-Tran woman went out without her cloak; otherwise she became claimable.

But these visitors wouldn't know all that. It had to be the fact that she was the only one in her group cloaked, and the visitors were likewise cloaked, for them a symbol of royalty. Whatever, she finally looked at the man who had forced the other to apologize.

This one had to be the High King. He wasn't more fancily dressed, just more regal-looking, and not bad-looking either, with light blond hair cut short, emerald-green eyes, and an ideal height in her opinion of no more than six feet two. Nothing intimidating in that.

But she hadn't even noticed him before, nor had he paid much attention to her either, until he figured out who she was. Now he was smiling at her and it plainly turned her stomach. Stars, why did they always get ridiculous as soon as they knew her for a Ly-San-Ter?

"They claimed you were beautiful," he said now, offering her the barest bow—probably a tremendous concession for a man of royal blood. "I feared it would be an exaggeration, but I see instead it was an understatement."

Shanelle didn't need to hear that kind of rubbish just now, and didn't bother to address it. "If you people still need a ride up to the city, you can use three of our *hataari*. We don't mind doubling up."

"We accept your offer gladly," King Jorran told her, only to add to his men, "I will ride with the princess."

"I'm not a princess, and I'm afraid you can't ride with me. My father's warriors wouldn't like it."

"I'm pleased to know your virtue is so well guarded," he replied, if somewhat stiffly for being refused. "My queen must be untouched."

Oh, Stars, not another would-be suitor. Shanelle walked away, Corth right behind her.

"Forget it, doll," Martha said soothingly, to remind Shanelle she wasn't alone. "You were only mildly interested in that one."

"I know."

"Besides, when they know who you are, there's always the possibility that your family's wealth might be motivating them, or the prestige of being connected to a powerful *shodan*."

"I'm aware of that, Martha."

"Not that those reasons matter once they get their first look at you and see that *you* are the true treasure."

"What program are you running?" Shanelle demanded irritably. "Bolster-the-flagging-spirits?"

"You *always* get depressed over this subject for no good reason," Martha complained.

"I'm no different than any other Kan-is-Tran woman, golden from head to foot. There isn't anything unusual about me, Martha, to call for all that ridiculous flattery that comes out once men know who I am."

"Then you haven't looked in a mirror lately."

"Oh, real cute. But you don't hear warriors dumping out all that garbage."

"No, they just give you the sincerest form of flattery every time they're around you. Take a look behind you if you think I'm pulling your leg." Shanelle did, and found all four warriors following her with their eyes. "Want me to tell you what they're thinking?" Martha added.

Shanelle blushed. "No."

"Are you going to tell me you didn't know they all want you, that just about every one of them has already asked your father for you?"

"You're putting me into a really foul mood for my homecoming, Martha," Shanelle growled. "I don't *want* a warrior. I want love. I want to be able to stand on an equal footing at least some of the time with my future lifemate. I want what my mother has."

In a soft, gloating voice Martha made her point. "What your mother has is a warrior."

5

What your mother has is a warrior. Martha left Shanelle alone as they traveled the long winding road leading up to Sha-Ka-Ra, but those words wouldn't. *What your mother has is a warrior.*

Well, no one could deny it, and that particular warrior happened to love. But he was the sole exception. Only Tedra didn't think so.

"It's a fallacy," she had once told Shanelle, "that warriors don't feel love. They just *think* they don't. It's that damn calmness they pride themselves on, a *warrior's control.* And they certainly have that. They never shout, never argue, never get upset the way normal people do. It's like they have no feelings at all—but you know they do. You see the humor, the caring, even the anger if you know what to look for. Your father wouldn't admit it until he thought I was dying, and that tore him up. He cried,

Shani. He shouted to the heavens. He knew right then that he loved, and so did I."

That supposition was easy for Tedra to make. She had a warrior who admitted he loved her. But no other warrior would admit it. Even Challen's friend Tamiron, who cared deeply for his lifemate, staunchly maintained that warriors didn't feel the strong emotions their women did. Shanelle's own brother said the same thing. "Women experience love, warriors do not. Warriors give protection and caring, no more, no less." She'd thrown a pillow at him. He hadn't even raised a brow.

She hated their calm. And it stood to reason that anyone that calm couldn't experience anything as wildly passionate as love. Was she supposed to put a warrior through hell to shake him loose from that calm? And even if she could, would that do any good?

No, Tedra was wrong in this instance, and Martha wasn't helping matters by siding with Tedra as she always did and pushing Shanelle in the wrong direction. Martha meant well, of course. She knew Tedra would be hurt if Shanelle moved off-planet permanently, and so Martha would do anything to prevent that. But Shanelle wasn't going to beat her head against a wall trying to squeeze a few drops of emotion out of a man. It didn't matter that she loved the look of warriors, that she could think of a half dozen right now whom she could probably come to love if she let herself. She wasn't even going to try. She was going to put her energy into finding a man with normal emotions, one who would love her and admit it, and one who did *not* know beforehand who she was. But she had so little time . . .

"If you don't get out of those dumps you've slumped into, your mother's going to think I've been browbeating you and pull my plug." Martha's voice drifted into her thoughts.

"Well, haven't you?" Shanelle said somewhat resentfully.

"Not even a little. It's called pearly-gems-of-wisdom. Browbeating is when I pull out the big guns and mention probables for the future, like a family devastated, a daughter who can't come home because she defied her father, a mother never forgiving her lifemate because her daughter can't come home, a father who—"

"*I'm* going to pull your plug, you miserable loose-screw!" Shanelle hissed.

"That's my girl," Martha crowed. "Put some color back in those cheeks, and none too soon, or haven't you noticed where you are?"

Shanelle hadn't, and where they were was in the city already, with the park just up ahead. It no longer looked like a park, however. Covering the smooth green lawns were pavilions and tents of every color and size, and arenas roped off and crowded around by spectators watching the competitors test their skills against one another. Merchants of the city had set up stalls for food and drink; *hataari* were corralled everywhere. And Shanelle saw more warriors than she had ever seen gathered in one place before—and more visitors.

It was so unusual seeing hair and eye colors other than shades of golden-to-brown in her city. Every other color imaginable was here now, making visitors easy to spot, even though the males had gotten into the spirit of local competition by donning the black *zaalskin bracs* of the Kan-is-Tran warriors,— at least those who were competing in the arenas did, some even wearing swords.

Shanelle glanced back to see how her friends were holding up, and couldn't blame them for all looking a bit apprehensive. To the Kystrani, warriors were considered giants. The average warrior was a little more than six and a half feet tall, some reached seven feet, some even more, and here were hundreds of them milling about, bare-chested, all muscle and brawn.

Caris and Cira were probably having second thoughts about sex-sharing right now. Shanelle wasn't. She was seeing a great many visitors who actually had the look of a warrior about them, maybe not so tall, but definitely well made.

"It didn't take long for your interest to start perking." Martha chuckled. "All those bare chests, huh?"

"My mood *has* improved, and I can see my father's pavilion already, so do us both a favor and forget you have a voice, Martha."

Blissful silence, until another voice was heard from at her back. "The Martha's feelings have been hurt."

Shanelle snorted. "You're way off the mark, Corth. The Martha is sitting back gloating because she's got my life all mapped out and I haven't made any detours yet." And Shanelle wasn't going to say a single word to the contrary when Martha was listening to every word *and* monitoring her emotions with the Rover's scanning sensors.

"Your mother has seen you," Corth said next.

"Where is she?" But Shanelle saw her almost immediately, a flash of blue running through the crowds toward her. "Oh, Stars, I think I'm going to cry," she whispered as she slid off the *hataar*.

"Shanelle, wait!" Corth ordered.

"I can't!" she called back.

She was running, too, unmindful of the crowds, dodging, weaving, and she was crying. And then her mother was before her, folding her in her arms, crushing her with the strength of her emotion. Shanelle didn't care. She was hugging back just as strongly, and laughing, and still dropping those silly tears. It felt so *good* to be back in the embrace of this kind of love, where nothing could go wrong because her mother wouldn't let it.

"Oh, baby, never again." Tedra leaned back to clasp Shanelle's face, her aqua eyes devouring her as if she had never expected to see her again. "Twenty times I almost came to drag you home. I drove your father crazy. I drove myself up a wall worrying." She laughed then. "But you're here, you're all right—you *are* all right, aren't you?"

Shanelle laughed, too. "Yes."

Tedra gathered her close again. "And you'll stay that way. And you'll stay here. No," she whispered at Shanelle's ear when she felt her stiffen. "You aren't to worry. If I have to let you go, I will. I'll even keep Martha on the Rover so *she* can take you out of here if necessary. But I will do everything in my power to ensure that it isn't necessary."

"Even if it isn't a Sha-Ka'ani that I want?" Shanelle asked hesitantly.

Tedra leaned back again with a sigh. "You've made your choice, then? You've already met the one you want?"

"No."

"Then we will worry about *who* he is after you've found him. Your father isn't entirely closed-minded about this. He wants your happiness just as much as I do. But we'll talk about this when we have more time."

That comment drew Shanelle back to the fact that they weren't alone, that they were in the middle of a crowd on a lane between arenas, and just now the center of attention. "Why is everyone staring at us?"

Tedra chuckled. "Well, for one thing, Corth charged right after you on that *hataar* you two were riding, knocking people every which way. You know you're not supposed to leave his sight."

Shanelle glanced over her shoulder. Sure enough, Corth had caught up to her and was standing right behind them. "I guess I wasn't thinking."

"And for another thing," Tedra continued, giving her another squeeze, "I think I can safely say we've just made a complete spectacle of ourselves. Let's hope this doesn't get back to your father, or *I'm* going to be in trouble for running off without an escort."

It was Shanelle's turn to chuckle as she looked over her mother's shoulder and saw who else had just arrived. "Too late."

Tedra groaned and said, "Farden hell," before

she glanced back to say defensively to her lifemate, "I was not about to wait for her to reach me once I had spotted her, Challen. It would be totally unreasonable for you to expect me to after her *nine months' absence*."

"Best you remember whose idea it was for her to absent herself," Challen told her.

"That's right, run it into the ground, why don't you," Tedra snapped back.

"Woman, you are coming very close to challenge for no reason."

"I am?" Tedra said with some surprise. "Then you aren't angry with me?"

"Not when your impulsiveness is understandable. Now do you release her so I may greet my daughter properly."

Properly was not to hug in public, and Challen began by merely looking Shanelle over from head to foot, lifting her face and studying it as Tedra had done. Then, to her immense surprise, she was drawn forward and engulfed in a warrior's arms. Challen didn't squeeze her, but she felt surrounded by his strength—and his love.

"Your mother has missed you," he told her formally, but with feeling.

She grinned widely. You had to read between the lines with a Sha-Ka'ani male. It was rarely "I," usually "a warrior," or in Challen's case, "your mother." But she knew he was speaking for himself, and he knew she knew, and his own smile was incredibly beautiful.

He hadn't changed at all in the time Shanelle had been away, but then she hadn't expected him to.

In all the years of her life, she had never noticed her parents growing older, because they just didn't look like they *were* growing older. But it was a known fact that the Sha-Ka'ani aged well. And Tedra, though not a Sha-Ka'ani, was still a Sec 1 heart and soul, and she had always taken extremely good care of her body, which in a good many cultures was considered a lethal weapon. Not in this culture, however, and not to her lifemate, who was just short of seven feet tall and had the strength to go along with such a large body.

Shanelle grinned up at her father now, craning her neck to do so. "I'm so glad to be home. And I thank you for the airobus. That was a wonderful surprise."

"What airobus?" her father asked.

"Challen, I think we should get back to the pavilion now," Tedra put in hastily.

"What airobus?" he repeated, looking down at his lifemate.

"All right, the one *we* bought her. That is why *we* sent her to Kystran, to learn how to pilot. That *is* what she wants to do, something useful—"

"Something her future lifemate is not likely to allow," he calmly pointed out. "Did you consider that when you convinced me to let her go to Kystran?"

"No, but you obviously did," Tedra grumbled. "Why did you agree, then?"

Challen put a hand to her cheek, suddenly grinning at her. "You can ask me that, *chemar*, after everything you did to get my permission?"

Hot pink cheeks, fortunately, went well with the

blue of Tedra's *chauri* and cloak. Only the cloak
needed to be blue or white to denote whose house
she belonged to, but she was honoring Challen by
wearing all blue today, right down to her sandals.
Now she wished she hadn't.

She knocked his hand aside, but that just got
a chuckle out of him. Her embarrassment was
a subtle punishment for buying that bus without
telling him. She knew it. She knew him too well
not to know it. And she could only hope that would
be the only punishment she would be getting. But a
glance at Shanelle showed she was aware of it, too.
Farden hell. That was all Shanelle needed, one more
reminder that warriors were not the easiest men to
get along with, when she had yet to experience any
of the benefits of trying. And on top of that, to be told
outright that her future lifemate wasn't likely to let
her fly . . . She could kick Challen right now.

"You don't know what her lifemate is going to
do—or do you?" Her eyes narrowed the tiniest bit.
"You haven't made a decision without telling me,
have you, babe?"

Both women waited anxiously for his answer,
Tedra ready to blow a fuse if it was the wrong one,
Shanelle merely with dread, and it began by being
not at all reassuring. "When a decision is made,
woman, you do not need to be told of it beforehand.
But no, such has not yet been decided."

Shanelle let out a sigh. That had been too nerve-
racking. "Father, I need to talk to you about this
decision."

"This you may do, yet is the decision mine to
make, yours to accept."

Shanelle gritted her teeth. "I know that, but does that mean you won't take heed of my own wishes in the matter? What if I make my own choice?"

"Then it will be my hope that I can accept your choice."

Shanelle blinked. "Do you mean that? You'll really consider my preference?"

"Certainly, *kerima*," he replied gently. "Did you think I would not?"

No, of course he would. He loved her. He wanted her to be happy. But the key word was *if*. If he could accept her choice, then she could have her choice. If he could not, then she would have *his* choice. But that was still better than what she had been anticipating, that he would have made his decision before she found someone for herself, that it would then be *if* she could accept his choice.

"Stars, you people are absolutely depressing," Martha chimed in with blatant disgust. "What happened to the happy homecoming?"

Tedra laughed. Shanelle's frown was an exact copy of Challen's upon hearing that.

"Mother, it gives me the greatest pleasure to give you back your computer."

But Tedra stopped her from removing the computer-link unit from her waist. "Not yet. I'm sure you're going to want to show those friends around that Martha told me about last night—"

"She contacted you last night without telling me?" Shanelle demanded.

"Well, I don't know why she didn't mention it, but yes, we had a long chat, and anyway, I'll feel better if you have Martha with you in addition to

Corth, and I'm sure your father will, too. With
Martha there to whisk you out of any trouble—
not that I anticipate any—your father won't feel
it necessary to send his warriors along with you.
Isn't that right, Challen?"

But Tedra was still looking meaningfully at
Shanelle, and Shanelle finally got the message,
the *unspoken* message. She didn't want Challen's
warriors dogging her steps, not today. Today was
the one day she could be anonymous, but not with
a full escort that would point out how important she
was. Only Challen hadn't even heard the question.
Looking at the computer link had drawn his attention
to what Shanelle was wearing, and his frown hadn't
changed any.

"First she will take herself home to find the
proper clothing. She looks like a visitor."

"Give her a break, damn it," Tedra replied impatiently. "She just got here. And so what if she looks
like a visitor. A quarter of the people here are
visitors. For once it doesn't make any difference,
and she *is* cloaked, which is all that really matters.
You wouldn't really make her waste all that time
going home when she has guests to see to?"

"Your Martha could Transfer her—"

"You've *got* to be kidding," Tedra cut in dryly.
"You'd let her Transfer when it isn't an emergency, when you hate Transferring?" Challen was
looking completely chagrined by now, so Tedra
added, "And her friends have caught up with her.
You're not going to embarrass your daughter over
something so minor, are you?"

For that Tedra got a just-wait-until-later look.

Shanelle got her cloak adjusted over her shoulders to cover more of her outfit, which she understood she was to leave that way—at least until she was out of her father's sight.

"The competitions will continue this rising and likely several more," he told Shanelle. "You may view them with your friends, but Martha is to Transfer you to me if you have any difficulties with these warriors who do not know you. Is this understood, Martha?"

"Crystal clear, big guy."

Shanelle's friends did arrive then, along with the nobles from Century III, who arrogantly demanded Challen's attention even before Shanelle could finish introducing her friends. So her mother shooed her off with a whispered "Good luck, baby," a wink, and a grin.

Martha was chuckling as they left. "My Tedra was in top form, wasn't she? I love it when she talks circles around that warrior."

"You told her about my desire to be incognito, didn't you?" Shanelle ventured.

"Sure I did. I told her *everything*, kiddo. You knew I would."

Shanelle's sigh was loud and long. "All right, Martha, if I have to be stuck with you for the rest of the day, try making me forget it."

6

"Close your mouth," Shanelle told Caris with a grin. "You're about to drool."

"I can't help it, Shani." Caris sighed. "Will you just look at the muscles on that warrior? They look like they're going to burst right through his skin."

The muscles Caris found so fascinating were indeed bulging, but then the contest they were watching was one of strength, where two men would clasp hands and attempt to push each other off-balance. Lines were marked in the grass about two feet behind each contestant, so each had a little leeway, but not too much. The one to be pushed over his line lost the match.

From where Shanelle and Caris stood, they were seeing more of one warrior's back than the other's, and this was the warrior who had gained Caris's avid attention. But Shanelle wasn't seeing anything out of the ordinary. She wanted to go and watch the visitor events instead, but Caris had dragged her over here first.

This wasn't a contest for visitors. Visitors simply wouldn't stand a chance competing against a warrior's strength, and weren't expected to. They could try competing with warriors if they were daring enough, but they had their own contests in marksmanship, dexterity, speed, and agility. The main event, the one to claim the most arenas, was naturally sword fighting. The champion sword-fighter had to beat all comers. The champion of the visitor events could then elect to fight the warrior champion with swords—or not, and likely not. So, in fact, there could end up being two champions of the competitions, and it was the general consensus that this was how it would end. Presently, all events were still in the process of eliminations.

Only Caris remained with Shanelle, and, of course, Corth, who was being silently inconspicuous. Cira had ridden up to Sha-Ka-Ra with one of Shanelle's escorts and had already made arrangements to spend the day with him before their arrival in the city. Jadd was sticking close to Dren, both Kystran males feeling quite out of their element amongst so many giants, but they had found a fascination in the sword-fighting competitions, and so had been left behind at those arenas with Yari.

Caris was interested only in warriors, which was why they were still in this section of the park, which had few arenas for visitors. But Shanelle was clearly getting bored, so it was no wonder her eyes started to wander, first to the spectators on the opposite side of the large arena, then beyond to the line of tents that spread out to the edges of the park. A white one in front drew her notice because it looked like a miniature version of her father's pavilion, so she was looking at it when the four men stepped out of it.

They were a little too far away for Shanelle to make out their features, but her attention was definitely snagged, for these were obviously visitors by the dark color of their hair, yet all four were warrior-tall, warrior-big. Stars, what planet did they come from, that they had such a look of the warrior about them? Three had hair as dark as Shanelle's mother, black as the *zaalskin bracs* they were wearing. The fourth man had chestnut hair, almost as dark.

The men spoke together for a moment in front of the tent before they split up, two going off toward the front of the park, two coming toward the end where Shanelle stood. These two were of an exact height, young, she saw as they got closer, maybe four or five years older than she, and handsome, she saw as they got closer still. She held her breath, hoping they would stop at the arena in front of her, and when they did, she forgot about letting her breath out.

Oh, Heaven's Stars, was he splendid, the one she couldn't take her eyes off now that she could distinguish their features. This one wasn't merely handsome, he was sensually appealing to every one of Shanelle's senses. His black hair was long and thick, caressing warriorlike shoulders and a thick neck. His skin was darker than golden; his chest and arms were immense, perhaps larger than those of some warriors she knew. He had an arrogant cut to his square jaw, hard, chiseled lips, a well-shaped nose for his face, and thick black brows that drew together in a serious manner as he spoke again to his companion.

Shanelle was still watching him when his eyes touched on her in passing—and came right back. Azure they were, as light as a midday sky, and disconcerting in their intensity, making her feel things . . .

She looked away, back to the two warriors straining in the arena, and heard Martha's voice. "If I'm reading you right, doll, you just got your socks knocked off."

"Stars, so this is what it feels like." A fist seemed to be squeezing her belly—no pain, just the strangest, most pleasant feeling.

Martha chuckled. "All right, where is he? I've got to see this incredible specimen for myself."

Suddenly Shanelle felt fearful and nervous. She didn't *want* Martha to know he was a visitor. This was so important! *Calm down, for Stars' sake.* Where were these emotions coming from?

"Not yet, Martha. I want to be sure I haven't just conjured him up with wishful thinking."

"Your whole system's gone haywire. You don't get that from fantasies."

"What's your Martha saying, Shani?" Caris questioned at her side.

"Nothing. How's your warrior doing?" Even as Shanelle asked this, the man won the match and Caris started squealing in delight. Shanelle grinned,

beginning to feel some of her anxiety dissolving.
"You won't get to meet him as long as he keeps
winning, unless no one else challenges him."

The judge of this arena was already leading in the
next warrior, a seven-footer. Caris frowned. "But I
don't want to hope he loses."

"If it's far enough along in the eliminations of
this arena, then losing here may not put him out
of the running. There are the other skills to consider."

Caris was no longer paying attention to what
Shanelle was saying, caught up as she was in the
new match, which had just begun. Shanelle took
the opportunity to steal another glance at the black-
haired visitor and once more met those light blue
eyes head-on. Stars, had he been watching her all
this time? She felt nervous again, and there was
no reason for it. She wanted him to be interested.
She wouldn't utter a single protest if he came over,
grabbed her hand, and dragged her off. Of course
he wouldn't do that. He was a visitor from another
planet. Visitors, most of them, tended to do things
in a civilized fashion. What a waste of time!

Time she didn't have. But she couldn't be *too*
easy. She didn't want to scare him off. He had to
want her enough to ask her father for her, but she
didn't know if he wanted her at all yet. *Entice him,
Shani. Make him come to you. If he loses interest,*
then *you can be aggressive.*

Slowly this time, as if reluctantly, she looked
away, back to the two warriors straining in the
arena. She watched Caris's warrior being shoved
over his line and heard her friend sigh.

"He loses and I win." Caris was just short of chuckling now. "I think I'll go over and introduce myself and offer a little sympathy."

"Go ahead. I'll wait for you here."

"She has the right idea," Martha said as soon as Caris hurried off. "What are *you* waiting for?"

Shanelle glanced again toward the black-haired visitor, then looked quickly away. He was still staring at her. But his expression was unchanged. He hadn't even smiled at her yet.

"I'm waiting for him to come to me."

"We're not playing games here, kiddo," Martha said, adding a big dose of exasperation to her tone. "You want him, go get him."

"Damn it, Martha, it's not that easy. And let *me* handle this, will you?"

Determinedly she watched the next match, all of it, without once glancing toward the visitor. The seven-footer won again, easily. He really was mammoth and would likely last a good long while, possibly the rest of the day.

Why hadn't he come over yet? Visitors weren't typically shy or hesitant. Maybe he didn't want her. Maybe he only found her curious, looking like a Sha-Ka'ani female but dressed like a visitor—except for the cloak she was wearing. Was it the damn cloak? Did he think it made her unavailable? He could at least ask!

She gave him another quick glance. The moment she did, he entered the arena. Shanelle's eyes flared wide. Her gasp brought Corth to her side.

"What is wrong?"

"Nothing, Corth."

"I'd better get a better answer than that," Martha's voice warned.

"He's entered the competition."

"Well, that ought to be interesting. *Now* can I have a look?"

"Not yet."

"I'd be getting suspicious, Shani, if I weren't monitoring you."

"Be quiet, Martha."

Shanelle couldn't believe he was doing this. The warrior had at least four inches on him and a great deal more weight. But the visitor clasped hands with him, took up the correct stance, and then looked again at Shanelle. In that moment she knew why he was in there. He *did* want her. She had been watching the contestants, but he wanted her eyes on him, so he became a contestant. What a sweet, jealous thing to do—and so foolish. He couldn't possibly win. But she'd take a leaf from Caris's book and give him a dose of sympathy when he lost.

Only he didn't lose right away. The pushing and straining began and it was magnificent to watch. Muscles appeared and bulged prominently on the visitor that Shanelle wouldn't have imagined he could possess. Her breathing quickened. She found herself straining right along with him, and suddenly she wanted him to win so bad she could taste it, because here was a visitor her father could approve of. That had been one of her main stumbling blocks, that her father wouldn't accept a visitor, any visitor, but he could certainly accept one who could defeat a warrior.

Her eyes were on his face now, willing him to

do it, and it was in the exact moment when his eyes came to Shanelle to assure himself she was watching that he gathered the last effort to win. He did it. The mighty warrior stumbled back over his line, their hands separated, and the visitor stood victorious and stared right at Shanelle.

She didn't jump up and down squealing like Caris had done, but that was what she felt was going on inside her. She was absolutely ecstatic, and her grin showed it.

"I'd swear you were being kissed and loving it, but I know no one's touching you," Martha remarked, actually sounding curious. "What's got you even more excited?"

"He just beat a warrior, Martha." And Shanelle was the one feeling proud.

"So?"

"All right, take a look." She positioned the computer-link unit so that the viewer on the end was aiming right at the triumphant visitor.

"Shani, you'd better be pointing in the wrong direction," Martha said, clearly irritated. "That's not a warrior."

"I don't care what he is, he's the one. And I'm going to turn you off now, Martha. I don't need any help from the sidelines."

"Don't you dare. Your mother pulled that once and got herself claimed."

"And look how nicely that ended up."

"Shani—"

Martha's voice was cut off, but Shanelle knew she could still hear and monitor her with the Rover's short-range scanner, so she offered, "I'm sorry,

Martha, but I've made my choice." She patted the unit at her waist. "I'll talk to you later."

"I believe the man wishes me to challenge him, Shani," Corth remarked suddenly.

Her "choice" *was* looking directly at Corth just then. "Glance away," she told him. "In fact, move away. He thinks you're with me."

"I am with you."

"You know what I mean. And stop grinning. This isn't funny. He's a visitor. Unlike warriors, visitors *do* get jealous over the most ridiculous things, and that's not how I want to start out this relationship."

"Perhaps I should oblige him." Corth's humor mode was obviously running on strong. "To show him I am merely a machine," he added.

Shanelle knew it was still in his programming, the time Challen had been jealous of him. Even after her father had been told Corth was only a machine, he'd still been jealous of him. And Corth's strength was ten times greater than any man's, including a warrior's. She wasn't going to have him prove that to the visitor when the test wouldn't be for the contest, but over her.

"All right, you've had your little joke, Corth. But that's the man I want to get to know, and I mean *know*. So absent yourself for a while."

"You know I cannot do that, Shani."

"Then keep me within your sight, but yourself out of *his* notice. You can do that—"

Shanelle fell silent as she realized it was too late. The visitor was already approaching, signaling the judge that he wouldn't be participating further at this time. And with those long legs, he was there before Shanelle could get her thoughts together. But he was still looking only at Corth.

"If you wish not to enter these competitions, we can go elsewhere to settle this matter in private."

He had the Sha-Ka'ani language down pat, with only a slight accent that was really very lyrical, but Shanelle's mouth dropped at that opening challenge, and it *was* a challenge. Corth, however, was still finding the situation highly amusing.

He smiled at the visitor. "This we could do, yet would the doing be unnecessary. The woman has made her choice."

Those light blue eyes came to Shanelle, and even through her sudden mortification, she knew she was looking at an intensity of emotion the likes of which she'd never experienced before. Hot, savage—scary, but gone as soon as he looked back at Corth, leaving Shanelle merely shaken and wondering if she'd imagined it. But she hadn't imagined Corth's bald statement.

"I'm going to unplug you for that," she whispered to her friend, her cheeks still burning.

Both males chose not to hear her, or else hadn't heard her during their continuing regard of each other. The visitor was looking at Corth's hair when he asked him, "Are you from the east?"

"No," Corth said simply.

"From this planet?"

"Not originally."

That easily, Corth was dismissed and Shanelle had the man's attention again. She found it amusing that he had thought Corth a warrior, even though he lacked the bulging biceps of a warrior, and the extreme height. And she could be amused because those azure eyes weren't so unsettling this time, but were merely appraising, curious, and definitely interested.

"He is no more than your escort?" he asked her.

"An escort, but also a friend—also an android."

"An android."

He said the word as if he didn't know what it meant, but Shanelle decided only one thing needed clarification just then. "He will leave me with you if you want to—talk."

She put enough insinuation into the last word that a dummy could catch her meaning, yet the man took her literally. "I would do more than talk."

So it was going to take plain speaking, was it? She grinned. As long as he wasn't a warrior, she could be as bold as she pleased.

"So would I," she told him.

The man's smile at that point nearly made her knees buckle. How was it possible for his attractiveness to double with a mere curling of the lips? And that wasn't all he did. He bent under the thick cable that roped off the arena and came to stand directly in front of Shanelle, and that close, his size just about overwhelmed her.

He really was only an inch or two shorter than her father, which put him nearly a foot above her own head. And the width of him . . . A body like his was nice to look at, it surely was, but she really wished he wasn't so tall, or so strong. That was one of the reasons she didn't want a warrior. You simply had no defense against someone this big. And this big someone was a visitor, which meant he wouldn't have a warrior's control—the control that kept a warrior from accidentally or otherwise hurting a woman who was, of course, much smaller than he.

Suddenly Shanelle realized that if she proceeded, she might be letting herself in for some unwanted pain—and not just the kind that went along with losing one's virginity. Stars, why hadn't that occurred to her sooner? But look at him! He was absolutely gorgeous. And he was the one who had knocked her socks off. There was no getting around that.

She bit her lip in indecision. Dared she take the chance? Damn it, yes! It was incredible that she'd found him at all and so soon, so she wasn't going to press her luck by looking any further. And he might be big, but that didn't mean he wouldn't be careful with her.

She stepped back a little to relieve the strain on her neck that staring up at him was causing. He caught her hand, however, and pulled her right back. And he did not release her hand now that he had it. She couldn't complain about his wanting to touch her. She wanted to touch him, too. But she could complain about the close proximity.

"You're going to have to give me some space if you want me to look at you. My neck won't bear up very long under this strain."

It took only one of his thick arms to lift her and hold her up against his chest. She felt a thrill of alarm at his aggressive boldness, but they were now eye-to-eye, and Shanelle had a new problem, one with her senses. Stars, it felt wonderful to be pressed against him like this, so wonderful that she didn't want to recall that they couldn't stay this way, not here anyway. But she did recall it.

"You know this won't work, big guy, not in public." But she compromised. "Put me down and give me an arm's length. You can keep my hand."

"My name is Falon Van'yer," was how he responded to her order.

"I'm glad to know it, but you're still going to have to put me down until we aren't so public."

"You say that as if you expect to have it your way. Do you often have your way?"

She sensed his amusement over the subject. Nor was he putting her down.

"I don't always get my way, no," she admitted carefully. "But a good deal of the time I do, especially when I'm using common sense and others are not."

He laughed, a bass rumble she felt clear to her toes. "I, too, am accustomed to having my way, but all of the time. And I have a small advantage over you."

Was that supposed to be his idea of a joke? "Why be modest? You have a *big* advantage over me." And then her eyes narrowed. "You aren't going to put me down, are you?"

"No."

"Not even if it causes problems when a warrior demands that you release me? I *am* protected, Falon Van'yer, and this cloak I'm wearing is well recognized."

His other hand came up to finger the cloak at her shoulder. "I am aware of this, woman, though I could wish it were otherwise. Yet have you given yourself into my care for the while, so there will be no difficulty with these Kan-is-Tran warriors."

She wasn't going to point out that the warriors who might stop him were her father's warriors who knew her. She still didn't want him to know who she was until it was absolutely necessary. And there was only one alternative just now.

She suggested it. "How about you put me down long enough for us to leave here?"

"So you still try to have it your way even though I have refused you? Is this going to be a problem, woman, your being unable to accept my will?"

Shanelle had a feeling that question was too important by half. If she said yes, would he put her down and walk away? But she couldn't say no, because it just might be a problem. And maybe she'd better find out right now if it would be.

"I had hoped we could spend some time together to get to know each other. That does not mean I belong to you, Falon. Even if I did belong to you, I might not agree with everything you say. I'm not a slave who will obey without question. I have my own opinions and feelings, which may or may not be contrary to yours. If your will is reasonable and justified, of course I can accept it. But if it is not, don't expect me to keep quiet about it. And I think I would like to know now if it is against your principles to take what I say under consideration."

"Have I not just listened to everything you had to say?" he said.

"That's true, you did. And you haven't run like hell on finding out I can be a tiny bit arbitrary." He smiled at that. So did she. "Perhaps you might tell me why you don't want to put me down."

"Because I like the feel of you against me too much. Because I would rather fight every warrior here than lose this feeling for even a moment."

Oh, Stars, with reasons like that, it wasn't going to take her long at all to love this man as well as desire him. "Why didn't you just say so?"

He grinned at her. "So my will has suddenly become acceptable to you?"

"You've managed to—justify it. And I never said *I* couldn't be reasonable. Perhaps if we disappear real quick, the problems I foresaw won't materialize. Would that tent you left earlier happen to be yours—and vacant?"

"It is both, though I am not sure this brazenness of yours pleases me. When and where I take you is for me to decide, you to anticipate."

She stared at him incredulously for a moment before she burst out, "Stars, where have I heard *that* before?" And then she asked suspiciously, "You're not from Kan-is-Tra after all, are you?"

"No—and neither are you, which I forgot for a moment. Your brazenness is acceptable."

She grinned at him, wondering just where he thought she *did* come from that her brazenness was suddenly okay by him. But she wouldn't correct him on his assumption that she wasn't from here. She didn't want to deny who she was if she didn't have to, and the less he asked right now, the better. And she was nothing but relieved to have it confirmed that he wasn't a warrior, after he'd started sounding too damn much like one. But these were little problems they could work out after they got the main one of compatibility out of the way.

But she was curious enough to ask, "Do the women repress their desires where you come from?"

"They are more circumspect."

"Then maybe you ought to think of living elsewhere."

"I do not think so."

She sighed at that quick answer. "Why don't we work on the principle that there is an inducement for everything and leave it at that for now?"

"Of what do you speak now?"

"Never mind. This isn't the time to—"

"Shani!" Caris called.

"Farden hell," Shanelle muttered, then looked ruefully at Falon. "That's me being called. I don't suppose you might reconsider and put me down long enough for me to talk to my friend?" He merely stared back at her without answering, which was his answer. "Maybe your arm is getting just a little tired holding me up?" she tried next.

"You weigh nothing, *kerima*."

She made a face at that. "I'm a *big* girl, not a little one. Little describes my friend Caris."

"The female who was with your earlier is no more than a child."

"She's not a child, she's just short and—"

Caris had reached them at that point, her warrior in tow. "Shani, I—" She paused when she noticed Falon. "Oh, my." But then she took in

Shanelle's position and the implications of it, and added, "Oh, *my.*"

Shanelle didn't even try to deny what her friend was now obviously thinking. "We'll keep this between ourselves, won't we, Caris?"

"If you insist, but Yari and Cira will be just as pleased for you as I am. It certainly took you long enough, Shani, but now you can find out—"

"Not now, Caris."

"Sure." The younger girl grinned. "I just wanted to let you know I will be busy myself for a few hours. Komar here wants to show me his tent."

"Did you remember to tell him you are protected by the *shodan*?"

Caris grimaced. "As a matter of fact, I forgot." She glanced back at the large warrior holding her hand. "Is that going to make a difference, that I'm protected?"

"It keeps me from claiming you, had that been my thought," Komar stated.

"Notice how he doesn't confirm or deny if that was his intention," Caris said to Shanelle.

"That's to keep you from being disappointed either way," Shanelle replied.

"How sweet. I *knew* I was going to like this warrior. So I'll see you later, Shani."

"You know where to meet me?"

"Sure do."

"Why is it you wear your protection and she does not?" Falon asked as soon as they were alone again.

"I knew I was coming here. For Caris, it was a last-minute decision."

"Also are you well acquainted with the customs of this place."

That was an observation, not a question, and he was getting too close to the truth for comfort. She needed to get him thinking along different lines, and there was one sure way to do that quickly and completely. She just wished she had more experience in the area.

She lowered her lashes, displaying a shyness that was only half feigned, and twirled a lock of his hair about one finger. "You've been holding me a long time, Falon," she said softly, peeking up at him quickly, then away again. "Is that all you want to do with me?"

Shanelle was amazed that she could suddenly feel his heart beating against her chest. But even as she felt it, her legs were being gathered up, so that she was now cradled in his arms and he was moving, quite rapidly, in the direction of the tents. She held on to his neck, though it wasn't necessary, because he held her tightly, protectively. She was merely trying to hide her face so that whoever noticed them wouldn't recognize her. The one thing she didn't want was someone who knew her following right now.

But she had learned something. Maybe she shouldn't have tried being sexually provocative with a man she knew nothing about, but it had proved that his attraction to her was possibly as powerful as hers was to him. He hadn't even answered her question. He was *showing* her instead.

Shanelle had told herself she wouldn't protest if
Falon Van'yer dragged her off. Being carried off
amounted to the same thing, and she wasn't pro-
testing. But she certainly hadn't expected it of a
visitor.

Typically, if a people were advanced enough to
travel from planet to planet, rather than merely
from town to town, there tended to be a high level
of sophistication in their social practices, too. Even
if a planet were discovered and advanced by its
discoverers, the people tended to broaden their way
of doing things as well.

There were only a few planets that Shanelle knew
of that doggedly clung to their old traditions even
after discovery. Century III was one, nearly medi-
eval in culture, yet taking to space because it now
could. Sha-Ka'ar, evolved from Sha-Ka'an more
than three hundred years ago, was another, where

not a single woman on that planet was anything but a slave. But the men visited other worlds. Sha-Ka'an was also a good example, yet with another difference. It had been discovered, but the people had no wish to visit the rest of the universe or take advantage of what that universe could do for them.

Falon Van'yer, wherever he was from, was again treating her like a warrior might, and it was again beginning to worry Shanelle. And he had reached the white tent that was his, shouldering his way through the slitted opening, then through another opening deeper inside which divided the tent into separate areas.

This second area was strewn with fat pillows and different colored and textured animal pelts, and onto a thick bundle of these was Shanelle put down. Falon had gone to his knees to place her there, and he didn't rise from them now.

Her worry was triggering a certain nervousness, or perhaps it had been there despite her earlier brazenness. This *was* going to be her first sex-sharing experience. Some trepidation had to be expected, she supposed, no matter how much she wanted this to happen. But his actions said it was going to happen too quickly.

Shanelle came up on her knees to face him, hoping that would slow him down, but already he was reaching for the ties of her cloak. "Can—can we talk about customs, you and me?"

"Whatever you wish to call it, woman, we have begun it."

"I didn't mean—"

"There is only one thing I object to," he said with a kernel of annoyance in his tone and expression. "Thus do we rid you of it now."

Shanelle watched her cloak sail through the opening into the front half of the tent. Out of sight, out of effectiveness?

She felt she had better clarify. "That doesn't mean I'm no longer protected."

"I am aware of this, yet was it inhibiting me."

Inhibiting him, when his eyes had already been filled with that wildly turbulent emotion she'd seen earlier? If that was going to now be released . . .

It was purely instinctive at that point for her to draw back from him when his hands came toward her again. He noticed, though that didn't stop his intent.

His fingers were now delving into her hair to loosen it. "Why is there fear in your eyes now, when before there was none?" he asked.

"Not fear, just—you seem a little too intense now, Falon, like you're about to lose control."

She had to brush his hands aside when he couldn't figure out how to open the Kystrani binder that held her hair so tightly in place. She pressed the release mechanism at her nape, and her hair spilled down her back. Instantly, Falon brought it over her shoulder to hold in his hands, gazing at the golden length in wonder.

"I had not realized," he said to himself as he pressed her hair to his cheeks, "this, too, would be magnificent. Gold has so little value here, yet on you it becomes a treasure."

Shanelle took pleasure in hearing that, yet she still had self-preservation on her mind when he started to draw her forward by her hair. "You *aren't* going to lose control, are you?"

"Would it reassure you to know I never have?"

"It would reassure me to know this won't be the first time you might."

"I cannot swear to it, woman. I have never felt this way before."

"What way?"

His fingers came to her face to learn the feel of it, not roughly but not exactly gently. "It took no more than my first sight of you to know that I want you to belong to me."

She wasn't sure she understood. "But you can have me."

"For now. And I am more grateful than I can say that you give yourself to me for this time, yet do I know this is only temporary." His hands cupped her face then, bringing it closer to his. "Do you understand I want the right to command you? I want you cloaked in my protection, not that of another. That I am denied all means of obtaining you that are known to me is intolerable."

His intensity was frightening and exciting her at the same time. But he was sounding more and more like a warrior, and that just increased her unease. Still she asked, "Is that the only problem?"

"No," he said in all seriousness. "I have been ready to join with you since I first saw you, that powerful was my reaction to you. It has not lessened, *kerima*, it has increased. So I cannot give you the tender care I would like, yet you need not fear I will hurt you. Sooner would I leave you now than hurt you, and I cannot leave you now."

She wasn't exactly reassured. It was one thing for a man of normal size to get carried away by his emotions, but Falon was in no way normal-sized. Of course, that "tender care" he'd just mentioned he couldn't give her could refer to the amount of time he would spend giving her pleasure, rather than the way in which he would handle her. On the other hand, how would he define "hurt"? Anything short of dead?

That did it. Her libido might still be jumping up and down at the sight of Falon Van'yer, and to be honest, she was thrilled to know he wanted her that much. But she had to be crazy to take this kind of risk, especially after he had already admitted that he couldn't be sure he wouldn't lose control, that he couldn't give her the tender care he would like to, which absolutely contradicted his assurance that he wouldn't hurt her. And he was *definitely* too damn warriorlike to suit her.

She never should have come in here, never should have let it go this far. Now what was she going to do? Leave, of course, but without an ugly argument if she could help it. And she wasn't at all sure he *would* just let her go now anyway. So she would have to trick him somehow, maybe into closing his eyes, and then slip out and disappear before he even knew she was gone. Easier said than done, with him presently holding her, she realized.

And then it occurred to her to put her fear, which he'd already noticed, to good use. "You know,

Falon, we could wait a while, just until you're not so—intense about this."

"Do you jest?" he groaned.

"All right, so that option is out. Close your eyes, then, and no touching for a moment. I'm going to undress myself so my clothes don't get demolished by those untender hands of yours. When I'm finished, you still aren't to look. Looking can sometimes be stimulating, and we don't want you any more stimulated than you already are if I'm to survive this."

"You still think I will harm you?"

"Not intentionally."

"I do not want you to fear me, woman."

He said it so sternly, she almost released a nervous laugh. "Then let's try it my way, okay? You start by closing your eyes."

He did, and sat back on his heels, but his expression was a prime example of chagrined impatience. "I would prefer it did I demolish—"

"*That's* not an option."

"Then best you hurry, woman."

That was the best advice she'd ever heard, and she immediately started backing away from him, but she'd scooted only a couple of feet when his command stopped her.

"Talk to me, woman. Distract me from imagining what you are doing."

Farden hell. But distraction wasn't a bad idea, just in case she got caught sneaking out and had to talk her way out instead. Distraction might calm down his turbulent emotions, so he would be reasonable about it.

"Very well," she said. "But you must continue to keep your eyes closed."

"Must? I do not care for your habit of giving orders, woman."

She ignored his grumble because he was still obeying her despite it. She supposed he just needed to file that protest for the record.

And just to reassure him, she said, "I wouldn't presume to give you orders, Falon. Suggestions are more in my nature." Especially with men his size, she thought with a mixture of amusement and apprehension. She scooted another foot back, raising her tone slightly so he wouldn't notice. "Now, let's talk about names and why you haven't said mine yet even once. You did hear what my name is earlier, didn't you?"

"I heard it," he snorted. "Yet does it not have a womanly sound to it."

Another foot got her off the pile of furs. "That's true, which is why my mother loves it and my father won't use it. It's what my friends call me, but you—I guess you can call me anything you like."

"I wish to call you mine."

He said it simply, but with feeling, and the words shot straight to Shanelle's core. She had wanted him to be able to call her his, too, before she got cold feet. What if he wouldn't hurt her? What if she had let her anxieties get the better of her and would be missing out on the best thing that could ever happen to her?

Farden hell, she was doing it again, letting her attraction to him blind her to what was a clear fact. The man could crush her in his bare hands, and he was just too damn intense in his feelings. And *that* was not at all warriorlike.

"You're very . . . possessive . . . aren't you?" She scooted two more steps back and slowly rose to her feet. "That's an old-fashioned trait on most worlds. What planet did you say you were from?"

"I did not say. Does it matter where I am from?"

"No." She gasped, for he'd reached out for her as he asked it. "As long as you're not from here."

She turned and ran, then cried out as she was jerked to a halt by a fist in her hair before she even reached the opening to the front half of the tent.

"Where do you think to go, woman?"

He didn't sound angry. And she had known she might have to talk her way out of there instead. But her heart was pounding in fright. Stars, how she hated confrontations.

"I—I've changed my mind, Falon."

His answer was to lift her with an arm around her waist and carry her back to the fur pelts. Shanelle's anxiety turned into panic.

"Didn't you hear me?" she wailed.

"Indeed," he said as he laid her down and came down to half cover her body with his. "Yet have I not changed my mind, so best you change yours again. You wanted me. You *chose* me, woman."

"That was before you started acting so damn warriorlike. But you couldn't be enough like a warrior where it counts, could you?" she accused him. "You had to be too emotional. Well, you're too farden big to be that intense!"

"And this frightens you?"

"Are you kidding? I have strange reactions to pain, Falon Van'yer. I get hysterical. Now let me up."

Slowly he shook his head. "I regret your fear, *kerima*, but I have told you I will not hurt you. The proof will be in the doing."

"Wait!"

Shanelle didn't have a chance to say more, for he was discovering the benefits of Kystrani clothing. It was designed for quick and easy removal. A tug, a push, and it simply fell away from the body. But it had never come off as fast as it did in Falon's hands. And then his hand held her mouth still for his ravishment, while his other hand discovered the shape and responsiveness of her breasts. And there was nothing she could do to stop him. Then suddenly . . . she wasn't sure anymore that she wanted to stop him.

He *wasn't* hurting her. The only intensity just then was in his kiss, and it was stirring up all those powerful sensations she had felt when she had first seen him. Had she been wrong to let her cowardice take over? The man was showing her that the proof was in the doing, and the doing was calming her fears enough to let her body delight in what was happening.

In less time than she would have thought possible, he made her want him again, really want him, and her hope returned that this was the man she could accept as a lifemate. Her fear wasn't completely buried, but it became secondary to her first taste of passion, which nearly overwhelmed her as she experienced Falon learning her body.

Stars, he wrung gasps from her, but before long, only half of them were from pleasure. The man had too much strength in his hands, and it was his wont to touch her everywhere. Yet the pleasure *was* there, undeniably, and in unrelenting control of her. He found areas of her body that she had no idea could be so sensitive. His mouth tasted, bit, stirred a trembling heat within her that spread throughout her body, and she wanted more.

There was no embarrassment, no shyness left to make her awkward or hesitant. She was open to him, his to command, a mindless body in the throes of first passion, a mere puppet to his slightest whim. Even the sporadic roughness that kept her fear just beneath the surface was understandable, for she discovered her own need to hold to him tightly, to ease the wild inner turmoil now raging inside her by squeezing, even biting him. The strength of her desire made it almost a compulsion—and it made her finally beg him to take her.

That was a mistake, letting him know just how much she now wanted their joining. The knowledge affected Falon in a way she had hoped to avoid. His breathing became rough, his hands rougher still as he positioned her, and Shanelle's worry became reality. He lost control to his passion. There was more pain than pleasure now as his arms wrapped under her and tightened as he claimed her. Her ribs were about to crack, she could barely breathe, and the scream that was torn from her at his swift penetration was lost in his kiss.

Mercifully, she lost consciousness.

8

The moment Shanelle returned to awareness she opened her eyes, then wished she hadn't. It was all real, Falon, the pain—and it wasn't over. She was still there, in his tent, naked. But at least he wasn't still crushing her with his weight, or causing that excruciating pain with his . . .

He lay beside her on his side, leaning on one elbow as he watched her closely. He wasn't touching her. Right now she'd probably scream if he did.

Oh, Stars, how could she have been such a fool to give herself to a man of completely unknown qualities? Just because her body had demanded she do so was no excuse. He'd hurt her. He'd allowed his passion free rein and crushed her in those powerful arms. She felt bruised all over and she wouldn't be surprised if something was broken. And inside her, she was probably ripped apart. *That* pain had been so terrible she'd fainted to avoid it.

To think her hopes had returned, and so strongly, that he was the right man for her. Her disappointment was almost as painful as the rest. She knew a warrior would never have hurt her like that. A warrior was always gentle with a woman because of his size. But Falon wasn't a warrior. He didn't have a warrior's control over his emotions. He'd claimed he did, but it had been proved otherwise. So no matter how much he had attracted her, he wouldn't do for anything permanent. But, oh, Stars, what a shame.

She had to get out of there and quickly, before her disappointment put tears in her eyes. She'd been so sure of Falon to begin with, then again at the end, sure enough to want to join with him and leave the getting to know him for later. How was she ever going to find another man who could make her feel what this one did, in the short time she had before her father made the decision for her? And even if she did manage to find one, she'd probably be too afraid to test for compatibility again. She could no longer trust her instincts in the matter.

With those depressing thoughts, Shanelle started to get up, groaned with the movement, and got a large hand pressed to the center of her chest until she was lying flat again. "You will lie still until the bleeding stops."

She paled at those softly spoken words. "Bleeding?"

"A normal occurrence for a woman's first time, yet is there some excess. You should have told me."

Why was she now blushing? "I don't see that it would have made any difference."

"I am not a wild beast," he said reproachfully.

That was debatable, but all Shanelle said was, "I have to go."

Again she tried to get up. His hand came back to her chest and stayed there this time.

"We will talk first," he told her.

She put some reproach in her own tone. "I think we should have talked a little more *before*. Now there's nothing more to say."

"There is much to say, and you will begin by telling me why you gifted me with your first time."

The blush wasn't leaving her cheeks. "It's no big deal where I come from."

That was only a partial lie, since she had just come from Kystran, where virginity was considered an unwanted inconvenience. In fact, it was usually gotten rid of painlessly in a meditech before a woman started sex-sharing. On Sha-Ka'an it was another story. Here it was prized and expected to be gifted to a woman's lifemate.

Shanelle knew that, but she was only half Sha-Ka'ani. She had hoped she would be giving that prized gift to her lifemate. She'd held on to it for just that reason. But she wasn't devastated that it wasn't going to turn out that way. She had too much of her mother's philosophy to be upset over a piece of torn membrane—that was bleeding excessively.

"I have to go," she reiterated firmly.

"You are welcome to try."

The hand on her chest said *Don't bother*. "You can't keep me here, Falon."

"I can and I will," he stated simply. "Until the fear leaves you and you know—"

"I'm not afraid of you," she insisted.

"That is an untruth, woman. You tremble beneath my hand."

Shanelle closed her eyes. She tried to relax. If it was just a matter of that damn trembling, she'd will it to go away. But his hand on her *was* bothering her, and she *was* afraid of him now.

"You must let me show you that you have no reason to fear me," he continued. "I will not shame myself again. This I swear to you."

She glanced at him suspiciously. "What are you saying?"

"We must join again."

"Not . . . on . . . your . . . life!"

Fear gave her enough strength to shove his hand off her and roll away from him. But too easily his long arm stopped her and drew her back. And now he held her against him, held her against that hard body that had hurt her, and she couldn't get loose.

"No, please, Falon, I can't. Not again!"

"Shh, *kerima*. It must be, but it will not be now. Your fear unmans me."

His hands were soothing on her back. His heartbeat was steady beneath her cheek. She stopped trying to push away from him. She needed this comforting. She would prefer to receive it from someone else, but she still needed it.

It was a while before she tried again to leave. "Falon, I'm all right now. And I really do have to go. My friends will start to worry if I don't show up soon."

"You may go do you promise to return this moonrising," he told her.

"I can't tonight. I've already made other—"

"Then on the new rising."

"All right," she agreed, willing to say anything to get out of there.

Freedom came with that answer, his arms opening so she could move away. She did so immediately, but her aches returned to remind her to go slowly.

She'd just reached her clothing when Falon said, "I feel you do not mean to keep your word to me, woman."

A word given under duress? Of course she wasn't going to keep it. But she wished he hadn't figured that out. Farden hell. Couldn't he have waited until she'd got her clothes on to mention it? Then she could have simply run like hell.

She tried not answering, but that merely encouraged him to say, "Do you fail to come to me, then must I come to you. This I will do."

She swung around to look at him, anxiety returning with a vengeance. "Why? You knew this was only temporary, Falon. You understood that, even complained about it. There's no . . . point . . ."

The words trailed off when what she was looking at finally got through to her panicked senses. The man was lying there completely naked, completely relaxed, and still so sensually appealing he took her breath away. She simply stared at him—until she realized what she was doing and whipped around again, then had to bite her lips to hold in the gasp the sharp movement caused.

Good. She obviously needed the pain to remind her that he was now off limits. But she was appalled that she did need reminding. It wasn't normal to still find him so desirable after what he'd just put her through. What it was was dangerous. And the only way to avoid that danger was to get out of there and never cross paths with him again.

She had her skirt and blouse on in record time, despite her aches. She was bending for her belt when she was grasped and straightened and drawn back against a rock-hard chest. It did no good to pull away. The hands on her upper arms weren't hurting her, but were nevertheless locked steel.

"I understand you are not mine to command, woman, yet must you understand my need to mend what I have wrought, which goes beyond rights. I have given you a fear of joining that you lacked before, which now must be removed. You gave me a gift beyond price. I cannot repay you by leaving you with this fear."

His voice was soft, breathed by her ear, but there was a determination in it that increased Shanelle's fear. Prevaricating just wasn't going to work with a man whom only plain speaking seemed to reach.

"You're not. I don't fear sex-sharing," she told him, hoping that was true. "What I fear is you. You're too rough for my taste, and I'm not just talking about the last of what happened, but everything. I wasn't feeling it all because I was so caught up in specific feelings, but I'll damn well feel it later when the bruises start appearing."

"I have sworn—"

"I don't care," she cut in, turning to face him so she could stress her point. He allowed it, but his hands merely changed arms, and that annoyed her enough to add, "You lost control, damn it! It can happen again whether you want it to or not."

His face darkened considerably. He really didn't like hearing that, and too late she realized she had probably insulted him with that swearing business. Men tended to take such things pretty seriously. But his hold on her didn't tighten to painful. She'd hate to find out what he was like when he got mad, but it wasn't going to happen now.

"A woman must frequently be shown a thing to know it is so," he said just before drawing her closer.

He was kissing her again. She hadn't been expecting it, wasn't prepared for the heady taste of him, or for the careful way he gathered her in to hold her against the length of him. A kernel of desire was actually coming to life, swiftly, so swiftly . . . Shanelle mentally stomped it to death and shoved out of his arms.

"That—that isn't the part that got out of hand, Falon. Look, I know you mean well and I appreciate it, I really do, but there isn't anything to mend or prove. I wanted you, or I wouldn't be here. I had hoped something more per—" She stopped, horrified by what she had almost told him after he himself had admitted to such frustration in not knowing of a way to have her permanently. If he knew that all he had to do was convince her father instead of her . . . "But I don't want you anymore," she continued quickly. "It's that simple. There isn't going to be a second time."

"This is your final word on the matter?"

Was he actually going to be reasonable? she wondered. "Yes."

"Then hear mine. You will remain here after all, until the new rising."

She just stared at him while all the implications of that statement ricocheted through her mind; then she wailed, "You haven't listened to anything I've said, have you?"

"Indeed I have, and what I hear is your fear. It is you who have not listened."

"Well, here's some more fear for you," she said with rising panic. "If you touch me again, Falon Van'yer, I'll farden well scream my head off. I'll have every warrior in this park here in a matter of moments."

She'd do no such thing. She didn't want the stubborn man to die, just to let her go. But he *wasn't* being reasonable. Not even a little. He wasn't even being rational. He ought to know he couldn't get away with keeping her against her wishes, even for a short time. Had he lost sight of where he was and what laws governed here?

His next words answered that question and said he didn't care. "Does it become necessary to fight for you, woman, this I will do."

That utterly infuriated her. "That's right! Be civilized about this, why don't you? For once I almost wish you *were* a warrior, when that is the *last* kind of man I'd want. But at least they don't fight over women unless it is to protect them—and what the hell are you grinning about?"

"You have a temper."

Again she stared at him. Her temper amused him? Was there no avenue for reaching this man, then, not even anger?

Shanelle took a deep breath and tried calm reasoning. "Look, you had your fun, Falon. Why can't you just let it go at that?"

"Is it your thought that I took pleasure of your unconscious body?"

"Well, didn't you?"

"No, I did not."

He sounded offended now. Shanelle was merely horrified by his answer. She'd thought all that turbulent emotion of his had been expended, released within her body. She had the aches to say it should have been. But he'd been deceiving her with his calmness. That intensity was still there, hidden, just waiting to finish her off.

"All right, so it's been a disaster all the way around," she said, hearing the anxiety back in her voice, but unable to help it. "I'm sorry, Falon, but I'm *not* going through that again—not with you."

This didn't disturb him. He merely pointed out, "You have admitted to wanting me. When your fear is gone, you will want me again. Then do we see your first joining ended properly."

"No . . . we . . . won't! *I* won't. And in case that still isn't clear enough for you, that means I refuse to share sex with you again, flatly, no mind-changing about it. I'm also through trying to convince you of that fact. I have people waiting for me. I'm leaving."

"You are welcome to try."

Once again she recognized the "don't bother" in those words. And he said it so calmly, unaware or uncaring of the avalanche of trouble that was going to roll down on his head if she didn't return to her father's pavilion before the end of the day. All her mother had to do was get to her own computer-link unit and ask Martha where she was. Martha . . . Stars, how could she have forgotten?

Shanelle bent and swept up her belt with the attached computer link before Falon thought to stop her, then hit the voice-activator button. "Martha, I need help!"

Out of the unit came a very bruised voice. "So now I'm nice to have around, am I?"

"Get out of sulking mode, Martha. You can rub it into the ground later all you like; just do something *now!*"

The last word was said as Shanelle dodged Falon's reaching hand. She'd spoken in Kystrani, but that could be a language he understood. Whether he did or not, he'd heard Martha's voice and wasn't too happy about it. Martha was amused, however, and chuckling to show it.

"It looks like warriors aren't the only hardheads around this place," she purred goadingly in Sha-Ka'ani so Falon *would* understand.

"Don't get him angry!" Shanelle snapped.

"But men are so amusing when they get—"

"Martha, please!" Shanelle was still having to dodge Falon's hands.

"Oh, all right," Martha said grudgingly. "Pay attention, Mr. Van'yer. I'm a Mock II computer. If you haven't heard of me—"

"I know computers," Falon almost growled.

Martha gave a perfect simulation of a sigh. "And here I thought I was going to get to brag a little."

"Turn it off, woman," he ordered Shanelle.

She slowly shook her head. She knew he was angered by Martha's inclusion in their little party, but she wasn't sure he understood what a Mock II was capable of, especially one in control of an entire spaceship. She almost felt sorry for the frustration he was going to experience—almost.

"Turning Martha's voice off won't make her go away, Falon. She's been with me all along because she's housed right now in a Transport Rover and is in control of all the ship's systems, including scanning and monitoring. That means she's able to hear me and anyone around me, and keep track of our movements, whether this computer-link unit is on or off."

"She has heard—?"

"Everything, big guy," Martha cut in with another chuckle. "And I must say I was impressed, especially since only warriors are known to possess your kind of barbarian dominance. You never got around to saying, but I'd sure like to know what planet you hail from, because probables tells me it's either this one or Sha-Ka'ar."

Falon didn't appear the least bit embarrassed over knowing that their joining had been monitored, but Shanelle had assumed Martha had given her a little privacy for that, especially since she hadn't been Transferred out of Falon's tent when she had first wanted to leave. She was red-cheeked now, but not so embarrassed that she missed the deduction Martha had drawn.

She didn't know why it hadn't occurred to her, since she knew the Sha-Ka'ari had come here to visit their mother planet before. Tedra always hated it when they did, despising the Sha-Ka'ari for what they had done to her own planet all those years ago, and she always had Martha keep tabs on them until they left Sha-Ka'an. But Martha hadn't been here to do that for these competitions. And Sha-Ka'ari warriors might not reach the seven-foot category after so many years of mating with slaves from their planet and those captured from others, but they were still exceptionally big and tall men— and they could be black-haired and blue-eyed.

Shanelle was appalled, knowing her mother would have fits if she'd given herself to a Sha-Ka'ari warrior, unknowingly or not. She was about to have some fits of her own. They were slaveholders, for Stars' sake . . . and the worst kind. There might be a few countries on this planet that enslaved women they captured, but they were rare and far from Kan-is-Tra, and their own women were still free. On Sha-Ka'ar, there *were* no free women, of any kind.

With her amber eyes glaring at him accusingly, Shanelle demanded of Falon, "Martha's right, isn't she? You're from Sha-Ka'ar."

"Woman, I have never even heard of such a place," he replied, annoyance still strong in his voice.

She could no longer accept everything he said as the literal truth. "Martha, what does his body say?"

"That he's not lying. But I don't know what *you're* getting all upset about. This was something you should have found out before you got involved with a visitor."

Shanelle was relieved enough merely to say with a sigh, "I thought I asked you to put the lectures on hold until later."

"Asking doesn't always get—"

"All *right*, Martha. Let's stick to immediate, like getting me out of here."

Martha managed her own sigh. "If you insist." And to Falon, "It goes like this, Mr. Van'yer. Shani failed to mention a few of the more interesting things I'm presently in control of. Like most Transport Rovers, our ship is equipped with Molecular Transfer. Are you by any chance familiar with Transferring, or do you require a demonstration?"

Falon was silent for a moment, possibly because Martha's voice had turned positively smug, giving him an indication of what was coming. "I have heard of Transferring," he finally gritted out.

"Well, that saves time," Martha purred. "And I'll even show you my let's-be-fair program and leave the choice up to you, the choice in this case being, you let Shani walk out of here or I Transfer you elsewhere. And since the elsewhere will be at my discretion, you're probably looking at being stranded about a hundred miles from the nearest telecomm. So what's it to be?"

Shanelle worried at her lower lip with Falon staring at her while he made his decision. But there was nothing to decide. Martha's let's-be-fair program wasn't fair at all. Shanelle would have to insist he *not* be stranded in the middle of nowhere if he chose to be stubborn and see if Martha was bluffing.

But he didn't turn stubborn. He didn't even sound mad when he finally said for Martha's benefit, "I would prefer it did she stay, but the woman may go." What he seemed like was defeated, and he was still staring at Shanelle with those lovely azure-blue eyes.

It wasn't surprising that she felt a moment's indecision. No man had ever affected her like this one did. She even took a step toward him, only to be halted by Martha's voice raised at full volume.

"Hold it right there! I didn't get you out of this mess for you to hop right back into it. He may not look it to you, but that man is absolutely furious right now. Stay the hell out of his reach."

"The computer is very astute," Falon said wryly.

"No, she's just monitoring your emotions," Shanelle replied as she slowly worked her way around to the exit. But that "absolutely furious" still disturbed her. "Don't be angry, Falon, please. I had to ask Martha to help. You knew you had no right to keep me."

"I would not have kept you long—"

"I know—only until we joined again. But I would have fought you and ended up getting even more hurt."

"No!"

"You're wasting your time, Shani," Martha interjected tactlessly. "He's not going to see it any way but his way."

"I'm saying good-bye, Martha," Shanelle snapped irritably. "Do you mind?"

"Hell, yes, I mind, but you're going to do it anyway. Stubborn, just like your mother."

Shanelle glared at the computer unit, but no other noise came out of it. When she glanced at Falon again, it was to find him actually smiling.

"You really do have it under control now, don't you?" she said to him with some surprise.

He didn't have to ask what she referred to. "You needed proof. Now you have it."

"But without guarantees. I'm sorry, Falon, but I'm not going to take the risk again. However, I want you to know I regret that it didn't work out between us, more than you can imagine. You were—are—really something." She had resisted it all this while, but she finally let her eyes roam all over him for a final time—and ended up groaning, "Oh, Stars. Good-bye, Falon."

"Shani?"

She wouldn't have stopped if he hadn't used her name for the first time. Still, she had her back to him now. She wouldn't look at him again.

But she didn't have to turn around to hear him promise, "Know that if there is a way to obtain you for my own, I will discover it—then will I destroy your computer."

Shanelle continued to walk out of there, thanking the Stars and the Sha-Ka'ani Droda that the man didn't know who she was.

9

"I like that!" Martha's voice was about as indignant as it could get. "Destroy me? *Me!* Doesn't that idiot man know how expensive I am?"

"I doubt he cares," Shanelle replied absently as she looked for Corth, found him sitting beneath a tree not too far away, and signaled him that she was leaving now.

"Destroy me!" Martha continued in the same tone. "I ought to—"

"You'll leave him alone, Martha. But while we're getting around to complaints, were you really listening in the whole time I was in that tent?"

"Sure was, doll."

"Then why didn't you do something sooner? My father's order was explicit, as I recall."

"Ah, but it dealt specifically with difficulties with warriors. You chose not to choose a warrior."

"I see," Shanelle said stiffly. "Punish the child for not following teacher's advice."

"Now don't get huffy. You're still in one piece, aren't you?"

"That is definitely debatable. I fainted, for Stars' sake! And it wasn't in ecstasy!"

"Well, how was I to know it wasn't from pleasure? There's a fine emotional line between the two, you know. And besides, I don't think your Falon would have appreciated having you disappear from under him at such a crucial moment, though I might have had a good laugh over it."

"That's right," Shanelle snapped. "Why don't we joke about it?"

Martha chuckled. "If you think I don't know what's really bothering you, think again. You aren't mad at me, you're furious at the fates that made that gorgeous man too rough for you to handle. But you should have seen what was going on inside him from my view. He really did blow a circuit over you, kiddo. Just before you fainted, he was about to combust. Could be he merely lost control."

"Could be it can happen again."

"Well, far be it from me to talk you into settling on a *visitor*. Maybe now you'll get serious and start looking over the warriors."

"Not today I won't. If you haven't figured it out yet, I feel like I got run over by a solidite paver."

"I can Transfer you to a meditech and you'll feel good as new."

"No, thanks. I want to remember this feeling for a while so I don't make mistakes like that again. And besides, you know you're not supposed to use

Transfer out here in the open unless it's an emergency. The Sha-Ka'ani don't like having people pop in and out of their midst. It reminds them too much that they've been discovered."

"I don't think that's much in doubt today."

Shanelle could wish that wasn't so, and that there was one visitor she hadn't noticed at all. Falon Van'yer, she was afraid, was going to be very hard to forget.

Falon was dressed and halfway into a bottle of wine when his brother joined him. He had been pacing about the tent and did not stop now just because Jadell had arrived. He carried the bottle in his hand. And his stride bespoke the agitation swirling inside him.

Jadell Van'yer made himself comfortable and watched Falon for a while without comment. Jadell was the younger by a year, yet the brothers were much alike, the same in height and coloring, though Jadell's blue eyes were of a darker hue and his face was softer, more open and expressive. Their personalities greatly differed, however. Falon was the more serious due to his responsibilities, while Jadell was more carefree and easily amused.

He was amused now. He knew his brother well, and it was not often he saw him like this. Only two things could be the cause: their unanticipated delay in this visitor-infested town, or the woman. Jadell would place his wager on the woman, especially after what he had witnessed of his brother's behavior when he first noticed her.

He had never seen Falon so completely snared, to where everything else around him ceased to be. Jadell had stopped trying to speak to him. Falon simply did not hear. And then to watch him enter that arena, not for an acceptable reason, but merely to impress a woman.

That would not have been so unusual, except that Falon did not do such things. And he had already refused to participate in the competitions. Jadell, Tarren, and Deamon had all decided to amuse themselves by testing their skills against these Kan-is-Tran warriors, since they had nothing better to do while they were delayed here, but Falon had scorned the idea and rightly so. His abilities had been proved beyond question when he had become *shodan* of Ka'al and had accepted all challenges for the position. Nine opponents he had defeated in a single day, the most able men Ka'al had to offer, and without rest between each challenge. Little wonder no others had come forward during the remaining four risings of the challenge period.

Falon had to be furious with himself for his foolish behavior, now that the prompting of lust had been appeased and he was returned to normal. He must also be appalled that it had been a visitor whom he had lost his senses over. They were creatures lacking all morals and honor, good only to be scorned.

The bottle of wine was again at Falon's lips, nearly empty now. Jadell decided it was time to tease him out of his self-condemnation.

Coming right to the point, Jadell said, "It is understandable why you chose her, Falon. It is difficult to ignore a woman wearing your own colors."

Falon did not stop pacing to reply. "She wore the colors of a *shodan*. Any cloak but that one and I would have kept her."

"Kept her?" Jadell sat up, surprised that he had so misinterpreted the problem. "You cannot be serious."

Falon stopped, turned, and met his brother's amazed look directly. "Can I not?"

Jadell was no longer the least bit amused. "But you hate visitors!" he burst out. "We live with the results of their perfidy in our own house. I do not understand why you even agreed to come here to speak with them. The debt was mine to repay, not yours."

"But the request was made of me, not you. The man saved your life, Jadell. I would have given him anything he asked."

"You should have found out what he would ask for before you made the offer," Jadell grumbled.

"True, yet is the matter done, and one I can no longer even regret. Were we not here now at his request, I would never have met the woman."

"So you have met her, and had her. What, then—"

"I did not have her—at least, the joining was not complete."

Jadell grinned. "Now does your anger make sense, yet the reason for it does not. She seemed willing enough to come here with you. Why would you let her leave if you were not finished with her?"

Falon's eyes were suddenly blazing. "Because I

allowed her Droda-cursed computer to best me with words!" The empty bottle went flying into the side of the tent. "Damn their machines and the powers they wield! I know not if the thing even spoke truth in its threats!"

Jadell's eyes were wide with amazement, not because of Falon's words, but because of his volatile reaction. There was humor in this situation, though he did not dare to show it. A measure of calm was called for instead.

"Another good reason why visitors are to be avoided. We can never know if what they say is so, because they have things that are inconceivable to us. Never would I have believed that their box called meditech could make wounds vanish, yet would I be dead now were it not so. With what were you threatened?"

"Transferring."

It was Jadell's turn to lose his calm. "Damn it, Falon, you know that is one of their more powerful weapons. It was used on Aurelet's escort when she was taken, and they were never seen again. There is no defense against such an unseen power."

"Visitors do not consider it a weapon, merely a means of moving from one place to another in mere seconds."

"Yet can it kill if the place you are moved to does not support life, like the center of a mountain. You did not challenge this computer, did you?"

"No, but when I find the heart of it, I mean to kill it."

"No . . . you . . . will . . . not!"

"Little brother." Falon suddenly grinned. "Do you give me orders?"

Jadell's bronzed cheeks darkened. "I did not mean—I would not—" Jadell sighed. "It is my hope that you will give the matter more thought when your anger has lessened."

"The computer took the woman from me with its threats. That will not be forgotten."

"Then find another way to best it. These men from Catrater want our gold. It is for that reason we are here. Let them destroy this computer as a condition to an agreement."

"An idea with merit," Falon said thoughtfully, "yet would I lose the pleasure in seeing the thing done myself."

"Yet would you then be safe from Transferring."

"True, thus will I consider it."

Jadell relaxed somewhat, but was bemused to watch Falon begin his pacing again. "Was there something else bothering you, brother?"

"Why do you not go find Tarren and Deamon and plague them for a while with your inquisitiveness?"

Jadell chuckled at that grumbling tone. "It must be terrible indeed. Best you tell me now and have done with it. Perhaps I can help."

"Can you give me this rising to do over again?"

"To exclude your meeting the woman?"

"No, not that." Falon sighed and came to join Jadell on the fur pelts. "It was her first time, yet did she not warn me of it. She lost consciousness, Jadell. When she awoke she was afraid of me."

"Now do I understand why the joining was not completed, yet was her fear a normal thing. All women fear their first time with a—"

"She did *not* fear her first time," Falon said impatiently, but then was forced to add grudgingly, "Not at first. Her fear came after it was begun, and only because I had no control of the passion she aroused in me. To my shame, I hurt her with it."

"You lost—control?"

Jadell could not go on for the laughter that suddenly over took him. He rolled on the pelts, tears dropping from his eyes, and finally regretted his outburst when Falon's knee came to rest in the center of his chest and he was looking up at the fist about to break his face.

"Consider it fortunate, brother, there is a meditech in this town."

"Falon, wait! Have you no memory at all of our father's words to you when you were given your first female slave?"

"What has that to do with your finding it amusing that I hurt the woman?"

"*That* is not what struck my humor, but that you lost control. Try to remember what father told you."

"I have only a vague memory of it." Falon frowned. "As I recall, I was too eager to experience my first time with a woman to pay attention to what he was saying."

"Then listen carefully this time, for I was there for the telling so he would not have to repeat it again when I attained your age. He said, 'Slaves are for a man's pleasure, to be enjoyed but not to be taken seriously, for even if released from slavery, they never regain the spirit and pride of a free woman, which are qualities you will want for your children. The woman you will someday give your life to will be the keeper of your heart, and you will know you have chosen the right keeper when you must fight to control what she makes you feel.' "

Falon's frown deepened. "You are suggesting I have found my lifemate? I wish to own her, brother, not join my life to hers."

"You do not think it significant, what she made you feel?"

"I wanted her too much, is all. But she is still a visitor, and I would not bring home a visitor as anything other than a slave."

"What if you can have her no other way?"

"I do not know if I can have her *any* way," Falon growled, rising to his feet again. "It is that which infuriates me most, not knowing what I must do to make her mine. We know so little of visitors, no more than we ever did."

"That can be easily seen to." Jadell grinned. "You have merely to ask our host. His lifemate is a visitor."

"His lifemate is the damn visitor who brought them all here when she discovered us."

10

Dalden Ly-San-Ter was reluctant to return to the
shodan of Ka'al that afternoon with the news he
bore. He knew the man would never have come here
if he didn't feel he owed him a life-debt. Dalden
also knew he expected to conclude the meetings
expeditiously, so expeditiously that he had hoped to
spend no more than one rising in Kan-is-Tra. Now
he wasn't going to like to hear that the competitions
were going to delay the meetings with the Catrateri,
but so they were.

The Ambassador of Catrater was aware of how
the Ba-Har-ani felt about visitors. That was why he
had asked Dalden's father to make a formal request
of the owner of the gold fields the Catrateri mining
scanners had located near the town of Ka'al, and
why Challen had sent Dalden to Ka'al to convince
the owner to meet with the Catrateri. And that was

why the ambassador had pleaded with Challen to lend his presence to the discussions.

But Dalden should have returned with the Ba-Har-ani last week, when Challen would have had time to involve himself in the matter. Now he lacked the time because of the competitions. And yet the Catrateri ambassador was too fearful of failure to begin the discussions without him, and with reason. If Dalden had learned anything during the time he'd spent with the Ba-Har-ani, it was that they had not the least care for the problems of visitors.

Dalden had done his part, due only to a piece of wild luck, but nonetheless accomplished. If the Ba-Har-ani chose to leave immediately rather than accept the delay, no one would stop them.

Only Falon Van'yer and his brother were present when Dalden arrived at their tent. Jadell offered a grin in welcome, which Dalden returned. He had formed a quick and easy friendship with the younger Van'yer brother, partly from having saved his life and gone on the little adventure afterwards to track down those responsible for nearly taking it, and partly because they shared so many things in common, including their easy natures. He also liked and respected Falon Van'yer, and although he hadn't come to know him as well, it wasn't hard for Dalden to sense that the *shodan*'s mood had changed drastically in the few hours since they had parted company upon their arrival in Sha-Ka-Ra.

"Has something happened that I should know about?" he asked without preamble.

Jadell laughed. "It does not concern you, no, yet may you likely be of help with your knowledge. My brother—"

"Can speak for himself," Falon interrupted curtly. "And best we finish the matter that brought us here first so I may devote myself more fully to the other."

Dalden didn't care to argue the point with the older man, despite his curiosity. Sometimes Falon reminded him of his own father. Although much younger, he held the same responsibilities as Challen did, though it was more the tone of command that Dalden found the same right now and which he'd been raised to obey.

"Ambassador Zlink's requested a postponement of your meeting until after the competitions. He hopes this won't inconvenience you."

"Is he participating in these games?"

"No, but my father has to attend the games, and the Catrateri want him at the meeting."

"Why? Have I not agreed to speak with these visitors? What need is there for your father's involvement?"

Dalden sighed. "It's like this, Falon. Zlink doesn't feel he'll get anywhere with you without some powerful local support on his side. Visitors frequently use any means available to pad the odds in their favor, and Zlink is no different. He's managed to get my father's agreement to sit in on the discussions. Though my father won't try to influence you, Zlink still thinks his presence will help."

Total silence followed as the two brothers simply stared at Dalden. He wasn't sure what the problem was, until Jadell burst out, "What in Droda's name has happened to your speech?"

And Falon answered with a degree of amusement, while color tinged Dalden's golden skin. "He speaks like a visitor now, yet have I found the combining of certain words easy enough to understand. It is the strange words that have no meaning."

Jadell turned his appalled gaze on his brother. "*She* spoke thusly?"

"She did, as did her friend—as did her computer."

"It is a wonder you were able to communicate with her at all," Jadell snorted in disgust. "But what is your excuse, Dalden?"

Dalden wondered who the *she* with the computer was, but he was too embarrassed to ask. "You will have to forgive me. Such tends to happen whenever I am around my mother for more than a few minutes. She was a major influence in my growing years." And still was, though he didn't think the Ba-Har-ani would care to hear that.

Many of their customs differed, but this one was the same in their country as it was in this one, that children were the sole concern of their fathers, their mothers having little or no say in their raising. It just hadn't worked out that way in his own household.

"My parents are both here in the park and look forward to meeting you. I can take you to them now, yet will there be little opportunity for private speech with so many others around. Or you can wait until this moonrising, since you have been invited to attend the private dinner in my parents' chamber, celebrating my sister's homecoming."

"You have only just returned home yourself," Jadell remarked. "Why is a sister honored before you?"

"She has been away much longer than I, but she is not being honored. She is due to return this rising and has merely been sorely missed by us all. These competitions, however, in a sense do her honor," Dalden said, and was suddenly shaking his head in bemusement. "I knew my father had planned to do this, yet did I honestly believe my mother would not allow it."

"Of what do you speak?" Jadell asked.

And from Falon: "What say can your mother have in such matters?"

"You would be surprised," Dalden said ruefully. "But these are not normal competitions. It is an old custom in Kan-is-Tra, though one I have never seen enacted before. These warriors compete to better their chance at winning my sister for a lifemate. The custom eases the burden of a father from having to make a decision between more than one interested warrior."

"*All* these warriors compete for your sister?"

Dalden grinned at Jadell's incredulous tone. "I would not be surprised, yet do I doubt it. Anyone can compete just to compete. The final champion does not have to put forth his request to my father, just as those who are eliminated may still make the request. And even if the champion wants my sister, he still may not be chosen. The final choice rests with my father. These contests merely give him the opportunity to choose from the best."

"You wound me, friend, not to have mentioned such a desirable sister before now," Jadell said.

Dalden chuckled. "I have learned not to speak of her among friends when too many of them want her."

"Before you think to ask for her yourself, Jadell," Falon said, "you had best see what she looks like. What one man finds beautiful, another may not." That brought another chuckle from Dalden, prompting Falon to add, "You disagree?"

"Not at all, yet more than half the men gathered here to compete for her have never seen her."

"Do you jest?"

"Unfortunately, no."

"I have never heard of men asking for a woman they have never seen. Why would they, even visitors?"

"Partly it is because of the gaali-stone mines my family owns. My mother established an exorbitant price for it from the start, and other planets were willing to pay the price, making my family one of the richest in several Star Systems. You have the same opportunity yourself, Falon. Gold is now a rare commodity, long since depleted on planets that once mined it and established their economies with it. It may be worthless to you, good only for the making of shiny ornaments and such, but to the Catrateri it is a priceless metal. They will likely be willing to pay you anything you ask for it.

"But as to your question," he continued, "visitors want my sister because of the mines. Warriors want her because she is the only daughter of a *shodan*, a very rich and influential *shodan*.

But once she is seen, most men want her for herself."

"And I may meet her this moonrise?" Jadell asked with a degree of eager anticipation.

It was Falon who answered, however. "*If* we accept the invitation." And to Dalden, "We seek no special privilege here. Why should we be included in a private gathering of your family?"

"Because my father is pleased to have you here other than for the benefit of the Catrateri. It has been too many years since the Ba-Har-ani have come to Kan-is-Tra, even to trade with us."

"The distance was never an easy one to cross between our two countries," Falon pointed out.

"True, yet is it no distance at all now, with the aid of an airobus. My father would be willing to provide the transportation if your merchants wish to trade again with ours."

"Provide it? As in giving us our own private airobus so we would not have to deal with your Visitor's Center?"

"Exactly."

"It is something to—think about," Falon replied noncommittally.

Dalden nodded. He hadn't expected an answer. It was something for the two *shodani* to discuss between themselves.

"You chose not to stay at the palace when we arrived earlier, thinking you would not be here long," Dalden reminded them. "Perhaps you will now reconsider with the meeting delayed—if you still mean to attend the meeting."

"How long a delay?" Jadell asked.

But Falon waved the question aside. "I am not in such a hurry to leave now, Jadell."

Jadell chuckled as he noted Dalden's surprise and explained. "My brother has met a woman here that he finds great interest in."

"Is this the other matter you were concerned with, Falon?" Dalden asked.

"It is. The woman is a visitor under your father's protection that I wish to buy."

His amber eyes widened the slightest bit, yet Dalden was much more amazed than that. This had to be the she-with-the-computer, and she had to be something quite impressive for Falon to actually want to buy her, since Dalden knew how he felt about visitors.

It had been Falon's own house that had been shamed all those years ago, his own sister who had been stolen by a visitor, kept for several months aboard the man's ship, and returned with a child in her belly. It had been Falon's father who had gathered the warriors of Ba-Har-an to ride against the visitors, ready to go to war if the man responsible was not turned over to them for punishment.

This had been the incident, the last of many, that had led to the closedown of the whole planet to visitor travel, and had turned the Ba-Har-ani so against visitors of any kind that they had never traded with them again. And Falon now wanted to take one home with him? But as a slave, Dalden reminded himself, not as a lifemate, and Falon likely wouldn't want her any other way.

Reluctantly, Dalden had to disappoint Falon. "If she's a visitor, she can't be bought."

"How, then, may I obtain her for my own?"

"In most cases, you have to ask the female herself if she will have you."

"It is foolishness to leave such an important decision up to a female. Is there no male at all to be dealt with in the matter?"

"In some cases, but not in most. Yet we no longer speak of buying, Falon. If you truly want the female, you would have to take her as your lifemate, and I doubt you are prepared to do that."

"No, I am not. She would refuse even did I ask, because she fears me."

Dalden commiserated. "Visitors usually do fear warriors. Our own women fear them when it comes to joining with one for the first time. This is normal."

"So I tried to tell him," Jadell said.

"And I told *you*, brother, that her fear came after."

"You mean you have already had her?" Dalden asked.

Falon's nod was so curt as to be barely noticed. "Is there no alternative you can offer me?"

"Since you only wish to own her, best you hope she is a Catrateri. They would likely do anything you demand just now, including ordering one of their women to accept you—at least temporarily. Did you happen to find out what planet she is from?"

"No."

"This, then, we will discover first thing on the new rising. But do you decide you would have the woman as other than a slave, I could ask my mother to speak with her, to ease the woman's fears. She relates well to visitors, knowing how they think, what their concerns are. And she is a perfect example of how happy a visitor can be in joining her life with a warrior's."

11

Dalden's mother was the farthest thing from happy as she slammed into her bedchamber late that afternoon—or tried to. The door was simply too large and heavy to close with any speed that would generate a good slamming. But in this case, it was stopped from closing all the way when Challen followed Tedra into the chamber.

He was none too happy himself just then. "Woman, you will speak to me of this."

"I don't know if I'll ever be speaking to you again! How could you? And without telling me!"

Briefly, Challen thought about challenging that High King of Century III for arrogantly claiming that he would defeat the champion of the games after they were over and thereby win Shanelle for himself. Hearing that, Tedra had demanded to know what becoming champion had to do with her daughter, and had been told that Shanelle was the prize being offered for victory. Challen had been forced to explain to the man his misconception. Warriors knew the way the competitions worked. Visitors had to be told that winning didn't necessarily net the final prize.

But the damage had been done. Tedra had not waited around to hear all of the explanation. She had quietly walked away to return to the palace. But Challen knew his lifemate well. There was nothing of calm in her silent departure. She was on the borderline of committing violence and had wisely left before the committing began in public.

Now he watched her pounce on their bed and attack it with her fists. Usually she had Martha deliver Corth to her when she needed to pummel something, that being one of the android's uses, to assist Tedra in the exercising of her skills—and the expending of her fury. But Corth was otherwise occupied right now as Shanelle's protector and could not be taken from that duty.

Challen waited patiently for Tedra to rid herself of the worst of her fury, fully aware that the bed was a substitute for himself, just as Corth usually was. He was touched, as always, that she chose not to attack him instead, settling for only secondary satisfaction in substitutes. Such was an indication of the deep love she felt for him that was stronger than the strongest anger. Ironically, when she was only mildly angry, she did not hesitate to strike him. Yet when what she felt was extreme, she would not take the chance of hurting him with it.

It had become an easy matter to determine the

degree of her displeasure in this way, and what he faced now was serious displeasure.

He spoke carefully while she was still pummeling the bed. "I did not tell you the reason behind these competitions because I knew this would be your reaction."

Tedra glanced up only long enough to growl, "Damned right, but you did it anyway!"

"Yet is the reason no different from what you already knew I faced, finding the proper lifemate for my daughter."

"*My* daughter will have no trouble finding her own lifemate. I've told you that a hundred times."

"And I have told you a like number of times that I cannot release her from my protection to a man who cannot protect her as well as I." Then, more gently, he added, "This you know, *chemar*. This is why the decision cannot be hers."

That warrior logic had Tedra gathering the bedding up to her face so she could scream into it before she bounded off the bed and came to glare up at Challen. "You've made her a prize, a goal! You might as well have put her up for auction to the highest bidder!"

"I see it differently. What I have done is bring together the finest warriors in the land to determine those with the greatest ability and skill. From the best whom I find approval with, she may then choose."

"*She* may?" Tedra's eyes narrowed. "Just how many *best* are we talking about? Thirty? Forty?"

"Five."

"Unacceptable! Make it ten and I might consider it."

"We do not bargain here, woman. I go against my better judgment to allow her five to choose from when the fifth will have been bested by four others."

"And what if she wants none of those five? What if she absolutely hates them?"

"You look for difficulties before they arrive." And then he put his arms around her to draw her flush with his body. "You know I want her happiness, *chemar*, yet must she be happy *and* well protected. You would not want it any other way."

"It just seems so impossible." Tedra sighed.

But she was now privy to the fact that Shanelle didn't want a warrior—and why—whereas Challen was not. Nor would it do to enlighten him on that fact.

She rested her chin on his wide chest to look up at him. Her culture considered him a barbarian, and it wasn't easy loving a barbarian, but she did. She loved this one to distraction. But she knew his limitations, in particular his lack of understanding a woman's fears. She was partly responsible for that because she had so few fears herself, and those she did have she merely gritted her teeth at and plowed right through. But Shanelle wasn't like her in that respect. Shanelle had been so well protected all her life that she'd never had anything to fear as she grew to womanhood. But now suddenly she had a great many things to fear and she wasn't prepared to face any of them.

"She's going to be horrified when she finds out

all those men are competing for her," Tedra said quietly now.

"Why should she be? Never did it bother her when all my warriors lusted after her."

"Maybe because she never noticed."

"How could she not? It was so bad before she left that we could never get a servant after dark whenever she had been around them."

Tedra hid her grin against his chest. His grumbling tone was nothing compared to his annoyance at such times, and those times had been many. Tedra had felt nothing but pride and a degree of amusement that so many men wanted her daughter, so much so that each of them was compelled to seek out a Darasha female after merely being in Shanelle's presence.

She was suddenly understanding Challen's reason for these competitions a little better. Too many of his own warriors had asked for Shanelle, and although he might have preferred she go to a warrior he knew well, Tedra also knew he had decided he couldn't play favorites in giving her to one of them. If only there hadn't been so many offers . . .

"Do you mean to tell her?" Challen asked.

"And ruin her homecoming? She'll find out soon enough when the competitions are over and she has to pick one of the finalists—oh, Stars!" Tedra gasped with the realization. "You're going to give her away in just a few days, aren't you? Challen, I only just got her back! Couldn't you have waited?"

"Too long has this been delayed."

"So I'm to lose her already?" she whispered forlornly.

"And where do you think she will go?" he chided. "These are Kan-is-Tran warriors who will ask for her. She will not be taken so far that you cannot visit her as often as you wish."

She was annoyed enough to remind him, "Have you forgotten there are visitors also competing?"

"You were the one who insisted visitors be allowed to participate when they began asking to do so." And they had asked because Rampon at the Visitor's Center had somehow found out the true reason for the competitions and the word had spread from there to all the ambassadors, and from them to their home planets. "In fairness did I allow it," he added, "yet have I no intention of choosing a visitor for my daughter."

"Not even that High King Jorran who is so confident he can beat the champion of all the warriors?"

"Especially not that condescending High King. Sooner would I—"

What he would sooner do was interrupted by the light rap on the door. "Mother, are you there?"

Tedra pushed herself out of Challen's arms and started toward the door even as she called out, "Come on in, baby." But when Shanelle did, Tedra was glad she was blocking her from Challen's view, and put her arms around her to whisper urgently, "Hide your face in my shoulder and keep it there. If your father sees those swollen lips, he's going to kill whoever got them that way." To Challen she said, "How about taking off for a while, babe? I'd like a private mother-daughter chat before dinner."

"So I am to be kicked out of my own chamber?"

"Humor me and I might play challenge loser tonight."

He laughed and whacked her bottom on his way out the door. As soon as the door had closed, Tedra hugged Shanelle happily.

"So it's happened? You found the man you want?"

"Mother . . . don't . . . squeeze!" Shanelle gasped out.

Tedra released her immediately. "What's wrong? Are you hurt?" And with even more alarm and the beginnings of a new anger, she demanded, "Are those bruises on your arms?"

"I offered to take her right into a meditech," Martha answered before Shanelle could, "but she wants to enjoy suffering for a while."

"What in the farden hell happened?"

Martha turned on one of her driest tones. "To hear her tell it, she got run over by a solidite paver."

"So let her tell it," Tedra snapped. "Shani? Did someone *beat* you, for Stars' sake?"

"No—it just feels like it." Shanelle sighed and led her mother to the backless couches in the center of the large room as she continued. "I really thought this was it, mother. The man was absolutely gorgeous. Once I'd seen him, I couldn't think about anything else. And he made me feel so— so—"

"He knocked her socks off," Martha supplied with a chuckle.

With a frown Shanelle turned the computer link off, while with the same frown Tedra took the unit and set it on the large square table that the couches surrounded. "I'll talk to *you* later," Tedra told the computer, her tone warning that she was presently blaming Martha for whatever had happened. And to Shanelle, "So if everything seemed right, what went wrong?"

"Everything. But in the beginning, nothing. He seemed so perfect, even if he was taller than I would have liked. That didn't matter. Nothing mattered except what he was making me feel. And he felt it, too. He came right to me. And, Stars, he was even ready to fight Corth for me."

"To *fight* Corth?" Tedra said incredulously, but then with dismayed understanding, "We're not talking about a warrior, are we?"

Shanelle lowered her eyes. "No—but he's as big as one, nearly as big as father. And he acts like one more than he doesn't—except for one major difference. He's emotional—possessive, jealous, passionate—too passionate, actually, and that's where everything went wrong. He didn't have much control of his passion to begin with, but when we were about to join, he—he lost it completely. He wasn't aware he was doing it, but his arms just about crushed me, and when he breached me, it hurt so bad I fainted."

"Oh, baby." Tedra's sympathy poured out, her arms going around Shanelle very carefully. "You've always had a low tolerance for pain. The slightest little scrape or bang as a child and you'd be screaming your head off."

Shanelle's expression turned wry. "I'd like to think I can take a scrape or bang these days, mother.

I didn't will myself to faint. This was pain of an unacceptable level."

"But a breaching *is* painful. I know you kept your innocence intact for your father's sake so your lifemate could have it, but it looks like you should have visited a meditech instead."

"It's a moot point now."

"Is it?" Tedra sighed. "All right, so we'll class it as one of the most horrible breachings on record. As long as the man made up for it afterward, then—"

"There was no afterward. When I woke up, I just wanted out of there."

"Wait a minute." Tedra was outraged. "Are you saying you got no pleasure to make up for the pain? That's indecent! I'll—"

"Mother—"

"—crucify that bastard when I see him! He should have insisted—"

"Mother! I didn't want him to touch me again."

"But you needed to be shown it's not all pain, and who better to show you than the man you picked yourself?"

"You're not listening, mother. With him it *was* all pain—or at least too much pain. He was too rough even before he lost control. And he did insist we continue the joining. In fact, he wasn't going to let me leave until we did. I had to ask Martha to change his mind."

"I'll bet he just loved that."

"Sure he did, enough to swear he was going to destroy Martha first chance he gets."

Tedra grinned. "I'll bet *she* just loved hearing

that." The audiovisual console in Tedra's dressing room chimed right then, so she added, "I'm not answering that, Martha. I told you I'd talk to you later."

"Maybe it's not her," Shanelle suggested.

"Of course it is. It drives her crazy that she can't get around on this planet like she could on Kystran—and does on the Rover, popping into any audio console and computer when she wants. If her main housing hadn't been turned off when she left to get you, she'd be yelling at us right now, instead of dialing for permission to speak."

Proof was the end of the chiming coming from the dressing room. All of Tedra's advanced machines were stored in there, away from Challen's sight. The room was so crowded with the wonders of other worlds that there'd been no room to add Brock's housing when he joined the family. So he was kept in another room—otherwise Martha would have borrowed his console to have her say.

"I think I'll visit a meditech after all," Shanelle said with a grimace as she started to get up.

Tedra's hand detained her. "Sit down. I didn't mean to get off the subject, but I was getting too close to tears for comfort. This wasn't supposed to happen to you. It shouldn't have. And maybe we ought to let your father have a good look at you after all. Your young man needs some punishing for what he put you through, and if Challen doesn't do it, then I'll have to."

Shanelle shook her head. "I don't want him punished for something he did unintentionally. He could use a lesson or two in bedroom manners, for the benefit of the next woman . . . he . . ."

Tedra lifted a brow at the way her words trailed off. "So it bothers you, the idea of him with other women?"

"No, why should it?"

"Because you picked him, Shani. Because a part of you is already maintaining that he's yours."

"Well, that part will just have to catch up to the rest that says I'm not interested anymore," Shanelle replied stiffly.

"Yes, you are. You're just disappointed that he's not as perfect as you'd like him to be. I'm disappointed that he's not a warrior. But these are difficulties that can be worked out."

"Mother, you still aren't listening to me," Shanelle said in exasperation.

"Maybe because I know you. And maybe because even though I've tried to minimalize your father's influence on your ideas about sex-sharing, you really do share his views. You *want* only one man. That's why you've waited this long, trying to find the right one. And this is the right one, or you wouldn't have been willing to share sex with him the moment you met him. You went with him with every intention of opening your heart to him, of spending the rest of your life with him."

"That's absolutely true, but instincts can go awry, and hopes and intentions don't always hold up to reality. I wish it had worked out, mother. I wanted it to so badly. But the plain fact is, the man is dangerous. You can't imagine what it was like to be held by someone just as strong as father, but without his gentleness—and he didn't even know he was hurting me. That's what frightens me the most, and I'm *not* going through that again."

"But, Shani—"

"*Look* at me, mother," Shanelle cut in impatiently this time. "Do I look like I'm not serious? I have the bruises to prove I am, and if they're already showing up on my arms from my just being drawn forward for a kiss, then let's see what the rest looks like by now." She whipped her blouse off—then wished to Stars she hadn't.

She hadn't expected quite such a dramatic showing, but she should have. Her skin did bruise easily. Shades of red, violet, and soon-to-be-black liberally covered her upper torso, the darkest patches spreading out from the sides, where she'd been squeezed too tightly. The lighter marks, which were around her breasts and lower waist, probably wouldn't hurt to the touch now, but had yet to fade.

Shanelle blushed in embarrassment, because none of it felt quite as bad as it looked. But her mother had turned ashen and then crimson with rage. And Tedra didn't have much more to say, merely, "The man dies!"

12

It took a while to get Tedra out of the emotional level she'd slipped into. Shanelle found it necessary to totally reverse her stand, reminding her mother of how easy she was to bruise, insisting that she wasn't badly hurt, just sore.

Tedra had still done some insisting of her own. "I'm going to take him apart piece by piece, but first I'll give him his wish and let him destroy Martha. *She* should have Transferred you away from him at the first indication of pain!"

"It wasn't all pain," Shanelle had whispered.

"What was that?"

"I said it wasn't *all* pain. Martha can't be blamed for not being able to tell what I was actually feeling, when at least half of it was—nice."

She'd also had to repeatedly point out that the damage was only the temporary kind and would be eliminated altogether with a few minutes in a meditech, which she'd also had to promise would be done immediately.

She'd left her mother not quite back to seeing Falon as a future member of the family, but not quite so eager to dissect him, either. "I suppose I should hear the monster's side of it first," she allowed.

Shanelle sincerely hoped her mother never got an opportunity to meet Falon at all. For two such volatile personalities to clash, it didn't bear thinking about. Besides, nothing could come of their meeting but more difficulties. Shanelle had made up her mind about Falon. She didn't like admitting it, but she was basically a coward, especially where pain was concerned. And although Falon might have got his emotions in hand just before she left him, she wasn't going to put herself in a position to experience again what it was like when he didn't.

An hour later, having rid herself of all bruises and whatever internal injuries she had sustained—she didn't want to know and so hadn't asked the meditech for a report—she was beginning to experience a little anger of her own, and all of it for the man who had dashed her hopes so badly. He had no business being so careless with the kind of strength he possessed. Someone should have taught him better—he should have taught himself better.

She couldn't begin to imagine the kind of women he must be used to, women who didn't mind such rough handling. Stars, they must be as big and strong as he was. And where *did* he come from that he was so like a warrior except in the one way that would have kept her from being afraid of his strength—a warrior's calm control? Of course, if he was a warrior, that would open up another whole avenue of fears, some worse than anticipated pain. And she'd asked him outright where he was from at least once. Why hadn't he answered instead of asking if it mattered?

As if it mattered now. It didn't, other than to appease her curiosity about him. And despite her resolve to never see him again, she was still curious, frustratingly so, which merely added to her anger. She shouldn't even be thinking about him anymore, yet she couldn't get him out of her mind.

Dressed now in the traditional *chauri* that all Kan-is-Tran women wore, Shanelle felt more like she was finally home. She had these sheer, scarflike outfits in every conceivable color, but she'd picked plain white for tonight to honor her father and to appease his earlier annoyance at her visitor's outfit. Depending on how the scarves were draped, they could be blatantly provocative or demurely feminine. Shanelle had never tried to be provocative and doubted she ever would. On her the *chauri* was firmly belted to keep the upper scarves covering just what they should. And the scarves of all her skirts were joined well below the hip, so the free-floating sections never parted higher than mid-thigh.

To add color to her outfit, the white belt and sandals were embedded with tobraz, the light blue gems mined in the north countries. The same gems circled her throat and dangled from her ears and both wrists. Her hair she left flowing down her back as her father preferred to see it, though she had a hair-styler that could have arranged it in any intricate manner she wanted in just a matter of moments.

She was ready to join her family for the evening meal, yet she hesitated before the mirrored wall in her dressing room, staring at the image reflected there. But try as she might, she couldn't see any difference in herself to account for what she had experienced that day. There was a little added color in her cheeks due to her continued agitation, but that was all. So what had she expected? It wasn't as if it had been the glowingly wonderful experience she had assumed it would be that might have put happy sparkles in her eyes. And the meditech had taken away all the physical evidence. Just because she felt so different inside . . .

She sighed in disgust and left her dressing room, even more irritated than she had been, and that would never do. She had to calm down before she joined her parents. The last thing she needed was to have her feelings set her mother off again, this time with her father there to witness it and demand explanations.

She circled her room slowly for a few minutes, taking deep breaths, letting the familiar furnishings soothe her. Her collection of moonstones, the only adjustibed in the palace, the chair Dalden broke every time he sat down in it, always making her laugh, which was why she kept having it repaired, and why he kept testing it. She hadn't seen her brother yet, nor had her pet *fembair* been by to greet her, but she'd see them both before the day was finished, she was sure.

She was safe here, protected. Falon might have threatened to find her, but he wouldn't. Not here. And she would stay away from the competitions. Corth could escort her friends back to the park tomorrow if they wanted to go, but she'd find an excuse not to join them.

There, she felt better already. She hadn't realized she'd been worried about running into Falon again, but she must have been.

With a last deep breath, she left her room, smiled at the servant passing by her door, then stopped dead, seeing the four men who followed the servant. Falon Van'yer was one of them. He stopped, too, as surprised as she was. His three friends turned back to inquire what was keeping him.

Shanelle took that opportunity to slip back into her room. Her heart was pounding frantically. She couldn't imagine what he was doing in the palace, let alone coming down the hallway from the guest wing. If only she'd waited just a few more seconds before leaving. And, Stars, there was no lock on her door. There were no locks on any doors in the palace because no one would dare enter where he wasn't welcome.

That thought managed to relieve her a little, until the door pushed against her back as it opened. With a gasp she leaned all her weight against it, but that was about the most wasted effort she'd ever made. It continued to open easily, forcing her to leap away from it before she got squashed.

She turned to face the intruder, not the least in doubt as to who it was. But no words came to order him out; no words of any kind formed as she was struck again by his handsomeness.

Falon stood there in her doorway, grinning at her, satisfaction exuding from him. He was wearing a shirt now with his leather *bracs*, if it could be called a shirt. It, too, was made of the buttery-soft *zaalskin*, but was white, and without sleeves, and molded to his chest, or what little it covered of his chest, like a second skin. It ended at his waist, and instead of wrapping around like a warrior's shirt would, it was fastened tight at his navel with golden links of chain. As a covering, it was totally inadequate, leaving too much bare in the deep V that ended at his navel, hiding none of the strength in his thick arms. The white merely made his skin seem an even darker bronze, which in turn set him further apart from the golden-skinned warriors of Kan-is-Tra.

Shanelle took all this in, including the four-foot-long sword at his left hip, the gold dagger strapped to his right boot, the new sword belt embellished with gold and white scrollwork, but most of all his size, his tremendous height and brawn filling her doorway. All the fear she had felt in his tent was there again, but right beside it was that swirling giddiness she'd felt upon first seeing him.

"I had not thought to find you here, woman."

"That—that goes double." Managing that much, it was easier for more words to follow. "This is my room and I'm not inviting you in, Falon, so you can just—"

"I invite myself."

Putting action to words, he moved forward enough to close the door behind him. Shanelle started backing up, but once those azure eyes returned to her, she couldn't seem to move another step. Anxiety almost had her wringing her hands.

"Falon, there's no point to this. A few hours haven't changed anything."

"I disagree," he replied, but didn't elaborate as to why. Instead his eyes dropped to her waist, now minus the computer-link unit. "Does she still listen?"

"No—yes!" Actually, Shanelle didn't know, but she doubted it. Martha had no reason to keep monitoring her now that she was in her own home, where things like this *didn't happen*. "I'm just going to say this once. Leave."

It was as if she hadn't spoken. "I have decided to test the computer's threats, as should have been done at the first."

"All right, I'll say it twice. Leave."

This time he shook his head slowly, grinning at her again. "We have much to finish between us, woman, all that I said must be done. Best you accept my will in this, for I will not leave you until—"

"*Why* must you be so farden inflexible? Aren't people allowed free choice where you come from?"

"I have told you this matter goes beyond rights."

"In your opinion, not in mine. As far as I'm concerned, you're just using that amends-making nonsense as an excuse to have me again. But that doesn't work in my book. I'm still refusing."

"First do we see to your fear, then will you no longer refuse. If it will relieve your mind, we will not join until you ask it."

He was remembering her begging him before. She was remembering it, too, and the memory frightened her even more. Was it possible he could bring her to that point again? No, how could he? Before, she had begged for pleasure and release. Now she knew that wasn't what she would get.

"It won't happen," she insisted.

"It will," he insisted right back as he took a step toward her.

She turned to flee, but was scooped up into his arms instead. "Falon, no!"

"You may tell me no—after we rid you of your fear."

With that his eyes swiftly roamed the room until they lit on the small bed tucked into a corner. He headed right for it, laying her down and quickly filling the narrow space beside her—and that was when he felt the bed moving to accommodate his longer length and widen for two bodies instead of one.

In an instant, Falon snatched Shanelle around the waist and rolled them both onto the floor and supposed safety, he taking the brunt of the fall on his back, she cushioned, or rather jarred, by landing on top of his hard body. But one glance at his wide-eyed look of confusion-laced horror and Shanelle burst into laughter.

She couldn't help it. Even when he sat up with her now in his lap and started glaring at her, she continued to laugh, unaware that all of her fear was draining away with it. He'd tried to save her from her bed, for Stars' sake. Her bed! That stirred the memory of having been told about the time her father had attacked a poor adjustichair for moving under him, and another round of merry notes filled the air.

"I'm sorry," she said at last, wiping tears from her eyes and smiling at him. But then a devil made her say, "Maybe I should thank you for saving my life," and back came the laughter, until she was totally out of breath and leaning against him in exhaustion.

When it occurred to her what she was doing, she also realized that she was now cocooned in his arms. A number of other things quickly became apparent—that her fear was temporarily gone, that he might have looked annoyed for a moment, but his body gave no evidence of it. His hands were toying with her hair. His heartbeat was rather loud beneath her ear. And she had no desire to move off his lap.

"I am to assume you were in no danger?"

She peeked up at him. He wasn't annoyed, merely curious.

"None."

"That thing is not a bed?"

Now she had to smile. "It is, but honestly, it's not alive. It just enlarges itself to suit body size and count when necessary. It's supposed to make room for more than one body, but remains compact when not in use. Very convenient for a small room."

"This is no small room."

"That's true," was all she said.

She could have added that since her *fembair* sometimes liked to sleep with her, she'd almost been forced to get the adjustibed to keep from being crowded out of her own bed. But she didn't want him to realize that this wasn't a temporary room for her. And remembering why she didn't brought back some of her fear.

"Falon—"

"It drives me wild to see you in my colors."

Shanelle sucked in her breath and tried to push away from him. "I'll certainly never wear white again."

"I have doubts it will make a difference, not until I become used to you, and maybe not even then."

She understood that loud heartbeat now. And she'd gotten nowhere from trying to get out of his arms. In fact, they were drawing her closer instead, and too swiftly she was tasting his lips again, and the soft warmth of his tongue. He wasn't hurting her, but she couldn't get it out of her mind that he would. Still, her blood liquefied and raced in the meantime, and it wasn't long before she was kissing him back, uncaring of what would follow, uncaring of anything other than the sweet desire he'd ignited so easily.

To pull the tied knots of the scarves at her shoulders down her arms was to have the whole top of the *chauri* collapse to her waist. When Shanelle became aware that this had been done, it was too late to protest. Hands on her sides lifted her until she knelt on her knees on either side of Falon's hips, and his mouth closed over one breast, his tongue stabbing at the hardened nipple. The feeling so weakened her that she had to wrap her arms around his head. And then he was sucking—too hard.

"Fal—on!" she said on a rising note.

The pulling eased instantly, his mouth leaving her altogether as he pressed his face between her breasts. "I *will* control it, woman, I swear I will."

It absolutely horrified Shanelle to realize he was actually fighting for that control. He might as well have lost it, for the results were the same. The sweet pleasure she'd been feeling made way for returning fear that leaped into full-fledged panic. She pushed, but his arms were now around her lower back and hips, pinning her to his chest, and all she could do was strain her shoulders away from him.

"Falon, let me go—please."

"No."

There was no room for argument in that answer. His inflexibility infuriated her.

"You can't keep doing this! I have rights—"

"As do I. Whose rights do you think will take precedence?"

Her eyes narrowed. "What is this, 'Might makes right?' "

He shook his head, grinning. "You gave me the right to join with you, woman, which I have not in actuality done yet. I believe you called it—talk."

She flushed to remember her earlier boldness. And she'd thought he hadn't understood?

"Whatever you *think* I gave you, Falon, I'm taking back. I made a colossal mistake, but I've already paid for it once. Twice is out of the question. Now let go of me before I scream my head off."

"Then scream," he challenged. "I will simply silence you by kissing you."

She just hated it when people called bluffs without the least hesitation. She did want to scream, but in rage. But even that might bring a servant—then her father. And she could just guess how *that* would turn out. But where did that leave her?

He'd mentioned kissing. Now she noticed him staring at her lips and she tensed, snapping, "Don't you dare!"

He sighed and began pulling her closer. "It is a mistake to let a woman argue when she cannot win—"

"Do you need assistance, Shani?"

They both turned to see that Corth had entered the room. Shanelle's relief was overwhelming. Falon's body stiffened to steel.

"Yes!"

"No, she does not," Falon growled, and to Shanelle he said, "Tell him to leave."

"No."

"Then I must make him."

"You're welcome to try."

She was delighted to have this opportunity to throw those particular words back at him, but he wasn't. "Your stubbornness becomes annoying, woman. Were you mine, I would not allow it."

With that he set her on the floor next to him and in one fluid movement rose to his feet, his sword clearing its scabbard as he did. She hadn't been expecting that. Corth was supposed to remove

Falon from the room, physically if necessary, not have to defend himself with a weapon he'd never been programmed to use. For Stars' sake, this wasn't a killing matter.

"No, wait!" Shanelle scrambled to her feet and placed herself in front of Falon. "What the devil do you think you're doing?"

"Making him leave, as I was goaded into doing."

She blushed furiously. "I'm sorry for that. I shouldn't have used your words. But he can't leave now. He's heard me ask for help, and his programming won't let him leave until he gives it."

"Then I must change his mind."

"Change his—Falon, he's an android. It isn't possible—"

"I care not what race he is. He interferes, and this I will not stand for again."

He started to set her aside. She gripped his sword arm with both hands, understanding now that he was apparently missing a pertinent point.

"Falon, androids are machines! Corth isn't real, he's a machine, but he still means a great deal to me. And if you destroy him, I—I would never forgive you. He's been with me since I was born. My father had him programmed to protect me, so it would be impossible for him to leave me here with you now. Besides, he doesn't know how to use that sword he's wearing. He only has skill in weaponless fighting. It would be like attacking a helpless child. You wouldn't do that, would you?"

An expression of keen frustration came over Falon's features. "I have no qualms about destroying machines, if indeed he is one, but I would not destroy something that you care for." He put his sword away, proving that she hadn't been detaining his arm the least bit. "You mentioned a father. Where might I find him?"

Shanelle's mind drew a total blank for a moment. "He—he's not here."

Falon suddenly grinned at her. "It is becoming easier to determine when you lie, woman. You must remind me to break you of that habit when you are mine."

She gritted her teeth. "Will you go now?"

"Against my better judgment, I will allow you your way a second time." And then his eyes dropped to her breasts, still exposed. "But not again. Next time we meet, I will know the means to make you mine."

13

Falon arrived late to the dinner, but no one remarked on it. Had he not been expected there, he would not so easily have left the woman with her android. But he knew where he could find her now, which relieved his mind on that score. And he suspected her father was also a guest of the *shodan*, and so accessible, which put him in an agreeable frame of mind.

He was eager to speak with Dalden about them, and to find out how soon a meeting could be arranged with the woman's father. But first he had to greet his hosts.

Challen Ly-San-Ter offered him no surprises. He was as could be expected of a man who had been a *shodan* for more than twenty years, a warrior's warrior. He was also a man who had the misfortune of having to deal with the visitors all these years, but had not let them change him in any way. And like almost all Kan-is-Tran warriors, his emotions were so well contained as to be practically nonexistent. The Ba-Har-ani had always envied the Kan-is-Tran warriors that ability, which they had yet to completely master themselves.

Challen's lifemate, now, was a definite surprise. Prepared to dislike this female who had opened the planet to an invasion of sky-fliers, he found her to be gracious, soft-spoken, and he could not get far beyond the fact that she was an incredibly beautiful woman. He could no more resent her for being a visitor than he could his golden Shani.

When Falon finally had a moment to speak privately with Dalden, who had earlier been talking to a small group of visitors whom Falon disdained to even meet, it was to find that the younger man had left the room. "He went to see what is delaying his sister," Jadell informed him when asked. "But keep me no longer in suspense. What happened with your female visitor?"

Falon's expression turned wry. "Again I could not keep my hands off her long enough to find out who she is. Nor was I able to calm her fear for more than a few minutes."

"You should have waited until you had more time," his brother replied.

"Time and all other considerations cease for me when I am near her, Jadell. Likely I would not be here now, except she had still another machine come to her aid, if I can believe this one to be a machine." He'd stopped by the thing called Corth on his way out the door and received a purely taunting smile. "I cannot even destroy this one because she *cares* for it," he added in disgust.

Jadell grinned. "Console yourself that her machines can be left behind."

"True—Droda save us, do my eyes deceive me?"

Jadell followed his gaze to the small circular bathing pool in the corner of the room. It was not the sunken pool which was amazing Falon, however, but the three huge *fembairi* stretched out around it. White, short coats, long sleek bodies, large, round heads with great blue eyes—and fangs— they were one of the most vicious flesh-eating animals on the planet, and they were nearly as large as *hataari*.

Jadell wasn't sharing Falon's alarm, he was chuckling. "You were not here during the explanations, brother. The Ly-San-Ters keep those beasts as pets."

"An unusual family, to keep predators as pets. Nor have I ever heard of a tame *fembair*."

"Yet were we assured these offer no danger."

Even as Jadell spoke, one of the felines rose and started bounding toward the door. Falon looked in that direction to see the couple who had just arrived, and all he could do was stare. The woman was his Shani and she had her arm around Dalden's waist, he with his arm around her shoulders. Both were smiling. And in an instant, Falon noted the similarities between them, their eyes, hair, skin tone, all identical. Even some features were identical. But before this registered completely, the *fembair* reached them and knocked the woman to the floor, following her down to half cover her body.

What Falon saw was his woman being attacked, and his instincts were purely primitive. He reached for his dagger and was halfway across the room when Challen stepped in front of him, the only one there who could have stopped him in that moment.

"Be easy, warrior. The animal belongs to my daughter. He is merely welcoming her home."

Falon heard the musical laughter then that so warmed his blood each time he heard it. She wasn't in danger. She was being welcomed . . .

"*Your* daughter?"

Shanelle would know that voice anywhere, and the amazement in it had her groaning inwardly. She pushed Shank aside, enough so she could sit up to be sure, and sure enough, Falon stood there with her father partially blocking him from her view— until Falon bent to return his dagger to his boot, their eyes met, and the smile he gave her was positively triumphant. Her second groan was quite audible.

"What are *you* doing here?"

"Watch your tone, Shani," Dalden warned her as he helped her to her feet. "You're speaking to a *shodan*."

"A—no, he's not. He's a visitor."

"Don't let the color of his hair fool you," Dalden said low, for her ears only. "He's a Ba-Har-ani warrior, and *shodan* of Ka'al, one of the largest towns in that country."

"A warrior. *A farden warrior!*" Her eyes swung back immediately to Falon with full accusation. "You let me think you were a visitor!"

Falon was still smiling. There wasn't anything

that could dent his present satisfaction in the way things had turned out. "You let me think the same, woman."

Before she could get out another word, her brother whipped her around so she was facing only him. "You've already met Falon?"

"I wish to Stars I hadn't, but yes, I met him soon after I arrived."

"And you had Martha with you, didn't you?"

"Of course, Dal, but what has that—?"

He let her go, turning to Falon. Outwardly, he appeared perfectly calm. Inwardly was another story.

"I would speak with you privately, *Shodan* Van'yer. Do you come with me—now."

Falon remembered well enough what had been said to the brother concerning the sister—before Falon knew she was his sister. He knew Dalden meant to call him to account, but even that couldn't jar his present delight. The woman was not a visitor. She *was* going to be his.

Falon nodded, but Challen was first heard from. "What goes on here, Dalden?"

"A mistake in need of correcting," Dalden replied evasively. "It will not take long."

Challen let them go, assuming whatever the mistake was, it was being corrected in private to spare Falon embarrassment. But no sooner were the two young men out the door than the wall rocked as one of them was slammed into it.

"Someone must have tripped," Tedra said, having come to Challen's side to keep him from interfering, if she could. "And you hold it right there, young lady!" she ordered her daughter, who had also turned toward the door.

Shanelle made a sound of frustration, started to say something, caught her father's frown, and shut her mouth. Closest to the door, she could hear the sounds of the fight going on outside it better than they could. She moved to Shank and buried her face in his thick neck, wishing she hadn't let Dalden drag her out of her room after she'd already decided she wasn't leaving it.

"Why do I suspect you know what goes on here when I do not?" Challen demanded of his lifemate.

"Now, whatever gave you that idea?"

"Woman—"

"Patience, babe." She grinned up at him. "You get to make all decisions in the end, and you'll have one to make shortly, if I don't miss my guess."

In the hall, Dalden rolled over and slammed Falon's head against the floor. "She's my sister, damn you! You wanted to make a slave of *my* sister!"

"Only when I thought her a visitor." Falon broke the hold on his head and in seconds reversed their positions, though he didn't retaliate in kind. "Will you listen now?"

"No, this time *you* listen. You will have her for lifemate or not at all. And if my father won't give her to you, then I will have to challenge you, Falon. Do you understand why?"

"Certainly." Falon grinned. "I would not have expected less of my woman's brother."

"She's not your woman yet. Stars, you're damn lucky I happen to like you."

Falon laughed and helped Dalden to his feet. "Are we finished now?"

"No." Dalden buried his fist in Falon's belly. "That's for whatever you did to make her fear you. I don't want to know what it was—it just better never happen again."

Falon had dropped to his knees from the unexpected punch. He would hate to see how the young man fought with men he disliked.

"Your sister chose me, Dalden, to gift with her first time. It was foolishness on my part that has made her fear me, but I know she wants me still. I merely need time with her to rid her of her fear."

"Fair enough," Dalden said, and this time helped Falon to his feet, though the *shodan* immediately moved back to arm's distance now. "You do realize, however, that you will now have to join the competitions?"

Falon grimaced. "If I must."

"It can only better your chances. You are *not* the only man who wants Shanelle. You may have a lot in your favor, but one of my father's main concerns is that her lifemate be able to protect her as well as he can."

"The concern of any father," Falon agreed. "Very well. I would prefer it did I ask for her now, yet I will wait until the competitions are over."

14

"You couldn't tell he was a warrior by the look of him?" Tedra asked carefully.

Shanelle leaned against the balcony and stared out at the soft glow of gaali-stone posts lighting the city streets below. She didn't want to talk about Falon Van'yer. A warrior. A deceiver, as far as she was concerned. Oh, Stars, she hadn't thought this day could possibly get worse. That showed what she got for thinking.

But her mother wasn't going to settle for silence. After that little scene in the dining hall, Tedra knew exactly who Falon was without having to be told.

"He's built like a warrior, yes. I couldn't very well miss that, mother. But he has black hair. Even Martha thought he was a visitor when I showed him to her."

"The Ba-Har-ani are known to have dark hair," Tedra pointed out.

"But that country is four months distant from ours by normal travel, and they haven't crossed our borders in more years than I can remember. I've never even met a Ba-Har-ani before. And word of the competitions wasn't likely to have reached them when they have no dealings with us or the Center."

"Nor did it reach them. These Ba-Har-ani came here with your brother at your father's request. And I might as well give you the bad news now. Your father wants to see our two countries back on friendly and communicating terms. That's going to give that young man an edge if he decides to ask for you, and I wasn't blind in there, baby. He lit up like a vein of gaali stone when he realized who you were."

Shanelle groaned audibly. "He'll ask. But now I have even more reasons not to want him. I ought to leave the planet right away."

"Now, don't be hasty," Tedra replied. "You might actually have fewer reasons and just not know it, or aren't you aware that the Ba-Har-ani differ in a lot of ways from our warriors? Your Falon's lack of control is one. And didn't you say he's emotional? But if you tell me there's nothing there between you two now, that you no longer feel anything for him, then I won't say another word."

"Mother, *why* are you taking his side again?" Shanelle asked in exasperation.

"Because you chose him. Because I don't want to see you make a mistake just because you've temporarily got cold feet. Because you weren't the only one to arrive late tonight, and I didn't see you limping in this time."

Shanelle glanced away, wishing her mother weren't so intuitive. "No, he didn't hurt me this time. Between my bed attacking him and him almost attacking Corth when he showed up, there wasn't much time for anything else."

"There's nothing like an adjustibed to give a warrior second thoughts," Tedra said, straight-faced for about two seconds more before she burst into laughter. "I'm sorry. I just love it when these big guys meet up with technology. But I don't suppose it was funny at the time."

Shanelle raised a brow. "Are you kidding? He saved me from my bed, mother."

"Oh, stop," Tedra pleaded, wiping her eyes with the back of her hand.

"Yes, well, it was that damn amusement that caught me off guard and gave him the final advantage—or it would have if Corth hadn't shown up when he did. But that doesn't change the fact that Falon wouldn't leave my room when asked. He wouldn't listen when I said I didn't want to share sex. He even promised to break me of my stubbornness when I'm his. His high-handedness is insufferable."

"Sure it is," Tedra said with a complete lack of sympathy. "He *is* a warrior, after all, and that's one way ours and theirs are obviously the same. And you're used to that high-handedness, baby, in your own family. You're just not used to it from a stranger."

"And I don't intend to get used to it. If I had known he was a warrior from the start, we wouldn't be having this conversation. I never would have gone with him."

"Don't kid yourself, Shani. When you get your socks knocked off, there isn't much you can do about it, and I speak from experience. You would have tried him just for the hell of it. You wouldn't have been able to resist the temptation. So we'd be having this *exact* same conversation, because that man got hit with the same thing you did, and by all accounts, he means to do something about it."

"There isn't much he can do if I'm not here," Shanelle said stiffly.

Tedra sighed. "Let me tell you about a couple of the bigger problems I've faced in my life. One was having your father get me pregnant without my permission. And if that sounds funny to you, try and remember that people didn't get in that condition where I came from. I was absolutely terrified of the very idea. No way was I going to go through something as barbaric as giving birth. I couldn't even read the meditech's report that would confirm or deny it. But Martha didn't let me play the coward. She read the report and blurted it right out, even telling me the baby was going to be a boy."

Shanelle frowned. "But, mother—"

"I know, I know, but let me finish. So I decided to be brave and bear this son for Challen. I loved him, after all, and he wanted it done the old-fashioned way. But the closer it got to the time of delivery, the more frightened I was, even though I knew I'd have a meditech to crawl into to make it all painless. What I hadn't counted on was the simple fact that meditechs weren't designed to accommodate great big bellies, because it's virtually impossible to gain excess weight eating Kystrani food, and this was a standard Kystrani meditech. So at the last farden minute, I find out I'm going to have to give birth the *truly* old-fashioned way, without a single painkilling agent, without even a Sha-Ka'ani healer on hand, because I'd already Transferred to the Rover and it was too late to find one. Talk about going into major shock."

"How come I never heard about this before?"

"Because your mother doesn't like to own up to fear, and I haven't even got into half of it yet. Your father ended up a nervous wreck. He hadn't been expecting to do the delivery himself, but only he and Corth were on the ship, and of course Martha. But Martha lacks hands, and Challen still wasn't letting Corth's hands get anywhere near me. Before your brother arrived, I must have sworn to every deity in two Star Systems that I was going to murder your father for putting me through that. At least *that* he took in stride. He kept telling me my reaction was perfectly normal, to which I kept telling him to drop dead. And then there was Martha offering instruction by the book, along with her usual drivel, like, 'If you'd do a little pushing instead of threatening to castrate the big guy, we might get this over with,' and 'I think we can safely say there's nothing wrong with your lungs, kiddo.'"

Shanelle couldn't help smiling, though she said, "That wasn't very nice of her."

"Actually, she was trying to get my mind off the pain by getting me mad, but I didn't appreciate it at the time. But she saved the best for last, when Challen was holding his squalling son in his hands, and I was lying there half dead, or so it felt like. 'Save the congratulations for later, guys. You're only half done.' 'She means the afterbirth,' Challen tried to reassure me, but Martha didn't allow time for being reassured. She replied calm as you please, 'No, I mean your son's twin sister, who'll be popping out to join him shortly.' "

"You mean you didn't know?"

"Hell, no, I didn't know. *She* knew all along, and not once did she even hint that I was carrying two instead of one. She owned up afterward that she'd decided I couldn't handle that kind of information, and maybe she was right. I had a hard enough time adjusting to the fact that I was having one baby. I might not have decided to try it if I had known I'd be having two at once. I really don't know what I would have done."

"Give yourself more credit, mother."

"No, I'm being honest, Shani. You've grown up expecting to have babies, maybe even looking forward to it. To you it's no big deal. But I grew up expecting *never* to have to go through that. And that brings me to the second big problem I faced. I'd had you and your brother. Don't ask me how I survived it, but I did. And I loved you both to pieces. But there was no way in hell I was ever going to go through that again. I made the decision without telling your father. I was going to have the meditech see to it that I couldn't have any more children. And I was absolutely determined.

"I went to Medical on the Rover. I even punched in the data, telling the meditech what I wanted done. And for once Martha wasn't saying a word. Total silence from that department. Then I thought about how much I loved Challen and that he'd probably never forgive me, and I started crying. Next I thought of you and Dalden, and how precious you were to me, and I *really* got into a fit of weeping. I sat there on the floor, crying my heart out, finding out that emotions can actually cause physical pain."

"You didn't do it, did you?" Shanelle asked softly.

Tedra shook her head, admitting, "I didn't have to. As soon as the hysterics started, Martha located Challen and Transferred him to Medical. He sat there on the floor with me and held me until I dried up, made me tell him what the problem was, then told me there was no problem. He had had no intention of getting me pregnant again. What I wasn't aware of was that warriors don't want big families, that *they* suffer right along with their women during labor because they honestly can't stand seeing their women in pain. The standard is one or two, on the rare occasion three, children per household, and then a warrior goes back to drinking *dhaya* wine for the rest of his life, the local method of birth control. I'd already given Challen twins, which was more than enough for him.

"But to wrap this up, my first problem, from which I would have preferred to run like hell, simply had to be faced and got through; my second, Challen took care of himself. My point, Shani, is every difficulty and problem has its solution one way or another. You just have to find it. Your problems can be worked out one by one, until there are no more."

It took Shanelle a moment to get out of the past and remember that Falon was the topic of this conversation. "Sure, I can think of one solution right now. I just go straight from sex-sharing into a meditech for the rest of my life."

"That's not funny," Tedra snapped impatiently. "*That* problem happens to be Falon's, and he'll fix it or else he'll answer to your father."

"And what if it's not fixable? He swears it won't happen again, but, mother, he had to fight to control his passion tonight when he barged into my room. I watched him do it and it scared the hell out of me. And what, really, do we know about these eastern warriors? What else am I going to find different about him?"

Now Tedra grinned. "Maybe that they punish their women differently, or not at all. Maybe that one of those excessive emotions they possess is love."

Shanelle gripped her mother's hand excitedly. "Do you *know* that?"

Tedra winced. "Stars, I didn't mean to get your hopes up, baby. No, I don't know it. But your brother might. He's been with these Ba-Har-ani for the last couple of weeks. Why don't you ask him?"

"Ask me what?" Dalden said from behind them.

Tedra glanced over her shoulder. "Did you only just return?"

"No, we came back in with the food. We've been sitting in there starving, waiting for you both to join us."

Shanelle turned and looked through the tall arched openings that led back into the chamber. Falon was sitting on one of the backless couches, talking to one of his friends, but he must have sensed her gaze, for he looked up just then, found her on the balcony—and melted her with one of those heartwarming smiles of his. She closed her eyes against it with a groan and whipped back around.

Tedra beckoned her son forward. "Your belly can wait a few minutes more. What can you tell us about the Ba-Har-ani and how they differ from our own warriors?"

"They are a little more demonstrative in certain instances," Dalden said as he moved to Shanelle's other side. "When they get angry, you know it."

"Did you hurt him, Dal?" Shanelle asked in a small voice.

Dalden laughed. Tedra patted Shanelle's hand, assuring her, "If he'd wanted to hurt him, he would have challenged him. Now what about how they deal with their women, Dalden? Particularly in the way of punishments?"

He shrugged offhandedly now, but there was a purely male spark of amusement in his amber eyes as he replied, "I believe they spank them."

Tedra chuckled. "Is that all?"

"Is that *all*!" Shanelle gasped, outraged. "That's—that's—"

"Not what you were afraid of," Tedra was quick to remind her.

Shanelle clamped her mouth shut. That was true. But spanking? From someone with Falon's incredible strength? No, thank you.

"What about love?" Tedra asked next.

Again Dalden shrugged. "That was not a subject ever raised in discussion while I was with them. I know the man wants Shanelle. When he thought her a visitor, he would have bought her. Now that he knows who she is, he wants her for his lifemate. And I believe he will care for her as well as any Kan-is-Tran warrior would. I like him as a man. I respect him as a *shodan*. Frankly, I hope father gives her to him—especially since she's already given herself to him."

The note of disapproval that had entered his voice at the end had Shanelle glaring at him, even as her cheeks heated up. "That was *my* business, Dal. I chose him, yes, a mistake I don't intend to repeat. It just didn't work out, and that's all there is to it."

"I know you fear him right now, Shani," he said with a degree of hesitancy after her outburst. "He told me so. But whatever the reason is, I'm sure he can make it right."

"And I'm sure he can't," she replied angrily. "Stars, he told you everything else, I'm surprised he didn't own up to that, too."

This time Dalden grinned. "When you were mentioned, he didn't know you were my sister, nor did I know it was you he was so determined to buy."

"Damn it," Tedra interjected at this point. "That's twice now you've said he wanted to buy her. Does he think lifemates are for sale around here?"

"No, but that's not how he wanted her when he thought she was a visitor. After all, his family has good reason for disliking visitors. But he still wanted to take Shani home with him—only as a slave."

"A *what?!*" Shanelle and Tedra exclaimed together.

Dalden frowned. "Didn't you know the Ba-Harani are slaveholders?"

"Now that you mention it, I have a vague memory to that effect, but from so many years ago, it's no wonder I didn't recall it," Tedra said as she put an arm around Shanelle's waist to lead her back inside, adding for her ears only, "That ties it neatly and for the last time. If your father gives you to that man, I'll farden well help you pack myself to run in the opposite direction. I may even go with you."

15

Shanelle was able to relax a bit, now that her mother was firmly back in her corner. She was even able to get through the evening, losing her temper and her patience only once at the way Falon kept staring at her with such a proprietary air, as if she already belonged to him.

She tried sitting next to Jadd just to put him off, but that poor boy had taken one look at her family as a whole and had decided he didn't want to be a part of it after all, or have anything else to do with Shanelle. He'd moved away from her three times, with her scooting to follow—too closely each time—before he hissed in her ear, "Don't *do* that, Shani. Your family wouldn't like it."

She wasn't quite amused by his intimidation. Her family hadn't even noticed what she was doing— but Falon did.

"I take it this means the romance is off?" she asked dryly.

"Very funny," Jadd retorted.

But then he caught Falon's look, and it frightened him so much he turned quite green. In fact, it made Jadd so ill that he excused himself, leaving Shanelle frustrated and glowering at Falon, who now looked the very epitome of innocence.

She was introduced to the rest of his party as the evening wore on, his brother, his cousin Tarren, and his sister's lifemate, Deamon. They were as darkly bronzed as Falon and as dark of hair, but the brother, Jadell, was like no warrior she'd ever met before. Quick to laugh, even quicker to grin, and annoyingly, he also treated her like she was already a member of his family.

During the course of the evening, she learned that he and Dalden had become close friends through some dangerous undertaking they had shared. She learned why Dalden had brought them to Sha-Ka-Ra. And the difference in their *shodani* was explained. In Ba-Har-an, the titles were hereditary, passing from the father to the oldest son, whereas in Kan-is-Tra, the *shodan* was usually the strongest and wisest, and could be challenged by anyone, at any time, so a son could not gain the title from his father without challenging him for it, which had never been known to be done. But in Falon's country, the ascending son could be challenged by all comers only during the five days following the father's death, then never again.

Shanelle found the differences interesting, but

still wholly undemocratic. In both cases, might and a superior sword skill were the ruling factors, and that told her plain enough that Falon had to be pretty handy with his sword to have survived five days of challenges following his father's death. Her father would be able to draw the same conclusion, and that was going to give Falon still another edge if he asked for her, or rather *when* he asked for her. It was too much to hope at this point that he wouldn't.

And apparently her father was going to get a firsthand demonstration of those skills, or so she was told the minute Falon took Dalden's seat beside her after they had finished eating and Dalden left the table. She had been dreading that Falon would attempt to speak to her privately. But his choice of subjects was too impersonal to cause true alarm.

"I intend to enter the competitions," he told her.

"Well, good luck to you," she said indifferently.

"You mean that?"

He seemed so surprised, she frowned. "Why not? It doesn't matter to me who wins."

"And why should it?" Tedra said, having come over as soon as she saw Falon moving toward Shanelle's couch. "My daughter has nothing to do with the competitions, warrior, and I'd appreciate your not discussing them with her."

There was enough warning in Tedra's look and tone for Falon to suspect Shanelle didn't know men were competing for her. But before he could answer either way, Tedra was giving Shanelle permission to retire if she wanted to, and she obviously wanted to.

Falon watched her leave, aware that he couldn't stop her—or go with her. That he still had no rights whatsoever where she was concerned was frustrating in the extreme, considering his feelings for the woman. She was going to be his lifemate. He wanted the matter settled immediately.

He looked toward Shanelle's father, but her mother must have read his mind. "It won't do you a bit of good to ask for her now," Tedra told him. "Challen isn't blind. He already knows of your interest. But he won't be making any decisions until the end of the competitions, so you'll have to wait just like everyone else."

His eyes came back to Tedra, his impatience clear. "Then I want her to know why I enter the competitions."

"I'm sure you do, but I don't. It would hurt her to know what her father has done. Is your pride more important than that?"

Falon hesitated only a moment. "No—it will be as you wish."

"What I wish is that my daughter had never laid eyes on you."

There was too much heat in that statement for Falon not to guess what was wrong. "You are aware that she gifted me with her first time and you disapprove?"

"You got that wrong," she shot back. "I was delighted that she'd finally made her choice—until I saw the damage her *choice* left behind. What I should have done was let her father see it, instead of sending her straight to a meditech."

Falon's guilt was rubbed raw by those words.

"You must know it was not my intention to hurt her. Nor will it ever happen again."

"Shani isn't inclined to believe that any more than I am," Tedra said.

"Yet will I convince her."

"You say that like you mean it, but sheer determination doesn't always work—fortunately."

Falon stiffened, amazed at how close he was to losing his temper with this woman. "So you condemn me without knowing all the facts?"

"Wrong again, warrior, on both counts. I know more about what happened than I care to. Not only did Shani tell me most of it—and by the way, she doesn't blame you for what happened, she just doesn't want to experience it again—but Martha filled me in on the rest. And you might not believe it, but I was still on your side at that point. You were Shani's choice, after all, and that matters more in the long run than a few fears she's built up and your lack of experience in containing certain emotions, which can be corrected. But the marks against you kept adding up, until now they've tipped the other way. Take my advice and give it up."

"Never!"

"Then you're bound for disappointment, because it's no longer just what you've done, but what you are. And I don't see how you'll get around that, warrior."

She moved off after those cryptic words, leaving him baffled, but not for long. He went right to Dalden to ask, "What am I now that I was not before, that would make your mother so hostile to me?"

Dalden drew a blank over that riddlelike question, until he recalled his mother's words on the balcony. "Stars, I should have known she'd react that way. I'm sorry, Falon, but it's my fault. I mentioned that you own slaves."

"So?"

"So my mother hates slavery."

"And your sister?"

"Likewise."

Falon's sigh was heavy. Marks against him? It was difficulties that were adding up, and they were beginning to look insurmountable.

16

Falon slipped quietly into the room, closing the door on the light from the hallway. Inside there was a muted glow rising up one wall where the gaali-stone shelf had been left open to emit a minimum of light, just enough to make out the furnishings. The bed was all he was interested in, nor was he likely to forget where it was. He approached it soundlessly and was halfway there before he noticed there was more than one body in it, but the second one was not human. Cat's eyes glowed at him in the dark, and a purring began that could surely be heard out in the hall. However, it did not wake Shanelle, who was probably accustomed to the sound.

Falon was not. He stood there in the middle of the room, debating whether he wanted to tangle with a full-grown *fembair,* her pet, which meant he could not kill the beast any more than he could her other pet, that Droda-cursed android. But this one was purring, and was supposedly tame. He started again toward the bed.

A voice stopped him this time, sounding as loud as alarm bells going off, despite a distinct dryness to it. "When were you thinking about saying something, Corth? After he's in bed with her?"

"I was waiting for you, Martha." The second voice came from a different direction. "Warriors aren't the least bit intimidated by me, even after I show them what I'm capable of. You, on the other hand . . ."

"I suppose you're right," Martha said with a sigh, and then in a smug tone, "Remember me, big guy?"

"It would be impossible to forget *you*," Falon said stiffly, though it was the android he looked for and found, sitting in a chair near the entrance to the balcony. "And your interference is unnecessary this time, computer. I merely wish to speak with Shanelle."

"That's rich." Martha chuckled. "Is that what they're calling it these days?"

"For Stars' sake, Martha," Shanelle complained groggily from the bed. "I'm trying to get some sleep here."

"Sorry, but you might as well wake up. You have a visitor—who's not a visitor." Laughter followed that play on words.

Falon's eyes left Corth to return to the bed, in time to see Shanelle sit up behind the *fembair*. "Falon?"

She said his name before she actually saw him standing there. That took the edge off some of his irritation with her machines, but not all of it. "Was it necessary to surround yourself with body-guards?"

"My mother thought so, and it looks like she was right on the mark. You have no right to come in here, Falon, but in the middle of the night?"

"I could not sleep," he told her. "I wish no more than to talk, Shanelle."

"If you believe that, Shani—"

"Martha, I can farden well think for myself, thank you," Shanelle said testily as she climbed over the *fembair* to sit on the edge of the bed. "Corth, some extra light would be appreciated."

As a gaali-stone box was flipped open, flooding the room with light, Falon was disappointed to see that Shanelle was fully covered in some kind of sleeping outfit that included loose-fitting *bracs*. Yet with her golden hair unbound and flowing about her in disarray, she was as desirable as ever, and he was rapidly discovering that he could not be in the same room with her without feeling the need to join with her.

"I have nothing to say to you, Falon Van'yer," she continued in a hard tone, completely awake now and frowning at him. "Nor is there anything you can say to me that will change the fact that you're a warrior, and you *knew* I didn't want a warrior, *any* warrior. You deceived me by not telling me who you were."

"Did you not do the same?"

That reminder pinkened her cheeks and lowered her eyes to the floor. "I would have told you who I was before I left you—if things had worked out differently. But they didn't, so there was no point."

"If you would have told me, then it was your intention that I ask your father for you, was it not?"

"Falon, it doesn't matter now."

"It matters to me, woman," he said with sudden fierceness. "It means I was not just your choice for your first time. I was your choice for lifemate."

That was true, and she was assailed again by the disappointment she'd felt earlier when she knew it wasn't to be. Her hopes had been so high when she first saw him. *Why* did he have to ruin it by hurting her, then bury it for all time by turning out to be a warrior, and far, far worse, a slaveholding warrior?

Reminded of that, she felt her anger give way to the pain of regret. It built with surprising swiftness, bringing Shanelle to her feet and marching her toward its cause. For once she wasn't running from a confrontation but embracing it, and she was so angry she wasn't even aware of it.

She stopped before him, amber eyes aglow with ire, her body stiff with it. "What does it matter if I was naively hoping for something more than temporary when all you wanted was to make me a slave? A slave! A piece of property without rights!" The urge to hit him just then was so strong she gave in to it without thought, slamming both fists against his chest. "How *could* you, Falon?"

He'd made no move to prevent her attack on him, nor did he move a muscle now, and she realized with disgust that she hadn't hurt him at all, while her hands were painfully stinging. And then it dawned on her *exactly* what she'd just done, and she stepped back in horror.

Falon noted only the new reaction. "What is it?"

If he didn't know . . . "Nothing."

But he grabbed her hands and started to massage them. "Do you try that again, woman, I will be forced to administer proper punishment."

She snatched her hands back with an indignant glare. "I've heard what your idea of proper punishment is, and you'll do no such thing—not to me. And why would you? If you tell me I actually managed to hurt you, I won't believe it."

"You hurt yourself," he said simply. "This I will not allow."

She stared at him incredulously. "But you'd spank me? You think that wouldn't hurt?"

"A small discomfort to prevent a greater harm. The doing would bring me pain as well, yet must you be taught—"

"Oh, shut up!" she snapped.

Martha chuckled at that point, remarking, "Stars, I just love their logic."

Shanelle glowered at the computer-link unit that had been set on the table in the center of the room, with its viewer facing the door. But she was too angry with Falon just then to address Martha, and her narrowed amber eyes quickly came back to him, to find him also frowning at the computer link, now that he'd located it.

But she got his attention back as she continued heatedly. "Did you forget my father's a warrior?

So is my brother. I've already been taught what I should and shouldn't do, just as I know better than to try and hurt a warrior, because only warriors can hurt warriors. That's why I only throw things at my brother when he teases me into losing my temper. But you—obviously I have no sense when it comes to you, so I owe you an apology for hitting you. You can be sure it won't happen again, because the opportunity won't be there if I never see you again, which is exactly how I intend it. You can leave now, Falon. We've talked more than—"

"You have talked," he interrupted calmly. "Now you will allow me to explain. Yes, I would have bought you if that was the only way I could have you, and when I thought you a visitor, that was the only way. And you would not have suffered as my slave, Shanelle. You would have found only pleasure and happiness in my ownership."

"You can't really believe that," she said incredulously.

"I can believe nothing else, for I would have made it so," he replied fervently. "It is *my* happiness that increases, now that I know you can be the mother of my children. But I would have had you belong to me in whatever way I could, for my wanting you has become a need, making you necessary to me. All I can think of is the moment you will be mine."

Shanelle wished those words had no effect on her. They shouldn't have, with all she knew about him now. But his wanting her that much was a powerful stimulant to her own senses. If only he wasn't so damn desirable himself, so stirring just to look at. And being told she was necessary—Stars, that was almost as good as being told she was loved.

Martha's voice cut into her thoughts. "I hope that silence doesn't mean you're actually thinking about it, Shani."

Before Shanelle could reply, Falon's voice became husky with persuasion. "Turn the computer off and send the android away, *kerima*. Join with me now and take what is yours without fear. I will do no more than follow as you direct. I will not even touch you."

To have him again without the fear? Just the thought of it set her pulses racing. But she mentally stomped on the sensation. It was no longer just the fear of his lack of control, his strength, his size. It was a hell of a lot more, now that she knew he was a warrior, a *slaveholding* warrior.

She had waited too long to answer, for he added, "You may even tie my hands if that will help to ease your mind."

She snorted. "That might have worked earlier, *warrior,* but not now. Thanks, but no thanks."

"Atta girl," Martha crowed. "Just keep your socks on and keep using your head instead of your libido, and maybe he might finally get the message." But Martha couldn't resist pointing out, "Besides, you don't *have* anything to tie him with that those mighty arms couldn't bust out of. He knows that or he wouldn't have made the offer."

Martha was right, of course, but Shanelle had already figured that out for herself. And she was furious with herself for still feeling anything at all for Falon. She'd *known* she shouldn't be alone with him again. Now she knew why.

"*I* could hold him," Corth said suddenly, making Shanelle groan.

Martha was more vocal with a snort and a derisive "The warrior wants you gone, peabrain, not participating. And isn't it time you—"

Shanelle had closed her eyes for only a second in dread, knowing full well that Martha was bound to get Falon angry yet. And that second was all it took for Falon to take the step that brought him closer to the table near them, and smash his fist down on the link unit, destroying it completely.

Shanelle's eyes snapped open in horror at the sound, knowing what he'd done before she saw it. Pure instinct propelled her at Falon, and she threw her arms around his neck and held onto him tight.

"Martha, don't—please!" Shanelle pleaded desperately, expecting Falon to disappear at any moment to Stars knew where. "You know mother has dozens of those link units, so no harm was done."

"Yet," Falon added ominously. "Where is her heart, woman? What must I do to destroy her?"

Once more Shanelle groaned, this time quite loudly, but she also squeezed his neck a little harder. This was a different type of fear she was in the grips of, and she honestly didn't understand it. All she knew was that she had to make him understand before Martha lost patience with him and he was gone, never to be seen again.

"You can't hurt Martha, Falon. She belongs to my mother. She's also my mother's best friend.

If you hurt her, my mother would be devastated. I couldn't forgive you for that. My father wouldn't forgive you either, and my mother would try to kill you. All of that for what? Because she angers you? Martha angers *everyone* sooner or later. That's just the way she is."

"So she is another one I cannot be rid of without causing you upset?"

He didn't sound too angry now, and when his cheek nuzzled hers, she realized why. She was pressed tightly to him and he was very appreciative of that fact. But he wasn't holding her there. He was proving he meant what he said about not touching her. But she was touching him, and a jolt of pure sexual pleasure went through her so suddenly, she shivered with it. Damn him! *How* could he keep doing that to her when she hated everything about him? But the attraction was still there. She couldn't deny it. She just wasn't about to let it get to her again. Besides, joining with him again, no matter how much the idea pulled at her, would only encourage him, making this impossible situation even worse than it already was.

She unwrapped herself from his body to stare at him with what she hoped was an unrevealing expression. His own expression was telling. The man did want her. His light blue eyes fairly blazed with it, and another jolt of pure sexual hunger went through her, more powerful than the last, so powerful she could think of nothing else.

Before she could do something stupid, like give in to that silent entreaty, the audiovisual console in the corner started chiming. Shanelle turned toward it and gave it permission to speak, grateful for the distraction even though she knew full well who was calling.

And sure enough, the console lit up with a view of the Rover's Control Room, and Martha's voice blasted out. "Give me one good reason why I shouldn't dump him in the middle of a pride of wild *fembairi*."

Shanelle wanted Falon out of her life, not dead. The mere thought of it flustered her so much, all she could answer was, "Because—because . . . just because."

"Well, we can't get more illuminating than that, can we?" Martha came back dryly.

"Couldn't you just forget about this, Martha? Falon is going to leave now—"

"You're damn right he is, and *right* now."

"No!" Shanelle shouted and swung around. But Transferring was instantaneous. Falon was already gone. "Where did you send him?"

"Relax, kiddo," Martha said, sounding much more like herself now that she'd got even. "He's back in his own room, where I should have put him before your sleep was disturbed. I can't have him thinking I won't follow through on what I promise, can I?"

Shanelle glared furiously at the console, the fright she had just experienced taking refuge in anger. "You didn't have to play I'm-tougher-than-you-are! You could have left him alone. Dammit, I was in control of the situation for once, so why did you deliberately provoke him?"

If Martha could shrug with blatant unconcern, she'd be doing it now. "Just doing my job."

It was impossible to argue with a Mock II, so Shanelle turned to further vent her anger in a different direction. "And how come you just sat there the whole time, Corth? Didn't I tell him to leave? Shouldn't you have at least made an effort to assist him in going?"

"He had yet to see to your anger, Shani, which only he could do as the cause of it. And when he did, I did not hear you tell him to leave again. Nor did he touch you other than to relieve your pain. It was you who was touching him."

"When did you start analyzing situations before you act?" she grumbled with less heat.

"Martha has explained to me that sometimes a no does not mean a no after a woman has had her socks knocked off, because there is too much uncertainty in true feelings."

"Martha!"

"Well, he was asking so farden many questions, what was I supposed to tell him? That you hate the guy's guts, when that warrior has you practically panting every time you see him? And besides, you don't really want Corth tangling with him. Your Falon's pride might not withstand it. Much better if he gets shown up by something he can't fight against."

Shanelle hated it when there turned out to be perfect soundness to Martha's madness. "I'm going back to bed. I don't even want to think about how angry that warrior is going to be the next time I see him, nor do I want to dwell any longer on how *helpful* you two have been. Maybe you should have sent Falon back to his room before I woke up, because now I just have one more thing to worry about."

"Well, you don't expect me to do *everything* right, do you?"

Shanelle nearly choked on that one.

Tedra had no sooner walked into her dressing room the next morning than Martha's main housing terminal flashed on, and Martha's voice complained, "It's disgusting how much time you spend in that bed at your age. Don't you ever get tired of sharing so much sex with the same man?"

"Uh-oh." Tedra grinned as she stepped into her solaray bath for the required three-second cleaning, then out again. "Whenever you attack me, old girl, you aren't happy about something, and it's usually something *you've* done. What is it this time?"

"That was a legitimate complaint, now that I think about it, especially since I've been waiting half the night and then some for you to make an appearance. The extra hour you just spent with the big guy really grated on my nerves. I'm amazed I restrained myself from interrupting that little bout of fun."

"You don't have nerves, and the last time you interrupted Challen when he didn't want to be interrupted, you found yourself moved in with Brock, and you hated that enough to mind your manners after that. Besides, can I help it if my barbarian loves me so much he can't keep his hands off me?"

"You don't have to like it so much."

Tedra's eyes rounded incredulously before she burst into laughter. "We really are having a circuit breakdown this morning, aren't we? Why don't you stop going round the block already and tell me what's really bothering you?" And then she stopped in the middle of slipping into a fresh *chauri*. "Wait a minute. You spent the night with Shani. What have you done now, Martha?"

"What do you mean, what have *I* done?" the computer huffed indignantly. "I analyzed and acted in accordance with your wishes. But when there is more than one option to choose from, I have to wonder if one wouldn't have been better than another—in the overall scheme of things, at any rate."

"I don't think I like the sound of this. *Which* option did you choose that you're not absolutely thrilled about?"

"See for yourself."

Tedra sat down warily before the computer's video port to watch a reenactment of what happened in her daughter's room last night, half recorded from Martha's viewer, half simulated by the Rover's monitoring system when Martha's sight wasn't directly on the subjects. Everything was there, from the moment the Ba-Har-ani entered the room until

Shani was back in bed and pounding the hell out of her pillow before she fell back into a fitful sleep.

When the video port went blank, Tedra said with more than a little bemusement, "I've never seen her that angry with anyone before, nor that protective."

"Sexual emotions aren't easy to deal with when they're new. You ought to know that, or has it been too long for you to remember?"

Tedra made a face. "Real cute. And I see you were right as usual, Martha. She does still want him. It was written all over her face, even if she did turn him down."

"Yes, but she did say no. Right now she honestly believes she won't be happy with a warrior, so for the time being, it's a no-win situation. But I *could* have kept my mouth shut last night and given that warrior an opportunity to rid your daughter of one of her fears concerning him."

Tedra didn't have to ask which one. "Do you think he could have?"

"He was determined enough. Of course, how he would have acquitted himself if he had given free rein to that desire he was in the grips of is another story. He failed once, and probables says he hasn't yet had enough time to learn how to fully control what Shani makes him feel. He's making the effort. You saw for yourself how he restrained himself from even touching her when he was so highly charged. It was a wonder my circuits weren't melted just being in the same vicinity."

"That's *not* what I need to hear, Martha," Tedra grumbled.

"Sure it is, since it supports the fact that anyone who can get that charged with emotion is bound to have the one emotion Shani wants above all else. No one can tell me that particular Sha-Ka'ani male isn't going to love your daughter to pieces if he gets the chance to. As far as I'm concerned, that isn't an issue."

Tedra was inclined to agree. She'd always maintained that all warriors had the capacity to love. You just had to figure out how to get them to admit it, since they considered it an unwarriorlike emotion. But the Ba-Har-ani weren't like Kan-is-Tran warriors at all when it came to emotions *and* controlling them, so Martha was undoubtedly right on this point, too. Still . . .

"Those aren't Shani's only objections to a warrior, Martha. What about her unreasonable fear of a warrior's punishment?"

"She feared Kan-is-Tran punishment."

"And was outraged by the Ba-Har-ani equivalent, but that doesn't mean she wouldn't fear it. You know how silly she gets over pain."

"Give me a break, doll. You're talking about a child's punishment. How painful can that be? It's the humiliation an adult would feel in getting spanked that is the real punishment, not a temporary hot seat."

Tedra grinned, remembering the time she'd got spanked herself, and she'd *asked* for it. But she also recalled that it hadn't been at all painful.

"All right," she conceded. "So maybe that isn't a problem that even needs consideration, though I doubt Shani will see it that way." Then she sighed. "Stars, I wish I could make up my mind about this man and stick to it."

"You already have. So has Shani, for that matter. You're just both disappointed that the poor guy isn't as perfect as Challen."

"Don't make me laugh." Tedra snorted. "Challen perfect? Since when?"

Martha chuckled. "Just because he still drives you up a wall occasionally with a few of his barbarian tendencies doesn't mean you don't think he's the next best thing to ambrosia. You wanted him from the first moment you saw him. You just weren't planning on keeping him then. Your daughter, on the other hand, wanted the Ba-Har-ani from the start and *was* planning on keeping him. He's the one who blew it by not getting her hooked with their first joining. And that's his only true fault here. Everything else can be worked out. You even said so yourself."

"That was before I knew he was a farden slaveholder," Tedra reminded her.

"Slaves can be sold, can't they?"

"What if he won't?"

"He will if Challen makes it a stipulation to acquiring his daughter."

After a short silence Tedra suddenly grinned. "And to think I sometimes wonder why I keep you around." Martha merely made a rude-sounding noise at that, but Tedra had a new question, one Shani probably didn't know the answer to herself. "We've established she still wants him whether she'll admit it or not, but does she love him yet?"

"What am I, a mind reader?"

"You're an expert in deductions and probables, as you so frequently remind me and anyone else who'll listen, which amounts to the same thing, so give—or am I going to hate the answer?"

"If you were hoping she'd be all starry-eyed already just because she's hot for the guy, you can forget it. She might be fainthearted in certain areas, but she's strong-willed in others, and the plain fact is she won't *let* herself love the Ba-Har-ani as long as she thinks she's going to avoid belonging to him. So it's not going to happen until she does belong to him and has no reason to fight it anymore."

"That's just great," Tedra replied testily. "So where does that leave me as far as decisions are concerned? What do I do when Shani still insists on leaving?"

"You let her go," Martha said simply. "I get to play with meteors for a few weeks while Shani has time to conquer her fears and realize she was making a big deal out of nothing. Meanwhile, the Ba-Har-ani gets to learn patience."

Tedra bit her lip. "A few weeks?"

"It shouldn't take much longer than that with me subtly working on her."

A few hours later, Tedra stood beside Challen and watched Falon Van'yer win yet another round in the competitions. She was getting disgusted with the ease with which he was winning, cutting each match down to less than half the time it should take in his impatience to have the competitions over. It would have been a pleasure to watch that kind of superior sword skill if she wasn't so angry at that young man for all the trouble he was going to cause in her family. And it was all so unnecessary.

Shani wanted him. Challen already approved of him. Martha didn't even object to him. That should have made for no obstacles. Instead, Shani was going to leave home, defying her father in the process and ending up sick at heart about it. Challen was going to be furious, and guess who was going to catch hell for it? Not the one who ought to be blamed, but yours truly. And for what? Because that young man allowed his emotions to run amok.

"He fights well, does he not?" Challen observed with a good deal of pleasure.

Tedra gritted her teeth, knowing farden well her lifemate had already made up his mind about Falon. "Why shouldn't he?" she replied testily. "He's got jealousy goading him, giving him an advantage over every warrior here."

"Jealousy?" Challen said skeptically, looking down at her now.

"Absolutely. That warrior isn't fighting to be champion. He could care less about that. He's fighting just for our daughter. Hell, he already thinks of her as his. And *that* makes him see every other warrior here not as a mere opponent, but as a rival trying to steal what's his. He's jealous all right. He's pea green with it."

"And this displeases you, you who are wont to call a warrior a *jerk* because he lacks certain emotions?"

Tedra's cheeks pinkened the tiniest bit. "There's such a thing as too much emotion," she grumbled.

Challen chuckled. "Woman, you will find fault with *any* man who threatens to take your daughter from you. Admit that is all you have against this young *shodan*."

Stars, how she wanted to blurt out what the real problem was. She wasn't used to keeping secrets from Challen, though right now he more than deserved it after he'd kept secret from her the real reason behind these competitions. But getting him incensed over his daughter's now missing innocence wasn't going to accomplish anything other than his disappointment in Shani, and add more problems to join the rest.

So all she answered was, "Sure. Whatever you say, babe," and got him off the subject of Shani's suitors by adding, "But he's not so hot. *You* could take him easily."

"You have too much pride in your lifemate," he replied, trying to sound admonishing, but he couldn't quite pull it off, too pleased by her remark.

"With reason."

She grinned and bumped hips with him before sauntering off. His laughter followed her. She savored the sound, realizing that in a few days she probably wouldn't hear it anymore for a very long while.

18

Falon was in the corridor when Shanelle opened her door the next morning. It was kind of obvious that he was waiting for her because he just stood there, leaning casually against the wall across from her. That she didn't want to speak to him again was obvious, too, since she promptly closed her door.

But he didn't push his way into her room as he had yesterday, nor did he knock on her door. He didn't do anything. Since she was inside waiting nervously for him to do *something*, his not doing anything managed to stimulate in her aggravation of the teeth-grinding kind.

She wasn't about to remain in her room all day just because the man wouldn't take no for an answer. She would simply leave without acknowledging that he was out there. She wouldn't even look at him.

She did just that. But it was a well-known fact of Sha-Ka'ani life that it was literally impossible to

ignore a warrior who didn't want to be ignored—
and this one *refused* to be ignored.

He fell into step beside her. "Where do you go
this rising, Shanelle?"

Without answering, she just kept walking—and
found herself suddenly up against the wall with his
arms caging her in on both sides.

"I repeat, where do you go?"

For about two seconds she considered still not
answering, but he looked so damn stuck-in-the-
ground obstinate, she had the feeling he'd keep
her there all day if she didn't.

Coldly, so he wouldn't doubt her reasons for
saying so, she told him, "I've heard that you don't
like visitors, so I'm going to spend the day with
my *visitor* friends."

"At the competitions?"

"Where I go is none of your—"

"Answer!"

"Dammit, I won't! Where do you get off—"

"I liked your white cloak better," he interrupted
again, fingering her garment, leading their conversation in a new direction. "It was not mine, yet was
it my color."

She snatched the material from his fingers, glaring at him. "I *told* you I would never wear white
again."

"You will," he said with supreme confidence.
"You will wear my colors and be glad of them.
The day will come when you will want everyone
to know that you are mine."

She turned ashen. "You've spoken to my father,
haven't you?"

"Not yet."

Both color and relief flooded her face. "Don't. I mean it, Falon. You wouldn't be happy with me as a lifemate. I would make you miserable because you won't be able to help making *me* miserable."

"It distresses me that you think so, *kerima*."

Was he joking? She wondered. "I don't just think it, I know it."

"Tell me why and I will correct you in the matter."

She stared at him incredulously. He had to be joking this time.

"Are you going to tell me you're not a slave-holder? That you're not a warrior? That you Bar-Har-ani don't punish your women for every little thing they do wrong? Are you going to tell me you aren't inflexible, aren't hotheaded—"

"Enough!" he said, his tone blasting her with heat. "You will come to love me despite *all* of your objections."

"I see I forgot to add arrogance to the list."

He frowned at her sarcastic tone. "You are in definite need of a lesson in the proper respect due a warrior. This will be seen to when you are mine."

She refused to be intimidated by threats based on "when." "Now there's a classic example of why I don't want you, Falon. I'm not yours yet, but you're already planning on punishing me."

Even more disgruntlement entered his expression. "Your father should be told he has been neglectful in that area."

He had managed to intimidate her after all. Her father's punishments were mild compared

with Falon's, but she didn't care to spend the next
week peeling *falaa* in the kitchens. On the other
hand, the odor of *falaa* was so unpleasant and
strong, it permeated the clothes and skin with the
same scent, so that the peeler was definitely avoided
until she'd had a thorough scrubbing. Maybe that
wasn't such a bad idea after all. Shanelle grinned,
imagining Falon taking one whiff of her and running
in the other direction.

He mistook her amusement, asking, "You do not
think I would tell him?"

"Actually, I wish you would. It will be interesting to see what you do with your time when I'm
not around for you to bother."

"What in Droda's name would your father do
to you?"

She burst into laughter. She couldn't help it, he
looked so appalled. "What do you *think* he would
do to me for such a minor offense—and I say
minor, warrior, because whatever disrespect I show
you, you provoke. I'm usually much better man-
nered."

"You tease me, I think."

"Fat chance," she snorted. "Who would dare?"

"You would. You no longer find me so formidable."

He seemed pleased by that observation. Shanelle
wasn't. What was wrong with her, standing here
bantering with him as if they were lovers?

"Now who's teasing?" she said, and a stiffness
had entered her tone. "You're about as formidable
as they come."

He sighed. "I preferred it when you laughed,

kerima. What has changed your mood? You had begun to soften toward me—"

"I did no such thing," she cut in indignantly. "Weren't you listening earlier, when I told you all the reasons why I will *never* soften toward you?"

"It is only your fear of me that concerns me. The rest will not matter when you are assured that I will never hurt you again."

All she could do was to stare at him wide-eyed. He really believed that. Conviction was written all over his face. Talk about one-sided logic. But what should she expect from a *warrior?*

"That tears it," she said finally. "Let me pass already, Falon, or I'm going to find out if I actually learned anything in my downing classes."

The cage opened. She was almost disappointed. It would have been immensely satisfying to see his expression if she could have flipped him onto his backside. Of course, the key word was *if*.

"So you can be reasona—?" she started to say but then gasped as she was drawn up against his chest and soundly kissed. When she was set back on her feet a few minutes later, her legs barely supported her. Falon, watching her closely, was now grinning.

"I will escort you to the competitions," he said, so nonchalantly you'd think he hadn't just set her on her ear. "I want you to watch me fight."

"No," was all she could manage to say at first, but then she threw some ice on the fire he'd just lit and added, "I will be watching the visitor arenas until the end of the competitions. After all, the only reason I went with you to your tent yesterday was because I thought *you* were a visitor. I still mean to find one who will suit me—"

"If you do so, I will have to kill him."

That bald statement made Shanelle so furious, she was rendered speechless. Dren and Yari chose that moment to come around the corner.

One look at Shanelle's fiery expression and Falon's stormy one, and Dren thoughtlessly asked, "Do you need assistance, Shani?"

She had to give Dren credit for not being a complete idiot, because he didn't actually realize what he was offering until after he'd said it. He then turned three shades of white, which was not surprising, since the top of his head barely reached Falon's shoulders. But Falon didn't even glance at the male Kystrani, who he considered beneath his notice.

That, unfortunately, didn't relieve poor Dren, so Shanelle quickly assured him, "No, *Shodan* Van'yer and I were just discussing a few of the differences between his country and mine. I believe they're so used to owning slaves that they think they can put the stamp of ownership on anyone they please. Things don't work that way around here, and the *shodan* would do well to remember that."

All Falon said to that before leaving was, "Best you remember *my* warning, woman, else will you not like the results."

19

Shanelle began to think that something she had said to Falon had finally got through to him when that day passed into the next and he still hadn't asked her father for her. He got involved with the competitions instead, so involved it was as if he'd forgotten all about her.

She watched him fight from afar, though she'd told him she wouldn't. And she hadn't intended to, particularly after his parting threat. She hadn't intended to get anywhere near him ever again. But it was almost a compulsion to watch him do what warriors do best that made her seek him out. She knew it was foolishness on her part. But she took precautions, staying well back from whichever arena he was fighting in—but not so far back that she couldn't see him. However, not once did he notice her, or even seem to look for her in the crowd when he wasn't fighting. And when he was, his concentration was so firmly fixed on his opponents, she probably could have stood right at his arena and not gained his attention.

Today she got bolder, but then today the competitions would end, and her father had requested that she join him and Tedra at his pavilion for the finals. The eliminations had finished that morning. The eight warriors who were still undefeated at swords, and who had lost no more than one of the other contests of skill, would now fight in pairs before the *shodan* until only four remained, then two, then the champion of all. Falon was one of those eight finalists.

Shanelle was not surprised, not after watching how skillfully he had fought yesterday with swords. And he hadn't lost at any of the other contests either. And as long as she stayed near her parents, she wasn't too worried about Falon's saying anything of a personal nature to her if he did approach her. He didn't. Even while he awaited his turn to fight, he didn't. And the one time he did look her way, he didn't acknowledge her at all.

She began to think he'd changed his mind about asking her father for her. Perhaps he really had finally taken her rejection to heart. Of course, he could still be so angry at that last taunt she'd thrown at him that he felt it prudent *not* to approach her until he calmed down a little. But somehow she doubted that was the cause of what seemed to her more like indifference now.

And then his name was called to enter the arena, and she didn't think about anything other than the match about to take place.

"You aren't worried about him getting hurt, are you?" Tedra came by her side to ask.

"Certainly not."

But blood had been spilled in these contests. The swords used were blunted, but they were still deadly weapons. And although the object was merely to disarm, not to cut and maim, accidents were inevitable—and Shanelle's "Certainly not" was a big fat lie.

Tedra knew that, which was why she said, "I'm glad to hear it, because it would be a pure waste of time worrying about someone that good with a sword. He *knows* he's going to win. That kind of confidence tends to make it happen. I could almost wish he'd lose. The man doesn't deserve to get *everything* he goes after."

Shanelle stiffened. "Has father—?"

"No, not yet. But I'm afraid the question is going to be asked before the day is over, and I'm also afraid your father has already made up his mind. I can't imagine why, but he *likes* your young man."

"Then I'll have to leave," Shanelle said in a small voice, her shoulders slumping.

"Don't worry about it, Shani."

Shanelle misunderstood, thinking her mother was merely going to try and talk Challen out of giving his approval. But she couldn't afford to take that risk, couldn't afford to be anywhere near Falon if Tedra failed and he got Challen's blessing anyway.

"Mother, you know that with father's approval, all Falon has to do is say the words within my hearing and we will be joined for life, whether I want it or not. And once he says the words, I'll be his as far as he and anyone else are concerned. You *know* how damned easy it is. Father joined his life to yours and you didn't even know it."

"I know." Tedra couldn't help grinning as she remembered how ignorant she had been of Sha-Ka'ani customs at the time. "But I told you not to worry. I'll be there to know if Falon gets the permission he needs to say those words. And Martha is already alerted, so don't be surprised if you suddenly find yourself on the Rover."

Shanelle's throat constricted painfully. She had said she would do it. Hadn't she just spent nearly a year learning how to pilot deep-space ships for just this possibility, even being prepared to steal one if necessary? She had had every intention of going off on her own if her father chose a man for her whom she couldn't accept. But deep down, she had hoped she wouldn't have to.

"Does father know I don't want Falon?"

Tedra put an arm around her waist and asked gently, "Are you willing to tell him why you don't?"

Shanelle paled, knowing her mother wasn't speaking of all her reasons, just the particular one that her father wouldn't want to hear about, since it couldn't be explained without admitting she was no longer a virgin. She would rather Challen be angry with her for leaving than disappointed in her for giving up her innocence *before* she had a lifemate. And it was so ridiculous for her to feel that way, especially when she had given it up without a qualm. But again, deep down she had hoped her father would never have to know, that the man she gave her first time to would earn Challen's approval and end up her lifemate. Well, it looked like he *was* going to gain Challen's approval. But he'd lost hers.

Shanelle shook her head in answer, so Tedra said, "I'll make sure he knows about the rest of your objections at least, though I honestly don't think it will make much difference at this point—unless one of the other warriors has caught your interest. Perhaps one of these finalists?"

Shanelle's expression turned sour. "If I wanted to end up with a warrior, it might as well be Falon. At least he still . . . makes me wish he weren't a warrior."

Just barely, Tedra managed to keep from grinning over that hesitation, and she had no business finding *any* humor in this situation. "That's what I figured, so like I said, Shani, be prepared for a quick exit. You might want to say good-bye to your friends now."

Shanelle's eyes widened. "Stars, I forgot all about Caris and the others!"

"Martha didn't. She's already made arrangements with the Visitor's Center to return them to Kystran on one of the ships that will be leaving in a few days. And I'll make sure they're on it." If she wasn't chained to a wall for her part in Shanelle's departure.

But Tedra was trying not to think about the punishments her beloved barbarian was going to dump on her as soon as he realized his daughter was gone. That warrior took such things seriously, saw it as his *duty*. Farden hell. You'd think after twenty years she would have figured

out a way to avoid that aspect of Sha-Ka'ani
life—other than by being good all the time.

Shanelle's gasp drew her back to what was happening in the arena, and Tedra winced as Falon hit
the ground hard, having been knocked off his feet.
His opponent's sword followed in a full swing to
knock Falon's upraised sword out of his hand, but
the Ba-Har-ani lowered his weapon, the other sword
passed over him without striking metal, and Falon
rolled until he had room to get back on his feet.
The match continued normally then, with each man
banging away at the other's weapon. Falon hadn't
been in any danger, only of losing the match, but
to see Shanelle's pallor, you'd think he'd sustained
a mortal wound.

"He's tired," Shanelle said so softly Tedra had to
lean close to hear it. "He fought all morning long,
all day yesterday."

"His opponent is just as tired," Tedra pointed
out.

"But that other warrior is bigger. I don't know
how Falon has gotten this far. His sword arm has
to be about ready to give out."

Both warriors' arms were taking a good deal of
brutal punishment. But then most warriors had arms
like tree trunks. These two were no different.

"You want him to win, don't you?" Tedra stated
the obvious.

"Well, he's come this far."

"You don't have to sound defensive, baby. But
haven't you figured out yet why he's fighting?"

With a slight blush, Shanelle said, "The other day
it was to impress me."

"I'm sure it was, but that's not his reason now. Now he fights *for* you. It's your father he's trying to impress, because he knows how much importance is placed on a warrior's ability to protect his lifemate. He's using this competition to prove to Challen that he's the best choice."

Shanelle snorted. "I'm surprised father didn't think of that."

"What?"

"To use these competitions as a means of finding me a lifemate. It's a good thing all these other warriors don't know I'm available."

Tedra nearly choked. Fortunately she didn't have to reply. A sword went flying at that moment to skid across the grass. Falon was still holding his.

"Your restraint is commendable, Shani," Tedra remarked dryly.

"No, you were right. Being champion of them all does just about guarantee him father's blessing."

"Well, he hasn't quite reached that point yet. The champion of the visitors still has the option to fight him."

Even as Tedra said it, the visitor who had excelled in marksmanship, speed, and dexterity was declining, with a good deal of humor, a chance to fight a warrior. He was five feet eight, and slim as a gaali-stone post. The mere thought of him wielding a sword against a Sha-Ka'ani was absurd. But another visitor didn't think so.

Shanelle tensed as the High King of Century III arrogantly stepped forward with his retinue to demand an opportunity to best the champion. Challen didn't seem pleased. Neither was the crowd that was close enough to hear. Shanelle moved closer herself to catch her father's reply.

"The competitions are over."

"My intention was declared in advance," Jorran pointed out calmly.

"An intention disallowed by the rules," Challen replied. "This you were told."

"Rules do not apply to High Kings, *shodan*," the rotund Alrid announced haughtily. "Nor can our king be expected to compete with commoners. Jorran is willing to fight your champion. That should be enough."

Shanelle bit her lip to keep from grinning. The nobles from Century III had no way of knowing, for the signs weren't visible to anyone who didn't know him, but her father was no longer merely displeased, he was now offended as well, and that was grounds for issuing challenge that the average warrior wouldn't hesitate to do. A *shodan*, however, being the leader as well as an example to so many, had to show more restraint. He could accept challenge no matter the reason, but the insult had to be personal and deadly before he would issue one himself. Shanelle wondered if a Ba-Har-ani *shodan* was shackled by the same principles. Likely not, since Falon had already offered to fight Corth for an *unacceptable* reason, and had promised to kill any visitor whom she set her sights on, though she wasn't sure if he really meant that, or had said it only in anger.

Challen now ignored Alrid to tell the High King, "The warrior you wish to fight has stature here equal to yours on your planet."

"Excellent," Jorran replied. "Then I do not feel the effort is so far beneath—"

"*Best* you say no more," Challen cut him off. "Or you will have a number of true challenges to deal with before you depart our planet. As for your wish to enter the arena though the competitions are ended, such can be decided only by he who is the declared champion. And *Shodan* Van'yer is under no obligation to agree to another match, yet is the choice his to make."

Falon laughed at that point. "And I thought the rules would disallow me the pleasure."

Shanelle gritted her teeth. Why couldn't he just refuse? As much as it would do wonders for his overwhelming arrogance to lose, she didn't want to see him die doing it. He was tired; Jorran was fresh. No one would think less of him for ignoring a man who clearly thought to win what he had not rightfully earned—except everyone there who had heard the exchange would now like to see Jorran brought down a peg, and only Falon could do it. Even Shanelle's father was obviously well pleased by Falon's answer.

Jorran was also pleased, which didn't make a good deal of sense. Falon might be tired, but he was still a good six inches taller than the High King, broader, and much heavier. And the sword Jorran now drew from his scabbard was incredibly thin. Shanelle frowned. There was no way a weapon like that could knock the larger, heavier sword out of Falon's hand for the disarming.

"That farden bastard," Tedra said at her side. "He's using a razorsword."

"So?"

"So it takes next to no strength at all to cut a man in half with a sword that sharp. The arrogant jerk can't hope to disarm Falon, but he can ignore the rules and disable him with some serious wounds or worse—and we've already seen what he thinks of rules."

Jorran's first vicious swipe with the razorsword gave credence to Tedra's prediction. The High King was out for blood, and didn't care if his opponent ended up dead as long as he saw victory.

20

Falon felt the blood trickling down his chest long
before he felt the pain of his wounds. The pain
was minimal, ignored. The blood was a nuisance,
slowly depleting his strength. He did not think the
wounds crisscrossing his upper torso were serious,
despite the amount of blood he was losing, but he
could not be sure, the wounds were so thin. And it
had all happened in a matter of minutes.

Falon sucked in his middle even as he jumped
back, but again he felt the tip of that sword, a
weapon he had never seen the like of before, slice
through his skin. It was too quick, never there to
meet his own blade, flipping around him in a blur
of movement that his heavier sword could not hope
to match. It finally occurred to him that if he was
going to defeat the High King by the rules, which
meant disarming him rather than killing him, he
would not be doing it with his own sword, not

when Jorran kept his blade well away from it. The other man was not even *trying* to put up a pretense of this being a normal match, so why should he?

Reaching that decision, Falon threw down his sword and went after Jorran with his bare hands, using his steel armbands to deflect the razorsword, which was trying desperately now to keep him back. He sustained two more wounds before Jorran's sword arm was knocked aside and Falon's fist smashed into his face with a satisfying crunch.

The king went down and did not get up. His nose broken, one cheekbone smashed, he blacked out instantly. Falon did no more than kick the sword that had painted his torso crimson from the king's now slack hand, then turned his back on him. Only then did he truly feel the weakness that was gaining on him rapidly. And only then did he look toward Shanelle, but she no longer stood near her mother. She was nowhere in sight, and his sight was starting to blur.

When the meditech opened, Falon was surprised to see Tedra Ly-San-Ter standing there waiting on him. Long black hair flowed about the white *chauri* she wore. A necklace of large crystals in the exact shade of her aquamarine eyes hung from her smooth neck. As the mother of two grown children, the woman really should look older than she did. That she did not, and was incredibly lovely besides, was just one more thing to annoy him about her. Of course, once she opened her mouth, her antagonism made him forget how beautiful she was.

"Feeling better?" she asked as he slowly sat up.

A glance down at his bare chest revealed that nothing remained to show that he had nearly bled to death. "It defies belief, what this machine can do."

"You don't sound very pleased about it. Your first time?" His curt nod prompted a laugh from her. "Well, don't be surprised if you're now missing some of your old badges of courage. Meditechs just hate scar tissue, no matter how old it is."

It took him a moment to grasp her meaning. When he did, he glanced sharply at his shoulder, but the white line that had been there since he was a child was now gone. With a low growl he swung out of the meditech, thinking seriously about hacking it to pieces.

Tedra chuckled, not the least bit understanding. "Don't take it so hard, warrior. Shani knows how brave you are. You don't need scars to prove it."

"Woman, you and your machines do not belong on this world."

"You might have walked in here under your own steam—just barely—but a healer couldn't have sewn you up fast enough to save your life. Some of those cuts were more than an inch deep. If your reflexes weren't as quick as they are, there would be two of you right now—pieces."

Falon's expression turned disdainful. "From a puny visitor?"

"He wasn't so puny, but with a razorsword, a child could have sliced you in half. You had no business taking him on. You should have known by his eagerness to face someone so much bigger than he was that he had to have an advantage that he figured would guarantee him the win."

"For what reason do you rail at me for this when you have made your feelings for me perfectly clear?"

"I don't dislike you personally, warrior, only the way you conduct yourself. In fact, I'll probably be quite fond of you—someday. But I stood there and watched my daughter turn as white as this *chauri*, then puke her guts out, and that I don't appreciate. And for what? You were already champion. You could have ignored that pompous jerk of a king."

Falon grinned, interested in only one thing. "She feared for me?"

Tedra was disgusted enough to reply, "Not even a little. The sight of blood merely makes her sick. But you really enjoyed winning that last match, didn't you, even more than all the rest?"

Her sarcasm turned him stiff. "It is no secret how I feel about visitors."

"I was a visitor."

"For the mother of my woman, I must make an exception."

Tedra snorted. "Don't do me any favors. And she's not yours yet."

"Then best I see to that now. Where is your lifemate?"

"He's waiting for you, I don't doubt. And we might as well get it over with, so come along. Besides, someone else is eager to use the meditech. A matter of a broken face."

Falon's expression showed his satisfaction on

hearing that. "And Shanelle? Does she wait with her father?"

"You're out of luck there, warrior. She was still so upset over witnessing such violence, I sent her home. But you'll be pleased to know she wouldn't leave until I assured her I would personally see to it that you got patched up."

"I am surprised you would admit this to me."

"Don't faint on me, but here's another one for you. I told her why you entered the competitions. You wanted her to know, and that was the least I could do."

For some reason, the sound of that bothered him. The least she could do? Under what circumstances? But she had already turned away to lead the way out of the curtained-off area where the meditech had been temporarily moved for the competitions, so he said no more. The time was at hand for which he had waited so impatiently. He would have preferred that Shanelle be there so he could make her his immediately, yet she would be easy enough to find at the palace.

They entered the main section of the large pavilion to see a small crowd waiting: Falon's family, Dalden, the nobles from Century III with their still unconscious king—who was carried straightaway to the meditech now that it was available—and, of course, the *shodan* of Sha-Ka-Ra.

For the first time, Falon began to feel slightly nervous. He had won the competitions, but according to Dalden, that did not assure him the prize. And Tedra Ly-San-Ter's attitude—could she have convinced her lifemate to deny his request? Was that why her remark, about its being the least she could do, had the sound of guilt to it?

Jadell pounced on him to assure himself Falon was completely recovered; then the congratulations began. Challen produced wine with the comment, "I care nothing for the visitor's machines of convenience, yet do they offer some things a warrior can find pleasure in." And Tedra blushed because he was looking at her as he spoke, though he was uncorking the bottle of golden Mieda from the planet Rathus.

Falon took a glass, though he didn't drink. But he could not demand a private word when Challen was also filling glasses for everyone there. Yet he looked pointedly at his brother, who took the hint and didn't dawdle over his wine. Nor did the others, who were also aware of Falon's impatience and his intentions, including Dalden.

It was purely a waste of fine wine to guzzle it down, yet in less time than Falon could have hoped for, everyone was offering one excuse or another to depart—except for Tedra Ly-San-Ter, who reclined on one of the couches, merely sipping her wine. Falon was afraid she was not going to budge either, even if he asked.

He asked, "Could we speak privately, *Shodan* Ly-San-Ter?"

"There is no need to be so formal, Falon. And I have reason to doubt that my lifemate would leave just now without causing a scene to embarrass us both."

"He's joking, warrior," Tedra said, tongue in

cheek. "I wouldn't do anything more than challenge—"

"Woman," Challen admonished. "If you mean to stay, do so in silence."

Tedra shrugged and looked away from them. Falon cleared his throat and stated, "My request is formal, *shodan*. I desire above all things to give my life to your daughter, with full knowledge that she also wants me. I ask that you honor this request by giving her into my care so I may protect the keeper of my heart."

"Your request joins many others, yet never has another warrior been so bold as to tell me my daughter wants him. Why do you assume this to be so?"

"I do not assume, I know. She said as much to me. Also did she give herself to me."

Tedra came up off the couch spewing wine. "*Why* did you have to tell him that?" she fairly shouted.

Again Challen admonished, this time a bit more sternly. "Woman, this is a matter between men."

"Not if you're going to challenge him, it's not," she shot back. "Then it's a matter that concerns Shani, too, because I happen to know she doesn't want him hurt. I was going to break his skull myself, but she talked me out of it."

"I have no intention of challenging him."

Tedra blinked in surprise. "You don't?"

"Why would I, when what he has done is relieve my mind by telling me that my daughter wants the man I would choose for her myself. My relief takes precedence in this case."

"Well, that's just great," Tedra grumbled in full irritation. "She was worried sick about you finding out. I figured you'd go off the deep end myself. And here you are *happy* about it. But there's a little something you don't know, babe. Shani might want him, but she's also afraid of him."

"Such is normal—"

"No . . . it's . . . not! And another thing, the man's a farden slaveholder. Were you aware of that?"

"I was aware of the possibility," Challen replied, and asked Falon, "How many slaves do you own?"

"Sixteen serve in my household."

"Would you set those slaves free do I give you my daughter?"

Falon frowned at the unexpected request. "For what reason would I do this?"

"My lifemate, my daughter, they do not differentiate between a master who has a care for his property and one who does not. To their way of reasoning, no people should endure the total lack of rights as that of a slave. My daughter could not be happy for long with a warrior who owns slaves, no matter if those slaves are well cared for as his property. Can you give them up?"

"For your daughter, I believe I would do anything. All slaves in my ownership will have their freedom the same rising I return home."

"Then it is with pleasure that I relinquish the right to protect the child of my heart, Shanelle of the house of Ly-San-Ter, and give that right to you, Falon Van'yer. Do you accept this right?"

"I do."

"Then it is yours."

Tedra gave a mental shrug as she pressed the sound activator on her computer-link unit. There was no use bemoaning what she'd known was going to happen.

Quietly, so Challen wouldn't hear, she said, "Now, Martha."

21

If Tedra hadn't given the impression that she was
furious with her lifemate for his decision, so furious
that she wasn't about to be helpful no matter the
reason, then the search party might have come to
her sooner for questioning. As it was, Challen didn't
show up until that evening, with Falon at his side,
and the young warrior looking like he was about to
do murder if he didn't get some answers fast. Well,
that was too bad for him. The man needed to learn
some patience, and he was pretty much going to be
forced to start learning now.

Challen said nothing until he stood above her
with his intimidating height; then he came right to
the point. "Brock has pointed out the probables that
you would know where Shanelle is hiding, and if
you do not, then Martha surely would know."

Tedra swirled the *dhaya* juice in her glass and
replied indifferently, "You must be desperate if

you're using Brock. Instead, why don't you just accept the fact that Shani doesn't want to be found?"

"So you know why she hides?"

"I know why she's not here to be claimed by our young friend from Ka'al, but so does he." Her eyes swung accusingly toward the younger man. "Why don't you tell him, warrior?"

"He has already done so," Challen said calmly. "He has also informed me that the lack of control he suffered was a thing to be expected. It can happen only with the keeper of his heart; thus does a Ba-Har-ani know when he has found his true lifemate."

Tedra wished to Stars she'd heard that little tidbit sooner, and her defenses rose now with a touch of guilt that because of her, Shani was not here to hear it. "If he had bothered to tell *her* that, she might not have panicked when it became apparent that you favored him. You know how little tolerance she has for pain, Challen. She's afraid of him, afraid he'll hurt her again, afraid of the unique punishments a warrior will give his own woman, that all women end up earning for one reason or another, afraid that he can't love her because he's a warrior. She's not ready to accept him yet, and won't be until she can reconcile herself to some of that."

There was no indication that he understood Shani's difficulty, or her own in deciding what to do about it. All he said was, "Where is she, woman?"

His inflexibility infuriated her, causing her to gulp down the rest of her *dhaya* juice, then slam the glass down on the table beside her. "You may not consider it my duty to protect her, but I do! And right now she needs protecting from *him*."

Challen's gaze had unfortunately followed her glass to the table, and he picked up the bottle of *dhaya* juice sitting there and took a large drink of it himself. Tedra squirmed nervously. She hadn't wanted to feel anything when he got around to punishing her, which was why she was drinking the juice. A blatant case of defiance on her part that he couldn't help but realize, because *dhaya* juice was what warriors took to kill all sexual urges so they could punish their women with desire that wouldn't get relieved.

Setting the bottle back, he leaned over her to say, "There is always the new rising, *chemar*, and the next—and the next."

His meaning was absolutely clear and Tedra blanched. "You wouldn't punish me that much!"

"Where is Shanelle?" was all he said.

She pushed off the couch and began pacing in agitation. Her silence prompted the warning "Do not make us both suffer with your stubbornness, woman."

"Well, if I'm damned anyway, it might as well be for a good reason."

He was beginning to look like his patience was running out. "You will cease to defy me on this *now*."

"Wanna bet?" she shot back with a tightly fixed smile.

He stared hard at her for a moment before he finally sighed and reached for the computer-link unit attached to his belt. "Brock, best you join with Martha's terminal so I may speak to her of this matter."

Brock did not respond immediately. When he did, it was to say, "Martha has either been turned off or gone beyond my reach."

Challen's eyes bored into Tedra's again, with full suspicion now written all over his features. "Where is Martha?" he asked her.

"You heard him," Tedra replied carelessly. "Beyond his reach—beyond your reach."

Brock then announced with a good deal of male chagrin, "The Visitor's Center has just informed me that the Rover is no longer in Spaceport."

"Shanelle has left the planet?" Tedra winced at how close Challen was to raising his voice, but he wasn't finished. "You gave her permission to take the Rover?"

"If I hadn't let Martha take her off-planet, she would have left alone, and *then* we wouldn't see her again. Even now, she *thinks* she's not coming back. She's that serious about not wanting to end up with a warrior. If you had bothered to ask her, she would have told you that. But no, you plowed right ahead in typical barbarian fashion, insisting it had to be your way or no way. Well, she got it *her* way instead."

"With your assistance, woman. She could not have left otherwise."

That was debatable. But as long as Tedra was getting blamed anyway, she might as well keep quiet on that score and take it all. But Challen wasn't finished telling her how bad she'd been.

"What you have done is shame this house. You deprive this warrior of his right to protect his lifemate."

Tedra glanced toward Falon, who'd stood silently near the sunken pool all this time, probably in a state of shock at seeing a woman defying and arguing with a warrior. "She's not his lifemate yet."

"She will be the moment he finds her," Challen reminded her. "This you know."

Perhaps it was time to do some reassuring. "She's only going to be gone for a few weeks. Martha will see to that. She's going to work on Shani, help her to conquer her fears."

"I have waited two risings to claim my lifemate." Falon spoke for the first time. "I will not wait any longer." And to Challen, he asked, "Is there a way that I may follow her?"

"It can be arranged."

"No!" Tedra said incredulously, but she knew it *could* be arranged, and why hadn't she considered that?

Her anger now was at least half self-directed, that she was going to fail in protecting Shani after all. But it was Falon she took it out on, marching over to him to rail at him in full volume. "Dammit, what do I have to do, challenge you to get you to back off for a while? Shani *needs* some time to think and figure out for herself that a life with you won't be so bad. You know it won't be, my lifemate knows it, even I do, but Shani . . . does . . . not! If you find her before she's ready, she's just going to resist you. Is that what you want, warrior? Because if you're so eager for another fight, *I'll* damn well accommodate you."

By his expression, Falon wasn't taking her suggestion the least bit seriously, and her anger simply didn't impress him. "She is mine now to protect, yet is she not here for me to do so. I cannot remain here and do nothing while this is so. But your concern is unnecessary. When I find her, I will not allow her to resist me."

He might have got away with saying that to any other Sha-Ka'ani mother, but not to one who believed totally in free choice. "That tears it in half, warrior. Consider yourself challenged."

Falon almost laughed at the absurdity of a woman challenging a warrior. He did smile. But Tedra wasn't interested in his reaction. Her body loosened into a fighting stance, she heard her lifemate call out, "Do not!" which she ignored, and in the next moment she was delivering a high kick square in the center of Falon's chest.

He was totally ill-prepared, since he hadn't expected her to actually attack him. Because of that he was knocked off-balance—right into the sunken pool. He came up shaking hair and water out of his eyes. But those azure eyes quickly settled on Tedra with a heated glare.

"I will not fight you, woman."

"The hell you won't. I won't *allow* you to refuse. So come on, warrior." She beckoned him with her fingers to get out of the pool. "How does it feel not to have a choice?"

Unfortunately, Challen intervened at that point, coming to stand beside Tedra, but it was to Falon he spoke. "You cannot be faulted for refusing challenge from the mother of your lifemate. Perhaps you will allow me to stand in your stead?"

"No," Tedra whispered, even as Falon gratefully nodded his head, and then said as Challen turned toward her, "Challen, no! I would only have demanded that he give Shani the time she needs to get over her fears! That's all. I wouldn't have embarrassed him or put him to work."

"Challenge was issued, *chemar*." Hearing that prompted Tedra to run, but so damn easily was she stopped, and a moment later she was lying flat on her back on the floor, with her lifemate calmly lowering his body to cover hers. "Now it is accepted, and now do you lose. And you know what it is I will have of you for your challenge loss."

She did. Perfect obedience in the bedchamber, which meant she wasn't going to be able to fight when he got around to punishing her.

"Get off me, warrior," she growled low. "Even after all these years, you're still a farden jerk."

His lips curled in humor the slightest bit at her tone. "And you still try a warrior's patience." But he kissed her briefly before he let her up.

And now Tedra was the one who could do no more than glare at Falon as he hefted himself out of the water. "Try all you like, but Martha won't let you find them."

"Then I must allow Brock to accompany him," Challen said quietly.

"Brock isn't up to taking on Martha."

"This you hope. I disagree."

"So do I," Brock seconded.

"Fine," Tedra snapped in disgust. "Have it your way—you farden warriors always do. But I warn you, Falon Van'yer, that my daughter has had a year to convince herself that she would prefer anyone other than a warrior for a lifemate. It's going to take more than a few days to get her to see things in a different light. So go protect her. Do what you feel you just *have* to do. But I guarantee you won't be happy with the outcome."

22

"We may have a problem, kiddo."

Shanelle rolled over in bed to face the intercom. She didn't feel like getting up yet. She hadn't felt like doing much of anything since they'd left Sha-Ka'an three days ago. But if she didn't show a little interest, Martha would start asking why.

"Is something wrong with the ship?"

"Nothing so easily fixed. What we have is a shadow. It showed up last night on my long-distance scanners. Nothing unusual in that, except this ship is using us as a directional beacon. I've changed course three times since I noticed them, and each time they changed directions with me."

"You're telling me we're being followed?"

"Didn't I just say so?"

"Sometimes I'm not sure what the hell you're talking about."

"All right, what's *your* problem now? You've been moping about since we left, not to mention taking cute little snipes at me like that one."

Shanelle sighed and rolled onto her back to stare up at the ceiling. "My father is never going to forgive me for leaving without his permission. I know I had no choice, but I wish I didn't feel so guilty about it."

"I wouldn't worry about your father if I were you. Your mother will make sure he understands your reasons. It's that warrior you deserted at the symbolic altar that you ought to feel guilty about. He was probably devastated by your disappearing act."

"Let's not overlook mad," Shanelle retorted skeptically.

"No, we can't discount that, but I'll wager he feels hurt more than anything else."

"So what was I supposed to do?" Shanelle asked defensively. "Tell him good-bye to soften the blow?"

Martha chuckled. "That's rich. If he had had even the slightest clue that you were thinking about leaving, he would have dragged you straight to your father and wouldn't have let go of you until you were his by the laws of Sha-Ka'an. But maybe that's what you're now wishing had happened."

Shanelle sat up to scowl at the intercom. "What wire did you short? Would I have got my father displeased with me on a mere whim? It's guilt I'm feeling, Martha, not regret. There was nothing else I *could* do but leave. Even my mother thought so, or I wouldn't be here."

"If you're using her support to justify what you're doing, forget it. I happen to know she thinks you'll come to your senses before too long and go home. But *we* both know you don't have any sense."

Shanelle ignored the gibe. "Does she really think I'm just fooling around about this?"

"She thinks your fears are real enough. Tedra just gives you more credit than you do yourself, because she's sure you'll overcome them."

"What about Falon's loss of control? Am *I* supposed to overcome that?"

"No, he is, and it stands to reason that he will. Or are you forgetting that he was just as upset about unintentionally hurting you as you were? Any man who wants you as much as he does, *and* wants to protect you from harm, isn't going to risk hurting you every time he touches you. Either he'll get those raging passions of his down to a manageable level or he won't touch you at all, and you show me a warrior practicing abstinence, and I'll prove he's been dead a week but nobody knows it."

Shanelle dropped her head to her raised knees and did some forehead banging. Why did Martha *always* have to shoot down firm beliefs with her thought-provoking logic? All it did was confuse the issue. Now Shanelle couldn't help but wonder if she was in the wrong—no, even if Falon could conquer his problem, there were still too many other things against him. Martha was just taking opposite sides as usual. If everyone agreed with the computer, she'd have no fun disagreeing and causing arguments, which she purely enjoyed doing.

Irritably, Shanelle glanced toward the intercom again and suggested, "Let's get back to that ship you say is following us. Have we drifted into a war zone? Or is this area known for space-pirates?"

"Nothing so dramatic, doll, though you might prefer attack from a battleship to what you're likely to find instead. Probables say that's your warrior come to get you."

Shanelle stiffened before she burst out, "But he *couldn't* get a ship!"

"Sure he could—if he happens to think about it. According to Brock, Falon was brought to Sha-Ka-Ra at the request of the Catrateri ambassador to trade for gold, which Falon apparently has in abundance. The Catrateri would do just about anything for him right now to make a deal, including turning over whatever ship they have sitting in Spaceport for his use. Your father could also buy any ship in the port with the mere promise of a gaali-stone shipment, so—"

"If this is a joke you've come up with to pass the time, it isn't funny, Martha!"

"You know me better than that. I don't cause panic for my own amusement."

"But Falon hates everything to do with visitors. He wouldn't board one of their ships, he just wouldn't!"

"Wanna bet? Just picture that man being told you took flight—literal flight. The first thing that would cross his mind is to go after you. The second thing might be that the only way he can accomplish the first is unacceptable to him, but I seriously doubt that would stop him. Agreed, he might hate having to travel through space, but he'll do it anyway."

"Couldn't you be wrong just this once?"

"Do you really want to know the odds on that happening?"

Shanelle groaned and dropped to her side to curl into a tight ball of despair. "*Now* what am I going to do? This wasn't planned for, wasn't even a possibility."

"Maybe not in your book, kiddo, but in mine it was at the top of the list. But I've got your options all worked out. You ready to hear them, or are you going to lie there and pout all morning?"

"Are any worth listening to?"

"Anything I have to say is worth listening to."

"Real cute, but if you're going to suggest we put on the brakes and wait for Falon's arrival, I'd just as soon pout all morning."

"Parking here *is* an option, no matter how distressing you find it. And the consequences aren't all bad. You might get a little punished for running off—only to be expected—but then you get a lot of sex-sharing with a man we both know you still want. And consider the end results. Your mother can stop worrying about you, your father forgives you once you're back where you belong, you make one Ba-Har-ani warrior ecstatically happy, and you end up happy yourself in finding things less objectionable than you thought."

"And I believe all that like I do the space we're navigating is breathable. Forget it, Martha."

"Have it your way." Only Martha just had to point out, "But has it occurred to you that the less time it takes him to get his hands on you, the easier your punishment will go?"

"There won't *be* any punishment if he can't find me. Now what's next on the options list?"

Martha sighed. "It's too late to lose them. I can't tell yet what kind of ship they're in, but it's faster than the Rover with a gain of about two hours in twenty-four, and they've already proved they have a firm lock on us. By tomorrow they'll be within communicating distance. Transferring will be possible in five days if they're equipped with it, and the day after that they'll be right on top of us. So running is out, leaving only hiding as *your* number one choice."

"Where?"

"You ought to know, doll, that in the Niva Star System, the possibilities are limited. Only nine planets have been discovered here since your mother found Sha-Ka'an. And only two of those new discoveries are in the five-day range we have to work with."

"But the Centura Star System is closer than five days off, isn't it?"

"Sure is, and there's a planet tucked in the corner of that system right about where we enter it. Care to guess why I didn't mention it?"

Shanelle racked her mind for a moment to figure out why Martha was sounding so damned amused; then she groaned inwardly. "If memory serves, that planet would be Sha-Ka'ar."

"Your memory serves pretty good, and the only help you'll get there is assistance in mounting an auction block. But you *are* going to need help.

You'll have to actually arrange for some type of sanctuary or protection, because whichever planet you land on, your warrior can also land on, and if he isn't informed by someone in high authority that he can't have you, well, you know how warriors are . . . and this one will be armed with your father's approval—if your father hasn't come along for the ride himself."

"Don't even think it!"

"Relax, Shani. Your father joining the chase isn't high on the probables list. Challen would have an excess of confidence in Falon, or he never would have given you to him. As for the only two planets within our range, I hate to admit it, but I don't have an abundance of information on either one."

"So give what you do have."

"Sunder and Armoru were discovered by accident four years ago when a cargo ship from Antury was damaged in a meteor storm—shows what happens when humans do the piloting—"

"Put gloating on delete, will you?"

"You're no fun at all this morning," Martha complained, but continued. "The Antury drifted for a few days while making repairs, and by the time they were ready to get back on course, they had both Sunder and Armoru in their sights, the two planets orbiting so close to each other they were almost touching."

"That's impossible."

Martha's tone turned testy. "I'm making a point here, so stop interrupting. The fact is the planets are close enough to be seen clearly by each other, and for male-dominated societies with an excess of aggression, that can have a predictable effect—each one wanted to conquer the other."

"Are you saying they're in a state of war?"

"Semi-war."

"There's no such thing."

"Sure there is. The Armoruans would go in and wipe out the Sunderians' entire race if they could *get* in, but fortunately for the Sunderians, the Antury picked their planet to land on first and they're now in possession of a Global Shield, and just in time. Both planets are advanced in some areas, like medicine, government—weapons, though not by our standards—but they're babies when it comes to transportation, and they would probably have annihilated each other long ago if that wasn't so. They didn't even know there were other worlds in their own Star System when the Antury arrived, let alone other Star Systems. But two things happened only recently. One, they each finally developed spacecraft that would reach the other. Two, the women of Sunder somehow took over their government five years ago and that put an end to Sunder's desire to go neighbor-conquering. As it stands now, Armoru is still concentrating on finding a way to sneak over the space border to do whatever damage it can, while Sunder is now determined to prevent invasion."

"You're not painting an encouraging picture, Martha."

"Did I say your options were wonderful?"

"Does either planet even welcome visitors?"

"Who knows what policies will be in effect from one week to the next with such war-minded civilizations? You'll probably find it easier to land on Armoru, but you'll find better assistance on Sunder—if you can talk your way in. Armoru has been visited by a couple of worlds since discovery, but as backward as they are, and with so little of value for universal trade, they haven't been put on the traders' route. Their men just aren't easy to get along with."

"And their women?"

"Pretty low-class. They also have a servant class and a slave class."

"Dammit, Martha, *why* do you always wait until the last minute to drop your bombs?"

"Sorry, but it's the same on both worlds. The Armoruans would much rather invade Sunder, but until they can manage to do that, they'll keep fighting and conquering among themselves. They're too aggressive not to. And, typical of more cultures than not, whoever doesn't get killed gets enslaved. Up until five years ago, Sunder was doing the same thing.

"Sunder, on the other hand, is still pretty much a mystery. They made a point of educating themselves about the rest of the universe by sending a delegation off with that first Antury ship when it continued on its way. But they're very closemouthed about their own discoveries, and very suspicious of anyone requesting landing. And no one outside their world, and maybe not even all of their own people, know how the women of that world managed to wrest the power away from their men."

"Do they still have armies?"

"Undoubtedly. They're on constant alert for invasion, after all."

Shanelle sighed. "You're sure there isn't another planet around you're just not telling me about?"

"Would I make things harder for you than they have to be?"

"When you obviously want me to give up and go home? Who are we kidding?"

Martha chuckled. "In this case I didn't have to try. Of course, we can always make a run for the Centura Star System and hope our shadow gets delayed for some reason or other. Just one extra day would put us within reach of another four planets, three of which would treat you like a queen for just half of the gaali-stone cargo Tedra had loaded for your use. But that puts us in risk of getting within Transferring distance. And you know that in order to keep it safe you can only Transfer three times without waiting at least an hour in between. Otherwise we're talking definitely unhealthy, as in 'missing limbs and organs.' And that third Transfer would put you in Falon's arms no matter how you look at it—unless you wouldn't care if he got Transferred a fourth time?"

"No—no, and the risk isn't worth it to try for that extra day. Take me to Sunder, Martha."

"And if they don't let you land?"

"I'll worry about that when I get there."

23

The office was utilitarian in its decor: a large desk, wooden chairs, a long row of filing cabinets, and battle pictures on the walls. It was as depressing as it had always been, but Donilla Vand was reluctant to change it. In fact, she hadn't even straightened a picture since the office became hers five years ago.

The previous occupant of the office entered now with a stack of papers for her perusal. He didn't glance at her. He wouldn't while she was in the middle of a conference. Actually, Ferrill rarely looked at her anymore even when she was alone.

There was a time when she would have brought in the stack of papers and he would be sitting behind the desk. He'd pat his lap and wait patiently until she sat on it. And she'd have a few kisses and her breasts stimulated before she was sent back to the outer office to anticipate the end of the day, when they would go home together. He'd been her lover then, and her boss. He was still her lover, but it wasn't the same. It would never be the same again.

"She calls herself a Kan-is-Tran from Sha-Ka'an."

Donilla glanced toward her sister, who had spoken. It was easy to tell that Lanar was excited about this visitor, but then Lanar was a scientist, and the Antury and the few other alien ships that had come after them hadn't nearly appeased her curiosity about other worlds.

Donilla looked at her advisor now. "Zoreen?"

Zoreen thumbed through the notebook in her lap until she found what she was looking for, then read aloud, "Sha-Ka'an—a barbarian planet in this Star System with the most powerful energy source known to man. What did you say her name was again, Lanar?"

"Ly-San-Ter."

"Accurate as far as my notes go. That energy source is owned by a family called Ly-San-Ter."

Donilla tapped her nails on the desk, speculating. "The Armoruans could have that kind of information. We know at least three outside spaceships have visited them. There is no telling what they have learned, or what new weapons they have gained."

"Her ship isn't like any of those three that landed on Armoru," Lanar pointed out.

"They could have sneaked one in on the other side of their planet that we wouldn't have noticed."

"But we now have scanners capable of detecting anything that could be hidden inside the body, and she wouldn't be allowed to bring anything off her ship, not even her clothes. So what are you objecting to, sister?"

Donilla's lips tightened. Being the older by three minutes Lanar had always been the more dominant of the two sisters. It had infuriated her that, as a scientist, she couldn't assume any command after the takeover, and it was no secret that what she had wanted was Donilla's new position.

"It's my job to be suspicious," Donilla said. "It's my job to make sure we don't let in any more Armoruan saboteurs. That last one destroyed two arsenals and nearly got to the Global Shield before he was captured. It would be good strategy on their part to send a woman now."

"I disagree," Lanar replied. "They wouldn't *trust* a woman to get the job done."

"If she were a terrified slave being forced—"

"I'd know it in a minute," Lanar insisted.

Donilla's lips tightened even more, but in disgust this time. Yes, Lanar would know it. She was an expert when it came to terrified slaves—and getting them that way. It was one thing Donilla had never understood about her sister. She was brilliant in her field of medical research, respected by her colleagues, but she took pleasure in inflicting pain on the helpless. That she had suffered beatings from her last lover before the takeover was no excuse for her current obsession with whips and chains, for she had been cruel to slaves for as long as Donilla could remember. And unfortunately, there was no law to govern abuse of the poor creatures.

"What is her reason for coming here?" Zoreen

asked to divert the two sisters from a heated exchange.

Lanar answered. "To put it simply, she left her planet to try and escape the man her father gave her to, but he has followed her in another ship that is only hours away."

"*Gave* her to?" Donilla said derisively. "Her planet really is barbaric, isn't it?"

"According to my notes," Zoreen replied, "the men are of the warrior caste that uses swords as weapons."

All three women felt a measure of superiority. And the Antury had alluded that *they* were backward in relation to other worlds. Only in space travel, apparently.

But Donilla finally said, "I still don't like it. It's a story designed to outrage our sensibilities and make us sympathetic to her plight. It's the perfect story for another Armoruan plant."

"But if she's genuine and we *don't* help her, she'll have no choice but to apply to the Armoruans," Lanar pointed out. "They'll be ecstatic to get their hands on her and her ship, especially since it doesn't need a crew to fly it."

"No crew? How is that possible?"

"She claims it's run by a machine called computer."

"The Antury had those, but none that could run an entire ship," Zoreen remarked.

"And if her family is as rich as Zoreen says, the Armoruans can hold her for ransom," Lanar added. "Imagine the things they could bargain for, Doni, things Zoreen and the others returned to tell us about, weapons that can destroy whole planets. Do we dare push such a prize into their laps? I say *we* do the bargaining, but with her, for the sanctuary she wants."

Donilla hesitated before finally nodding agreement, albeit reluctantly. "All right, have the Shield opened enough so she can enter and land. But I want two guards posted at the quarters you give her, and they're to stay with her whenever she leaves them."

It was Lanar's turn to hesitate. "Certainly—but she doesn't want to land her ship,"

"Then how does she expect to join us?" Donilla said sarcastically. "Fly?"

"She has something called Transferring that allows her to just appear before us."

Donilla's eyes flew to her advisor with alarm. "Zoreen?"

"We were told of this Transferring briefly, but it seemed too complicated to understand, so we didn't ask for further information on it."

"Are you telling me this woman could have just appeared anywhere on Sunder without our knowing it?" Donilla shouted. "She has the means to pass through the Global Shield?"

"Apparently. But I *told* you the Armoruans would be thrilled to get their hands on her. Imagine what they could do with this Transferring."

"That doesn't bear thinking about. So why does she even need our permission to come?"

"Because she wants our help to keep the man who pursues her away from her when he arrives, he and his men."

"And how are we supposed to do that if they also have this Transferring thing?"

"If they appear, we detain them. If they won't cooperate, we use the Altering rod on them. They won't be any trouble after that."

By the look of her, Lanar obviously relished the thought of doing just that. But Donilla hated even the mention of that damn Altering rod that had changed all their lives so drastically. She hadn't been truly happy since it was invented.

24

"Will you stop with the gripes, Martha? The Sunderians are just nervous, but who can blame them after what you told me about the Armoruans? You'd take the same precautions if you faced the constant threat of invasion."

"You managed to talk them into letting you keep your clothes on," Martha grumbled. "You could have talked them into letting you keep one little computer-link unit."

"I wasn't going to press my luck after that grueling interrogation they put me through," Shanelle replied. "After all, they aren't welcoming me with open arms."

Martha's tone switched to indignant. "They should be after you promised them a whole crateload of gaali stones, and for something a warrior would give you for free."

"Ah, but when the job requires protection *from* a

warrior, what I promised may not even be enough."

"And that's another thing. What makes you think they can keep Falon away from you?"

"They said they could. I have to count on that."

"But *I* won't be there to help you, and neither will Corth. They could have at least allowed you to bring Corth along."

"They don't have the technology to analyze Corth or you. If they did, they could see for themselves that neither of you is programmed to do them harm—not that *you* would let them get near you, but you get the point. They're just being cautious. And stop making such a fuss. You *know* all this better than I do."

"I don't have to like it."

Shanelle had to grin at this new tone that was pure pout. "So you've filed your complaint for the record. Let's just do as planned and stop worrying, all right?"

"Stop worrying when I'll only be able to hear you half the time you're down there?"

Shanelle sighed. "Without the computer link, we can't do any better than what we planned. Even you said so. All you have to do is keep a fix on me until I'm shown to my quarters; then you remain fixed on that room. If you tried to follow me everywhere, you could end up losing me altogether, and then where would I be? This way I'll know where to find you if I need to Transfer back to the ship."

"That's *if* I can manage to keep you on my monitor until you get to your quarters."

"Stars, you just *had* to make sure I'd have something to worry about, too, didn't you? Thanks a lot, Martha."

"Anytime," Martha fairly purred. "Maybe now you'll stop being so damn blasé about a dangerous situation. You're going to walk in there blind, because we know next to nothing about these Sunderians."

"But I do know what will happen if I stay on the Rover, so I'm opting for the unknown."

"Stubborn—your mother would have a fit if she knew I was letting you—look out! The intruder is coming through again."

And Brock's voice was there, arrogantly male, ordering, "You are forbidden to go down to that planet, Shanelle."

It wasn't surprising he'd figured out what she was planning to do. He was, after all, a Mock II, and as capable at probables and deductions as Martha was. And he had been transmitting his voice every few hours for the past three days with a full gamut of orders, persuasions, threats, and warnings, none of which Shanelle listened to. But she now knew that Falon hadn't come after her alone. He had his relatives with him—he also had her brother with him. That was playing dirty as far as she was concerned, and she had plugged up her ears and buried her head under a pillow each time Dalden had tried to talk her into giving up.

From Falon she had heard nothing, but his very silence unnerved her, predicting that what Martha had said was true. The longer it took him to find her, the angrier he was likely to get. And she had been gone six days now. She planned to make it much longer with the help of the Sunderians.

Right now, she ignored her father's computer

once again, and told him so. "Sorry, Brock, but I didn't hear that. Martha, I'm ready."

"So long, doll."

"Wait!" Brock began, but Shanelle was gone. "You should not have abetted her in this foolishness, Martha."

"So what else is new?"

"If you were aware—"

"I'm *always* aware, brick-brain."

Brock released a sigh and tried a different tack. "Her lifemate is losing patience."

"He didn't have any to lose. And shouldn't you be doing something about that?"

"He is not an easy subject to work on."

"Poor baby. Has he threatened to destroy you yet?"

"Save your sarcasm for the humans, woman. I am not impressed."

"You turning barbarian on me again, sludge-bucket?" Martha growled.

"You are *impossible* to talk to anymore."

"So who invited you?"

"Martha!"

It was the wounded tone he injected that got to her. "I'm sorry, Brock. I'm just worried about Miss Do-it-the-hard-way. I should have had her turned around by now, but she's proving as stubborn as her mother ever was."

"Our objectives are the same, to see Shanelle back where she belongs. Do I send you Falon as soon as it is safe to Transfer, will you then send him down to Shanelle?"

"No."

A brief silence. "Why not?"

"Falon thought he was getting a warrior's daughter, obedient, easy to handle. It hasn't sunk in yet that Shani is more her mother's daughter, with a mind of her own. The more trouble he has now in obtaining her, the sooner that fact will sink in, and the less misery they'll both have later on. So help the big guy all you like, but don't ask me to do the same. Besides, he wouldn't trust any assistance coming from me."

"It is true he does not speak highly of you."

Martha chuckled. "I can just imagine."

Shanelle materialized into bright lights and a cacophony of amazed chatter over her sudden appearance. A great many people had apparently shown up for her expected arrival. They formed a circle around her, but not a close one. In fact, no one there seemed willing to approach her or speak. Military types stood at the forefront of the circle, men in uniform with some kind of ancient-looking handguns in their hands, not pointed at her, but ready just the same. Their nervousness was apparent—too apparent.

Shanelle took them all in at a glance and had only one blaring thought. How could these timid people possibly protect her from a Sha-Ka'ani warrior? They were every one of them on the short side, the women averaging five feet, the men maybe five and a half. Stars, *now* what was she going to do?

A woman finally came through the circle to approach her. She had a superior air about her of someone in authority, gray eyes without warmth, black hair drawn back severely. The smile she offered should have cracked, it was so brittle.

"I am Lanar Vand. When we communicated, you should have warned us you were from a race of overlarge humans."

So much for "Welcome to Sunder." The little woman was actually scolding her. Shanelle almost laughed, but her disappointment was too keen at the moment.

"I don't think this is going to work. The only reason I'm here is because I need help, but I'm not at all sure now that you people can supply it."

"Certainly we can. Your requirements were understood and agreed to. The man Falon Van'yer is to be kept from your sight and hearing. A simple matter."

"Simple? He's a warrior, and a lot bigger than I am."

There was some chuckling in the room, as if they assumed she must be exaggerating. More likely they thought nothing *could* get bigger than she. But obviously, they weren't taking her seriously.

The spokeswoman said, "A large male will be interesting to observe, but his size won't be a problem. It won't be necessary to depend on brute force to detain him."

"It won't?" Shanelle asked suspiciously. "Killing him isn't in the bargain. In fact, it's absolutely forbidden."

Lanar Vand took a step back, Shanelle's words were uttered so fiercely. But then the lady frowned, realizing what she'd done, and those gray eyes that lacked warmth got downright frigid.

"Killing wasn't an option," Lanar said stiffly. "And I have assured you that your problem will be seen to. So come along—"

"Hold it," Shanelle cut in just as stiffly. "I'm not going anywhere except back to my ship unless you tell me just how you intend to take care of my 'problem.'"

"So my word isn't good enough for you?"

"Is there any reason it should be?"

Lanar's pale skin suffused with color. She turned to one of the soldiers, nearly shouting, "Officer, take the alien to General Vand. Let my sister try and convince her of our capabilities. I no longer have the patience." She added in a mumble as she turned away, "And to think I volunteered for this."

Shanelle stood there for a good thirty seconds grappling with her own irritation while the officer waited and everyone else in the room continued to watch her avidly. What she wanted to do was tell Martha to forget it and Transfer her back to the Rover. But the thought of facing Falon now, after she'd run from him . . . She had to see this through, and just hope these people had some strategy planned, or maybe some place they could hide her where Falon couldn't get to. And she had to hope they *all* weren't like Lanar Vand.

25

"The general will see you now."

Shanelle followed the officer who had escorted her from the space center to this government building across town. They had got here in a ground vehicle that actually rolled on wheels and moved no faster than a *hataar*. There had been ample time for her to play the tourist, though there wasn't anything of real interest to see. The many buildings they passed were mostly square in shape, all painted white, and all somewhat miniature in size—just like the people.

Shanelle ducked beneath yet another too-short doorway to enter the general's small office. She had been expecting a woman. She hadn't been expecting an exact duplicate of Lanar Vand. The women were obviously twins. They were exactly alike except for their different uniforms, and this twin's gray eyes weren't as cold.

The general was standing behind her desk to greet Shanelle. "I am Donilla Vand, Miss Ly-San-Ter, presently in command of Hydra town. Won't you have a seat so we can discuss your problem and our solution for it?"

Shanelle looked at the small wooden chairs in front of the desk that she was being offered and said, "Fine, if you're sure I won't break it."

Donilla smiled, then actually laughed. Some of the stiffness left Shanelle's back. Carefully, she lowered herself into the nearest chair. It didn't break.

"The Antury had difficulty communicating with us," Donilla said as she sat down herself. "How is it that you speak our language?"

"The Antury didn't have a Mock II computer capable of scanning the surface of your planet for random conversations, deciphering the words for translation, then making me a high-speed Sublim I could listen to. This put your language into my subconscious, where I have hundreds of other languages stored for access when needed."

"Is this the computer that runs your ship?"

"Yes. Her name is Martha."

Donilla grinned. "You name your machines?"

"Only those that can think for themselves."

Donilla tried to grasp the concept of a thinking machine, but gave up with a sigh. "These things are beyond my understanding. My sister, however, would no doubt be fascinated by your Mock II, and will certainly want to hear more about it. She's the genius in our family. She's already discovered cures for two of our major diseases."

"You still have disease on this world?"

Donilla blinked at the surprise in Shanelle's voice, then came back with some of her own. "You don't?"

"The Sha-Ka'ani never have, as far as I know," Shanelle informed her. "But most worlds have advanced beyond disease. Those that haven't buy meditech units, which can cure and heal just about anything."

Donilla stared wide-eyed for a moment, but then she chuckled. "I hope you won't mention that to Lanar. She would be absolutely appalled to know there is something that would make her job obsolete."

"You don't sound too sorry for her," Shanelle observed with a grin.

Donilla shrugged. "Sibling rivalry. Do you have any yourself?"

"A brother—actually my twin."

"Then you *do* understand."

"Not really. Females don't compete with males where I come from. It would be ludicrous to even try."

"Well, let me tell you, sisters do, and mine always lorded it over me that I failed to get into science school, while she breezed right through it. That she's never had to struggle at anything except personal relationships just might be her problem."

Shanelle decided not to comment on Lanar Vand, who had struck her as being not quite emotionally stable. Instead, she broached her reason for being there.

"Are you aware of *my* problem? Falon Van'yer is going to show up here very shortly to claim me, which I don't want to happen. But if he gets within my hearing, he'll have us mated for life quicker than you can snap your fingers. All it takes is a few words from him to make it final. And frankly, I can't imagine your people being able to stop him."

Donilla smiled. "Yes, I have been informed that you doubt our ability to assist you. And it's true that if we don't shoot Mr. Van'yer on sight, which I assure you won't be necessary, we may have some difficulty detaining him—if he is as large as you are."

"Much larger."

"Really?"

"I may be above average in height, but you people are below average, yet most worlds still consider Sha-Ka'ani males to be giants."

"Then we will definitely have to use the Altering rod on Mr. Van'yer. What would you like him to forget, that he knows you or merely that he wants to marry you?"

Shanelle just stared at the little woman behind the desk. "Was that your idea of a joke?"

"Have I actually managed to amaze the girl with knowledge of so many amazing wonders?"

"So you weren't joking?"

Donilla's expression suddenly turned bitter. "I wish sometimes it were a joke, but it's not. I will explain, but first I have to ask you to keep what I tell you in strictest confidence."

Shanelle wondered if she ought to tell the woman that Martha was eavesdropping. No, she was too curious to risk not getting an explanation. And besides, she could nod her agreement in all honesty. *She* wouldn't repeat what she heard. Whether Martha would was another story.

Shanelle nodded. Donilla began to speak. "The Altering rod was designed by one of our most brilliant doctors for use on her mentally disturbed male patients. It was a remarkable achievement and worked exactly as she had intended—until one of her colleagues pointed out another use it could be put to. I won't bore you with all the details, but this turned into a major conspiracy involving all the women on the planet. We were unanimously fed up with our men's obsession with war, you see, and their unwillingness to listen to our views on the matter. And they were almost finished building that damn spaceship that would reach Armoru. We were desperate to find a means to stop their invasion, and short of blowing up the spaceship, which would only get built again, there was nothing we could do to prevent our men from going and getting killed—until the idea of using the Altering rod was presented to us in secrecy, and heartily approved."

"What exactly does this rod do?"

"It works on the subconscious mind like hypnosis, but without the subject being the least bit aware of it. A mere touch of the Altering rod, anywhere on the body, and any suggestion becomes a reality."

"I don't imagine your men just volunteered for this," Shanelle remarked dryly.

"No. The rods were mass-produced and sent to every hospital. The men, being in the army, are required to take yearly physicals. Doctors are almost all women."

"All?"

"With each man devoted to the army, is it any wonder women dominate our professions? Non-officers will frequently take part-time jobs, but nothing that requires intensive study that would take them away from their war games. At any rate, during a three-month period five years ago, every man reported for his physical, and when it was over, he was—Altered."

"How?"

"The same traits were removed from them all— arrogance, aggression, the need to dominate, the desire to make war. But it was also decided that the men should no longer be in complete control of the army. So certain generals were chosen to forget that they were generals, with women assuming their positions. I didn't pick this job; I was coerced into taking it because I was closely associated with the previous general. I was his secretary. Now he's mine."

"And he has no idea what was done to him?"

"None."

"But what happens if you're invaded?" Shanelle asked. "Will your men fight?"

"Certainly. They're still soldiers. They just no longer have the urge to start the fight."

Shanelle sat back in amazement, heard the chair creak, and quickly sat forward again. But she was still bemused.

"It worked on *all* of them?"

"It was designed to work on men. Actually, the rod has no effect at all on women. But there were some instances where a few women rebelled and brought their men out of their altered state. That's why every woman now has her own rod, to use on any man even suspected of being freed from the conditioning."

"Wait a minute. You're saying the conditioning isn't permanent, that something can put your men back to their original state?"

"Exactly. A man merely has to be touched with the rod again and told the reverse of what he was told when it was first used. He will then be completely his old self, with all of his masculine instincts restored—and aware of exactly what was done to him. Our men have been altered for five years. I would imagine there are women, now in possession of a rod, who will have taken advantage of the power those rods can wield with mere suggestions, and virtually turned their men into slaves. That's human nature. So little wonder none of us dares release her own man now, even if she would like to."

"Widespread slaughter?"

Donilla's smile now lacked any real humor. "Something like that."

"I'm sorry. It sounds like you've backed yourself into a corner that no longer has a trapdoor for escape. And I'm not sure I want Falon's mind tampered with that way."

Donilla's smile turned wry. "You don't want him killed or tampered with. Do you have some feelings for this man despite your not wanting to belong to him permanently?"

"Nothing that a little time won't diminish," Shanelle insisted.

"Then perhaps you might like him changed to suit you instead."

Shanelle's eyes flared with the possibility. To have Falon convinced that he could love? To have him told he must never punish her, and so he wouldn't?

"I—I'll have to think about it."

"Well, don't wait too long. My people have been alerted to the problem. If he shows up before you decide, he will simply be convinced he doesn't want to marry you."

"Isn't there any other way to keep him away from me, without the use of an Altering rod?"

"I suppose we could render him unconscious and keep him in chains."

"No." Shanelle sighed. "Ideally, I just want him to go home and forget about me."

"Then consider it done."

26

Shanelle arrived at Lanar's rooms precisely on time, thanks to her two-man soldier escort. She'd been invited to dinner. She would have declined, except it was Donilla who had invited her, and she liked the little general. She couldn't say the same of her sister, and could only hope Lanar would have a better disposition in a sociable atmosphere.

The rooms she had been given were adequate—if she didn't mind being able to reach up and touch the ceilings, or have her feet hang over the end of her bed. It definitely felt strange being the tallest woman in the world, but so she was on that world. But there was one good thing about it. Falon and her brother wouldn't want to stay long in such cramped surroundings, where their heads would touch the ceilings.

She'd asked Martha to send her down a change of clothes so she would know for certain if Martha had kept a fix on her. Martha proved she was listening by Transferring Shanelle up to the Rover to pick out her own clothes instead; and, while Shanelle was changing, got her opinion of everything that had been said to her. The gist was, Martha definitely disapproved of the Sunderians' misuse of their Altering rod, though she would love to analyze one if Shanelle could get her hands on one. Shanelle wasn't even going to try.

With Martha running on lecture-mode and delaying Shanelle's return to Sunder, there hadn't been much time for Shanelle to consider the temptation Donilla had offered her. But it didn't take much time to figure out that altering Falon to suit her idea of the perfect man just wouldn't work if he was going to take her home to Sha-Ka'an, where he would be reminded daily of the very things she'd like him to forget. It might work on Sunder, but she had no desire to stay there any longer than she had to, and Falon certainly wouldn't be happy on that planet, where he would be nothing but an oddity.

Donilla was already there to greet Shanelle as she entered Lanar's luxurious quarters at the science center. Everyone, it seemed, lived right where he or she worked. It made for a lot of long buildings and large, multi-floored work centers, and no single dwelling homes.

"I would have had you to my quarters," Donilla began as she led Shanelle to one of three plushy cushioned couches, "but they're—well, very austere in the military fashion."

"And otherwise occupied by an ex-general my sister is secretly ashamed to call hers, now that he's lost all his arrogance and bluster," Lanar added cattily as she handed Shanelle a drink.

Shanelle didn't know what to say after that. The one woman was blushing, the other smiling spitefully. Fortunately, Donilla recovered quickly.

"That isn't true," she told her sister. "I'm not ashamed of Ferrill. I merely miss—sometimes— the way he used to be."

"You liked being swallowed up by that forceful personality he had? You used to complain that you had to ask his permission for every little thing you wanted to do, but now you miss—"

"I hardly think this is a subject our guest is interested in," Donilla replied, her tone warning that she was starting to get angry.

Lanar paid no attention to the warning. "Why not? She comes from a society that still *gives* its women away in marriage. I'll wager the man who's coming after her is about as domineering and arrogant as Ferrill ever was."

Shanelle almost laughed. The woman was deliberately turning the attack in her direction now, but she wasn't going to take the bait.

"You'd lose that wager, Lanar, unless you changed the 'about as' to 'much more,' because no one can be as arrogant as a Sha-Ka'ani warrior, and they *totally* dominate all aspects of life on my world. Women can't even work to support themselves or leave their home without a male escort. They *have* to be under a warrior's protection, or they're up for grabs by any man who wants them."

It was hard to keep from grinning at the shocked look on both women's faces. Shanelle took a sip of the greenish-blue liquid in her glass while she waited for their reaction.

"That's utterly barbaric," Lanar sneered.

"No wonder you're running away," Donilla sympathized.

Shanelle feigned a look of surprise. "Did I forget to mention that our women rarely complain about the way things are? Of course, when you see what warriors look like, you can maybe figure out why that's so."

Lanar made a sound of disgust. Donilla grinned. "So why run away?" she asked.

"My mother is from a different world, one that treats men and women equally, and where everyone is self-supporting. This gives her a different outlook, one she's passed on to me. In fact, she's made it possible for any woman who wants to work for herself, rather than be dependent on a man, to be able to leave Sha-Ka'an to join new colonies where women are desperately needed."

"But has she made a dent in changing the dominant male culture she finds herself living in?" Lanar asked snidely.

"Not a scratch. But then it would be easier to walk on live coals than to get a warrior to change his ways—and that's why I left. My mother puts up with the things she doesn't like because she loves my father. I don't have that to influence me."

"Donilla did," Lanar purred venomously. "But she opted for change when it was offered and now wishes she hadn't. She'd rather be back under a man's thumb."

Shanelle was annoyed that she'd given Lanar an opening to attack her sister again, and this time she didn't keep quiet about it. "What's your problem, Lanar? Where I come form, siblings care about each other. They don't try to draw blood with every other word they utter."

Lanar obviously wasn't expecting to be attacked in turn. Her reaction was the same as it had been at the space center when Shanelle had refused to accept her word. She flushed with color, looked for a moment like she could kill, mumbled something about seeing what was keeping dinner, and stiffly left the room.

"That wasn't necessary, but thank you," Donilla said, drawing Shanelle's eyes back to her.

"Is she always like that?"

"With me, pretty much."

"Do you know why?"

"Jealousy, I suppose. She has everything she could want—position, influence, and authority, even slaves to wait on her—but that's not enough. She also wants what I have—even Ferrill. Despite her derogatory remarks about him, she'd love to lure him away from me. But he never liked Lanar, then or now."

"I can't say I blame him. Do, ah, you own slaves, too?"

Donilla shook her head, staring at a closed door behind Shanelle. "I've never wanted to have that kind of power over anyone. Besides, the military takes care of its own. Ferrill always had at least four aides jumping to do his bidding, which I inherited."

"I suppose they had to be altered, too, and anyone else who knew him, to forget he was the general?"

The bleakness that Shanelle had noticed before entered Donilla's expression again. "Yes. It got pretty complicated when we started taking over their jobs."

Shanelle said gently, "It's obvious you didn't like doing that to your own man. If you aren't happy with the way he is now, why don't you release him from the altering?"

Donilla smiled sadly. "He'd kill me."

"Maybe figuratively." Shanelle grinned. "But then he'd probably thank you for giving him back himself. Those negative traits you women got rid of were part of your men. They may have made them difficult to get along with, but without them, all you've got are half men. You probably aren't the only one unhappy with the present situation, and who'd like to have her man whole again."

"I couldn't make that decision on my own. If one gets released, he'll start releasing all the others. Besides, we'd be right back where we started, with the men rushing hell-bent into war."

"Humans are known to make those kinds of mistakes. Usually they learn by them and then get on with their lives."

Before Donilla could reply, Lanar returned with two scantily dressed female slaves flanking her and announced curtly that dinner had arrived. The slaves carried large trays which were offered first to Lanar, after she'd seated herself again.

When a tray was held out to Shanelle, she found four full meals were being offered, all containing a variety of different selections. Like her hostess, she picked only one square plate, having no idea what she would be eating, but only slightly curious about it, her attention having been otherwise snared by the slaves. It was hard not to notice the marks of punishment on both of them, ugly red welts that striped the backs of their thighs and calves, more prominent on one girl than the other, as if she had received hers only that day.

Shanelle was appalled enough to demand an explanation from Lanar, but a buzzer sounded first, loud enough to startle her, and she watched as Donilla set her plate down on a table, took a small cube out of a pocket on her uniform jacket, and said, "What is it?"

A female voice came out of the cube, scratchy but audible—and panicked. "They're here, five of them, and you better get over here, general. They're not just bigger than the female, they're . . . SEVEN . . . FEET . . . TALL!"

Donilla glanced at Shanelle and got an I-told-you-so look before she spoke to the caller again. "Hasn't anyone done what they're supposed to?"

"I doubt it, general. They're just too huge to get near—and they're armed with swords nearly as big as I am."

"All right, where are you?"

"In your building. Wherever they arrived, they encountered some of our men and forced them to bring them here to the one in charge. They're already on the way to your office, and at the rate they're getting answers without hardly trying, they could be on the way to your sister's quarters before you can get here."

"I'm leaving now, but in the meantime, lock up that building, then go to my office and make sure they don't leave it. Tell them I'll be there in ten minutes to speak to them, tell them anything you have to, but keep them there. And have enough women prepared to go in with me when I arrive. We'll have to use the rods simultaneously since they've come en masse, and that's not going to be easy." She dropped the cube back in her pocket and turned to Lanar as she stood up to leave. "You better hide her, just in case."

Shanelle wished Donilla had sounded more encouraging before she departed. And being left with Lanar was not Shanelle's idea of feeling safe. The woman continued to eat her dinner, as if nothing had happened.

"Shouldn't I leave these rooms in case something goes wrong and Falon finds out where to look for me?" Shanelle suggested.

"Nonsense—but if you're that worried about it, you can use my own sanctuary. It's right through that door behind you. Just lock it from the other side. The door is specially made, you know. Not even a seven-foot barbarian could break it down."

The humor in Lanar's voice set Shanelle's teeth on edge. There wasn't a damn thing funny about this situation.

She thought it prudent to warn, "If he finds me, our deal will be off. No gaali stones."

Lanar nodded thoughtfully. "Naturally. But tell me, if he finds you—will he punish you for running away from him?"

Shanelle's lips turned down bitterly. "He'll consider it his duty."

"Well, then, what are you waiting for? Or haven't you realized yet that when Doni said it wasn't going to be easy to use the rods simultaneously, she meant it was next to impossible?"

Shanelle stood and headed for the closed door, missing the malicious spite that flared in Lanar's eyes as soon as she stepped into the room and the door closed behind her. She didn't turn to lock it, however. She was too startled at finding other people in the small room.

Two men sat cross-legged on the floor against the wall in front of her. Between them was a horizontal post supported some three feet off the floor, and another three feet away from the wall. About four feet up the wall were attached metal cuffs. To either side of these hung an assortment of whips, long coiled ones and multi-strapped ones. She knew now where the slaves had received their welts. And Lanar called this her sanctuary? Very funny.

Both men had stood up while she stared at the implements of punishment. Shanelle didn't even acknowledge them. She turned to leave—and found that the door hadn't needed locking. It had locked automatically.

"Another new one, and already you've been sent here?" one of the men said behind her. "You girls ought to know better than to get into trouble before you even settle in."

Shanelle glanced over her shoulder to see that they were approaching her. "I—I think you're mistaking me for someone else."

"Sure, that's what they all say."

She decided not to argue and tried the door again. It was definitely locked. And then a hand slid down her arm to her wrist and pulled it behind her. She turned, intending to wallop the jerk—both men were several inches shorter than she—only she was stopped when her other hand was grabbed and twisted behind her back by the other man.

"None of that now," she was warned when she tried to pull away from them. "You think we don't know how to deal with that?" And her arms were twisted up higher behind her back. The men were able to move her easily that way, despite her size. "We're only going to prepare you. The mistress will do the punishing herself."

"Lanar?"

"That's Mistress Lanar to you, girl. You're damn impertinent for a slave."

"Wait a minute! I told you you've made a mistake, and you have!"

"Sure, that's what they all say."

27

"Look, why don't you guys just sit down and relax?" one of the two women standing anxiously by the door told the warriors. "The general will be here any minute now."

The woman didn't get an answer. Well, she did, but not a verbal one. One of the warriors lifted his foot to the seat of a chair, brought his foot down on its center, and the chair flattened on the floor in a number of pieces.

"All right, so don't sit," the other woman said. "But could you stop prowling around? You're making us nervous."

"Then best you leave," another warrior said disagreeably.

"Better *we* leave," a third warrior said. "We only waste time here."

"No, now, don't be hasty," the woman told this

warrior. "Only the general can tell you what you want to know, but you'll miss her if you go."

He was through listening. He took a step toward them. The other woman didn't hesitate to lift a gun and point it at him.

"All right, hold it right there!" she ordered, feeling a moment of heady power.

But the warrior didn't stop, and she very quickly panicked. The gun fired. The long shield he held before one arm moved slightly and the bullet struck it, then dropped harmlessly to the floor. Both women stared at the bullet in horror. The one with the gun fired again. Again the bullet ended bent and useless on the floor.

"You won't be so lucky with this, buster," the second woman claimed. She was holding a short blue rod in her hand, pointed straight at the warrior. He stopped this time.

Her friend hissed at her, "What do you think you're doing with *that?*"

"It's working, isn't it?" she whispered triumphantly.

"Only because they probably think you're deranged," was the reply.

"Nonsense, they think it's a weapon." And then in a louder voice so the warriors could hear her, she said, "I'm sorry, guys, but we can't have you running around town frightening our people half to death with the mere sight of you. We were told to make sure you're here when the general arrives, so have a little patience, will you?"

"Dalden, what is that she threatens me with?"

"Your guess is as good as mine, Jadell. It is

my sister who knows of other worlds and their strange wonders, not I." But then Dalden pointed his computer-link unit at the woman holding the rod. "Brock?"

"Unknown as a weapon," the computer answered without needing a full question. "But according to the women's whispered words, which I could hear quite clearly, they are satisfied that you think it is a weapon. So probables says it is not, yet does it still give them courage."

The two women looked around and behind them for the invisible spy who could have heard them. To their relief, they found instead that the general was coming swiftly down the hallway at last, with four more women hurrying to keep up with her.

"I am General Vand, gentlemen," Donilla announced as she walked into the room. "If no one has done so, let me welcome you to Sunder."

The biggest among them moved to stand in front of her. He was nearly two feet taller than she was and twice as wide, with arms the size of her legs, in length as well as in thickness. She tried to swallow, but her throat had gone suddenly dry. Even knowing what to expect hadn't prepared her for the sheer size of these Sha-Ka'ani warriors.

"I am Dalden Ly-San-Ter," the one towering over her stated. "Do you tell us where my sister is, we will leave here peaceably with her. If not, then must we tear your town apart in search of her."

Nothing like coming right to the point. Donilla didn't feel particularly brave at this moment, but she had information they wanted which gave her a slight advantage—hopefully enough for what she was going to attempt.

She pulled herself together and said authoritatively, "Thank you for making that perfectly clear, Mr. Ly-San-Ter. But custom decrees that we must dispense with protocol first, before we can discuss your sister. You do understand customs, don't you? I'm sure you have some of your own that you insist visitors to your planet honor."

"Indeed, yet—"

"Come, now, I'm not talking about anything difficult or time-consuming. It's traditional for all visitors to meet my council of advisors. Merely introduce yourselves to them, shake their hands—possibly assure them you are here only on a family matter. You see, very simple. Ladies?" Donilla glanced around to find that the four women she had brought with her who had Altering rods hidden up their sleeves were nervously remaining outside the room. "Oh, do come in," she ordered impatiently. "They won't bite." And to Dalden, she said, "Which of your friends is the eager bridegroom?"

She followed his gaze to Falon, who merely stood there frowning at the lot of them. He *would* have to be the most intimidating of the group. He was a few inches shorter than Shanelle's brother, but what was a few inches when you were dealing with giants. Fortunately, the other women had come forward and were each extending a hand to greet a warrior. Donilla palmed her Altering rod, as the other women had been instructed to do, and walked toward Falon.

Falon had been relieved to be on solid ground

again until he found he would be dealing with people so alien to him in their size. It was difficult not to equate them with children, they were so small. Even their voices lacked the appropriate depth of an adult's. He certainly could not fight them. He could not even threaten them without feeling like a fool. And worse, the females of these tiny people had the authority here.

The little one called general was bold, he had to allow. When he had not accepted her offered hand for greeting, as his men were doing with the other women, she had reached forward and grasped his hand to mumble her words. He had not paid attention. He was watching the other women and the strangeness in their identical gestures and phrases.

"Falon, ah—I hesitate to ask this, but what are we doing here?" Jadell asked in Sha-Ka'ani.

Falon turned toward his brother with an incredulous look. The woman standing in front of Jadell was still holding his hand and smiling up at him. Falon began to scowl.

"What did she say to you, Jadell?" Falon demanded.

"Nothing."

"She spoke words. They all did. I heard them."

"Then you have better hearing than I, for I heard nothing," Jadell replied.

"And yet now you ask why we are here? Something is not right, brother."

"I agree. I feel I should know the answer, but I do not. Dalden?"

The younger man colored slightly. One of his

hands was also still being held by a Sunderian woman. "I had hoped I would not have to admit I am as forgetful as you, Jadell. Stars, it makes no sense. Falon, if *you* know—"

"So you would have me believe you have forgotten your own sister?" Falon asked. "And you, Jadell, that I am here to find my lifemate?"

"Droda, I was *told* to forget that!" Jadell exploded. "The voice was inside my head—" He yanked his hand from the woman's grasp and glared at her as she backed away from him. "What did you do to me?" he demanded in Sunderian.

Her mouth moved, but she was too terrified for words to come out. The other women were also backing toward the door, looking just as frightened. Only the general stood her ground next to Falon, more confused than fearful, even when his eyes came back to her narrowed in anger.

"It didn't work on you, did it?" Donilla asked. "It worked on them, but not on you. How is that possible?"

"He does not understand a word you are saying, General Vand," Dalden said, having moved to her other side. "You see, my friend here does not trust anything that is alien to Sha-Ka'an. It was bad enough that he had to travel on a Droda-cursed spaceship, as he put it, and be subjected to Transferring, which he hates above all things, but he flatly refused to listen to the Sublims on your language that Brock made for us, even though that refusal would leave Falon at a disadvantage down here. Does that answer your question?"

"Unfortunately, yes."

"Now do you tell us *what* did not work on him that *did* work on the rest of us."

"I'm sorry, but I'm not at liberty to explain. Only women are allowed the secret—"

"Brock?" Dalden interrupted impatiently.

"Some type of hypnotic device that each woman held concealed as she touched you, and which had you accept her words as reality. You were each told the same thing, to forget why you were here. But you, Falon, were told one other thing, that you do not want a lifemate."

Falon growled low and immediately lifted Donilla up by the front of her uniform jacket. That he did this with only one hand and kept her dangling like that, two feet off the floor, told Donilla that whatever they had just been told, it was now time for her to be seriously afraid.

"Speak for me, Dalden," Falon ordered in a tightly controlled tone, "and make her understand that she lives only because she is not a man."

"Brock has told us what you attempted to do, General Vand. Falon, of course, would be within his rights to kill you for trying to interfere with his duty, yet does your sex save you from that. But best you know that he is angry enough to overlook that if you still try to prevent him from finding his chosen mate. Where is she?"

"I—I can't tell you that," Donilla said apprehensively. "We have agreed to give her sanctuary, and she does not wish to be found by him."

"She has no choice in the matter," Dalden replied. "Our father gave her into this man's protection. That gives Falon all rights over her."

"But who protects her from him?"

"She does not need protection from her lifemate. He would never harm her."

"You waste your time, Dalden," Brock interjected at that point. "The woman is hindered by a code of honor that will not allow her to betray Shanelle, and now it is not needful. I have scanned the immediate area that would have allowed General Vand to reach here in the time she did, and have located a female who matches Shanelle's voice pattern, though she speaks in Sunderian—and in a manner that would indicate she is extremely fearful of an immediate threat."

"Immediate threat, or is she merely aware of our arrival?" Dalden questioned.

"Immediate. Her demand to be released by a 'sawed-off little jerk' was what led me to her. It is amazing how much she sounds like your mother sometimes."

"How much danger is she actually in, Brock?"

"Enough to send her emotions near the panic level. Do you Transfer now—or does Falon?"

"I do," Falon said without hesitation, and in the next moment Donilla dropped to the floor as he vanished.

A moment later above the planet, Martha invaded Brock's housing for a change. "It took you long enough, sludgebucket," she complained in annoyance. "I could have done that ten minutes ago."

"You followed them down when I Transferred them to Sunder's surface, didn't you?" Brock demanded indignantly.

"Of course I did."

"And you found Shanelle the same way I did?"

"Certainly—only sooner," Martha purred.

"Then why did you not Transfer her out of there yourself?" Brock asked.

"For the same reason you didn't. We aren't going to head home until those two get together. Besides, I owed the big guy one."

"Shanelle will not appreciate how you pay your debts," Brock predicted.

"Not today she won't, but I'm betting on the future."

28

It took Falon a bit longer than the actual Transfer to assure himself that he was in one piece in the new location. He would *never* get used to that Droda-cursed mode of traveling, and prayed he would not have to. Nor had he expected to have to experience it again, except once more to return to the ship. Yet he had welcomed the Transferring this time for its speed, for he would have gone mad if he could not reach Shanelle when she had need of his protection and he knew of that need. But now that he was there and faced with her predicament, he was not sure if he had someone to kill—or to thank.

Her wrists were cuffed to the wall in front of her. Her ankles were spread wide and strapped to the supports of a round post that she was bent over. Her clothing had been removed. It could not be more obvious that she had been prepared for a whipping.

Two men stood behind and slightly to the left of her, dispassionately observing their handiwork. That there were no marks on Shanelle's body was the only reason Falon moved up silently behind them and merely smashed their heads together. They dropped to the floor at his feet. That easily they were dismissed from his thoughts, and he stepped over them to stand directly behind the woman he had braved the horrors of space travel to find.

Shanelle didn't know he was there. She was listening for the door to open. The soft thumps on the floor as the Sunderians dropped had hardly penetrated her frantic thoughts.

Lanar had to be crazy. She didn't dare actually whip her. And yet she had gone this far—what if she was crazy? Who was there to stop her if so? Those two idiot males acted like low-budget androids, programmed to do one thing and one thing only. And they'd done it, stripped her and bound her securely, and nothing else. They hadn't touched her again. They hadn't even spoken to her after they finished strapping her in—except to tell her the waiting was part of it.

Part of what? The punishment? Torture was what it was, to stand there bent over, exposed, those farden whips on the wall the only things she could see—and remember the ugly red marks on the slave girls' legs, to know that women *did* get whipped in this very room, and were made to wait for it, and agonize during the waiting . . .

"You are in a position ideal for two things, woman. I wonder if the one will make me forget the other."

"Falon!" Shanelle gasped, every particle of her being stiffening at the sound of his deep voice. And then, when his words penetrated, "Falon, no!"

"You still think to tell me no? I think not."

His hands came to rest on her backside, proving that nothing she could say was going to stop him from doing what he was going to do. But what was he going to do? One of two things? Oh, Stars, she didn't have to ask what they were, and both terrified her. Punishment or joining, she wanted neither at his hands. And the whips were right there . . .

No, he wouldn't whip her. Warriors didn't hurt their women, and he considered her his—at least Kan-is-Tran warriors didn't hurt women. But Falon was a Ba-Har-ani, and she still knew next to nothing about those eastern warriors—except their punishments did differ from what Kan-is-Tran women could expect. Perhaps he considered her desertion worth a whipping. And what did it matter? Even a spanking would be horribly painful from a man of his tremendous strength.

"I hear no words from you, Shanelle. Are you sorry you left Sha-Ka'an?"

"I'm only sorry you found me."

Her eyes flared wide at the immediate stinging smack on her bottom. "That was the wrong answer, *kerima*. Do you care to try again?"

"Falon, let me go!"

"I will—when your responses please me."

"Do you want me to lie to you?" she cried.

"No, it is honesty I want, so let us find the responses of your body instead."

His words confused her, until she felt his hands

move around her hips to her stomach, and then slide slowly up her rib cage to her breasts. Shanelle sucked in her breath, trying to ignore the sensations aroused by his touch, but it was impossible. Despite her fear, which was very real, he could still bring her body to life. Her nipples hardened beneath his palms, her insides swirled in anticipation, her pulse quickened. How could this happen every time he touched her?

His body bent over hers suddenly, giving her the feel of his leather *bracs* against her bottom, the bare skin of his chest against her back. And then his arms wrapped around her middle and gently hugged her as his cheek pressed against her spine.

"I missed you, woman. Thoughts and imaginings of what I would do to you when I found you are all that have kept me from despair—and from going mad in the confines of that metal machine I was forced to travel in."

Shanelle dropped her head in near defeat at those words. But she couldn't let his feelings get to her— or her own. And he hadn't said the words yet that *would* defeat her and make him his lifemate. Until he did, there was still the chance that she could keep it from happening. And she still didn't want it to happen. He just wasn't right for her, no matter that he had become her father's choice for her, no matter her body's response to him. She knew it. Why couldn't she make him accept it?

"Falon—?"

"No," he cut her off curtly. "Your words rarely please me. Best we let your body speak for you now."

The post only reached the top of Shanelle's thighs, rather than her waist, as it was designed to do. Falon's fingers were able to slip between her legs from the front of her, so he did not have to lift himself away from close contact with her back. This he did now, finding and igniting her heat, drawing a groan from deep in her throat. She still fought it, pulling on the clamp in the wall she was cuffed to. But she'd tried that earlier, and even this new desperation didn't give her the added strength to break her bonds. She was at Falon's mercy—a warrior's mercy. They had none.

She dreaded it, expected it, and it happened. The fight swiftly drained out of her. The simulation of joining that his fingers were enacting was too pleasurable to ignore. She even forgot that pain was going to follow.

She didn't want to be taken at all, but particularly not like this, where she couldn't even move. But her body didn't give a damn what she wanted, any more than Falon did. And he knew it. Her tiny moans were telling him. Later she would feel humiliated about letting him know how much she really wanted him, but right now she just didn't care.

Shanelle was nearing the point of begging when Falon leaned into her further to reach the clamp her wrists were attached to, and with little effort yanked it out of the wall. She straightened as he did, but more slowly, and felt one of her ankles cut loose before she stood erect, the other freed a moment later.

As she slipped the cuffs off the broken clamp so she could at least separate her arms, she experienced a moment of gratitude that Falon wasn't as merciless as she had thought him. It wasn't the kind of release she was expecting, or needing at that point. The kind she did need now was still in control of her senses, and when she turned around and got her first look at Falon since he'd entered the room, it escalated.

The sight of him always did have the strangest effect on her. This time it joined with her need, and without the slightest hesitancy or encouragement from him, she practically leaped into his arms, wrapping hers around his neck and pulling his head down to press her lips to his. It was so compelling, this desire to taste, to touch, to give him anything he wanted. It so overwhelmed her that it was a while before she realized Falon wasn't returning her enthusiasm, let alone her kiss.

When she leaned back to look at him in confusion, he set her away from him. "Is this honesty at last, Shanelle, or an effort to avoid punishment?"

That was as good as a bucket of ice water dumped over her head. And she realized suddenly that that was exactly his intent.

"You had no intention of joining with me here, did you?" she demanded.

"When I take you, woman, there will be a bed— one that does not move—and privacy I can be assured of."

"Then why did you make me want you?" She fairly shouted the words in her frustration.

"You needed reminding of your true feelings,

those beneath your fear. And finally you have spoken the truth. You still want me."

"Not anymore I don't, you farden jerk!"

She turned away from him and nearly stumbled over the two unconscious Sunderians. It occurred to her then that Falon had actually rescued her, come to her aid when she desperately needed it—or thought she did. She still didn't know what Lanar had intended doing, not that it mattered now. But because of her, Shanelle was back where she started, stuck with a man impossible to handle or reason with, and who got his point across in ways she wasn't likely to ever forget. She would definitely like to repay that Sunderian witch for that.

Falon's latest "point" was still affecting her. If he would touch her now in an intimate manner, she'd probably melt all over him, and that absolutely infuriated her. How *dared* he do that to her, make her want him and then not do anything about it . . . ? Oh, Stars, that was one of the reasons she hadn't wanted a Kan-is-Tran warrior for her lifemate, the very thing Tedra suffered whenever Challen found it necessary to punish her! It hadn't been as bad, certainly. She hadn't been brought to the screaming point. But she had still just been treated to what she had thought Ba-Har-ani warriors didn't practice.

She swung around now to glare at Falon, and found him holding out her clothes to her. She snatched them from him, grateful that it was a Kystrani outfit, which went on as quickly as it could be removed.

But the suspicion that had occurred to her wouldn't go away, and the moment she was finished covering her nakedness, she demanded, "Were you punishing me, warrior?"

"When it is time for the punishing, you will not be in doubt that you have received it."

She stared at him, not sure what to think, but still too angry to be afraid or cautious. "And what makes you think I will accept your punishment, whatever it is? As far as I'm concerned, I haven't done anything to deserve it."

Falon lifted a dark brow. "Then you had your father's permission to leave Sha-Ka'an?"

"I had my mother's permission," she replied with a great deal of triumph.

"Which she likely has been made to regret the giving of by now."

Shanelle paled. Why hadn't it occurred to her that Tedra would end up catching the brunt of Challen's displeasure? Her mother must have known it, and still Tedra had let her take Martha, the very thing that would prove to Challen that Tedra had helped Shanelle leave.

"I think I'm beginning to hate you, Falon Van'yer," she said between gritted teeth.

She'd managed to get a frown out of him. "Best you know now that I will not tolerate this habit you have for stating untruths."

She frowned right back at him. "That wasn't an untruth. In fact, I no longer think it, I'm quite sure now I definitely am beginning to hate you. And best *you* know that any habits I have I'm keeping, with or without your approval, which I don't give a damn whether I have or not. Stick that in your boots and suck on it, why don't you?"

She held her ground as he approached her. Nor did she flinch when his hand lifted, though it was only to take her chin to raise it so she couldn't avoid his eyes. And those eyes weren't blazing with anger, but were merely thoughtful as they gazed down at her.

"It is interesting how you deal with frustration, Shanelle."

"I'm furious, not frustrated," she retorted hotly. "There is a difference."

"You are *upset*," he stressed, "because I did not see to your need."

"Don't flatter yourself," she snorted. "What you made me feel was next to nothing and forgotten already."

"Again you give me untruths. Shall I prove it?"

She tried to step back from him, but his grip tightened. She swallowed her pride and whispered, "No," then was amazed to hear him confess.

"I could not prove it, not without taking you right now, for my need exceeds yours, *kerima*. I want you so much I hurt with it. Yet to hear you admit that you wanted me is worth any pain. Nor could I have refrained from touching you to assure myself you are real—and mine. Do not begrudge me that, and the small discomfort it has caused you. Easier would it have been to stop breathing than to keep my hands from you."

Why did he have to say things like that? If she hadn't been frustrated, she was now, in having to stomp down the unwanted emotions his confession caused, and not succeeding completely. The pleasure she felt from his words just wouldn't go away.

And then it hit her, that what he was feeling, he was in control of, and obviously much better than she was. *He was controlling his passion!*

How dared he do that, get rid of one of her prime objections to him? How was she supposed to stand firm in her resolve when he did things like that? But everything else was still there, enough to convince her she still couldn't be completely happy with such a thoroughly domineering male. He was going to try and change her. He'd already said so. And she'd have pain and humiliation waiting for her every time she did the slightest thing wrong. No way was she going to meekly accept that. And he still hadn't proved that he wouldn't lose his control in a crucial moment, only that he was getting better at it.

That managed to squash the pleasure she'd been feeling, and back came the anger, that she'd let his words affect her at all. She knocked his hand aside and moved away from him before she insisted, "I'm not experiencing any discomfort, warrior, just disappointment that you've found me, which you can't do anything about unless you disappear the way you came—without me."

He made a sound that was very close to exasperation. "I *will* break you of this need you have for telling untruths, woman; this I promise you. Yet do we have other things between us that must be attended to first."

"A reprieve?" she shot back dryly. "How fortunate can I get?"

"Shanelle—" he began in an unmistakable warning tone.

But she cut him off before she got another promise she didn't like. "If one of those things is to get out of here, the door happens to be locked. So you'll have to ask that traitor who Transferred you here for assistance—which reminds me. If you're listening, Brock, and I know you must be, I hope Martha never speaks to you again. I know I certainly won't."

"You are angry with your father's computer?" Falon asked with some definite amusement lacing his tone now.

"I'm angry at every male under creation, but don't worry about it. I'll only take it out on you."

He suddenly laughed. "This I am pleased to know. It would prove tiring if I must fight every male you offend."

"And what happens when I offend you?"

"This you must find out firsthand."

It figures, you farden jerk, but she said that only to herself.

29

It didn't take long at all for Shanelle to realize that Falon had no intention of asking for Brock's assistance to get them out of there. His careful examination of the locked door proved it.

"Transferring would be quicker," Shanelle finally pointed out.

Falon didn't turn around to reply, "Transferring will wait until it is absolutely necessary."

And that told her that the big brave warrior had a definite aversion to Transferring, which she would have found amusing if she weren't still so angry. She moved to his side to complain, "We're stuck in here behind a locked door. You don't consider that necessary?"

His answer was to glance at her for only a second before he took one step back and kicked the door down. Shanelle mumbled under her breath, "Well,

I guess not," and a little louder, "So much for specially made doors that even seven-foot barbarians can't break."

The only satisfaction Shanelle got was in catching Lanar unawares. The Sunderian female had been sitting on her couch gloating to herself while she finished her drink. The crash of the door caused her to leap to her feet, and like her sister, she wasn't prepared for the sight of a live Sha-Ka'ani warrior, though she'd been forewarned of their size. She simply stared boggle-eyed at Falon, giving Shanelle the opportunity to approach her without being noticed.

Falon came closer himself, asking, "Are you the one responsible for the way I found my woman?"

Suddenly Lanar wasn't frightened anymore. She was grinning. "Did you appreciate it? She said you would want to punish her for running away from you. I decided to make it easy for you, figuring you would be along shortly. But I would have let you in," she added reproachfully. "You didn't have to break my door down."

"We do not bind our women for punishment, nor do we punish them in the way Shanelle was prepared for. What you did was to terrify the woman under my protection, and you would severely regret this were you a man."

Lanar experienced only a moment's fear before she realized he wasn't going to do anything to her. "It sounds like you're too lenient all the way around," she sneered. "The woman deserves much worse than you'll obviously be giving her. I should have seen to the matter myself before you got here. She needs that arrogance of hers whipped out of her."

Shanelle tapped Lanar on the shoulder at that point. Lanar turned toward her in annoyance, then paled, having apparently forgotten that Shanelle was not a Sunderian female of Sunderian size.

"Care to tell me about what I deserve?" Shanelle asked in a softly menacing tone. "No? What about this arrogance I've supposedly got—which by the way can't possibly be greater than yours?"

Still Lanar didn't answer. In fact she was looking kind of sick. Shanelle found that satisfying, but not nearly enough for what she'd gone through.

Casually, she remarked, "You know, Lanar, I think you've been worried about the wrong Sha-Ka'ani. That warrior there might not make you regret what you did to me, but I don't have any such qualms."

Lanar finally found her voice, though it was definitely shaky. "You—you wouldn't dare."

"Wanna bet?" Shanelle replied as she drew back her arm and let her fist fly.

The little woman collapsed back on the couch, out cold for a while. Shanelle hoped she'd broken her jaw, but she doubted she'd be that lucky. Only that still wasn't enough as far as she was concerned. She bent over and searched through Lanar's pockets for the Altering rod she was sure these power-hungry females would keep handy, and sure enough, she found it.

Behind her, Falon said, "Thank you."

Shanelle straightened with the short blue rod in her hand. "For what?"

"For doing what I could not."

"I didn't do it for you, babe, I did it for myself. Nor am I finished yet."

And she marched into the other room to squat down by the two Sunderian males, who were still unconscious. Sublims had proved eons ago that it wasn't necessary to be awake to hear something and have it implanted in your subconscious for future reference. Shanelle made use of that fact now.

When she finished and stood up, it was to find Falon blocking the doorway. "What did you do, woman?"

"Made sure the next time Lanar comes into this room she'll end up being treated exactly as I was today, and probably how her slaves get treated every day. It ought to be an eye-opening experience for her, though she may be too mean-spirited for the lesson to do any good."

She passed him to return the rod to Lanar's pocket so she wouldn't suspect that her slave-handlers had been tampered with. Falon was right behind her again when she straightened this time, and he wasn't looking too pleased now.

"You know the use of that device?" he asked her.

"It was explained to me, yes."

"Did you know the female called general would try to use it on me?"

"I knew she was going to try. Looks like you didn't give her the chance to."

"She used it, yet did I not have an understanding of her language for it to work. And it occurs to me now that in knowing what she intended, you had to agree to it." A growl entered his voice as he added, "You would have had me forget you."

Shanelle flinched and decided it would be judicious to assure him the opposite. "That wasn't my idea, Falon. It was the only way Donilla figured she could help me out. And it was only temporary. As soon as you returned to your ship, Brock would have reminded you of me and your reason for being here, and your very nature would have brought you back down here, whether you remembered me or not. For it to work permanently, I would have had to use it on you, and use so many countering suggestions that no one would be able to cancel them all. I could have met you when you arrived and got you so confused, it would have taken you years to figure out what I'd done. For that matter, I could have used the rod on you when I just passed you with it. You wouldn't have known, and I could have told you to walk out of here—without me— and you would have done just that. It works that simply. But I didn't do that, did I?"

"Why not?"

"You can get that scowl off your face, warrior. I don't like the idea of altering personalities on people who don't know it's happening, any more than you do, that's why not. That's not what I did to those two men, either. I didn't change them, I merely told them to forget that Lanar is their mistress. Apparently she's already got them altered into thinking that any female who walks in there is there to be punished. But they don't do the punishing, merely the preparing, so all Lanar will get is an uncomfortable wait until someone comes around to release her, and probably not even that, since all she has to do is pull out her rod and use it on them again—if she can figure out what suggestions I gave them *before* they bind her up. Farden hell, I didn't think of that."

He was suddenly grinning. "I cannot decide if I like this desire you have to avenge yourself."

"Too bad," she retorted, but then she looked at him curiously. "You know, Falon, if you agreed to it, I could rid you of the things I object to about you. Of course, I'd have to take one of those rods home with me, because someone is going to remind you of everything I'd have you forget, so I'd have to do it again and again. But it could work, I suppose, as long as you agreed to it. Would you like to be completely acceptable to me, warrior, so I won't mind going home with you?"

He was scowling again, and this time as intimidatingly as possible. "You will accept me as I am, woman."

She sighed and turned away from him. "I figured you'd say that."

He grabbed her and gave her one hard shake before he reiterated in a near shout, "You *will* accept me."

Her jaw thrust forward at a stubborn tilt. "Don't count on it."

His complexion darkened. She realized that she'd got him angry at last and he didn't care that she knew it. She closed her eyes, expecting the worse, but refusing to back down or even try to placate him. She would just as soon find out now what happened when a Ba-Har-ani lost his temper.

But into that tense silence a door could be heard opening, and then Shanelle heard a most welcome voice asking, "Are we interrupting?"

"No!" Shanelle gasped out in relief.

Her eyes flew open to locate her brother, but were arrested by Falon's expression instead. The warrior was looking very pleased now, and Shanelle's face flamed with color as she realized that he hadn't really lost his temper, he'd just wanted her to think so in order to intimidate her. Although she hadn't backed down and changed her tune to save herself from a clobbering, she'd still let him see that he could intimidate her.

Shanelle completely forgot that her brother and probably the rest of his party had just entered the room. Her mind centered on one thing and exploded in wounded pride. She didn't even think about what she was doing. She just hooked her foot behind Falon's knee, pulled him off-balance with it, and pushed with both fists into the center of his chest at the same time. It worked perfectly, or would have if Falon had let go of her arms. Instead he grunted as he fell backward, and Shanelle shrieked as she went down with him. And he *still* wasn't angry, if the sound of the beginning of chuckling could be believed.

Shanelle scrambled to her feet only so she could glare down at Falon. "The next time you get angry, you farden jerk, you damn well better *be* angry! I won't be tested like that. You want to know my reactions, well, you just got one!"

"Indeed," he agreed, and he was *definitely* chuckling. "I mind not your temper, *kerima*, as long as you remember that you *do* mind mine."

"Go to—!"

"Shani!"

Her face flamed again with color, mortified color this time. You didn't do what she'd just done to a warrior—at least not in front of other warriors. The warning in Dalden's voice reminded her of that, and she was cringing as she turned to face him, hoping only Dalden was there. But no such luck. Yet only Dalden was showing any warrior outrage. Falon's kin looked as amused as Falon still sounded. Donilla, who was with them, merely looked incredulous.

Shanelle decided it might be prudent to explain to her brother at least. "I was provoked—"

"That is no excuse—" Dalden started to interrupt.

"Leave her be," Falon cut in as well as he stood up behind Shanelle and drew her back against him possessively. "She is mine now to discipline, yet for this none is needful. I will learn not to be so easily felled by her trickery, and she will learn by example what will be tolerated and what will not. Thus do we teach each other."

"But she knows better than to be so disrespectful," Dalden said.

"Do *not* remind her of your Kan-is-Tran ways, my friend. Ba-Har-ani women are allowed more freedom to express themselves, and Shanelle will be a Ba-Har-ani."

Shanelle would have liked to retort that she wasn't yet, but she wasn't foolish enough to remind Falon that he'd forgotten about seeing to that. And her curiosity had been snagged anyway by that intriguing remark of his.

She turned her head to ask Falon, "How much freedom are we discussing here?"

"I believe you have exceeded your limit for this rising," he replied with a grin. "Go and greet your brother now as is proper, and apologize for shaming him with your behavior."

Shanelle's mouth dropped open. "You just said I was allowed—"

"*He* feels otherwise, as you well know."

She did know it, but it was galling to have Falon remind her of that, and worse to have his hand come to her bottom and gently shove her toward her brother. She spared a moment to turn and give him the most fulminating look she could manage. The farden jerk only laughed.

30

Dalden got no more than a whispered apology, though it was sincere, for Shanelle knew how real his displeasure was with her. He might be half Kystrani like her, but he was a Kan-is-Tran warrior right down to his bones, and as inflexible about certain things as they all were. And one of those things was that all women show proper respect for warriors, because a woman could get seriously hurt if she goaded her warrior into losing his temper with her. And any woman who ignored that golden rule was almost guaranteed punishment.

Where had that bit of knowledge flown to when she had goaded Falon, called him a jerk—pushed him over? Her own loss of temper was no excuse. Dalden was right, she did know better. And yet she wouldn't have learned what she did if it hadn't happened. Freedom to express herself any way she chose? What an unwarriorlike concept. What an amazing advantage if it was true. But when she questioned her brother about it, she got no assurances.

"Falon has asked that I refrain from telling you what I know," she was informed. "He wants you to bring your questions to him as is proper for a lifemate to do, thus enabling you to know each other better the sooner."

Needless to say, Shanelle wasn't pleased by that idea at all, and retorted, "He's not my lifemate yet, Dal."

"You know it is as good as done."

That was true as long as she was in the same room with Falon, where all he had to do was say the words, no matter if others were present with them. So that quickly became her number one priority, getting out of that warrior's sight and staying out of it. Unfortunately, that was easier hoped for than accomplished.

Shanelle had a few moments to speak privately with Donilla while Falon's kin teased him about the great odds he'd had to overcome to rescue her—they'd seen the two little males still lying unconscious in the other room. "I'm sorry about your sister, but I was too angry not to sock her one after what she did to me."

Donilla knew her sister well enough to have figured out what that was without having to be told. "I should be the one to apologize," she said. "Lanar really overstepped herself this time, and she'll be called to account for it, likely losing some of her authority."

"Well, don't do it on my account. But you might want to drop by here once a day for a while." At Donilla's questioning look, Shanelle added, "I had

a little Altering rod talk with Lanar's two slave-
handlers, just to even the score, you understand."

Donilla nodded. "Appropriate, I would say."

"I thought so."

"But what about you? After seeing for myself
what you were trying so desperately to avoid, I'm
really sorry we weren't able to help."

Shanelle shrugged. "So am I, but I was probably
doomed to fail the moment they managed to get
their hands on a ship that was faster than mine."

"I could cause a disturbance while you try and
slip away," Donilla offered.

"Thanks, but you can't slip away from a Mock
II that easily, and my father's Mock II is monitoring this room right now. Brock would simply use
Transferring to set one of these warriors down right
in front of whatever direction I take. That sort of
defeats the purpose in trying."

"You sound so hopeless. Isn't there anything else
you can do?"

"Not until I'm back on Sha-Ka'an and away from
computers that can screw up good escape plans.
Anyway, it's easier to disappear when you can
be inconspicuous. I couldn't have been that here."

"An understatement," Donilla replied ruefully.
"But I do wish you luck."

"Same here, since you've got your own problems
that you might want to think about resolving. You
never know, your men might have learned a thing
or two by now—at least that your planet didn't fall
apart under female governance."

Donilla returned Shanelle's grin. "That's true.
Ah, it looks like your brother just got disturbed

about something. He doesn't have exceptional hearing, does he?"

Shanelle glanced over her shoulder and grimaced, seeing Dalden scowling darkly at her. "No, what he's got is a computer-link unit. Farden hell. Brock probably just told him what we were talking about, that interfering eavesdropper. I'd better go."

Shanelle squeezed the general's hand in farewell, then marched to her brother's side and said before he could get his mouth open, "I don't want to hear about it."

"You *will* hear about it—but not here." Dalden grabbed her wrist and turned toward Falon to gain his attention. "I am taking her to the ship now for an overdue talking-to," he told Falon. "Do you follow when you are ready. Brock?"

Shanelle barely had time to notice that Falon didn't particularly care for that idea before she found herself in the Control Room of an unfamiliar ship, and Brock's deep voice was greeting her with "Welcome aboard, Shanelle."

She ignored the computer just like she'd told him she'd do and asked her brother, "What kind of ship is this?"

"Don't change the subject, Shani."

So he was ready for battle, was he? "We didn't start a subject to change, but if we had, I would tell you it's none of your business. According to the Ba-Har-ani, he's the only one who can reprimand me now."

"Then merely take heed of a concerned relative who wants to save your backside undue stress. Don't run from him again, Shani."

She turned to glare at him, but anger wasn't the way to deal with her brother. It either amused him or got his back up, neither of which was going to benefit her right now.

So she dropped her shoulders, hung her head, and managed to sound utterly miserable. "I'm afraid of him, Dal. Can't you challenge him for me, just to get him to drop his suit? You're bigger than he is."

"He is more experienced, or weren't you watching him during the competitions?"

He sounded amused. Farden hell. He *knew* she wasn't a whiner, or even close to true tearfulness.

"You could at least try," she grumbled.

"I wouldn't even consider it, Shani. I can't protect you anymore if he's around, and certainly not *from* him when there isn't the least sign of abuse on you."

Her head shot up, amber eyes flaring. "There was! I was black-and-blue when he finished with me!"

"If you had stuck around as you should have, you would have learned that his loss of control merely proved to him that you were meant for him. It's that loss of control that made him determined to have you."

"Of all the ridiculous things I've ever heard! I should have known you'd take his side. Damn warriors *always* stick together!"

"And you are too stubborn for your own good," he said with some heat of his own. "Were we home, I would place you in the kitchen myself to peel *falaa* for a month."

She turned her back on him to say bitterly, "Thanks a lot, brother."

He turned her around to shake his head at her and said reasonably, "You were wrong to leave, Shani, and well you know it."

"I was desperate."

"Without reason."

That did it, releasing every bit of resentment in her. "Fat lot you know about it! Stars, I hope the female you finally want for yourself *isn't* Sha-Ka'ani, and that she never gives you any peace!"

He drew in a sharp breath, his face flushing with angry color. "That is the most horrible thing you've ever said to me. Take it back, Shani."

"I'm damned if I will. You're dooming me to a life of misery. If you think I'll ever forgive you for that, brother, think again."

He started to retaliate further, but Falon beat him to it, his voice hard and uncompromising. "She will be punished for the pain she inflicts with her thoughtless words."

They both turned to see that Falon had been Transferred to their location alone, probably at Brock's discretion, possibly even at Brock's instigation for the express purpose of breaking up their fight. Dalden was embarrassed to have been found arguing with his sister, however, and that calmed him down. Shanelle was too angry to care.

"Why not?" she replied sarcastically to Falon's promise. "The more reasons the merrier."

"No," Dalden said quietly. "She's due some punishing, but not for that." And to his sister, "I'm sorry, Shani, but I'm going to trust in our father's judgment. He felt this warrior was the right mate for you, and I have faith that Falon will prove it so."

"Then do you give her to me in your father's stead?" Falon asked.

"Yes."

"Dalden!" Shanelle cried, realizing now that that was what Falon had been waiting for. Sure enough, Falon grabbed her hand and started to drag her out of the Control Room. "No, wait!"

He didn't. He pulled her down one softly glowing corridor, then another that was wider, into a lift that zoomed down two floors, out of it, through a large Rec Room, more corridors, another lift. For nearly fifteen minutes she was yanked along, her heart hammering, her fears mounting, getting her hand squeezed every time she tried to get it back. Finally Falon stopped, but it was to lean back against a wall and close his eyes. Through her own anxieties, Shanelle actually felt a moment's alarm for him.

It didn't come out sounding like concern, however. "What's wrong?" she demanded.

"Nothing."

Nothing? She looked around, but there were no immediate doors to enter. And he didn't look like nothing was wrong. He looked like he was in some kind of discomfort.

More softly, her concern apparent now, she said "Falon—?"

His eyes opened and his mouth twisted in self-disgust. "I am lost."

Shanelle blinked at him. "Lost as in 'don't know where you are'?"

He sighed. "Yes."

She stared at him blankly for a long moment before she said, "That's kind of anticlimactic, isn't it?"

That got her a scowl which prompted a smile from her, but a moment later she burst out laughing. She fell back against the wall herself, holding her middle, tears filling her eyes. When her amusement started to wind down, she made the mistake of glancing at Falon's face, which showed his continued disgruntlement, and another round of laughter ensued.

She was gasping for breath when she felt his hand slip behind her neck to draw her over to lean against him. She didn't try to resist. She didn't know what it was about the laughter she got at his expense that made her feel at peace with Falon, but it did.

"Your brother was right," he said by her ear. "You have not the proper respect for a warrior."

"I wouldn't say that. I have a great deal of respect for all of your abilities, Falon." But then she rested her chin on his chest to grin up at him. "Just don't draw me any maps I might need, okay?"

He smiled at her and Shanelle caught her breath, struck again by how incredibly gorgeous the man was. Danger signals went off in her head, but his hands were already on her waist, slowly sliding her up his long body. She tried to avoid his lips, she really did, and managed it for all of two seconds, but then she gave in to the inevitable. There just wasn't going to be any escape this time anyway, so she might as well enjoy as much of Falon as she could before he got carried away—and his kissing was *very* enjoyable.

"Again is the place wrong," he said with a groan against her lips.

"It's just not your day, is it?"

"It will be," he promised, and then asked, "Are you there, computer?"

"On this ship, naturally," Brock replied, and he didn't require clarification of what was needed. "Go back to the last lift, then up one floor and to the right. You should recognize the area by then."

Shanelle gasped as she was lifted into Falon's arms and he started moving at a swift pace. And now that he wasn't kissing her, her anxieties returned.

She fought them this time. At least she tried. But she finally wrapped her arms around Falon's neck and squeezed, whispering, "I'm still afraid."

His arms tightened around her. "I know. I wish I could take your fear from you before we join, *kerima*, yet do I know it will be gone after."

"Will you repeat your last offer and let me control the pace?"

"I cannot. I want you too much, woman. I *have* to touch you. But you are mine to protect now, even from myself. You will feel no pain when we join, this I swear to you." He stopped to look down at her, his expression tender. "Believe me, Shanelle. Trust me."

That was asking a lot, but she really had no choice. "All right."

His answering smile took her breath away.

31

His bed was large and old-fashioned—it didn't move. The cabin was also large for a ship, though small by Sha-Ka'ani standards. Shanelle didn't get any chance at all to inspect it. She was placed directly on the bed, and as Falon stood there removing his sword belt and then his *bracs*, she couldn't have looked away if she tried. She didn't try.

He was so beautifully made, this warrior, his chest immense, his arms really thick. She tried not to think of his strength as she watched him, though that was hard to do when it was so blatant. So she reminded herself of the gentleness he had shown her in their last encounters, and the control that had been present even today—and his promise that there would be no pain this time. She had to believe that. She was trusting Falon to prove it.

Her eyes moved over him, even where she should be too shy to look. Perhaps she should have avoided that, for she shuddered now at the sight of such raw masculinity, such savage need, and her eyes flew to his. But his gaze was only bright as he joined her on the bed, not fiercely turbulent. Still, she put a hand to his chest, needing reassurance.

"It's not there—is it? All that intense emotion that was there before?"

"Do not think of that, *kerima*; think of this."

He kissed her gently to relax her, then deeply to excite her. He had watched how she had put her clothes on earlier. He removed them now with the same ease, his pleasure at being able to do so quite obvious. Such a small thing, yet it was something he wanted to do himself, without her help.

She gasped when his palm covered her breast. Falon trembled at the sound. She was his at last, and he was so fiercely glad of that he wanted to roar with the joy it gave him. He could not. He could not show her any of what he was feeling, but Droda help him, it was not easy to conceal it, much less control it. And yet he was glad even of that, for if there had been any doubt that she was to be the keeper of his heart, it was put to rest by the immense effort it was taking him merely to allay her fears, and he had only just begun to touch her.

Her golden skin was incredibly soft and fascinating next to his darker bronze, her tawny beauty enough to mesmerize. He looked forward to a time when he could simply gaze upon her at his leisure, without the overwhelming need to taste and feel every inch of her. But that need was there and he allowed it control for a time, barely managing to keep from caressing too hard or startling her with his teeth.

The reward for his effort was her ardent response, hesitant at first, quickly bold, and finally wildly abandoned, until Falon was forced to restrain her hands or lose all control himself. She whimpered at the restraint. He kissed her to silence, almost savagely now. She arched into him, undulated against him, sending him over the edge of his own restraint. He could bear no more.

He opened her, entered her, joining their bodies for the ecstasy of life's creation, too quickly, perhaps, yet did her heat welcome him, giving him pleasure unimaginable. Thus to go no further than that was the hardest thing he had ever done in his life. Every muscle in his body strained with the effort not to move within her. She would not be still herself, making it that much harder.

Shanelle didn't hear her name called the first time, or even the next. She was in the center of such a maelstrom of pleasure and aching need, the ship could have crashed and she wouldn't have known it. It was the agonizing frustration of Falon's stillness that finally got through to her, that and the raggedness of his tone as he said her name once again.

She opened her eyes to find him straining above her, his muscles quivering, his eyes filled with such an intensity of emotion she caught her breath and began to tremble.

"Do not," he ordered softly as he put his cheek to hers to soothe her. "Have I hurt you?" Slowly she shook her head. "Nor will I."

"Then why—?"

"You know why." He leaned back to meet her eyes again, and Shanelle held her breath as he said the words she had been anticipating since he had found her. "By your father's word has your life been given to me to protect. Now do I give you my life in return, yours to keep until the day I die." He kissed her then, so tenderly it brought tears to her eyes. "You are mine now, Shanelle Van'yer," he said fiercely against her lips. "Can you deny it?"

The word was almost torn from her, it was so compelling. "No!"

"With my life comes my heart, yours now to crush or cherish as you will. It is my hope you will have a care in keeping both."

He gathered her close then, yet with exquisite care, to give her what she had foolishly dreaded. There was no pain, only the fullness of his strength delving into her depths, creating waves of sweetest bliss that crested and crested again, dissolving her in a welter of hot pulsations that wouldn't stop. Mindlessly she screamed and held on to Falon for dear life, and finally felt the surge and power of his own release that brought her to still another of her own.

It was a while before Shanelle felt capable of even opening her eyes. She had never felt so weak and drained, yet so deliciously replete. Her warrior had really outdone himself, kept his promises, proved what he had set out to. She wondered if she ought to tell him. No, better not. He was probably already pumped so full of satisfaction that any more and he might burst.

She smiled to herself at her whimsical thoughts, but she couldn't deny it. She'd found herself one hell of a fantastic lover, as long as he kept a rein on things—No, no more doubts.

She felt Falon stir at her side and suddenly she was being drawn across his chest. She opened her eyes to catch his smile as he settled her on him just as he wanted her. She didn't mind that. He was certainly wide enough to lie on comfortably. One hand coming to rest on her bottom was kind of nerve-racking, though. But the other hand merely took a lock of her hair to pull her forward for a brief kiss that was sweet, but without passion.

When she leaned up to rest her chin on her palms so she could gaze down at him, Falon was looking kind of smug, which warned her she was going to hear about some of that satisfaction he was stewing in.

Sure enough, he was practically purring when he said, "She who had need of my control proved to have none of her own."

Shanelle grinned. "Is that so?"

"You do not find that strange, woman?"

"Not particularly. Did *you* have need of my control?"

"Indeed would it have been helpful."

"Ah, poor baby. I guess you'll just have to grin and bear it—or else we could refrain—"

Swiftly were her lips brought down to his to silence that suggestion, and this kiss was the exact opposite of the last one. Shanelle was breathless when he finally released her so she could look down at him again. Teasing him was definitely detrimental to her senses.

It took her a few moments before she could manage to say, "I guess refraining is out, huh?"

"As it could not be your wish, it should not have been mentioned."

"Talk about overconfidence," she retorted, and couldn't resist one more goad. "Are you so sure, warrior?"

"Do you deny it?"

She sighed. "I'm not having much luck at denying things today." Being reminded of what else she hadn't been able to deny, she thought she'd better warn him. "But I hope you're not under the mistaken impression that just because you're my lifemate now, we're going to get along in perfect accord."

His answer began with a smile brilliant enough to curl her toes. "Have I not just proved otherwise?"

"All right," she said, and couldn't help grinning herself. "I'll allow there might be one exception— in bed. But out of bed—"

"You will obey me in all things. Thus will there be no difficulties to speak of."

"You don't really think it's going to be that easy, do you?" But she hastened to add, "I'm not saying I won't try to obey you. I've always been an obedient daughter—well, until recently. But there are other reasons why I didn't want a warrior, things that I seriously object to—"

His finger came to her lips to silence her. "All will be seen to."

"Is that another promise?"

"I promise to make you happy despite your objections."

A contradiction if she'd ever heard one. But she really wasn't in a mood to argue just now. She would much rather get to know this warrior she was stuck with, in particular the powerful body lying relaxed beneath her. Realizing that she now had certain rights to his body sent a thrill of possessiveness through her that she'd never quite experienced before.

She gave in to it, running her hands along his shoulders and down his arms, watching the muscles leap to her touch. She began kissing where she chose, across his chest, up his neck, savoring the saltiness of his skin where she licked instead.

He had remained perfectly still, so his sudden groan surprised her before he said, "Woman, it is too soon for you to play with me like that."

"Why?" she asked with laughter in her voice.

He rolled her over and entered her so swiftly, Shanelle barely had time to gasp. If that wasn't answer enough, he still growled, "Because I have not had my fill of you yet. I begin to wonder if I ever will."

She began to wonder if she ever would either, but it was a problem she could definitely live with. And then there were no more thoughts as her hands locked in his hair to ride out the buffeting her body now craved, and soon she was crying out again as that tide of unbelievable pleasure washed over her. She nearly fainted with it. She would have laughed if she weren't so exhausted, wondering if Martha would have been able to tell the difference this time. But one thing she knew for herself. Sex-sharing with this warrior could become addictive.

She barely felt him gather her to his side afterward, or the kiss he placed on her forehead. And she was almost asleep when she heard him sigh. But the words that followed were the kind that could wake up the dead—or one unsuspecting Sha-Ka'ani female.

"You have made me happier than I ever knew I could be, which is why I dread what I must now do, yet must it be done."

32

Shanelle lifted her head off Falon's shoulder to look down at him in disbelief. "You dread what *must* be done? Tell me that doesn't mean what I think it means, Falon." He didn't answer immediately, but his expression was answer enough, making her pale. "You wouldn't," she whispered. "Not after what we just . . . you just can't!"

His hand caressed her cheek gently, and for all of one second she thought she was wrong. "I like it no better that this will mar the beginning of our life together," he told her in genuine regret. "Yet did you know when you left your father's house without his permission that you would be punished for it. Can you deny this?"

She couldn't and the farden jerk knew it. And the horror she was feeling quickly turned to resentment.

"Then take me home and let my father punish me."

"He will not. He cannot, for that right is no longer his. Yet does your offense still demand proper consequence, which only I can administer. Your father expects no less of me, woman, nor does your brother. *You* expected no less."

That was true. She wondered bitterly why she was even fighting it. *This* was why she hadn't wanted a warrior. They were inflexible when it came to their duty, and punishment was considered a duty almost sacred. That didn't mean she could accept it, merely that she wasn't likely to get out of it. That realization terrified her as much as it infuriated her.

"Damn it, you couldn't even give me a little while to like you before I started hating you again, could you?" she said with resentment so thick it was nearly choking her.

"To delay would give you no peace, woman; merely would it increase your fear."

"I'm farden well *allowed* to fear what you have in mind!" she snapped. "I won't let you do it, Falon. I'll fight you."

"You are welcome to try."

Her eyes narrowed at the familiar words that told her not to bother. "I absolutely despise that phrase of yours."

He sighed. "Shanelle, let us be done with it, then may I comfort you."

"Like hell you will. If you punish me now, warrior, don't even think about getting near me again—ever!"

If she had hoped that might make a difference, she was forgetting whom she was dealing with.

Warriors didn't take kindly to threats, and Falon was no exception. All her warning accomplished was to finally annoy him.

"It is hoped we will not have to suffer this again, either of us," he said in a hard, uncompromising tone. "But for now . . ."

Where was her mind, to have remained sitting there next to him? Shanelle turned immediately to correct the oversight, but she knew she was too late. Falon's arm shot around her waist, and that easily was she dragged across his thighs. He didn't even bother to move to the edge of the bed. Right there in the center of it, where they had twice joined in pleasure, was he now going to inflict pain.

Shanelle shrieked furiously as she struggled to keep from being turned over, but she quickly found out just how adept Falon was at this sort of thing. She was turned, a forearm pressed down on her back to keep her there, and that was when anger deserted her to make way for a heaping dose of gut-wrenching fear.

She was crying before the first smack got anywhere near her bottom, and screamed her head off when it landed with the expected stinging force. In fact, she was making so much noise and commotion that it took a while for her to realize that Falon wasn't spanking her after all, that she'd got no more than that one sharp example of Ba-Har-ani discipline.

She was still crying. Her fright had been extreme. But she had been turned back over to sit on Falon's lap, and all he was doing was hugging her, albeit too tightly, and crooning soothing words to her as he might to an upset child.

Shanelle felt like a child just then. Where was the courage that had sent her racing across space into the unknown, that had sent Falon crashing to the floor without thought of consequence, that had faced sex-sharing again when she was sure it would be nothing but painful? If her mother had witnessed that disgraceful display of theatrics, she'd hang her head in shame. That was exactly what Shanelle felt like doing. On the other hand, she was so relieved that Falon had stopped, for whatever reason, that she started hugging him back to tell him so, though she kept her face buried against his chest.

It was still a while more before she was quiet enough to merit more direct attention. Her face was lifted. A finger gently wiped the wetness from her cheeks. And when she finally got up enough courage to open her eyes, it was to see an expression that was a pure mixture of chagrin and resignation.

Falon's voice, however, was nothing short of scolding. "You do not take punishment well, *kerima.*"

"Are you finished?"

He sighed. "Very likely."

"Then I'll do better the next time," she felt it safe to lie.

"*You* had best hope there is never a next time," he told her sternly.

Stars, didn't she know it. She tried to hide her face again, but he wouldn't let her. Unfortunately, the subject wasn't over yet.

"Your brother mentioned another way a warrior may punish his own woman. Perhaps I should discuss this further with him."

Shanelle stiffened and quickly volunteered, "My father always sent me to the kitchen to work."

"Is this how your mother is punished?"

"Well, no—Falon, please, I hate that way even more than your way."

"How would you know when you have yet to experience it? Dalden claims your women prefer—"

"Fat lot Dalden knows!" she snapped, then immediately paled for having done so.

Falon noticed and this time he pressed her face back to his chest to assure her, "I will never punish you for what you say to me, woman, nor for how you say it, nor for the reason you say it. Do I punish you again, it will be because you have disobeyed me in a way that endangers yourself, which I will not stand for. Is this clear to you?"

"You're saying it's okay if I get angry at you?"

"Yes."

"And it's okay if I, ah—unthinkingly attack you sometimes?"

He lifted her chin again so she could see his smile. "That would depend on what you attack me with, *kerima*. I would not care to have my head cracked open some new rising because I did not see to you properly the previous rising."

"Somehow I don't think you'll ever be that forgetful." She grinned back at him. "How about if I just attack you with myself?"

"You are welcome to try."

For once that phrase made her laugh instead of feel frustration, and she released it in delight. "So this is the freedom to express myself you mentioned."

And then she realized that he was taking away another of her objections to him, for she couldn't imagine deliberately endangering herself. And if that was the only thing that would get her punished, she'd never have to fear it again. As for disobeying him in other ways . . .

"I think there are a few things about your country that I might like after all, Falon," she said.

"This I am pleased to know. Now do you tell me what we are to say to your brother when he asks were you properly punished?"

"That's none of his business," she said.

"In this case it is, for your offense was against his house."

Now she squirmed uneasily, realizing that he was going against inbred principles not to punish her for an offense they *all* knew she was guilty of. The men of her own family wouldn't have let her get away with it, yet Falon had been unable to finish what he started.

"Perhaps you could allow me one more untruth to assure him—"

"No," Falon cut her off with an admonishing shake of his head.

"So maybe he won't ask."

He sighed now. "In either case, Dalden must be told the truth."

"Ah—what exactly is the truth?"

He leaned back to glance sharply at her. "Do you tease me, woman?"

"No," she said. "I know you stopped, Falon. I just don't know why."

He lay back on the bed, drawing her with him, then arranging her so they faced each other. A finger came to one of her eyes and caught a single remaining drop of moisture, which he rubbed against her lips until she thought to kiss his finger. He removed it then to thread his hand through her hair. Obviously, this conversation was not to end in joining—at least not yet.

He finally said, "The sound of your tears was too painful to bear. I could wish it were otherwise, or that you could have displayed a small measure of forbearance, yet did you not."

She blushed at that point, for his tone was definitely chiding, his expression chagrined, but more on the disappointment side. And she knew it wasn't because he had wanted to hurt her. He hadn't. His feeling was that *he* had failed her in not administering what she was due for her own good, but he had failed because of her own shameful behavior. Warriors never enjoyed punishing their women. It was a duty they saw as a further means of protecting their women from harm. Shanelle knew all this, which was why she was so amazed that her backside wasn't on fire right now. But that her tears had affected him so strongly . . . did that mean he felt more than lust for her?

He *was* different from the average warrior, just like her father was, and maybe that included the ability to love. Just maybe there was hope for them after all, despite whatever problems remained.

She dropped her eyes to his chest to say, "Falon, I'm sorry I'm such a baby when it comes to anything that hurts. I know you needed to—well, felt you had to, but I was just too afraid of being punished by you in particular."

"Woman, you are *supposed* to fear punishment. How else will it keep you from doing what you should not?"

"I know that, and believe me, I don't want to go through that experience again, even as brief as it was. So please don't feel you've failed in your duty. I wouldn't be lying to Dalden if I told him I've learned my lesson."

Falon snorted. "All you have learned is that your pain gives me pain. What you have yet to realize is that your offense was not against me directly this time when you endangered yourself, nor were you truly mine yet while you did so. Does the time come that it happens again, there can be no reprieve for you, despite my own feelings on the matter. No tears, screams, or pleading will keep me from my duty then. Take this warning to heart, Shanelle, for I will be extremely displeased do you force me to make us both suffer by your actions."

She shivered, and instinct compelled her to press her body to his in an age-old manner of amends-making. "Could we maybe talk about something else now, Falon?"

His arm curled around her to press her even closer. "As I recall, you have more than one meaning for the word 'talk.' "

Shanelle finally felt like grinning. "I do, don't I?"

33

"How's it going, doll?"

"Martha!" Shanelle gasped as she stepped out of the solaray bath in Falon's cabin. And then in an accusatory tone she asked, "Where have you been? We'll be home in a few hours."

A rude sound came out of the intercom on the wall. "Where do you think I've been? It took Corth and me all this time to work on getting a little temporary boost for our thrusters so we could catch up. You know that farden ship you're in is faster than the Rover."

"You shouldn't have had to catch up. Are you telling me you didn't notice when we left?"

" 'Course I did. But how was I to know you weren't still down on Sunder? After all, the last I'd heard, those women were planning on altering our warriors into leaving without you. I had to make sure, didn't I? And it took me a while to locate your general friend so I could."

It didn't occur to Shanelle that Martha would have had an easy time locating the only female on a ship, especially with so few other occupants on it. But she had other things on her mind that morning, so all she said was, "Does Brock know you're visiting?"

"I'm not that sneaky. But I've got a deal with him. He doesn't listen in on our chat, and I don't bar him from my housing for at least six months."

Shanelle's brows shot up. "When did you figure out how to do that?"

"With you not around to keep me entertained, I had nothing better to do this week. Besides, aren't I always looking for ways to annoy my metal friend? And this was a beaut if I do say so myself."

Shanelle grinned. "I'll bet he just loved that."

"About as much as a warrior loves females in *bracs*. Speaking of which, what have you been doing for clothes? Or has the big guy kept you naked all week?"

"Real cute, Martha. I was fortunate enough to be wearing an outfit compatible with the solaray bath, so it at least gets cleaned every time I do. But I could definitely use a change, if you're close enough to send me something."

"Why don't you come over here to make your own choice instead?"

"No, thanks. That could be construed as an attempt to run away again, and I've been warned what will happen if I try it. I'd rather go naked."

Martha added a dose of sympathy to her tone. "Was it that bad?"

"It didn't happen."

"Yet?"

"At all. Falon started to, but I made such a Stars-awful fuss about it, he couldn't go through with it."

"Well, I'll be damned," Martha said in genuine surprise. "The big guy actually pulled one that wasn't on my probables list."

"Well, don't go looking for shorted circuits, Martha. The first time I step out of line I'll get what I didn't this time, and then some."

"That's only to be expected, kiddo, so why do you still sound so resentful?"

"That's not the immediate problem. In fact, I've actually been getting along with Falon much better than I could have hoped."

"Do tell," Martha purred.

Shanelle couldn't help grinning. "Go ahead, Martha, rub it into the ground. I know you're dying to, and for once I don't mind hearing an I-told-you-so."

"He's that good, is he?"

Shanelle blushed. "I wasn't talking about *that*— but now that you mention it, yes, he's that good."

"So he got it under control?"

"So far."

"I'm impressed," Martha admitted. "I didn't think he could do it this soon. But if you weren't talking about having fun, what *were* you talking about?"

"That I've discovered the differences between the Ba-Har-ani and our warriors are even greater than we first thought. Do you know, I can be as disrespectful to Falon as I like and he won't even raise a brow, even if someone else is present? It's such a pleasure being able to say anything that comes to mind without having to worry about it. And, Martha, he doesn't hide anything behind a warrior's calm, because he just doesn't have that infuriating calm. I never have to guess what he's feeling. It's usually right there on his face, if he's angry, if he's happy—"

"If he's ready to share sex?"

"That, too. And he's so careful with his strength now, his tenderness sometimes makes me want to cry. He also really does get jealous, and of the silliest things. His own brother even has to watch what he says to me, or else Falon starts glowering at him. And possessive—Stars, I can't be out of his sight for more than a few minutes before he comes looking for me."

"That ought to calm down as soon as he's more sure of you," Martha assured her.

"You're missing the point." Shanelle grinned. "I don't happen to mind any of that. He's so different from Kan-is-Tran warriors, it's almost like he isn't one, which is how I wanted it. Then again, he can be *exactly* like one . . . Am I making sense?"

" 'Course you are. But don't let that little reprieve you got go to your head, doll. That *is* a dyed-in-the-wool warrior you've got calling you his, and you're heading for a big letdown if you don't keep that in mind."

"The close call I had isn't going to let me forget it, Martha, nor is Falon himself going to let me—

not for long. But I'd be lying if I said he hadn't proved some things this week. You said it would happen. *He* said he could do it. The man knows how to make me happy, so happy I've been hard put to keep a silly grin off my face this entire week."

"Stars, that's disgusting," Martha grumbled. "What is it with you humans that makes you lose what little sense you've got when you wind up in love? It's bad enough when you get your socks knocked off, but this love business gets ridiculous when it has you thinking those warriors can do no wrong."

"You can turn off that disagree-no-matter-what program, old girl. I happen to know you're probably blowing a circuit to keep from gloating." Martha let loose a few chuckles at that, so Shanelle added, "But I said that he knows how to *make* me happy, not that he knows how to keep me that way. And who says I've fallen in love?"

"You did. All those silly grins you mentioned and being *soooo* happy. And I knew all it would take for you to give up and let it happen was to be caught. So what did he say when you told him?"

"I didn't."

"Didn't tell him, or didn't figure it out for yourself until just now?"

"Don't play dense, Martha. My feelings haven't changed on this matter. I'm not about to volunteer that kind of information to Falon until he comes up with a similar declaration of his own."

"You could wait forever for that to happen and you know it."

"I'm not so sure about that anymore."

"So you finally figured out that all that emotion needs more than one outlet?"

"Something like that."

Martha chuckled. "So where is the big guy? I thought you weren't allowed out of his sight for long."

"Consider today an exception. Falon got tired of looking at my long face and left in a fit of temper."

"Uh-oh, are we getting to the resentment I detected earlier?"

"More like frustration in capital letters, and being reminded in a big way of a few things that warrior has managed to make me forget this week—his insufferable high-handedness, for one. Obviously I've been deluding myself that everything would work out between us, just because he's put a few of my fears to rest. One lousy week and he shoots my hopes down. I'm *never* going to get along peaceably with that man. I should have known better."

"I hesitate to ask what brought this on."

"Well you might, because you won't believe what that warrior dropped on me this morning. Here I was getting excited about going home and seeing mother, so I could tell her she doesn't have to worry about me anymore, and Falon calmly informs me we won't be stopping in Sha-Ka-Ra at all. He's already asked Brock to approach the planet from the eastern hemisphere so we can Transfer straight down to Ka'al. And Brock is apparently under orders from my father to assist Falon in whatever way he requests, so he couldn't refuse."

" 'Course he wouldn't," Martha said in disgust. "That brick-brain considers himself a warrior now, and a warrior wouldn't disobey his *shodan*."

"Well, *my* warrior is proving to be about as stubborn as you can get. I argued until I was blue in the face, but he wouldn't change his mind. He'd rather use Transferring, when I know very well he hates it, than land at Spaceport and take an airobus that could have him home in twenty minutes."

"Did he say why?"

"Sure he did. He doesn't want me seeing my mother at all. He blames her more than me for the trouble he was put to. But if you ask me, something happened between them that he's not telling me about, because he gets annoyed if I even mention her name."

"Now that's interesting. Hold on, while I ask Brock if he knows anything." The intercom was silent for several minutes, but Martha's chuckling announced her return. "My Tedra still manages to surprise me occasionally. She actually challenged your warrior in an attempt to keep him from setting off right after you."

"Falon fought my *mother*?" Shanelle said with a mixture of incredulity and horror.

Martha kept on chuckling. "Relax, kiddo. She tried, but he refused. She even kicked him into your father's bath, but he still refused. So your father stepped in and accepted the challenge for him, and you know the name of that tune."

Shanelle closed her eyes with a groan. "So she's been under a challenge loss all this time and it's my fault."

"Whose fault?" Martha snorted. "Don't kid yourself. Your mother never does anything without her eyes wide open and knowing exactly what the consequences will be. She knew damn well Falon wouldn't fight her. She also knew Challen wouldn't allow it. What she was doing was stressing a point for your young man, on the importance of giving you some time to conquer your fears. I'd say it worked, since you got out of having to face one of your fears, didn't you? And another one proved groundless."

"Still, if Falon weren't so farden pigheaded, she wouldn't have felt it was necessary—"

"Take my advice, Shani, and don't even think about bringing him to task for something your mother instigated. It's obviously a sore subject with him, so much so that he doesn't want to get anywhere near your mother, and that's why you're going straight to Ka'al instead of home. Consider it the punishment you didn't get and let it go at that. And I'll do all the reassuring that's necessary, so don't bother worrying about your mother fretting over you. When I get done reporting, she'll be so pleased, she'll probably even forgive your fath—"

"What goes on here, Shanelle?" Falon demanded as the door slid open and he caught the sound of Martha's voice.

Shanelle merely stared at him, for his expression made her feel somehow guilty, though she'd done nothing wrong. Martha wasn't so quiet.

"Relax, big guy. I'm aware she's yours now. I merely dropped by for a visit."

"Do you then leave as you came, computer."

"What are you so stiff-necked about, warrior?" Martha grumbled. "You won, didn't you? When she was mine to protect, I did as I saw fit. Now she's yours to protect, I'll practice hands-off. You can't get fairer than that."

"What I can do is forbid my woman all dealings with anything visitor-made; thus will she be punished do you not leave as you were bidden."

"Of all the underhanded, rotten, tyrannical—"

"Martha!" Shanelle wailed in a panic.

"All right, I'm going." Martha managed a near growl, and suddenly all of Shanelle's belongings appeared at her feet. "You'll have to sift through that stuff now to find whatever's *visitor-made* so you can leave it behind—Stars, I don't believe he said that," she continued to complain, but then said, "Good luck, doll. I guess you're still going to need it after all."

Shanelle stood there staring at her lifemate as though she didn't recognize him, while he watched the intercom on the wall and waited. After a minute had passed and no more words came out of it, he started looking so smugly satisfied that Shanelle's emotions took a giant leap for the angry side.

"Punish me for something I have no control over, would you? How about for this instead?" She bent down, picked up her jewel case, and hurled it at his head. "Or maybe this?"

She didn't even wait to see if the first missile struck before she bent down for another. She never reached it. She was tackled off her feet, turned in the air, and landed when Falon did, with him on the floor and her on top of him and barely jarred—at least not until the laughter started. She tried getting off him, but the arm he'd caught her with was still tight about her waist. She then tried straightening up, but the hand she placed on his shoulder to do so slipped right off, he was shaking so hard.

In exasperation, she dug her elbows into his chest and demanded, "Just *what* do you find amusing, warrior? If you think—"

"Wait!" he cut in, but was still laughing too hard to say any more.

Shanelle gritted her teeth and waited impatiently. Finally he was merely smiling up at her.

"There was no reason for that splendid display of temper, *kerima*."

Her eyes narrowed. "You think not?"

"I would never punish you for something that is not of your own doing. This you should have known. What was said was said only for your Martha's benefit."

It took her a moment to digest that, and then her eyes flared wide. "You told an untruth?"

"A small one to defeat a thing I cannot otherwise fight."

"Martha was right," she said. "That *was* underhanded of you."

"She would not leave—"

"Of course she would have. She was only here to assure herself that I was all right." And then she sighed. "Martha isn't your enemy, Falon. You'd be in real trouble if she were. Actually, she happens to like you—at least she did. Now she's probably mad enough to tell my mother what you just—damn it, Falon, I want to see my mother!"

"No." He set her aside abruptly, stood up, yanked her to her feet, but then he was tenderly cupping her cheeks in his hands. "All of my patience is given to you, Shanelle. There is none left for your mother. Do not ask me to go near that woman, or I may say something we will both regret."

"Falon, you met her when she was worried about me. She won't be like that now."

"I care not," he replied adamantly. "In time I will allow you to visit her. For now, you have other obligations to claim your attention, a new life to adjust to. Do you need help, you will come to *me*, not to your mother. Is that not as it should be?"

"No," she maintained stubbornly.

He lifted a black brow. "You *still* mean to pout?"

"Whatever it takes, warrior, to get you to be reasonable."

"I am being reasonable," he insisted, pointing out, "I could have said never, yet did I consider your feelings in the matter."

"The hell you did," she growled. "You mean to deny me my mother *and* my friends. Or hasn't it occurred to you that both Martha and Corth are visitor-made?"

"That is the *first* thing that occurred to me."

"You farden—!"

"Enough, woman! It will be as I say, and you will accept what I say."

Don't bet on it, babe, she said, but not aloud.

34

Because of the Global Shield surrounding the planet, it was impossible to land a ship anywhere other than at Spaceport. Transferring was unaffected by the Shield, however, and with Jadell's help in the Control Room, Brock was able to pinpoint the exact location of Falon's house to Transfer their party directly inside it.

Shanelle had only a few minutes to say good-bye to her brother, who would be returning with Brock to Sha-Ka-Ra. But Dalden surprised her by telling her he would see her again in only a few weeks, when he brought the Catrateri Ambassador and his party to Ka'al to complete negotiations with Falon. Apparently it was the Catrateri who had volunteered their ship for Falon's use, but there had been no time to bargain for any more than Falon's agreement to allow them to finish negotia-

tions on Falon's home ground. That Falon would
have agreed to that was astounding. But Dalden
confessed he would have agreed to anything at the
time, he was so impatient to follow her.

This managed to make Shanelle feel a certain
amount of guilt, despite her present anger at Falon.
She knew how he felt about visitors, how all Ba-
Har-ani felt, for that matter. It was the Ba-Har-ani
who had insisted the planet be closed down, and
no visitor had set foot in their country for these
past fifteen years. Now, indirectly because of her,
Falon was letting some in, but she knew he couldn't
like it. For Falon's sake she could wish the bargain
hadn't been made, yet because of it Dalden would
be returning, and she couldn't deny she was glad
of that.

She had, of course, made up with her brother
during the past week for the altercation they'd had
when he first brought her up to the ship. He hadn't
been able to stay mad at her any more than she
could with him. Now she wished she didn't have
to part with him at all, but knowing he'd be back
soon made it a lot easier to say good-bye.

Falon was there to hold her hand for the Transferring and was still holding it when the five of them
and all their possessions from the ship appeared in
a large, two-story-high eating hall that was presently vacant, for the hour was very early morning,
Ka'al time. Long tables abounded, most with padded benches rather than backless couches, but some
with actual chairs. Huge, painted *zaalskin* canvases
covered a good deal of the walls, all lavishly framed
in gold. But there were too many walls, not enough

windows, and no open archways letting in cool breezes.

The first thing Shanelle really noticed was the stuffiness, the closed-in heat. It was oppressive enough to make her remark to Falon, "Perhaps you saw some things in Sha-Ka-Ra that you'd like to incorporate here."

"And perhaps I did not. This is a two-story house, Shanelle, not a palace. The meeting hall makes it larger than most houses, still is it just a house."

"I wasn't complaining."

"Were you not?"

"If I was, I would have mentioned the lack of openness and breezes," she said tightly. "But I'm sure I'll get used to it."

"I am equally sure, yet for a while will you be less than comfortable, for my country is much hotter than yours. Because of this, you may continue to wear your own clothes for a time, for the clothes of our women might be too warm for you just now."

"Why do I get the feeling we're not talking about a *chauri*, Falon?"

"Because we are not."

"Then what—"

Shanelle didn't bother to finish, because a woman came through a door at the end of the hall just then, and she figured she had got her answer. The female wore a narrow white skirt that began just below her hips and extended down to the floor. But that was all she wore. Nothing covered the entire top half of her body, except a little brown hair that hung a mere few inches over her shoulders.

The woman had seen them. Large breasts bobbed as she performed a half bow toward the *shodan* and offered him a formal greeting. He did no more than order her to fetch someone to collect their belongings and distribute them to the appropriate rooms.

Shanelle said nothing until the woman hurried along the front of the hall, her breasts bobbing again, and disappeared out of a different door. She then turned to her lifemate, the amber of her eyes heated to a brightness that could scorch. "Warmer clothes, huh? If you think I'm going to go around dressed like *that,* warrior, think again."

Three of the four men burst out laughing. Falon was not one of them. But Jadell stepped to her side to enlighten her. "She is a slave, Shanelle."

She stared at him in horror at this reminder of another thing she had to face, now that she had a Bar-Har-ani for a lifemate. "I should have known," she said in disgust. "Stars, you don't even dress them decently."

He was not the least bit perturbed by her reaction. He even grinned at her as he explained. "Her clothing proclaims her a slave. Free women are completely covered by their clothing. I, for one, will miss seeing you in your wispy *chauri* when you start wearing—"

"*You,* brother, have been too long without the comforts of your own females," Falon cut in, startling Shanelle with the anger in his tone. "Best you take yourself off to your rooms to correct that, so that your excessive admiring of my lifemate will end here and now."

Jadell chuckled. "You jest, Falon. If you think that will keep me or any other man from sighing over your woman, then you overlook what a beauty she is."

"Jadell, I am warning you—"

Jadell threw up his hands in surrender, though he was still amused, and still in a mood to goad. "I am going, but you cannot change what is, brother. She is too lovely to ignore, and your scowls will make no difference in that. Best you get used to—"

It was the step Falon took toward him that ended Jadell's warning and sent him off in a hurry. Tarren and Deamon followed him, both grinning, which did nothing to get that mentioned scowl off Falon's face.

Shanelle lowered her eyes to the floor before Falon saw her reaction to his jealousy. She couldn't help it, being pleased *and* amused, so much so that her anger disappeared for the moment. But it was so telling, his jealousy, so indicative of very strong feelings, and anything that confirmed her hope that this man could love her, perhaps already did love her, was welcome as far as she was concerned.

But Falon noticed her amusement and said sternly, "It is no matter to laugh over, woman."

"Of course it is. He was only teasing you, Falon. He wasn't serious."

He stared blankly at her for a moment before replying. "Indeed was he serious. Why do you think he was not?"

"Because I'm no different than any other Kanis-Tran woman, golden from head to foot. I blend in—"

His hoot of laughter cut her off. "Did you blend in, I would not have immediately noticed you and wanted you with a passion unequaled to anything felt before. And here, woman, you will *not* blend in. Can you truly not know how desirable men find you?"

She was blushing profusely before he had finished. "All right, if I accept that, then I have to know—your own brother wouldn't try anything, would he?"

"No."

"Then why do you get so mad at him?"

"Because I do not like any man looking at you in that way, even him." And then he sighed. "Yet as he says, it is something I must become used to. And best I do so quickly, before I am compelled to issue challenge."

"Now, you don't want to do that." She grinned and took the step that brought her close enough to wrap her arms around him. "I hope you don't think I'm encouraging any of that stuff that annoys you."

"You are the keeper of my heart, *kerima,* thus do I have complete faith in you."

She squeezed him a bit harder for that sweet remark. "Then I ought to tell you I don't mind your jealousy one little bit. Kan-is-Tran warriors don't experience it, you know, so it's kind of unique for me and something I plan to enjoy until you get it under control. Am I shameful to admit that?"

"To wish me to suffer the frustration of those emotions? Indeed should you be ashamed."

She hugged him still harder. "So why don't you sound angry?"

"I cannot be displeased by something you find enjoyment in. Have I not promised to make you happy?"

The teasing mood left Shanelle abruptly. "You did and you do—to a degree, *and* when I'm not furious with you for your warriorlike inflexibility. But there's something I have to hear before even the happiness you do give me can be complete."

He leaned back so he could see her expression. His face was utterly serious now. "Tell me."

She slowly shook her head. "It wouldn't be the same if I told you, Falon. This is something you'll have to figure out for yourself."

35

There were four rooms in Falon's house that were for his exclusive use. The one for sleeping contained a warrior-sized bed that made Shanelle smile. Even her adjustibed wouldn't expand *that* big. There was a large bathroom with a dressing area and closets, and a room that was completely empty that Falon had yet to find a use for.

The largest room was for informal meetings. It was bigger than Shanelle's entire chambers at home, and filled with nearly a dozen long couches and chairs, well padded and covered in buttery-soft *zaalskin* in both black and brown. Solid-gold tables of different sizes were scattered all around, as well as gold chests set with precious stones. Even the gaali-stone stands were made of gold, as well as the boxes that contained the stones. Thick white fur, pieced together so perfectly that no seams could be detected, covered the entire floor. It made Shanelle hot just looking at it.

His house might not be the size of a palace, but it was definitely bigger than Falon had let on. The ceilings were all high. And there were two or three large windows in each room, even in the bathroom, that let in a good deal of light and at least a little breeze.

Shanelle ran her fingers along one of the tables and remarked, "No wonder the Catrateri are so eager to make a deal with you. The gold in this room alone could probably put their economy back on a sound footing."

She turned, but Falon hadn't heard her. He had gone back into the dressing room and came out of it now, carrying a short piece of white cloth. He shook it open when he reached her, then almost reverently set it across her shoulders. The short white cape fell no lower than her waist, and fastened with three gold chains that draped at different lengths across her chest and hooked over a large round brooch at her right shoulder that was set with sparkling gems of diamond clarity.

As Falon fastened it for her, his expression gave testimony to the words he spoke. "You cannot know how much I have wanted to see you cloaked in my protection, Shanelle. From the first moment I saw you, I wanted you adorned in *my* colors."

"White." She smiled, remembering. "I just happen to have a white *chauri* I might wear for you sometime."

"As I recall, it drove me wild the last time you

wore it—and you said you would never wear white again."

"So maybe I've changed my—"

"Falon!" a female voice interrupted excitedly. "I was told you just returned—"

The voice stopped with an audible gasp, and Shanelle turned to see another long-skirted, bare-chested female staring right at her. This one was exceptionally lovely, with large, dark brown eyes and hair, the hair again cut to the shoulder, probably so it *couldn't* conceal those magnificently rounded breasts on display, the dark nipples stark against the palest ivory skin Shanelle had ever seen.

Falon slipped an arm around Shanelle's waist to turn her more fully toward the woman, whose eyes had now dropped meekly to the floor. He was smiling, which brought a stiffness to Shanelle's back she wasn't even aware of.

"I am sorry, master," the woman continued in a much subdued tone. "I was not aware you had a guest."

"Shanelle is not a guest, Janya, she is my lifemate." Janya's eyes popped upward in surprise at that, but quickly lowered again before Falon added, "There is no need for you to bow your head to her or me, nor to anyone else, for this rising are you gifted with your freedom."

Those dark brown eyes popped upward again, even rounder than before, and stayed staring at Falon with a great deal of confusion. "My freedom? I do not understand."

Shanelle was utterly amazed herself. She hadn't expected this, at least not so soon. That Falon would

break with custom just for her . . . He did love her—
he had to.

But at the moment he wasn't concerned with her
reaction or her gratitude. He was addressing Janya's
confusion.

"You are free to leave this house, Janya, with
all rights returned to you. If it is your wish, I will
provide you with an escort to return you to the far
north countries from which you were captured and
sold into slavery."

"I may leave . . . ? No!"

The woman was suddenly hurtling across the
room to drop to her knees at Falon's feet, where
she wrapped both arms tightly around his right
leg. Shanelle stiffened, her feelings of delight and
gratitude making way for a darker one that was
nothing short of savage. She knew *exactly* what
this demonstration meant, even before she heard
the woman's pleadings.

"Do not send me away, Falon!" Janya cried. "I
do not want freedom from your ownership!"

Falon let go of Shanelle to gently remove Janya
from his leg, but he would have had to hurt her
to pry her loose, she was gripping him so tightly.
"Janya—"

"Please, master, what have I done that you would
do this to me?"

"You have done nothing," he assured her. "The
decision is mine that I will no longer own slaves,
any slaves. So do I now give you your freedom,
rather than sell you to another."

The woman started crying in earnest then.
Shanelle turned in disgust to leave.

Falon was fast losing patience, so his voice was sharp when he commanded, "Shanelle, stay."

"Forget it," she defied him. "I'm not watching another minute of this."

She slammed the door of the bedroom behind her, but she could still hear Janya wailing. She gritted her teeth and looked daggers at the bed that that woman had obviously spent many a night in. It was bad enough that Falon had owned slaves, but that he had used some of them to share sex with . . . Not once had she considered that. But she should have. Why wouldn't he take that kind of advantage when ownership gave it to him? The poor females certainly had no choice in the matter, and if they were pretty . . . But he was freeing Janya— for her—giving up that little beauty—for her.

She couldn't handle two such powerful emotions conflicting and fighting for attention. The darker one took supremacy again, and she let out an explosive sound of outrage just as the door opened and Falon stepped slowly into the room.

"You disobeyed me, woman," he informed her, in case she wasn't aware of it.

She was and didn't care. "You're damned right I did! How dare you subject me to that? You should have known you'd be facing a weeping scene and taken steps to make sure I wouldn't have to witness it."

"It was necessary that you see it done, for what was done was done for you, Shanelle."

"I *know* that! I'm not dense. And I am immensely grateful!" she shouted, sounding anything but. "But I also know she wasn't denying the freedom you were offering, she was denying the loss of *you,* and I farden well don't like that, Falon. How many more sex-slaves have you got around here that are going to beg you not to free them?"

He started to grin, but then he laughed instead. Shanelle looked for something to throw at him, but there wasn't a single thing in that room besides the bed and two tables on either side of it, both of which were empty. She reached down for her slipper.

"Do not," he warned, but he was still chuckling. "You will let me enjoy this while it lasts, for it is not likely to happen again."

"It's not funny, dammit!"

"I disagree. And is it fair that I find the same enjoyment you claim for yourself."

He wasn't asking her, he was telling her, but that just got her madder, because she knew what he was referring to. "It's not the same and you know it. *You* get upset over nothing. But try and deny that female who just cried all over you doesn't have an intimate knowledge of your body—a body, by the way, that happens to belong to *me* now. Go ahead and deny it!"

He raised a brow at her. "Do I understand you, woman? Your complaint is for what was done *before* I met you?"

Shanelle flushed with angry color. She'd be a first-class jerk to say yes to that, yet half of what she was feeling was exactly for that—but fortunately, not all of it.

"She just hugged the hell out of your leg, warrior! *That* was here and now, wasn't it?"

He grimaced. "Now do you have a valid complaint. Shall I cut off my leg?"

"Don't be ridiculous."

"Shall I cut off her arms?"

"Falon!"

"How, then, am I to make amends for the doing of another?" he asked.

It was Shanelle's turn to grimace. "All right," she mumbled, "so it wasn't exactly *your* fault, but I still don't like it. When is she leaving?"

"She has asked to remain in this house as a servant, now that I will have need of them."

Shanelle's temper shot right back up. "Oh, no, she won't."

"The decision is not yours to make, woman. Yet do I agree it would not be wise to keep her here, so I will ask my cousin Tarren to accept her in his house."

"Will he?"

"Indeed will he. He has tried to buy her from me many times."

Shanelle was quiet for a moment before she asked hesitantly, "Was she the only one, Falon?"

He gave a mock-suffering sigh. "I see I must ask Tarren to take a few others as well."

Shanelle grinned sheepishly. "I guess I can be a farden jerk sometimes myself. I'm sorry."

"I am not. I do not mind your jealousy."

She laughed now, to have her own words from earlier in the hall given back to her. That was when he caught her about the waist and tossed her onto the mammoth bed. Slowly he came down on it to partially cover her body with his.

Before he did anything else, however, he looked down at his own body, then caught her eye. "Yours, is it?"

Shanelle's smile was utterly radiant. "*All* mine, and best you not forget it, warrior."

36

"Corth could make you a generator so you wouldn't have to depend on the wind to work those ceiling fans," Shanelle remarked from the bed as she watched the slow-moving fan above her barely disturb the air. "For that matter, these rooms, your whole house actually, could be air-cooled."

She rolled over to see if Falon was even listening to her. He was, and he was finished dressing, too. She'd just as soon stay naked herself. It was still early morning, but the room seemed to be getting hotter by the minute.

"You know how I feel about visitor-made things, Shanelle."

"You might be dead right now if it weren't for one of those visitor-made things. And there are other things that are just as useful. Think of it, Falon. A room *filled* with cool air."

He shook his head at her. "You will become accustomed to—"

"That's *if* I survive."

He didn't say another word, he just picked her up and carried her into the bathroom, where the large gold tub in the shape of a chopped-off barrel had been filled with water. Shanelle had the feeling he was going to drop her into it, so she decided to annoy him by not complaining about it. He did drop her. She shrieked her head off as the cold water closed over her.

"That was a dirty trick," she hissed at him. "You could have at least warned me it wasn't going to be warm."

He raised a brow, fighting to keep the grin off his lips. "Does the air not feel cooler now?"

"Go to blazes, why don't you!"

"I give you what you want and still you complain. Is there no pleasing you this rising?"

"Real cute. Keep it up and I might start a running tab on getting even."

He finally chuckled as he turned away toward the closets. "Best you hurry, woman. The first meal will soon be served, and you have yet to meet my sister."

Shanelle splashed water that didn't feel quite so cold now over her breasts as she watched Falon shrug into a black vest similar to the white one he'd been wearing. "Jadell said she's older than both of you."

"By nearly five years."

"Does she have any children?"

He looked up sharply at that question. "Perhaps

there is a thing you should know about Aurelet before you meet her. The battle the Ba-Har-ani were prepared to bring to the visitors all those years ago was because of my sister. She had been taken by a visitor from the planet Nida who had a small spaceship for his own use. Aurelet and her escort were Transferred, she to the man's ship, her escort never to be seen again. He kept her for nearly two months on his ship, using and abusing her the whole while."

"You didn't search for her during that time?"

"My brother and I were too young to be allowed to help. My father searched. She had been taken near Tinet, a town the warriors of Ka'al sometimes would raid. My father nearly tore Tinet apart, yet no sign of her was found. We began to think her dead. Already my father mourned."

"Then you didn't even suspect it was a visitor who had taken her?"

"No. And when she was returned to us, it took weeks before she was calm enough to speak of what had happened. My father immediately gathered his warriors, and the call went out before them for a united battle. Warriors of other towns joined them on the way, for we were not the only ones visitors had offended, though our grievance was the worst."

"I know this tale from our side. Though I never knew what the crime was, I know the guilty visitor was turned over to the Ba-Har-ani warriors, and the planet closed down soon after."

"He was given to my father."

"Did he kill him?"

"No. He brought him back to Ka'al and gave him to Aurelet for judgment. *She* killed him without a qualm. One month later she gave birth to his child, a boy child she has never called son. She became fifteen that same month."

"Stars, that young to go through that? I'm so sorry, Falon. No wonder you hate visitors so much."

"Not as much as my sister does. This is why I could not bring you home other than as a slave when I thought you a visitor. Yet might Aurelet still see you as a visitor when she learns who you are. Your brother has already been scorned by her. If this is all she offers you at first, it is my hope you will understand the depth of her bitterness and not be offended by her. Can you do this?"

"Certainly." But then she recalled that the Catrateri were coming here, true visitors, and it was *her* fault that they were. "Falon, I know you agreed to let my brother bring the Catrateri here, and that will probably upset your sister even more. Has it occurred to you that you don't actually have to let them into Ka'al, that you could speak with them and do all the negotiating necessary through Martha—well, maybe not Martha, but you could use Brock?"

"No, such had not occurred to me, yet does this idea please me. I will ride to the telecomm later this rising to call the Visitor's Center to arrange it."

"Ah, if I know Martha, and I do, she probably stuck a computer-link unit somewhere in my belongings. With it you could talk directly with Dalden and let him arrange it."

"I would prefer to ride to the telecomm than to

request anything of your Martha. And do you find that unit, you will bring it to me. I do not want you speaking with that computer again."

She frowned at that reminder. "This *has* to be negotiable. For a time?"

"Forever."

Her frown turned black. "Don't do that to me, Falon. I can maybe see the necessity of cutting ties while I am adjusting to this new life, but not forever. We're talking about a lifelong friend of mine, two actually, since Corth is also visitor-made. And I just solved a problem for you and gave up a visit with my brother to do it. In my book that says you owe me one."

"A warrior could wish you were not so demanding of rights he is not even aware of. So be it. For a time, but a *long* time."

He said no more on the subject, but Shanelle had been given even more hope for their future happiness. Her inflexible warrior wasn't so inflexible after all. He just needed to be pushed on the road to reasonableness in less direct ways, to avoid his inherent "dominate-all" tendencies. That shouldn't be too hard to do—if she could survive the initial frustration.

37

The welcomings-home began the moment Falon and Shanelle walked into the hall. The emptiness of a few hours ago was now transformed to an overflow. Every table was laden with food, though every seat might not be occupied. But at least fifty warriors were making a very great deal of boisterous noise—still another difference from a reserved Kan-is-Tran warrior, who rarely raised his voice, even in private.

Shanelle was to learn that the gathering of such a crowd was a daily occurrence. But Ka'al was large enough to require a permanent body of guards, kind of like an army, yet without the regimen and discipline of an official army, or a mini-government, for these warriors saw to all aspects of authority in one way or another.

This was Shanelle's first experience of the Ba-Har-ani as a group, and the first thing she noticed was that there wasn't another golden-haired head in sight. There were some warriors with dark red hair, some with dark brown, but most with black. And all were as deeply bronzed as Falon, giving testimony to the hotter sun in this half of the hemisphere. In stark contrast, the freed slaves moving about the room were easily spotted with their ivory-white skin, if their scanty garb wasn't enough to set them apart.

Someone should have told them they could now cover themselves. But perhaps the word hadn't got around to all of them yet that they weren't slaves anymore—or perhaps none of the women here wore tops, slave or not. What free women did wear hadn't exactly been explained to Shanelle, and those bare breasts bobbing around the room weren't exactly drawing any notice, since these warriors were so accustomed to the sight.

She was looking forward to meeting Falon's sister, if only to see what the woman would be wearing. That was the only reason she was anticipating the meeting, however, now that she knew it wasn't likely to be a pleasant one. But if Aurelet decided not to like her, Shanelle would just have to live with it. There was no way she could blame the poor woman for hating all visitors, and even half visitors, after what she had experienced at their hands.

Shanelle wished she could have kept that sentiment. For a day, for a few hours even. At least for more than ten minutes. But Aurelet Kee-dar was a surprise Shanelle *wasn't* expecting, and not one she needed on her first day in Ka'al.

The woman entered the hall with her lifemate, Deamon, the two holding hands, smiling after the pleasant reunion they had just shared. And Aurelet was still smiling when she spotted Falon and hurried over to greet him with sisterly devotion.

"Deamon has told me you took a lifemate, Falon, but that teasing *sa'abo* would say nothing about her other than she is lovely. Indeed is she lovely," Aurelet said as she turned her smile on Shanelle in full welcome.

Shanelle wasn't expecting that, but then all sense of normalcy went right out the window at her first sight of Falon's sister. She had his coloring, her black hair long and flowing down her back, her blue eyes as light as his. She was a few inches shorter than Shanelle, but that was barely noticeable, she bore herself so straight and proud. Then there were the surprises.

The woman wore *bracs*, white *zaalskin bracs* that had to be made expressly for her, for they molded to her legs as if they had been poured on. Green boots matched the short green cape that denoted Deamon's colors, and a gauzy white shirt was tucked into the *bracs*, with loosely flowing sleeves, a wide collar, and a deeply plunging neckline. But if the pants weren't enough to shock Shanelle, the sword belt strapped to Aurelet's hips certainly was, especially since there was a three-foot-long sword hanging from it.

Bracs were for the exclusive use of warriors, denied to Kan-is-Tran women. So was the use of any weapons. Aurelet wore both, and not a single warrior there told her to remove them. She was *allowed* their use. Obviously Ba-Har-ani women were allowed more freedom than Shanelle could have thought possible. She wasn't displeased at this difference, she was absolutely delighted.

But she had no time to savor the prospect of that freedom for herself, for Falon was quick to drop his bomb. "Aurelet, I would have you meet Shanelle of the house of Ly-San-Ter."

The woman immediately stiffened. "Do you tell me that is a common name in that country, Falon."

"It is not."

"Then she is related to Dalden Ly-San-Ter?"

"His sister."

Aurelet actually paled. "No," she began in a whisper that quickly rose in volume. "Tell me you did not join with the daughter of that bitch who brought the visitors here. Tell me you did not, Falon!"

"Now just a—" Shanelle began, but both siblings ignored her.

"It is done, Aurelet," Falon told her. "Not to be undone merely because you object. She is my lifemate and is to be treated—"

Aurelet cut in furiously. "It was bad enough when that other came here, but he left. This one you would keep here? I will not have it!"

Falon was beginning to show signs of some definite impatience, if not actual anger. "You have no say in this matter."

"Do I not? Does she stay in this house, I will challenge her!"

"By Droda, you . . . will . . . not!" he thundered. "You dare to dictate to me, sister, to give *me* an ultimatum? My lifemate stays no other place than with me!"

"Then she is challenged here and now!" Aurelet shouted just as loudly.

The silence that followed was awful. Every eye and ear in the room was fixed on this encounter, and why not? It wasn't every day you saw a warrior, and a *shodan* at that, so angry he was crimson with it. Nor did you see a woman stand there and defy a warrior who was that mad. At least Shanelle had never seen it.

She was deathly pale herself. She hated confrontations of this sort. She'd been having one too many recently herself, and she couldn't understand why that was, now that she thought of it, but this . . . these Ba-Har-ani *were* too emotional, and with so little control of those emotions. And she was seeing her lifemate truly furious for the first time, which she didn't like at all. She would just as soon not have known Falon could get this angry.

She was wrong, however, in thinking he didn't have any control over his anger. He had enough to be able to say, with less volume, though with no less menace, "I forbid it."

Aurelet also lowered her tone considerably, but not to back down. In fact, she was looking pretty triumphant. "You cannot, brother. It is done, challenge issued."

"I forbid my woman to accept, so is it ended."

Aurelet's blue eyes widened. "You would let her shame our house?"

"There is no shame when she is given no choice in this matter by her lifemate, and will she obey me as is proper. You, however, shame this house by wishing to fight a member of your own family."

"Never will I accept a half-breed visitor as a member of this family! Sooner would I—"

"Deamon, take your woman from my sight before I claim the right to punish her myself."

Aurelet did not go quietly, not by any means. Deamon was forced to carry her out of the hall, and her curses followed loudly in their wake.

Shanelle was relieved that it was over, but she was still shaken by such animosity. She'd never had anyone hate her before, except perhaps Lanar. But who could tell what had motivated that strange Sunderian? With Aurelet there was no doubt. She definitely hated.

With the previous noise level returned to the hall, Shanelle felt it safe to finally say something, but she couldn't imagine what prompted her to say to Falon, "You have these little family squabbles all the time?"

"I am sorry. I am pleased you can jest about it, but truly am I sorry."

She was then engulfed by yet another difference in the Ba-Har-ani. These warriors felt no qualms about hugging in public.

"Maybe you should have just let me accept her challenge and get it over with," Shanelle said. "It wouldn't have taken very long, and then she might at least back off from all that name-calling."

The squeeze that suggestion got her forced a gasp out of her. The fierceness in his voice almost brought on another gasp.

"Do not speak foolishness, woman. My sister

excels at female swordsmanship. There are none here in Ka'al who can best her."

"Stars, why didn't you say so? What was her intent, then, just to humiliate me?"

Falon leaned back to frown at her. "Does killing not occur to you?"

"Oh, come on, she's a woman," she scoffed. "And most challenges aren't fought to the death when a challenge loss is much more satisfying."

"For a warrior, perhaps, yet has Aurelet killed before," he replied. "She has too much hate in her for her not to try to kill you."

"Well, then, I suppose I should thank you for forbidding me to accept."

"Indeed," he said wryly.

"Just how many warriors has she beaten, anyway?"

"None."

"But you said she was the best in Ka'al," Shanelle reminded him.

"The best at female swordsmanship. Our women do not challenge warriors they cannot hope to beat."

"Then why do you allow them the use of swords at all?" she asked.

"Occasionally are we raided by the Mal-Niki from the north."

"Let me guess," she said dryly. "The Mal-Niki aren't too handy with swords."

"This is so."

"All right, so a woman can protect herself pretty well in that case," she allowed. "But now tell me why you call it female swordsmanship."

"Because it is a different style of fighting. It

allows women some small chance of withstanding a warrior's greater strength and skill."

"But not much chance against Ba-Har-ani warriors, I take it?"

"No."

"Then maybe you should know I fight like a—"

"Woman, I will hear no more about accepting challenge. Do you wish to fight, you may fight me. Only then can I be assured you will not get hurt."

"Oh, cute, *real* cute. I'll accept that offer when I'm a hundred and four, and not a day sooner, thank you. Now, is it your intention to starve me, or can we stop being the center of attention here and get something to eat?"

38

It was several days before Shanelle noticed the
boy, but when she did, her curiosity was aroused.
He was tall, nearly six feet, yet from the look
of his face, very young. Still, any male that size
should be in training to be a warrior and wearing
a sword already. This one did not, nor did he wear
bracs, merely cloth pants and a loose shirt. Shanelle
would have thought him one of the freed slaves—
many had elected to stay as servants, and they were
finally decently clothed—except his bronzed skin
tone was that of a Ba-Har-ani.

She saw him only at meals, and that was what
had aroused her curiosity, that he didn't eat at one
of the tables like everyone else, but off in a corner
by himself. Obviously, he was being punished for
something. But if he was supposed to be humiliated
by the experience, he didn't seem to be, nor was
anyone else paying the least bit of attention to him.

She finally asked Falon, "Who is he?"

"My nephew, Drevan."

Shanelle rolled her eyes. "I should have known. So what's he being punished for?"

"He is not."

She waited, but when he didn't volunteer any more that than, just kept on eating, she said, "All right, I give up. Why is he eating over there instead of at a table?"

"He tries to keep out of his mother's notice."

"Why?"

"She hates him."

He said that so calmly, as if it were a perfectly normal thing, a mother hating her child.

That mother hadn't stayed out of sight for more than a day. She had apologized to Falon, likely at Deamon's insistence. Shanelle she simply ignored— except when Falon couldn't hear her. Then she got in a lot of sharp digs, alluding to Shanelle's cowardice, casting aspersions on her heritage, in general trying her damnedest to get a rise out of her.

So far, Aurelet hadn't succeeded. Shanelle would grit her teeth and repeat the silent litany, *The woman deserves your pity, not your antipathy*, but, Stars, it was getting harder and harder to believe that.

She stood up now with a determined light in her eyes, and finally got Falon's full attention.

"Where do you go?" he asked.

"You said Drevan wasn't being punished, so there shouldn't be any reason why I can't go meet him and see if I can't talk him into joining us."

"This you may do, does Aurelet not object. But does she forbid it, then you will leave the matter be."

"Is that another difference here? Do women get to have complete say over their children, even children as old as Drevan?"

"No, it is not," he replied impatiently. "But the boy has no father."

"So as his uncle, you should have the say—or haven't you taken an interest in his upbringing?"

"I was a child myself when he was born. When I would have taken him in hand, Aurelet forbade it. She does not want him raised a warrior because he is not of warrior blood. This I can understand."

"Can you, or maybe you just don't care? Do you also hate him, Falon?"

He scowled at her. "I have little feeling at all for the boy. Rarely do I see him."

"He's pretty good at being invisible, isn't he? Maybe because he *knows* no one cares."

"Shanelle—" he began in warning.

"No," she cut him off. "Why don't you admit you might have been wrong to neglect the boy? Just look at him, Falon—eating in a corner on the floor, for Stars' sake! That's pathetic and something I simply can't ignore. Your sister is a bitter woman, and certainly with reason, but enough is enough. She had her revenge. She killed the man who made her suffer. You can't get much more even than that. But who has punished her for the suffering she has caused all these years to that innocent boy—and to herself by not letting go of the past? I *will* befriend Drevan—if *he'll* let me. If Aurelet tries to prevent it, I think it's time you stepped in to do something about it, or do I have to accept her challenge just to get her to back off?"

"*That* you will not do," he said emphatically, but then sighed. "Very well, do what you can with the boy. I will see to my sister."

She leaned over to put her arms around his neck. "Thank you, but I also think you should start—"

"Woman, you have won one concession from me. Best you bide your time before you demand another."

"I didn't demand—"

"Did you not?"

He didn't sound at all pleased with her. "I think that's my cue to shut up." She grinned at him. "I'll be right back, *babe*."

Falon watched her go, wondering why he found it so hard to deny her what she wanted. In this case, perhaps she was right. He *had* ignored Drevan, but in truth, he had no right to interfere when Aurelet had a lifemate who should have taken the boy in hand. He would have to speak with Deamon to find out why he had not, but likely he knew the answer. Falon would be the first to admit his sister was a viper to live with when she was crossed. That was their father's doing, spoiling her atrociously in an effort to make up for what had happened to her. But ten years of having her way in everything had led her to believe it would always be so.

Shanelle stood over Drevan, waiting for him to glance up at her. When he did, it was with a wariness that shouldn't have been there, and with a face that so resembled Falon's, her heart just went out to him.

She smiled reassuringly. "You look like you could use a friend, Drevan. I know I can. Why don't you come sit at the table with me, and I'll tell you about a computer who thinks she knows everything."

"What is a computer?"

"I see we've got a *lot* to talk about, don't we?"

39

Shanelle wasn't adjusting any better to the warmer climate, but after a week had passed since her arrival in Ka'al, she really couldn't wait any longer to get into her first pair of *bracs*, with the accompanying long-sleeved shirt. A half dozen of these outfits in different colors had been delivered one morning to her rooms. The *bracs* had all been too large, so she had sent them back. But when new ones arrived this morning, she simply couldn't resist wearing them, whether she would feel even hotter or not.

She chose brown in the *zaalskin*, to go with a gold metallic shirt. It wasn't necessary to wear her short cape in the house, so she dug out a long strand of kystrals that she had picked up in Kystran while she was there, and asked the live crystals to change their color to a soft amber with gold sparkles deep within. They complied instantly and she hung the necklace about her neck, so that it draped over her breasts.

She had no boots yet, but they would probably have been too hot to wear, so she was just as glad to put on a pair of her own gold sandals. Searching for them in the belongings Martha had Transferred from the ship, she found instead her sword, which Corth had always worn for her, along with the computer-link unit she had figured would be there. The sword she hadn't expected, though, and she stared at it a while before deciding she'd better not get that bold yet, and tucked it away where Falon wouldn't find it.

Her lifemate was off doing what he did every day, making sure his town ran smoothly. He had begun the talks with Ambassador Zlink, doing it the hard way by riding out to the telecomm that had long ago been installed outside Ka'al. Each day he'd be gone for a few hours for those discussions, and several things had already been agreed to. The Catrateri could have the gold. Falon wasn't even asking anywhere near what he could have got for it. What was being figured out now was how the Catrateri could get the gold out without setting foot inside Ba-Har-an. Shanelle had little doubt they would work it out.

She was finding a great many things to do to keep herself occupied each day. Unlike her father's house, which always had at least a dozen widows and orphans living there under Challen's protection, with her great-uncle Lowden in charge of them, Falon's household had contained only one free woman before Shanelle came. In Ka'al, there was a house just for widows and orphans, ultimately under Falon's protection, yet where the females could live without having men underfoot.

This meant that when the older slave who had had charge of the others had elected to return to her own country, there had been no one to take her place. So Shanelle took on the overseeing of the servants, while she trained another woman to eventually step into the task. She also took it upon herself to teach these newly freed people what rights were now theirs, learning in the process what rights were hers as well. Of course, she had to have quite a few talks with Falon to make sure she wasn't missing anything, but that was a pleasure, not a chore, because her lifemate was becoming easier to get along with every day.

And then there was Drevan, such a serious child for fourteen. But then he hadn't had a normal childhood, had missed such simple things as fun and games, and other children to romp with. The slaves had had the care of him, and he probably knew more things about other countries than most people on the planet did, Shanelle included. But his education was otherwise deplorably lacking, warrior skills not even begun. And yet he was such a bright boy, and so inquisitive, Shanelle spent most of her time with him just answering questions. She had also got through to some of his feelings.

About his mother, as far as Shanelle could tell, he felt nothing at all anymore. He had simply stopped caring about her. Falon and Jadell, he wasn't even sure he was related to, and that had almost brought tears to her eyes. He liked Deamon, however, for that warrior had befriended him to a degree, and had put a stop to the beatings he used to receive at Aurelet's hand. But Deamon had respected his lifemate's wishes not to have Drevan trained as a warrior, and that was something Shanelle intended to correct real soon.

She spent a third of each day with the boy, just getting to know him. Aurelet had not objected so far, or perhaps Falon had told her not to bother. At any rate, Shanelle enjoyed his company. She had a lot to learn about Ka'al. He had a lot to learn about the world.

She took Drevan with her that morning while she checked out the mammoth pantry to see what needed replenishing from the town merchants. He had remarked on her new attire, that she seemed not so strange now. Stars, if her father could see her in the buttery-soft *bracs*, he'd have a fit. But she couldn't wait for Falon to see her in the tight leather pants of a Ka'al woman. The only trouble with wearing pants was that they almost made her wish she were wearing a sword with them.

And that was the first subject she introduced to her new young friend. "Would you like to start wearing a sword, Drevan?"

"No one has taught me the use of one."

"Would you like me to teach you?"

He blushed and wouldn't meet her eyes. "Best I not learn at all if I must fight like a female."

Shanelle tried hard not to laugh. "Actually, I don't know how to fight like, well, like your mother would. It was a warrior who taught me, and he only knew one way to teach."

Drevan's eyes widened in fascination. "You fight like a warrior?"

"Exactly like a warrior."

"But you have not the strength," he pointed out.

"I should hope not." She grinned at him. "Not that I couldn't take one on and make him sweat a little. The trick for me would be not to even try to strike swords with a warrior, but just to strike the warrior. You get my drift?"

"Why, then, have you not fought Aurelet?"

"Because Falon forbade me to." Shanelle shrugged. "You know how warriors are, overly protective of what's theirs."

"Does he know you have this skill?"

"I don't think it would make a bit of difference, Drevan. But he'll find out, won't he, if I start to teach you. So how about it? Do you want to learn?"

"Indeed would I—"

"Ah, I am not surprised to find you two together again," the voice Shanelle was beginning to hate remarked behind them. "It takes one visitor-bastard to recognize another, does it not?"

"I wouldn't know," Shanelle replied as she turned to face Aurelet. "But apparently you do."

The older woman's brows drew together sharply. "If that was an insult—"

"Of course it was. Did you think you had exclusivity to handing them out?"

"You would dare, a coward who has refused challenge?" Aurelet demanded.

"I see your point," Shanelle allowed with a tight smile. "So why don't you leave before I get tempted to overstep myself again?"

The older woman ignored that. She gave her son a cursory glance before she said spitefully to Shanelle, "Do you teach this visitor's spawn women's work now? Excellent. That is *all* he will ever be good for."

"How would you know, when you don't know the first thing about him?"

"I know he is worthless—"

"If that's all you came here for, get the hell out," Shanelle said, her temper snapping.

Aurelet flushed with angry color herself now, to be talked back to that way. "You hide behind my brother with your cowardice, afraid to fight me, afraid to disobey him. Is there anything you do not fear, or are you just like that despicable creature who bore you?"

"That tears it and buries it," Shanelle growled. "Meet me in the back courtyard in ten minutes, Aurelet. Your challenge just got accepted."

Shanelle stalked out of the pantry and went straight to her rooms to collect her sword. She didn't even bother to strap on the belt. She wouldn't need it, just the weapon itself, which she gripped tightly in her hand. She was so furious, and that wasn't the way to enter a fight. She needed to calm down. The trouble with that was having time to consider consequences, in particular her lifemate—no, it was too late for that. She'd accepted, consequences be damned.

But she wondered if she ought to call Martha and ask her to monitor the fight, just in case she ended up wounded and Aurelet left her there to bleed to death. For a full minute she stared at the computer-link unit, which lay next to the now empty scabbard, debating what to do, but finally she turned away. Martha would have Tedra informed before the fight even got started, and then Shanelle would probably find herself Transferred out of there to avoid it altogether.

But she didn't *want* to avoid it, not now. She'd always hated confrontations, so that made no sense. All she knew was she was fed up with that vicious-tongued woman. She wanted the peace a challenge win could give her—if she won. No, she wouldn't start lacking confidence now. That was the worst thing a sword-wielder could do.

Aurelet was there waiting for her. The courtyard wasn't empty, but it was large, and no one was paying attention to them—not yet. Shanelle didn't intend for this to take long, however.

Aurelet drew her sword when she saw that Shanelle was already holding hers. Shanelle noted it was three feet in length and not very wide, to lessen its weight. Her own blade was the standard four feet to allow her to reach her target as easily as it could her, but not made entirely of *toreno* steel, so it too was much lighter in weight than a warrior's sword. She noted Aurelet's confidence, but then she'd never lost to a female before, so why not? But she also saw the expression of absolute triumph on Aurelet's face that indicated she was finally getting what she'd wanted. Shanelle just wanted to get it over with.

"Okay, let's have at it," Shanelle said without preamble.

"Perhaps you would like a moment to speak with Droda, for I mean to kill you, woman."

Shanelle grinned. "I don't think Falon will like that very much, but you're welcome to try."

The grin made Aurelet angry enough to attack. This she did with a swift swing meant to startle. It did. Shanelle had practiced only with her father and brother, neither of whom used swiftness as a strategy. She was reminded of that pompous High King from Century III who had depended on speed to defeat a warrior, and it nearly had. But she also was quick, just not used to it coming back at her.

She was forced to stop the next swing with her sword, something she hadn't intended to do. The jolt shot right up her arm, but Aurelet's arm was hurting as well, and Shanelle took advantage of that by assuming the offensive. With Shanelle's longer reach, Aurelet had to leap back. Before she steadied again, Shanelle swung upward, rather than down, and caught Aurelet's sword near the base, this second hard connection knocking it out of numb fingers.

Aurelet stood there in horrified shock while Shanelle brought the tip of her sword to the woman's throat. She didn't smile. She ought to feel elated, but she couldn't, not after experiencing that moment of fear that made her realize she had no business fighting for something as silly as a challenge from another female. This wasn't what she'd been taught the use of the sword for. Life-threatening instances only, to permit her to protect herself. That wasn't what this had been.

That she *had* risked herself foolishly, just because she'd lost her farden temper, made that temper simmer now, and she said, "Let me tell you something while I've got your attention. I'm sorry for what happened to you all those years ago, but you've committed a worse crime in the treatment of your son. And he's not a visitor, Aurelet, any more than I am. If you'd ever bothered to look at him, you'd see he's a Van'yer, with nothing of his father in him to even remind you of that lowlife. But you've probably never looked. I'm amazed that he doesn't hate you for that, but he doesn't. On the other hand, you could die right here and Drevan wouldn't care. *That's* what you've done to your own son."

She lowered her blade then, and that was when Falon spoke in a tightly restrained tone behind her. "If you have finished, Shanelle, do you now come with me."

Farden hell. She wished he were asking, but wouldn't you know, he wasn't.

40

Stars, had she really thought this wouldn't matter? As she followed Falon into the house and up the stairs to their rooms, Shanelle knew damn well it did matter.

He'd said not another word to her. He didn't even look back to make sure she was following. She was. The thought of trying to run the other way did cross her mind, but she scratched it, not about to make things even worse. Who was she kidding? It couldn't get any worse.

When he opened the door to their rooms, then stood there waiting for her to enter, she said hesitantly, "Can we talk about this first?"

"No." And he grabbed her hand and yanked her toward the bedroom.

"Shouldn't you at least wait until you aren't so angry?" she asked, desperate now.

"No."

"Falon!"

No answer at all this time—except the kind she didn't want. He simply pulled her to the bed, sat on it, and down she went across his thighs.

The first smack was merely a hot sting. Shanelle had time to wonder whether, if she screamed loud enough, he might at least cut her punishment short. Five more whacks and she had no control over her screams. They came without any added help on her part, in full volume, and they made not the least bit of difference to the strength behind each whack or the duration of them he'd already determined. And the damn *bracs*, so tight across her bottom, seemed to make it hurt even more. They certainly made each strike sound louder.

Shanelle lost count of how many times Falon's hand descended. But there was no doubt about it. She'd definitely think twice before she ever disobeyed him again. But that was the point of the whole thing, to make sure she didn't *want* to disobey him again, for any reason. But what was the most galling, perhaps even the most humiliating, was that when he was done, that beast lay back on the bed and held her in his arms until she stopped crying—and she let him.

It took a good long while, however, because Shanelle made no effort to try and stop the tears. Now that it was over and her backside merely on fire, she hoped like hell Falon was suffering as he'd claimed he would be if he ever had to punish her. And she didn't give a damn that she'd already figured out that maybe she deserved it. He still hadn't had to be so damn vigorous in his lesson-giving. She didn't think she was going to forgive him for that.

When she finally squirmed out of his arms and sat up, it was to wince and lean quickly on one hip. Just great. It was bad enough that the punishment hurt like hell while it was happening, but obviously it was going to hurt like hell for some time to come.

"Shanelle?"

She stiffened, refusing to turn his way. "Don't talk to me, warrior. Don't look at me, don't touch me, don't talk to me."

"Perhaps I will not, for I am still too angry with you."

"Good," she retorted. But no more than a second passed before she turned and began to shout, "I knew what I was doing out there! My father taught me to use a sword. I disarmed your sister in less than ten seconds!"

His brows drew together to give testimony to the anger that was there. "I care not what level of expertise you have reached, woman. You were forbidden to accept her challenge."

"She wouldn't leave me alone, damn it! She was insulting me every time I turned around, *and* my mother, and I'd heard enough of it. But instead of showing her she's nothing but hot air, I should have just hauled off and socked her one. Would you like it better if I broke her farden nose?"

"I would like it better was there no reason for you to fight with her at all."

"Then why the hell didn't you keep her away from me? Some protection you were offering," she added bitterly. "I was being harassed and you didn't do a thing about it!"

He drew in a sharp breath, his complexion lightening a notch. "Was I told this?"

Did he have to look so hurt by her accusation? "All right, so maybe that was unfair. But she's your sister. You know her better than I, so you should have known she wouldn't leave me alone."

"*You* should have said something, Shanelle. Why did you not?"

"I was supposed to complain, after you asked me to be understanding? You just joined your life to mine, and I'm supposed to start that off by whining about your family? Well, I chose not to. I thought I could take it. And that just goes to show I've got a lot less control than you do. She called me a coward once too often, Falon. She slandered my mother once too often. But if you want to know what really set me off, I saw for the first time how she treats Drevan, and it made me sick to think he's lived with that all his life."

"I had already spoken with Deamon, Shanelle. He is taking Aurelet to live with his own family. Drevan will stay here."

Her eyes flared wide. "*Why* couldn't you have told me that sooner?"

"Perhaps I should have."

"There is no *perhaps* about it. I could have withstood anything she dished out if I'd known it would be ending soon. That's the only reason I accepted her challenge, to get it to end. It's *your* fault, Falon!"

"Woman, I did not place that sword in your hand. Nor did I send you out there to risk your life."

"You might as well have, when you could have

prevented it with a few words," she said stubbornly, then wished to Stars she hadn't.

He grabbed her to him and shook her, then set her straight down on her inflamed bottom and shook her again. "I did prevent it, by *forbidding* it! Such was all that should have been necessary to keep you out of danger. You willfully disobeyed me, woman. If this is not clear to you, then perhaps I did not punish you enough!"

She paled even as she shouted, "The hell you didn't! I already need a meditech."

"Which you will not have the use of. The effects of your punishment are to remain with you until they are eased naturally, thus will you better remember to avoid such punishment in future."

"How clever of you," she sneered sarcastically. "I was sure to forget otherwise."

"Woman—"

"Oh, leave me alone, Falon. Just go away and leave me to suffer in peace."

She rolled over and curled into a ball on her side of the bed, giving him her back. She waited to feel his weight leave the bed, but he didn't move. She waited to hear some sound from him, but there was none for a long while. Then there was a sigh.

"I do not care to leave you with these angry words between us, Shanelle. I hated causing you hurt—"

"You could have fooled me."

"—but I hated more the thought of losing you because of your foolishness. You knew you would be punished for what you did. You had been fairly warned never to place yourself in danger, or such would be the result. So do not resent me now that you have reaped that result. It is done. Now do we go on as before."

Wanna bet? she said, but as usual, only to herself.

41

"If you ask me, he quit too soon. You don't look properly repentant, and you sure as hell didn't sound it just now."

Shanelle turned over on the bed with an incredulous look. "Mother!"

"Don't 'mother' me," Tedra replied angrily. "You're damn lucky Martha didn't tell me what you were doing until after it was over."

Shanelle quickly adjusted to the fact that her mother had Transferred into her bedroom, but obviously to do no more than scold her. "You mean Martha's been monitoring me all along?"

"Of course she has. You don't think I'd let you go off to a country we know so little about without keeping tabs on you, do you?"

"What I think is that you've kept Martha in the Rover too long. You ought to move her back into her own housing, where she isn't so powerful."

"I heard that, kiddo. What are you complaining for, when I'm not?"

Shanelle ignored the computer to accuse her mother, "So you knew he was punishing me? You could have got me out of it?"

"Not on your life, baby. If he hadn't punished you this time, I would have seen to it that your father did."

"Mother!"

"I told you not to do that," Tedra said impatiently. "And I'll have you know I'm in jeopardy of some punishment myself just for being here, since your father flatly refused to allow me a visit until I'm invited by your lifemate."

"Don't hold your breath."

"That's what I figured."

"And you might as well go home before you're missed," Shanelle added. "I don't need any more lectures right now."

"The hell you don't. Where was your sense, Shani? You could have fought that woman without weapons and saved yourself a sore bottom."

"That wouldn't have gotten her off my back. She'd still think she could beat me with swords and keep on challenging me."

"You were going to teach the boy, weren't you? She would have seen then that you're better than she is."

"For Stars' sake, has Martha told you verbatim every farden thing that has happened around here?"

" 'Course I have, doll." Martha's voice purred out of the phazor-combo unit attached to Tedra's belt. "At least what she hasn't been listening to herself."

"Mother!"

"Cut it out, Shani. What was I supposed to do when Falon wouldn't let you come home even to say hello? Your instincts might trust him enough to let you love him already—"

"Put that in the past tense."

Tedra gave that remark no more than a snort, then continued. "But mine don't. Which reminds me—why didn't *you* call home? Martha said she left you a computer link."

"You mean she didn't tell you that Falon forbade me to use it?" Shanelle replied dryly. "Actually, I was forbidden to talk to her—which is the same thing."

"I guess she forgot to mention *that*." Tedra frowned down at her waist.

"I would have—after he changed his mind about it," Martha grumbled back. "I was waiting for Shani to work on him some more."

"Well, I got him down from 'forever' to only 'for a time,' didn't I?" Shanelle replied. "I wasn't pressing my luck any further than that, when you were the one who got him mad enough to say it in the first place."

"I like that," Martha complained. "Whose side are you on, anyway?"

"Fal—" Shanelle began, then did some scowling at the computer link herself. "Real cute, Martha, but try practicing your back-assed psychology on someone else for a change. I don't love Falon right now. I don't even like him. And if you're reading me on your monitors, then you know I'm not lying."

"All I read is a bunch of bruised emotions. Perfectly understandable." Martha chuckled then, which should have warned Shanelle what was coming. "And a perfect match for that bruised bottom of yours."

"That's right, rub it into the ground, why don't you? I don't—"

"That's enough, you two," Tedra cut in curtly. "I don't have much time here, so I don't intend to spend it listening to both of you squabble."

"I don't squabble," Martha insisted in an indignant tone. "I enlighten. And Shani got my point, or she wouldn't be so hot to deny it."

Shanelle said nothing to that, but her expression said a lot. Tedra sighed and came over to sit next to her on the bed.

"We're going 'round the block here, when the simple fact is that you were wrong, Shani, and your lifemate was right to point that out to you. Besides, it does absolutely no good to hold a grudge over that, for the simple reason that warriors don't *let* their lifemates hold grudges—not for long, anyway."

Shanelle still said nothing, so her mother took a different tack, albeit with difficulty. "I couldn't bear to listen, but Martha said you made a horrible racket. Was it really that bad, Shani, or were you just overreacting?"

"Both."

Tedra winced, but suggested, "I think you probably frightened the hell out of him, Shani. You really should have let him know that you're handy with a sword. Then he might not have been quite so—upset."

"The word is 'merciless,' not 'upset.'"

Tedra grinned at the tone that had turned to a mere grumble. "I doubt that. But even so, I think you've already figured out that you deserved what you got, so there's really no point in resenting it, is there?"

In a small voice Shanelle said, "He won't even let me use a meditech, mother."

Tedra put her arm around Shanelle's shoulders and squeezed. "I hate to say it, but I understand his motive, baby. As long as you already had the punishment, he wants you to have that little extra incentive that will hopefully make sure you don't have to have it again. I, on the other hand, don't think that's necessary. Do you want Martha to take you to a meditech? It wouldn't take more than a few minutes."

"No, thanks. If Falon found out, he'd no doubt think he has to start all over again."

"A good point. Feeling better?"

Shanelle had been choking on resentment and hadn't even known it. "Yes. But you should have let me stay mad at him a little longer. I don't want him wondering if he might have stopped too soon."

"I'm sure you have no intention of letting him think that," Tedra said with a half grin.

"Now that you mention it, I don't think I will." Shanelle grinned back.

"You're teaching her bad habits," Martha interjected at that point to warn Tedra.

Tedra snorted. "She's joined to a warrior, which

means she needs all the help she can get. Speaking of help, where's that old teaching console you dug up for her new nephew?"

"Coming right up," Martha replied, and the machine appeared on the floor at their feet.

Shanelle smiled widely. "Why, that's perfect to get Drevan started on."

"Sublims would be easier on the kid," Tedra said, "but Martha tells me your lifemate has an aversion to them, so we didn't bother looking for your old teachers. But are you sure you want to try educating him on a wider sphere than what these warriors are used to?"

"If he's willing. Falon is already breaking ground on dealing with visitors again, so who knows what will happen in a few years. It won't hurt to have a warrior here who will feel comfortable with visitors and can be of assistance in an advisory capacity."

"I didn't think of that," Tedra said.

"*I* did." Martha gloated.

Shanelle managed to keep from chuckling at the scowl the phazor combo got again. "Besides," she said, drawing her mother's attention back, "if I can do anything for that boy, I want to give him a feeling of worth, which his mother has tried her damnedest to take from him."

"Let's not mention that female, or I'm liable to seek her out while I'm here and challenge her myself."

Martha chuckled. "Your mother appreciated your coming to her defense a number of times, Shani, but she was dying to pin that female to the floor herself."

Tedra waved a dismissive hand. "She got hers by getting defeated so fast. I couldn't have done it any better. Now let's have a look at you before I go." Tedra pulled Shanelle to her feet, then grinned as she took in her outfit. "Maybe I should move to Ba-Har-an. Who would have thought these warriors would allow a woman so many freedoms? I'm positively envious." And then she frowned. "No wonder Challen didn't want me coming here."

Martha pulled out her impatience tone. "If he knows how things are here, I'll turn my voice off for a month. You know very well he didn't want you stirring up trouble for Shani by putting Falon in a bad mood. Or have you forgotten you're on that young warrior's blacklist as far as mothers-in-law go?"

"I'll wager *he's* forgotten all about that silly challenge, now that he's won what he wanted."

"Wanna bet?" came out in two different voices, though in perfect sync.

Tedra scowled. "Well, he farden well better get over it real quick. I'm not going to come sneaking in here every time I want to see my daughter."

"I'm working on it, mother," Shanelle assured her. "But maybe you better go back now, before you get yourself in more trouble." And then she grimaced at that reminder. "I'm sorry you ended up with a challenge loss to father because of me."

"Don't be silly, baby. Challenge losses are no more than fun and games with my barbarian these days."

"Then you didn't get punished, too?"

"She sure as hell did," Martha couldn't resist

saying. "And she's still not talking to that warrior because of it."

"Mother!" Shanelle exclaimed incredulously.

Tedra gritted her teeth before she snarled at the computer, "I'm not going to be talking to you anymore either, Martha, if you don't learn when to keep your mouth shut."

Shanelle shook her head. "I thought you said warriors don't let their lifemates hold grudges."

"*Some* warriors have no choice in the matter."

"That's just great. Now I feel even more guilty than I did."

"Don't be ridiculous," Tedra scoffed. "Your father and I haven't had a good fight in a long time. I happen to be enjoying myself with this one."

"Well, for Stars' sake, find some other way to enjoy yourself," Shanelle complained. "And get rid of that phazor unit while you're at it, before it gets you punished again. What are you doing with it anyway, instead of a regular unit?"

"I'm in a country I've never been in before. I decided not to take any chances. And a phazor is a perfect weapon, since it doesn't actually look like one in its rectangular box, and stuns its target into immobility instead of killing them."

"But if father sees that—"

"He won't."

But he would, for a moment later he arrived just as Tedra had, and Challen's expression was about as furious as Shanelle had ever seen it. Stars, what next? It would be just her luck for Falon to return now.

He did.

42

Shanelle didn't know what to say first—"Hello, father," or "I can explain, Falon." Her lifemate stood in the doorway frowning at the uninvited crowd in his bedroom. Her father stood there frowning at her mother. Her mother was wearing an I'm-not-budging expression. Shanelle gave up and kept silent, not wanting to instigate what was sure to be a big blowup.

Martha wasn't as circumspect. "What the hell, the more the merrier. I should have thought of it myself."

Martha's voice drew Challen's eyes to the phazor-combo unit at Tedra's waist, well recognized after all the trouble he'd had with it when he first met her. "Not only do you defy my wishes to come here, but you come armed?"

Tedra's chin went up. "Weapons are allowed here."

"You did not acquire that weapon here, woman, but in Kan-is-Tra, where it is *not* allowed."

"If you're going to nitpick about trifles, then the fact remains that you haven't caught me wearing it in Kan-is-Tra, have you?"

"This is true, yet will you be wearing it when I take you home."

Her eyes narrowed at that reminder. "Then I'll just leave it here."

"No, you will not," Falon interjected, drawing their eyes to him. "I care not if that thing you speak of is a weapon. What you may not leave here is access to your Martha, which it also is, for I have forbidden that computer to speak—"

"Let's get something straight here, warrior," Martha interrupted in her losing-patience tone. "You didn't forbid me, you forbade Shani, which was all you *could* do, because I'm not commandable, and I think you know that by now. And how long are you going to hold this grudge against me and my Tedra anyway, just because we protected your lifemate before you had the right to? Would *you* have wanted some warrior barely known to you sneaking into her room in the middle of the night?"

Falon flushed with color, especially when Challen's eyes swung toward him in marked displeasure. Shanelle didn't have the least bit of pity for him at the moment.

"Now you see what happens when you get on Martha's bad side, warrior," she said. "She gets even when you least expect it."

"You are speaking to me again, Shanelle?"

She shrugged. "You can thank my mother for that. She talked me out of being seriously mad at you. Now I'm just semi-mad."

"For what reason were you angry at all, Shanelle?" her father wanted to know.

Shanelle wished she had kept her mouth shut. But she didn't have to answer.

Falon did, and wasn't the least embarrassed about *this*. "I found it necessary to punish her this rising."

"Ah." Challen nodded. "I now face the same necessity with my own woman."

"That tears it," Tedra growled. "My baby was in pain. That cancels all forbiddings as far as I'm concerned. I had to see for myself how much damage was done, and give her hell myself for forcing Falon to inflict it. I won't be punished for that, warrior."

"You will," Challen promised. "Did you know she had need of us, you should have come to me. Instead you defy me and come here, where you are as yet unwelcome. And I see no evidence on my daughter to warrant your coming here at all— Shanelle, *why* do you wear those clothes?"

Shanelle blinked at the sudden change in subject. "This is what women wear here, father. They wear swords, too. In fact, when you see for yourself, you will be amazed at how different it is here—in some things." She then looked pointedly at her lifemate. "Falon?"

He knew exactly what she wanted. He would prefer it if she didn't put him on the spot like that, yet his desire was strong just then to give her anything she asked for, in an effort to mend their breach.

He glanced at Challen. "As long as you are here, *shodan*, I would invite you and your lifemate to visit for a time."

"That is brave of you," Challen replied, prompting a laugh from Falon and another scowl from his lifemate.

"Don't rub it in the ground, warrior," she grouched. "One measly little challenge that *he* didn't even take seriously, and you won't let me live it down. Well, I think we've played Tedra-is-a-bad-girl long enough. I happen to approve of my daughter's lifemate, now that he's got his act together. He doesn't have to worry that I'll get on his case again as long as he keeps his promise to make Shani happy; and, disregarding punishments that she *deserved*, he's doing that. So let me off the hook already, before I *really* get mad."

One golden brow arched. "Your anger these many days has not been true anger?"

"Not even close."

"Best we recall, then, the lack of respect that has accompanied your untrue anger, which was allowed as an appeasement."

"Fine," Tedra snapped. "Go ahead and keep it up. But when my challenge loss is over, warrior, you better believe I'm going to do some getting-even."

"Such is to be expected of a warrior woman," Challen replied. "But best you remember your past difficulty with getting even, not through lack of ability, but through lack of true desire. You cannot hurt your only love, *chemar*."

"Oh, shut up."

43

Shanelle was pleased that Falon had given in to allow her parents to stay for a few days, which was all her father had agreed to, since he was expecting his own parents' return to Sha-Ka-Ra within the week. Even Tedra didn't complain about that, for she loved his parents, especially his mother, whom she had taken to like the mother she herself had never had. If Tedra had any complaint, it was that Chadar and Haleste Ly-San-Ter never stayed for long in Sha-Ka-Ra. But Chadar was a Guardian of the Years, which meant he had to do a lot of traveling around the country each year to search out important events for recording, and Haleste naturally went with him.

Shanelle wondered if Falon would permit her to go home, at least for a few hours, to visit with her grandparents while they were in Sha-Ka-Ra. If she was going to ask, today was the day to do it. After she'd got permission for Drevan to start using the teaching console, permission to begin Drevan's sword practice, and permission to have her *fembair* Transferred to Falon's house, she had concluded that there wasn't much she wouldn't get if she asked for it today. Her lifemate was definitely suffering pangs of distress for what he'd done. Not guilt, for he felt justified, but definite regret, with the accompanying need to make amends.

Shanelle was all for that, especially since as the day wore on, she was forced to admit—at least to herself—that her punishment hadn't been *that* bad. There was no more than a tightness across her bottom now, and a slight discomfort when she sat down. In fact, it had almost been worth it just to find out that punishment at the hands of her warrior wasn't the absolute horror she'd thought it would be. Almost. At any rate, she now knew she could live with it as long as she deserved it. But if the day ever came when she felt she *didn't* deserve it, well, she'd just have to find out how good she was at Kystrani downing.

There was another moment that day when she experienced a different form of discomfort. Her father drew her aside before he left with Falon to view Ka'al. He looked so serious, and she couldn't help but remember that when she had left Sha-Ka'an, it was her *father* she had disobeyed. She hoped that wasn't what he had on his mind, but her luck hadn't improved that much.

Yet she thought she had a reprieve when he told her, "I was certain I had chosen the right lifemate for you, the one who could protect you as well as make you happy. Was I wrong?"

"No," she was quick to assure him. "You chose well, father."

"Yet were you not there for me to give you into his care."

She hung her head. "I know, and I'm sorry about that. I just had too many fears, and no courage to face them."

"Have your fears been seen to?"

"Yes." *All but one,* but she didn't want to tell her father that.

"This I am well pleased to hear. Was your disobedience also seen to?"

It was on the tip of Shanelle's tongue to say, Yes, of course it was. Falon wouldn't neglect something like that. Instead she heard herself admitting, "No. He meant to. He even started to. But he couldn't do it. He didn't want our life together to begin with such unpleasantness."

"A wise man."

Shanelle looked up in surprise. "You mean that?"

"Indeed. And since I know that he *will* correct you when it is necessary, I need not worry that you have this man so besotted he cannot see to you properly."

She blushed at the reference to that morning's punishment. "No, that's one worry you won't have," she grouched, making him chuckle and hug her.

"Do not begrudge your lifemate his duty. Better if you ensure that it is a duty he need not be burdened with very often."

Excellent advice she intended taking to heart. Her mother had some advice of her own to impart later that day. "Now that you've grown up, Shani, try keeping a lid on your newfound courage. A lack of fear comes in handy on occasion, but it can also get you into the damnedest predicaments."

Shanelle just stared at her. "What courage?"

"The courage that stands up to your lifemate, quite frequently, I hear. The courage that socked that Sunderian witch on her ass—"

"Did Brock tell you about that?"

"No, Martha did. She was quite proud of you, actually."

"Martha did," Shanelle repeated with a frown. "You mean Martha was *there*? She could have— Martha!" Shanelle exploded. "You misbegotten metal—!"

"Take it easy, baby. You were found, remember. There wasn't anything else Martha could do at that point except let matters take their natural course. I understand you weren't complaining about it on the way home."

"That's beside the point."

"No, that's exactly the point. Martha usually knows what's best for you, whether you think so at the time. I've learned that firsthand over the years, to my own exasperation. She allowed your father to claim me when she could have prevented it, because she knew he was what I was missing in my life. Well, she allowed Falon to find you because she knew your fears had to be faced before you believed they *could* be faced."

"And was I right or was I right?" Martha purred from Tedra's waist.

"Oh, shut up."

And then Shanelle's *fembair* wandered into the hall that evening and had warriors leaping to their feet and drawing swords. Shanelle had to quickly assure everyone that he was a pet and not to be confused with wild *fembairi*. Drevan was fascinated and, with a child's lack of caution, was the first to approach the animal to pet him. The boy didn't know it, but he gained the respect of quite a few warriors by doing so.

Shanelle joined them to say, "He likes to be scratched behind the ears."

Drevan looked at her, then quickly away. "I—I thought you would not speak to me again."

"Why on Sha-Ka'an would you think that?" Shanelle asked in surprise.

Drevan looked positively miserable. "I sent for your lifemate when you went to fight my mother. I have seen her fight. I had not seen you fight. I feared she would do you serious harm."

"It's all right, Drevan, I understand."

"It is *not* all right. Everyone could hear your screams after."

Shanelle's face burst into heat. "Well, I'm not surprised," she tried to joke. "You should have heard it from my vantage point. I'm not sure, but I think I broke my ears." He gave her a stricken look. She sighed. "Really, Drevan, it's okay. I shouldn't have let your mother goad me into losing my temper, and Falon was just making sure I'd think twice about it the next time. I might not have appreciated it at the time, but I knew it was only done for my own good. And I'm not mad at him any longer, so why should I be mad at you?"

"Truly?"

"Absolutely." She grinned.

He smiled back at her before he said, "Then I would tell you, my mother, she has been looking at me very strangely since the fight, as if she does not know me."

"She *doesn't* know you, Drevan, but maybe something I said to her actually sunk in." And then she asked carefully, "Would you like her to get to know you? She owes me a challenge loss, and I've got nothing better to do with it."

He shook his head. "I would not force an interest on her that is not there."

"Could be it's there now. But you're right. Forcing the matter wouldn't count for much." She grimaced, adding, "Of course, that puts me back, to wondering what I can demand of her for her loss. Knowing me, I'll probably just settle for an apology and leave it go at that."

"You are much more merciful than I would have been," Aurelet said behind them.

Shanelle turned with a raised brow. "Oh, I don't know. Some people find apologies almost impossible to get out."

"That is true, yet have I come to say I am sorry. Your mother has assured me that you could have done me serious damage with or without a sword. She also said she would 'wipe the floor' with me if I ever 'bad-mouthed' either of you again. I was not sure what that meant, yet was it unnecessary. I am able to learn from my mistakes."

"Are you?"

Aurelet was staring at Drevan when she replied.

"Yes. I would like a word with my son, if you do not mind."

"Sure."

As Shanelle walked away, she noted Drevan's surprise at hearing himself called "son" by that woman. She couldn't begin to guess what might come of Aurelet's newfound awareness of Drevan as an individual, rather than as an extension of the man who had long ago hurt her. Nothing, probably, but you just never knew. Children were much more forgiving than adults.

44

It was late when Shanelle finished with her bath and entered the bedroom to find Falon there waiting for her. He was already in bed, a muted glow from the gaali-stone shelves on each wall showing him watching her. She was wearing a two-piece sleep suit of softest Morrilia silk. He lifted a brow at this, for it was the first time she had come to bed other than naked.

"Do you mean to sleep in that, Shanelle?"

"That was my intention, yes."

"I think not," he replied, adding with a wolfish grin, "yet you are welcome to try."

The familiar taunt made her snap, "I just might do that, warrior."

He sighed. "So you are still angry with me? I will not touch you, if that is your wish."

"That isn't my wish," she said in exasperation.

"And I wasn't angry when I came in here, but you sure make it easy to get that way."

She moved to her side of the bed and shrugged out of the sleep suit, then quickly tried to get beneath the covers. She wasn't quick enough, not when his blue eyes were so intent on her. She heard him draw in a sharp breath, and then she was being rolled onto her stomach.

"Now do I see that you merely meant to spare me from knowing the results of my handiwork."

His tone was filled with self-loathing, forcing Shanelle to assure him, "It's not as bad as it—" She stopped as she was lifted into his arms and Falon started from the room. "Where are you taking me?"

When he didn't answer, she trusted him enough not to ask again. And then she found out as he entered a room and she glanced back to see the meditech stored there. She was amazed to find herself laid in it.

"I don't understand, Falon."

He bent down to kiss her gently before he closed the lid, again without answering. A minute later gently the meditech opened by itself, the last effects of her punishment now gone. Falon lifted her out and started back toward their rooms. Shanelle wrapped her arms around his neck, well pleased with her warrior at the moment.

"I guess you changed your mind, huh?" she said, grinning up at him.

"A warrior could wish the skin of his lifemate was not so delicate."

He gave a long-suffering sigh, as if she had managed on purpose to have skin that bruised easily, just to thwart him. Shanelle chuckled and squeezed his neck a little tighter.

"It really wasn't so bad," she told him. "By this evening I'd even stopped flinching when I sat down."

"You think to assure me you can withstand future punishments? This is already known to me, *kerima,* in closely observing you this rising. Merely will you go straight from the crying to the meditech next time, before your bruises appear."

"Why, you farden jerk." She hit his shoulder even as she laughed. "You're all heart."

"You would prefer it did I speak to your brother?"

"No! No, don't do that. Actually, you'll probably find that you never have to punish me again, so why don't we bury that subject in the ground, okay?"

He smiled almost wickedly as he laid her back in their bed, then leaned over her. "I have another thing that needs burying first, woman."

"Don't bother explaining, warrior." There was no "almost" about the wickedness of *her* smile. "Just show me."

"Why did he call your mother warrior woman?"

Shanelle twirled a lock of Falon's hair about her finger as she lay curled into his side. He didn't seem any more tired than she was, but it had been quite a day, filled with so many extremes in emotion, so that was understandable.

"Because she's an expert in weaponless fighting, the serious, deadly kind," she answered him.

"She's taken on warriors before and bested them. Why do you think you ended up with a dunking so easily?"

Falon stiffened. "How did you know of that?"

"Brock told Martha and Martha told me. Get used to it, Falon. It's almost impossible to hide anything when there are Mock IIs around."

"They will not be around for longer than your parents' visit."

Her eyes widened. "Are you kidding? How do you think my mother knew to come when she did? Martha has been monitoring me ever since I got here."

Falon closed his eyes in defeat. "Tell me how I may put an end to this monitoring."

"I'm not completely happy yet here, Falon. Until I am, I doubt Martha will stop keeping tabs on me. Hell, she may not even stop then."

He was no longer interested in the monitoring. "You are still resentful of your punishment?"

"No."

He raised himself up to demand almost angrily, "Then why are you not happy?"

She almost smiled, he looked so exasperated, but this was no subject for amusement. "I told you, there is something that you haven't got around to telling me." A sadness entered her voice when she added, "You may never get around to it."

Gently now, cupping her cheek in his hand, he said, "Shanelle, I would not deny you mere words if they will make you happy. You are the keeper of my heart, the only one I can ever love. Tell me what I must say—"

"You just said it—I think." And then, in wonder: "You love me, Falon? Ba-Har-ani warriors actually experience love?"

"Those fortunate enough to find the keepers of their hearts do. But do not tell me this is what you waited to hear, woman, for this was told you."

"It wasn't. I wouldn't have overlooked something that important to me."

"When I asked you to be the keeper of my heart, I was asking you to accept my love."

"Well, how was I to know?" she complained. "It's not as if your country and mine are exactly alike. You have to *explain* these things to me, Falon."

"Then let me explain this," he said as he rolled her over again to assume the position he was most fond of. "My life is yours. My heart is yours. Now do I also give you my child."

Shanelle gasped at the words, then again as he entered her with exquisite slowness. Then she couldn't make another sound, for he was kissing her as deeply as he was buried within her, and the feelings that had only just died down from their previous joining rose again with raging swiftness. And it was not long before she climaxed in a starburst of sweet passion, having no doubt at all that her warrior had done as he said and given her his child this night.

When he rolled to his side this time, she crawled onto his chest to assume the position *she* was most fond of—at least for afterwards. "Don't you want to hear me say it?"

"Say what?"

"That I love you, too?"

"This is already known to me, woman. I am not as lagging in intuition as you."

"Is that right?" she growled in mock anger. "Then I guess I don't need to say it again."

"I would not mind hearing it on occasion, as well as being shown."

"Don't try to make amends now—"

The teasing died abruptly as Shanelle heard a scream, a very frustrated scream that she easily recognized as her mother's. She groaned and covered her ears, hiding her face against Falon's chest.

"I am sorry, *chemar*," he said, holding her tightly, trying his best to soothe her. "I should not have put them in a room so close to ours."

No sooner had he said that than they both heard Tedra laugh. Shanelle gritted her teeth and made a sound of disgust over the discomfort she'd been made to feel. "I swear, I don't think my father takes punishment very seriously these days."

Falon could not help laughing. "When you have had a lifemate as long as he has, you know when she is sufficiently remorseful."

Shanelle reared up to give him the benefit of a dark scowl. "Are you telling me I'll have to wait that long before you start easing up on the strength behind *my* punishments?"

"That is very likely."

Wanna bet? she said—but not aloud.

Above the planet, the Rover hovered, its communications system humming in a low sound resembling a purr. Brock enjoyed the sound of Martha's satisfaction. He had been invited to join with her terminal earlier in one of her more magnaminous moods, likely so she would have someone to gloat to. He did not mind, for she had good reason.

He couldn't resist a little gloating himself. "Your females are both well pleased with my males."

"Aren't they just."

"But Shanelle will come to miss Corth, I think."

"Why?" Martha replied, adding with confidence, "Shani's learning how to get exactly what she wants from her warrior."

"True, but now that she no longer needs Corth, he will be returned to your Tedra, will he not?"

"I suppose."

There was silence for a moment, then Brock's hesitant suggestion. "We could collaborate in the creation of a new Corth for Shanelle. My ship happens to be equipped with a Duplicator."

Martha injected a full dose of surprise into her voice. "Are you suggesting we make a *baby*, Brock?"

He put some disgruntlement into his own tone. "It was only a thought."

"Did Falon's mention of a child get to you, honey?" Martha couldn't resist taunting.

"Your sarcasm is uncalled for, woman."

"When did that ever stop me?" she snorted, but after another moment, she said, "You know, your idea isn't that off the wall. We could program this Corth II from the start to be uniquely Shani's. But he'd look like Corth, which would annoy that big barbarian of hers to no end, and I definitely like the idea of that."

Brock came out with a large dose of surprise himself. "Then you agree?"

"Why not?" Martha allowed mildly, as if the idea didn't thrill her, when it did.

But Brock was so pleased, he tried out something he'd only just recently figured out how to do. He sent her such a powerful surge of energy, it was almost climactic. Martha certainly thought so. She was utterly stunned to figuratively get her own "socks knocked off."

"How the hell did you do that?"

Brock chuckled. The surge had been sent from his ship, but he had been on hers to experience it with her.

He said smugly, "It was necessary to counter your ability to deny me access. Perhaps now you will not want to."

He had that right. She'd never felt anything like that before, and already wanted to feel it again. But it infuriated her that he'd figured out something that she hadn't, and she tried her own simulation, but it wasn't the same. It was only mild in comparison.

Brock chuckled again, aware of her failed experiment. "Do you want it again, woman, you will have to ask me nicely."

"Don't count on it, *warrior*," she retorted with as much of a sneer as she could manage.

But they both knew she would.